FAIRY TALE

I0835830

Fairytale

By

Tracy Broemmer

Women's Fiction

Published by Tracy Broemmer

Edited by Jeanne Smith (First Edition), Lexie Broemmer (Second Edition)

Cover Design:

All Rights Reserved

Copyright:

First Edition © 2021, Second Edition, © 2026

ISBN#: 978-1-965331-24-8

Names, characters, and incidents depicted in this book are products of the author's imagination or are used fictitiously. Any resemblance to actual events, or person, living or dead, is coincidental and not the intent of the author.

No part of this book may be reproduced or transmitted in any form or by any means without permission in writing from the author.

A NOTE ABOUT FAIRYTALE

This book was originally published in 2008 under the pen name Therese Kinkaide. It is the same story with updated editing, a new ISBN, and a new cover.

Fairytale was written in 2007. It was the second book of two that I published under the pen name. While the book cover and the editing had a glow up, the story is the same—every chapter that is in "present day" is actually current to the writing date, so present day in the story is 2007/2008.

A NOTE ABOUT FAIRYTALE

This book was originally published in 2008 under the pen name Therese Kinkaide. It is the same story with updated editing, a new ISBN, and a new cover.

Fairytale was written in 2007. It was the second book of two that I published under the pen name. While the book cover and the editing had a glow up, the story is the same—every chapter that is in "present day" is actually current to the writing date, so present day in the story is 2007/2008.

RAPUNZEL

One

June, 2008

Springfield, IL

'Caroline.'

The name—her name, she is told—means nothing to her. The sound of it on the man's lips stirs nothing inside her. There is nothing about him, the way he looks or talks or the words he feeds her the same way he'd fed her ice chips when she'd first regained consciousness, that is familiar. She's still afraid, though she must admit, this man has done nothing to harm her, nothing untoward. The room she's in now is cozy; it's better than the hospital room she'd first opened her eyes to—how could it not be?—but nothing here speaks to her as if it belongs to her.

Days have gone by, but she doesn't know how many. She doesn't know what day it is, and though she knows the nature of her injuries—she could catalog them almost as clinically as a nurse—she doesn't know how she sustained them. The man, he'd said his name was Miles—and come to think of it, he'd sounded sad when he told her his name—insists that she will know about the accident soon enough. He's told her several times he doesn't believe she is strong enough to know the truth yet.

He is good looking, but there are no clues as to who he is in his deeply chiseled face and jaw. His thick brown hair is unkempt but sexy, and his green eyes are too sorrowful to sparkle. In the beginning, she'd been so careful of what she'd said. This man—*Miles*—had been at her bedside during her every waking hour, and from the way he'd grown more haggard looking as the days wore on, she assumes he'd spent the nights cramped in the uncomfortable hospital issue recliner. Finally though, she'd had enough. Enough of his hang dog expression. She needed to concentrate on why every inch of her body hurt as if she'd exploded and recently been glued back together. She couldn't do that when overwhelmed with guilt for causing this stranger so much grief.

His eyes had shone suspiciously bright when she'd snapped that day two weeks ago. Or had it been three? She doesn't know, and that's the hell of it. She doesn't know who the hell she is, but she is someone and that someone inside her claws to get out. He'd rubbed his stubbled jaw and pushed his fingers—he wears a gold band on the ring finger of his left hand—back through his hair. His face had seemed harder in that moment, as if his hands had sucked all the compassion from his blood and through his skin. When he'd drawn a ragged breath, she'd braced herself, assuming he was going to argue. Instead, he'd simply lifted one shoulder in a half shrug and turned and walked out of the room.

The door had locked behind him. This man—*Miles*—had not harmed her, and yet, he'd been keeping her prisoner in this cozy little room for an unknown length of time. When she awoke, in the hospital, she'd been terrified to find her arms had been restrained. He tells her it was for her protection, that she'd been acting violently in her dreams. Swinging to hit people unseen to him and the doctors. It seemed for a while that she should believe him.

Now and then, disorganized thoughts and haphazard images flash through her mind. They don't fit this room, the lavender walls and the thick navy down comforter on the bed. She sees a woman's face, but it's the eyes that draw her attention. Blue eyes, but not the ice blue that can cut right through a person. Big, warm blue eyes. Lips pressed hard together, as if they might unleash a cry of anguish if they open. And then she hears it. A fist in a face or a gut. A fist on flesh. And a cry of pain. She sees blood. She sees way too damned much blood for it to be a simple fistfight. And then it slips away before she can grasp it and push herself to remember more. If she is remembering.

The pin in her leg does not seem to be healing well. She walks with a limp. At the moment, she does not know how old she is, but she thinks she's not old enough to walk with a limp. The man—*Miles*—has not allowed her to see herself. But she's touched her face, and she knows there are enough stitches and scars there that even if she saw herself, she wouldn't recognize her face and know who she is. She doubts that he purposely tries to keep her identity from her. Probably he is afraid for her to see her patchwork face.

Perhaps she looks like Frankenstein now. Perhaps she looks worse.

"Caroline."

Who is he? Who is this man who seems to have devoted his life to her recovery and yet keeps her in this room hour after hour, day after day? He's allowed her to open a window and feel the fresh breeze on her face; she's no flight risk. A drop from her third story window would most likely break her leg again and possibly break something else in the process.

She turns from the window to look at him when she hears the door click behind him. The sound reverberates, but she doesn't have time to wonder about it. *Miles* is not alone. There is a woman with him. A tall, lithe woman with blonde hair cut in a stylish wedge.

The woman stares at the floor, as if she is afraid to look Caroline in the eye. She is dressed in designer clothes; seems unfair that Caroline remembers the names of designers and musicians and movie stars, but she can't remember her own name. A gold bangle bracelet adorns her right wrist, but it is the only jewelry Caroline sees.

"Caroline, this is Dawn."

The name means nothing to her. Dawn lifts her head, finally, to look at her. Caroline hates her instantly, just because of the pity in her brown eyes. She doesn't need their pity. She needs only her freedom. She could function in society, even if she has to start over. She's not at square one. She has not forgotten *life*; she's simply lost who *she* is.

"Caroline."

Caroline glances behind her, at the window. Suddenly chilled, she wants to close it. But Miles carries something in his hands. A book. A photo album. She narrows her eyes at him. This is the day then, the day when her re-education will start. Remembering Caroline. Except that she doesn't want to remember Caroline through this man, through *Miles*.

Who is Dawn, she wonders, that she must be here for this momentous occasion? Why, suddenly, on the day *Miles* chooses to introduce her to her past, does he bring her another visitor?

Caroline, still cold, hedges her bottom close to the bed and finally sits. Curls into herself and folds her arms across her chest. Miles moves closer to the bed, sets the photo album close to her, as if to entice her. Instead she watches Dawn move hesitantly across the room, to the open window.

When the woman looks at her, Caroline sucks in a sharp breath. She doesn't know the face, but she sees the blue eyes in her memory. The lips pressed together to hold in the cry.

"Caroline."

She jumps when she feels his fingers cautiously touch her shoulder. He does not touch her. He never touches her. She has not been touched, except by doctors and nurses, for medical reasons, since the accident. Possibly longer, she doesn't know.

Suddenly suspicious, she watches as his hand trails lightly down her arm and reaches to take her hand. To pull her hand away from her body. Uncurl her fingers and place something in them. Dawn cries softly when Miles closes her hand around the object. Caroline watches Dawn, intrigued by her tears.

"Who are you?" Her voice is raspy. She hardly uses it, because she has nothing to say to Miles and he is the only person she sees on a regular basis.

Dawn sobs and turns away from her. Miles squeezes her hand. Whatever he put in her hand is round. Small and circular. She opens her fist and slowly looks away from Dawn.

It's a gold band. With a beautiful princess cut diamond.

"You're my wife." The words crawl out of his mouth and stick to his lips and his face. He winces as he waits for her to react to his announcement. Grimaces, actually. As if it pains him that she's his wife. Probably not that. Probably that she's his wife and doesn't remember him.

"And who is she?" Caroline asks, because she knows without knowing that this woman standing in this cozy prison is a link to who she used to be.

Dawn clicks her tongue against the roof of her mouth and turns back to them. "Caroline," she whispers and then she breaks and she cries again and Caroline sees the unhappy curve of her lips, as they strain to hold in her feelings.

It's not that his words are not stuck like tar and sand and huge heavy chunks of gravel in her throat. It's not that she didn't hear him say "you're my wife." It's more that with those words, the fear inside her just metastasized like a rapid growing cancer. Those words. Why, in God's name, did this man bring this woman with him on the day he decides to remind her that she is his wife? The woman—Dawn—still struggling to control herself, finds something fascinating to study on the floor at her feet.

Caroline needs to stop this train before it wrecks in a heap at her feet. She remembers nothing, and yet feelings are clicking and falling into place inside her. Though Miles has never hurt her, at least not since she's regained consciousness, she does not trust him. Seems there should be implicit trust between a woman and her husband.

"Dawn is your—"

"No." Caroline lets the ring drop from the palm of her hand. "No." She turns her back on the photo album, on the ring, and on her husband and pushes herself from the bed. Her leg throbs now. She hitches, in her uneven gait, to the window. Brushes Dawn's shoulder as she passes. "I need to be alone."

"It's time," Miles says firmly.

"And who are you to tell me it's time?" Her voice is clipped and cold. She doesn't recognize it, but then she doesn't know her voice to recognize it.

"Your husband, Caroline," he reminds her.

She bows her head, as if in submission. "Why would my husband feel the need to keep me in a prison?" She looks back at him and sees that her words don't hurt him. Instead, he climbs gracefully to his feet. His eyes are cold with anger.

"For your own safety."

"So you say." She shrugs.

She stands now, so close to Dawn, she smells her perfume. A rich fragrance. She winces and closes her eyes. The light in the room is too much. Her head hurts. The flashes, visions, whatever, seem to make her sensitive to light. She hears laughter, bawdy, raucous feminine laughter. The sound almost brings a smile to her lips. These are the memories she wants to find. The ones that ignite inside her and melt away the fear and the dread she's been living with for an unknown length of time.

"You don't remember me?" Dawn says softly. Caroline turns to study Dawn's face. Here, she sees the compassion, true sadness, that is curiously absent from this man's face. This man, who claims to be her husband.

Thin, blonde eyebrows arch over haunted brown eyes. High cheekbones and pale, thin lips. A faint scar that disappears under the chin. Caroline, with a boldness that is foreign to her, touches Dawn's face and lifts her chin with her fingertip. The scar trails nearly an inch toward the woman's neck. She traces it with her fingertip, as if it is Braille for those who no longer remember life. As if this scar alone will bring her back the woman she used to be.

Dawn's eyes fill, and when she blinks, tears wet her face. Caroline ignores the impatient sigh behind her. She lets her hand fall to her side and shakes her head in answer to Dawn's question.

"No," she whispers and adds when the word seems to slice the woman like glass, "I'm sorry. I don't."

"Caroline," Miles says again. "The photo album."

"I can't right now." She shakes her head. Gives him her back and closes the window.

"You will right now," he answers.

"What's your hurry, all of a sudden?" she asks when she turns back around to him. "How long have I been here? What's this sudden hurry to make me remember?"

"Because Max is here to see you." The words seem to drain him. He looks shorter and pale and broken. There is no mistaking the sadness in his eyes now. Who the hell is Max, and why does he have this power over this man?

"Who's Max?" Caroline asks with a shake of her head. She glances at Dawn, when the woman sobs out loud again.

"Our son." Miles sighs and lowers his head. "He's waited all summer to see you, Caroline. He just wants to see you. He's scared. I think he's scared that I'm lying to him. That you didn't survive the—that you didn't make it. He needs—"

"How old is he?" Caroline lifts a hand to halt the emotional barrage.

"Four."

"Oh my God." She covers her mouth with one hand and clutches her stomach with the other. She's afraid she might be sick. Her body had given birth to a child and she now has no memory of carrying him. Birthing him. Loving him. "Oh my God," she says again. The tears are warm on her face and then when they trail over the bandages on her face, she feels oddly numb and then they touch her skin again and she feels them and she tastes the salt on her lips.

"The pictures," Miles clears his throat, "in the book are mostly pictures of Max. You and Max."

~

He's a beautiful child, with longish black hair that hangs in his eyes. Eyes that are blue, not green like Miles'. She wonders, as she watches his short, skinny fingers piece together a puzzle, if that could mean she has blue eyes. And then she cringes and hates herself for thinking about her own puzzle when she should just relax and get to know this boy. Get to know her son.

Hard not to wonder, though. Hard not to wonder what Max could do with the puzzle of her memory, since he's made short work of this twenty four piece puzzle of Mickey Mouse. His smile is crooked, one corner of it sits so high on his face, it almost touches an ear. Small, shell like ears. A tiny, upturned nose with just a smattering of freckles over the bridge. A dimple under the lower corner of the smile. Someone made this boy beautiful. She finds it hard to believe she had any part in it.

Shy, but hopeful, he sits next to her at the card table Miles has put in her room. Something else she supposes she should worry about later. Giving Miles hell for the card table. Why in God's name she can't leave this room and venture out to a family room or a kitchen is beyond her and still nothing she need discuss with a four year old. He doesn't say much, but he turns to look at her every few seconds, as if to make sure she is really there.

"You're very smart," she tells him as he drops another colorful cardboard piece into place.

He leans over the table on his elbows, but he looks back at her now, over his shoulder. The look of tired wisdom on his face is disconcerting. "Daddy said you wouldn't remember." His whispered words hurt more than her leg on a damp, cold day.

"I'm sorry, Max." Her own voice is barely more than a whisper. "Maybe some day I will."

"Daddy says you won't," he answers with a shrug of defeat. Her eyes devour the line of his neck under his hair, the lock the curls around the shell of his ear as he studies the puzzle pieces in front of him. Why would Miles say that? Why would Miles tell a four year old that his mother would not remember him?

"You know what might be even better?" She wishes her voice did not shake.

Clearly intrigued by what could be better than her remembering him, Max moves back from the table and rests his denim clad butt on his feet, on the seat of his chair. He wears a brand of jeans she doesn't recognize, but from the looks of his knees, he's hard on them and probably goes through several pair every few months.

"I'm getting to know you when you're already four," she says and knows as the words dive out of her mouth how lame they sound and that this intelligent child is not going to buy any bullshit from her. "Besides the fact that you're very handsome, I'm getting to know you when you're already a big boy. And I can like you for who you are, and not just because you were my baby and I had to like you." He's staring at her, undecided as to whether or not to believe her or like what she said. "Dirty diapers and all." This, at least makes him giggle.

"We do puzzles," he tells her. "Me and you."

"You and I," she corrects him automatically and assumes she must do it often when he rolls his eyes.

"Dawn hates puzzles."

She arches an eyebrow but says nothing as he turns back to the puzzle. Dawn. Who in the hell is Dawn, if Miles is her husband and Max is her son. Where does Dawn fit in?

"What does Dawn like?" she asks, knowing if she asks direct questions of Max, regarding the memories she's lost, he might clam up and not tell her anything.

"She reads to me," he answers. "Bedtime stories."

Dawn. *Dawn* reads him bedtime stories. Why is that? Why doesn't *Miles* read him bedtime stories? "What's your favorite bedtime story?" she asks him. She rubs her hands on her jeans. She takes a deep breath, careful not to let Max know how hard it is for her to do that. Not because of any injury. Because she doesn't understand Dawn's role in this Rapunzel soap opera in which she now stars.

Max looks at her again and lifts a shoulder in a half shrug. She sees Miles in him in that action, and any doubt she may have had about Miles being his father is gone. "When you read to me all the time, I liked 'Twinkle Twinkle Little Star.'"

Well, she knows the song, but she can't remember a book. "What does Dawn read to you?"

"'Who Wants a Baby Dragon?'"

"Do you like it?"

"It's sad." Max stands and goes to the window. He's done. She doesn't know him, but she knows that by walking away from the table and the puzzle, *from her,* he's finished talking about Dawn and probably Miles too. "I'm hungry."

She doesn't have any snacks in her prison to give him. She can't just open the door and take him down to the kitchen and bake him monster cookies, just the way he likes them, with just a little bit of extra peanut butter. She can't even open the door and yell for Miles to tell him Max is hungry. She lowers her head to her hands and rubs her eyes and her forehead and her searching, probing fingers bring tears to her eyes.

"I'm sorry," she says, but she knows Max does not hear her and at four, he does not believe her and so she cries harder. She is still sitting this way, five minutes later, when Dawn comes for Max. Max is curled in a ball on her bed. She watches Dawn tease him and cajole him into coming with her.

She stands, when Dawn picks him up. The woman meets her eyes, and Caroline reads the fear, as if her face were an open book.

"I can't—" Dawn shakes her head.

"Why?" Caroline demands. She moves as quickly as she can, but Dawn sidesteps her and hurries to the door. "Why? Why am I locked in this room, Dawn?"

"Do you know me?" Dawn whispers. Max lays his head on her shoulder. Caroline feels a flash of hate burn through her. This woman has her freedom and her son, and she doesn't even know who in the hell she is.

"No."

Dawn swallows hard. Caroline wants to push her, but she knows it will get ugly because she hates the desperation clawing in her throat right now and she needs someone to shoulder her rage. Max does not need to hear anything so ugly.

Instead she waits until the door closes and she hears the lock click, and she picks up a candlestick. It's heavy; she knows it is probably crystal, but she doesn't care. She draws back and lets it fly. Feels a tiny bit of relief sprinkle over her as it shatters against the far wall. Let Miles say something. She's ready for a fight. While Dawn is downstairs, making Max his favorite cookies.

His favorite.

She tries to swallow. His favorite. Max's favorite cookies. How in the hell does she know that, if she doesn't know Max? She doesn't. She does not recognize his face or his voice. The only thing familiar about him was his little half shrug and that is only because she has seen Miles do it so often since she's been locked up in this Godforsaken room.

And yet, she knows monster cookies with extra peanut butter are his favorite cookies. She can feel the dough in her hands. The sugary peanut butter and the oatmeal flakes. Stunned by this tactile memory, and desperate for something more, she backs on trembling legs to the bed and then falls to sit there, waiting. Waiting for something, anything, more to come to her.

Dammit all, she can *taste* the cookies. But she can't remember Max's face.

~

"WHO ARE YOU?" SHE WHISPERS TO THE FACE IN her mind. There's no answer, of course. *Dawn* is not here in her prison, but she can't get the woman out of her mind. She *knows* her, but she does not remember her. She just feels it, in her gut. Dawn is as important to the events that have led up to her injuries and her imprisonment as Miles. Funny, she feels closer to Dawn, trusts her more—far more —than she trusts the man who claims to be her husband.

Claims to be? She sighs and groans long in frustration and climbs out of bed to wander her room. It's dark, but she doesn't want the light. Miles had come in some hours ago and studied her for a moment before going to clean up the shattered crystal against the far wall. She'd stared at him as he did so, daring him to chastise her for what she'd done. To rave about the cost of the candlestick. He'd said nothing at all.

That's worse, she thinks now. That he'd come into her room and remained cool and aloof and said nothing when she was raging for a fight. For something other than the nothingness that has plagued her for so long.

She opens the window and rests her forehead against the glass pane. When had she decided Miles is just *a man who claims to be her husband?* She doesn't really know when she'd begun to feel that way. She only knows that Miles makes her stomach twist into knots and her palms sweat and her heart race like a runner after a one hundred yard dash. Not in a good way, but in the way she might feel if she suspected someone was following her down a dark, deserted alleyway.

Her visit with Max had proven to be a power drill on her nerves. She closes her eyes now, but the moonlit hills beyond her window are etched upon her eyelids. Max is a beautiful child. If she were a normal woman, a normal *mother*, she would love to see him again. To sit with him while he works diligently with puzzle pieces or to hold his small, trusting hand in hers as they walk. To soak his essence into her skin through her pores and carry something of him in her body now, since she does not remember carrying him the first time. But she's not normal. And sitting with him today had been more painful than the first days of her recovery, when she'd said silent prayers to simply die in her sleep.

How is it, Caroline wonders, as she watches Max run ahead of her in the yard, that a boy can amass so many bruises and scrapes and even a few small, crescent shaped scars and his mother does not remember how they came to be? The sun finds strands of red and even a bit of gold in Max's dark hair as he launches himself at the dog, and she imagines, adds yet another scrape to each knee he lands on. Skipper, the large, unruly mutt of a dog, rolls over for Max to scratch his belly. Four giant hairy paws skim at the velvet blue sky so far above their heads.

Miles had allowed her freedom, ever so small. Then again, is it really freedom when she is only outside, in the yard with Max, because Miles thought she should be? If she had *asked* Miles if she could come outside and walk in the yard for a while, would he have let her? The breeze feels good on her face. It is hot outside, she can see the beads of sweat on Max's forehead, when he gives his longish bangs an impatient brush out of his eyes. Hot and the midday sun is relentless, but Caroline feels new and whole here, as the sun warms away the chill of the only past she knows, *remembers.*

She watches the boy and the dog play; it's obvious they have not been locked away as she has, to heal or to worry about her. They play together often, the dog barking and running in big circles, only to come back and drop at Max's feet. Her leg aches from walking so much, and from walking on the uneven grass, but she won't complain. She does sit, however; she climbs up to sit on the picnic table. Her elbows rest on her knees; she cups her chin in her right hand. Max's laughter is the only fitting soundtrack to this moment, though she hears the low hum of an engine from somewhere down the street. Probably a neighbor mowing the lawn.

Max is a mess of skinny, bony angles and tawny skin. The legs of his black shorts hang low, past his knees, but when he falls to the ground, they fall slack up on his thighs. She could love this boy so easily; it's remembering that is so hard. Seems like she should take advantage of Miles' generosity or his agenda. Take a moment to study the green, the yard that must ramble on for an at least an acre. It is not yet full summer, despite the heat and the roaring sun. The burnt rug of dried brown grass is last summer's memory. She is surrounded by vivid green and blue.

The house, to her right, is old but beautiful. Her eyes climb slowly from the first floor windows to the second and finally the third. From where she sits, she can see that the white paint on the window trim is beginning to crack. Miles had painted it, but she figures it has been a couple of years. She glances back at Max, who is still playing with Skipper, and then searches the third story windows to find hers. It is this side of the house, because the hills beyond this yard are the only scenery she's seen in weeks, possibly months.

She'd wanted to move. The three story brick house is beautiful, yes, but she had argued with Miles that it was too much. Too much house, too much expense for the three of them.

Suddenly aware of her thoughts, Caroline climbs to her feet. Struggles to stand, but the grass is tilting upward, coming at her quickly. Miles had insisted the house was the only house he would live in. There was no need to uproot Max and start over. She'd argued that Max was too young to know the difference. He hadn't even started school yet—

Her throat burns. She is going to be sick. Her hair clings to the back of her neck, and her palms are damp, but when she wipes them on her shorts and then touches her legs, they are ice cold.

Sick.

She can't be sick. Not with Max here.

Miles had gotten angry. His face had purpled in rage, and she'd stared at him in stunned silence. She hadn't seen—

"Caroline?"

She raises her head now, when she hears the name. *Her* name. Dawn is hurrying across the yard to her. For a moment she is relieved. She needs someone to steady her. To hold her up for just a moment. And yet, she is afraid of Dawn. The woman has given her no answers. What if she tries to rush Caroline back inside, up the cramped staircase, and into that room? That damned prison that has robbed her of any hope of a memory, any sense of self she might have had.

"Caroline, are you alright?" Dawn is out of breath from running across the yard. "I saw you out here. I thought you were going to pass out."

Caroline concentrates on breathing. If she looks as she feels, Dawn might think she is not really Caroline. Not substantial, not made of flesh. Pale as a ghost. She swallows hard and looks away from Dawn's inquisitive eyes. Wonders if Dawn was on patrol, standing at a window and watching her. Watching her for what? To make sure she didn't pass out? Or to make sure she doesn't take off, with or without Max.

"I'm fine," she answers. Her voice is quiet but firm.

"Are you sure?" Dawn reaches for her, but Caroline jerks her shoulder back and Dawn's hand falls away without making contact.

"I'm sure." She gives Dawn a curt nod and looks back over her shoulder. Max is watching her uncertainly. She squints; the sun that had been a friend earlier is now harsh. Stepping back from Dawn, she lifts her hand to shield her eyes and then she offers Max an encouraging smile. He studies her silently for a moment, as if deciding whether or not to trust that she is okay, and finally turns back to the dog.

"You can fool him, but you can't fool me, Caroline." Dawn's voice is firm. Caroline looks down as Dawn's fingers curl around her arm. "If you're weak, say so. It's hot out here. You need to come inside."

Caroline snatches her arm away from Dawn and takes another step backwards. "I have been inside for God only knows how long," she hisses. Her heart knocks so hard against her ribs that she wonders if Miles can hear it, wherever he is. Does he hear it? Does it sound like a desperate prisoner pounding away at the walls that confine her? "I don't know who you are or why you're here, but you need to back off."

"I'm your friend," Dawn whispers. Even the whisper breaks, and Dawn averts her glassy eyes. Caroline thinks she is either a friend or a damned good liar. She seems sincere, and yet, why isn't she more willing to talk? To *help?*

"So you're my friend." Caroline's voice is tinged around the edges with bitterness. Sharp bitterness and blunt pain. "What do you do as my friend?" She narrows her eyes at Dawn. "Spy on me? Report to Miles what I'm doing while I'm out here? Play nursemaid to my son?"

"I'm here to help!" Dawn snaps, her voice thick with tears.

"Here to help me?" Caroline says softly with a shake of her head. "Or Miles?"

Dawn flinches as if Caroline's words are fingers that sting her face in an angry slap. "We were college roommates, Caroline."

Caroline sinks her teeth into her lower lip. She doesn't remember college. She doesn't remember classes or textbooks or parties or roommates. She doesn't remember Dawn. As she opens her mouth to say this to Dawn, she hears music. Dawn groans and pulls a slim silver cell phone from the front pocket of her denim shorts. Before she can flip it open, Caroline grabs her wrist and wrenches her hand so she can see the caller ID.

1. *Miles Wolfe.*

~

HER FACE ITCHES. THE WOUNDS ITCH AS THE doctor—she doesn't remember his name,

has never been bothered to try—peels away the gauze. He is cautious, careful not to hurt her. How can he know that it already hurts? That she fears the first glimpse of her face? Fears looking into her own eyes and finding a stranger staring back at her?

Miles stands at her bedside, hands dipped in the pockets of his gray dress slacks. The navy and silver and white tie around his neck is loose and crooked. His hair is disheveled. Apparently he's had a long day at work. His eyes rove her face, take in the mystery beneath the gauze, gauge the scars the medical care can't erase, all without ever meeting her gaze.

Humiliation swells inside her when the doctor is finished, and he looks to Miles for a comment. Her face is unveiled, and these two men stand over her and communicate without words, and she has no mirror. She still has no self. The air in the room—neither cold nor hot—feels strange against her newly uncovered skin.

"That's incredible," Miles finally says and she wonders what is incredible and why the hell she has not been given a mirror.

"Could I see?" Her words are no more than a croak. Neither man looks at her. She clears her throat and repeats herself, this time a bit louder.

"In a minute, Caroline." Miles waves a hand at her, as if to dismiss her. An incredible rush of angry heat rolls up into her chest. She scoots to the edge of the bed and stands. Turns her back to them and wonders what wrong she had done in her former life to deserve this treatment, this confinement now.

The doctor speaks in quiet tones about avoiding infection and the need for proper care of both the face and the stitch sites. The face. Not Caroline's face. The face. She licks her lips and sighs. Crosses her arms over chest and waits. She turns back just as the doctor and Miles shake hands. When the man turns to look at her as he pulls open her door, she stares at him coldly. The son-of-a-bitch is another of Miles' pawns in a game he is playing with her. A game she doesn't fully understand yet, but she knows damned well it is a game.

"I want to see my face," she says boldly when they are alone in the room.

"Of course you do." He nods and smiles at her. It looks like a friendly smile. But her imagination paints sharpened tips on the edges of his teeth and a feral glow in his eyes. "I'll get a mirror, and I'll be right back."

She stares at the door when it closes. Why he couldn't let her go to a mirror escapes her. The bathroom adjoining her room here does not have a mirror. There aren't even any small flaws in the wall to suggest there was a mirror, and it had been removed. There aren't any flaws anywhere in the paint in the bathroom or this bedroom, come to think of it. Almost as if it had been redecorated recently.

The door crashes open, and she startles. Jumps and then looks at Miles, certain he can read her thoughts. He carries a small mirror in his left hand. The one with the wedding band. Hers lays on the dresser. She can *not* yet make herself put it on. Dawn and Max traipse in behind him. Frustrated, she closes her eyes and turns her head. This is a moment for solitude. At the very least, a moment for a husband and wife, not an audience.

Dawn folds her hands, as if in prayer, and raises them to touch the tips of her fingers to her lips. She looks hopeful. But for what? Max stares at her with huge eyes, dark with an emotion she can't name as Miles hands her the mirror.

"You've waited for this for a long time, Caroline," Miles tells her. He stands directly in front of her as she looks down at the reflection of her face. She is shocked to see flawless skin. No jagged Frankenstein scars. No bolts holding her head together. Smooth, perfect skin and warm blue eyes stare back at her. She doesn't know this woman who stares back at her. Blue eyes and all, she is a stranger and her presence here in this room drains Caroline.

She'd wanted so damned badly to see a friend in the mirror. And now she still has nothing, no one, not even herself.

She looks up when she hears Max crying. Presses a fist to her heart as Miles picks him up.

"That's not my mommy."

CINDERELLA

Two

1994

Bloomington-Normal, IL

Caroline Evans watches the orange ball—Beth claims it is hibiscus or at the very least, a *mix* of hot pink and orange—roll down the wooden lane. She hears a groan of disgust behind her as the ball hooks half way down and begins to curve toward the head pin. With a resounding smack, the ball takes all ten pins down. Caroline, competitive to a fault, throws her arm up in a victory whoop and turns around to grin at Dawn Rafferty.

"You suck," Dawn mumbles with a laugh.

"Um, no." Caroline tosses her long honey blonde hair over her shoulder and laughs. "You suck."

Dawn drains the brown bottle in front of her and stands. "You want another?" She reaches for Caroline's beer bottle.

"Sure, why not?" Caroline shrugs. She moves to sit at the computer as Dawn leaves her and goes to the bar. The bowling alley is dead tonight. Then again, it's Monday night, and it's too damned cold outside for normal people to be out, and this is exam week. She'd been ready to dig her fingernails into the walls and climb to the ceiling just for kicks, at the apartment studying for her history exam. Thank God she's got a stronger will and maybe hotter blood, because she'd managed to make Dawn think that walking the six blocks to the bowling alley for a beer and a cheeseburger was a good idea.

Dawn hates to compete with her, whether it's bowling or Poker or tennis, so Caroline had promised herself she wouldn't suggest actually *bowling* once they got here. Just a beer or two. Something to eat. A change of scenery. Dawn had been dozing, face first in her accounting book when Caroline had thrown a pillow at her from across the room. She'd been good though. They'd eaten burgers and fries and drank two beers before she'd looked at the pool tables, ready to suggest just one game. Unfortunately all four tables were being used, so a quick game of pool was out of the question. Dawn had said no, before Caroline even twisted on her bar stool to look at the allies.

"We need to go back up to the bar," Dawn tells her. She leans over Caroline's shoulder and sets her beer down in front of her.

"Why?" Caroline lifts the bottle to her mouth.

"Hot guys shooting pool." Dawn raises her eyebrows.

"Hot like Joe Tangey?"

"Please." Dawn rolls her eyes. "Hot like Brad Pitt."

“Thank God you didn’t say Harrison Ford.” Caroline looks back over her shoulder. She can see the pool tables, but from where is sitting, she doesn’t see the guys Dawn is talking about.

“I’m not Beth,” Dawn reminds her. “And Joe Tangey isn’t hot.”

“Was last weekend.” Caroline lifts one shoulder in a lazy shrug. “So you said.”

Dawn shakes her head as a laugh bubbles up inside her. “Shut up.”

“Finish the game. We’re in the ninth frame.”

“What if we miss them?” Dawn sets her beer down and reaches for her ball. Blue. Unmistakably blue. Lighter than the hibiscus hot pinkish orange ball but still. Just one color to go by. Then again, Beth isn’t here, so the color of the bowling ball isn’t a factor tonight.

“Fresh batteries,” Caroline answers.

Dawn barks a loud laugh. Caroline shakes her head as she watches Dawn stand, ball in hand, ready to bowl. They’d met freshman year at Illinois State University. In fact, they’d been roommates, and within two weeks of classes, had become inseparable. Caroline remembers the first day they’d met, when Dawn had stepped into the dorm room, loaded down with duffel bags and backpacks, followed by her Mom and her aunt, both of them loaded down with boxes and more bags. Caroline had pitched in and helped them all get Dawn’s stuff put away, essentially helping to get Dawn settled in, when she herself, had just settled in. When all the handshaking had been done and Dawn’s mom and aunt had hugged her goodbye and all the noise quieted down, Caroline and Dawn had been left standing in the dorm room, looking at each other. Caroline, always one of the crowd but still somewhat of a loner, had stared at Dawn thinking 'what do I do with you?' Now, just three years later, Caroline watches Dawn bowl and thinks what would I do without you?

"Okay, Ace, how do I pick that up?" Dawn asks of the seven ten split on the lane in front of her.

"Wing it and say a prayer to St. Brunswick," Caroline suggests with a shrug.

"You're a lot of help." Caroline waits for her to pick up the ball, but Dawn stands very still, eyes on something behind Caroline. "Don't look now," she says quietly. "But there's some guy really watching you."

"Really?" Caroline jumps up and turns to look. She sees two guys at the bar, but neither of them is looking at her.

"What part of don't look now do you not understand?" Dawn yanks Caroline's arm and half pushes, half pulls her back to sit down at the computer. They both struggle to control their laughter.

"You said guy—"

"I know." Dawn snorts. "And you salivated on command." She leans over the computer and ducks her head because the guy is looking their way again. "Don't look. He'll think we're high school kids."

"What's he look like?" Caroline whispers, with a giggle dangerously close to slipping out.

"You don't have to whisper." Dawn clears her throat. "He's tall. Dark hair. Kind of longish and messy. But it's sexy."

"What's he wearing?"

Dawn eases up her grip on Caroline and looks the other way. Caroline assumes the guy is watching them now. "Jeans. Beige sweater. Loafers. Leather bomber jacket hanging open."

"Tom Cruise or Pierce Brosnan?"

"Tom Cruise."

"And he's watching me?"

"Well, us. But he was looking right at you a few minutes ago."

Caroline takes a drink of her beer. "Okay. Well. You still have to finish this frame."

Dawn nods and raises her eyebrows. "Yeah. Right. Okay."

Caroline feels eyes on her back as Dawn bowls her next ball. She wants to turn around and look, to see him for herself, but she doesn't want to be obvious. She's not desperate, only curious, so she doesn't want to provide false advertising.

When the game is over, she and Dawn change their shoes, gulp down what's left of their beers and head back up to the bar. The guy is standing at the bar now, nursing his own beer. Caroline gives him the once over and decides Dawn's right. The guy is hot, and suddenly she feels desperate. Thankfully, Dawn grabs the back of her shirt and steers her to the shoe rental counter.

"Be cool," Dawn reminds her. "Make him come to you."

Caroline raises her eyebrows. "Maybe he wants you."

"Either way, let him come to us." Dawn turns and smiles at the guy who takes their shoes. She still has a young face, young and cutesy, but Caroline thinks one day she'll grow into the curves and angles of her face and body. She'll be drop-dead gorgeous, while Caroline is still sitting here at college blonde and passable. "Here he comes." Her lips don't move. Caroline stands up straight, a flash of heat surging from her belly out to her fingertips. Funny how you can still feel the nerves and the excitement of a guy or the first meeting with a guy, even after you've fallen in love the first time, played with sex the first time, and had your heart broken down to nothing the first time.

"Can I buy you ladies a drink?" His voice is deep, a little bit gravelly. Something that undoes Dawn Rafferty completely. Caroline looks at Dawn out the corner of her eye. Sees the way her eyes get a bit bigger and almost laughs, thinking the guy could say another word or two and charm Dawn into the backseat of his car.

"We were..." Dawn stammers and looks at Caroline. She wants to accept his offer, but she's making sure it's okay with Caroline first.

"Yeah." Caroline nods. "Thanks."

He slides an arm around Dawn's waist and lays his other hand on the small of Caroline's back and ushers them down to the bar. "Miller Lite?" he asks and Caroline realizes he *had* been watching them. They've both already downed four Miller Lites. They both nod, and he catches the bartender's attention and asks for three. When the bartender sets the three bottles in front of him, he takes one and turns to Dawn, on his right side. Caroline is surprised when he leans toward her and brushes her lips with his.

"For you." She hears him say. So he *is* interested in Dawn. Too bad, because he is definitely easy on the eyes. But she's excited for Dawn anyway. "What's your name?"

"Dawn."

Caroline smiles and reaches for her beer. Before she can pick it up, he does. She leans back out of his reach as he turns to hand her the beer. "And you are—"

"Caroline," she says softly. His eyes are green, and they have flecks of gold in them. His jaw is firm and strong, and his hair dips low on his forehead. She catalogs his face—the scar on his forehead, his long eyelashes and his soft looking full lips—quickly, nervously. She tips the bottle to her lips, but he shakes his head and leans closer to her. Touches his lips to hers.

Disgusted, she wants to slap him. She's not into this kind of game, and she thinks Dawn isn't either. But he smells good. He smells crisp and masculine and when he teases her lips apart with this tongue, he tastes like mint.

"Do you always do that?" she asks bluntly when he pulls away from her.

"What?" he asks. He sits up straight and glances back at Dawn, who still looks enraptured by him, and then back at Caroline. He wears a look of innocence, but he grins at her and then takes a drink of beer. "I'm sorry," he says with a small, almost bashful laugh. "You're both gorgeous. And I figure my luck I'll never see either one of you again, so I thought I'd take my chances and get a kiss from each of you now."

Caroline shifts only her eyes to look at Dawn. Raises her eyebrows when Dawn gives her a nearly imperceptible shrug. She's not sure if she should be pissed—if *they* should be pissed or flattered or what. The kisses had been bold, but soft and undemanding. At least, hers had been. And now he looks sheepish and embarrassed. And he's still hot.

Dawn tips her beer bottle and takes a big drink. They should go home. Nothing good is going to come of this night, and they both have exams tomorrow.

"What's your name?" Caroline asks him. Dawn has a mouthful of beer. Beth, their other roommate, is not here. Only Caroline can talk to him at this exact moment.

"Miles," he says, still wearing the sheepish grin. "Miles Wolfe."

Beth Summers yawns and turns a page in her physics book. The fingers of her left hand are curled absently around a small glass of orange juice; her right hand is now flat against her book. Her hair, the color of sun on a sandy beach—she hates the mix of little bits of blond and too much brown—falls from behind her ear and hangs in front of her face. With a sigh she abandons the orange juice glass and tucks the offending shank back behind her ear.

"Wait." She clears her throat and looks up at Caroline, who stands at the gray and lavender speckled laminate counter. Beth hates it, likens it to a couple of cartons of Easter eggs dropping and cracking and then spreading and growing together and now here they are with this disgusting counter top. What's worse is that Caroline *likes* it. Caroline throws back the last swig of orange juice in her glass, as Dawn pops the top on her Mountain Dew. Beth eyes her with a shiver. "That's disgusting."

"No worse than cold pizza in the morning," Dawn mumbles and shrugs.

Beth looks back at Caroline. "This guy kissed you? Last night? This guy kissed you at the bowling alley?"

"Yep." Caroline nods.

"But you said he kissed you." She turns to look at Dawn.

"Mm-hmm."

"Well, I hope neither of you—" Beth's mouth drops open. She lifts an eyebrow in question and then looks back at Caroline. "Did you guys—? With him? You two—?" She shrugs and lifts both hands to dance in front of her, as if the silly gesture can take the place of the words she can't say. "Together?"

Caroline stares at Beth, a silent laugh edging its way up from her stomach. Dawn snorts Mountain Dew and then coughs and laughs until her eyes water. Beth sits back in the chair, physics book and exam now forgotten. "Do tell," she says sweetly to Caroline.

"He bought us both a beer and kissed us—"

"Both of you," Beth interrupts Caroline to clarify this point. "He kissed both of you."

"Yes," Caroline hisses and laughs. "And then he offered to drive us home."

"Hope he had a big backseat," Beth says on a whistle.

"Shut up." Caroline rolls her eyes. "He was a nice guy. He dropped us off out front and left."

"So this guy," Beth begins. She stands and moves aimlessly around the small kitchen and finally rests a hip against the Easter egg counter top. She's not sure why she got up, except that she feels compelled to stand, as if being on Caroline and Dawn's level, she will understand their story. "This guy flirts with both of you. Buys you both a beer. Kisses you both. Drives you home. End of story."

Caroline and Dawn look at each other and then back at Beth. "Yep." Dawn takes another long pull on her soda.

"Who got his phone number?" Beth folds her arms over her chest.

"I didn't want his number." Dawn shakes her head and shivers, like she's got the willies.

"You didn't?" Caroline asks, surprise evident in her voice and her eyes. "You didn't think he was hot?"

"He kissed us both," Dawn reminds her. "and he lingered with you. I think it was clear who he was interested in."

Caroline's long blonde ponytail swishes as she shakes her head.

"Can't blame him." Beth shrugs. "You're both adorable."

"Yes, of course we are," Dawn agrees. "He was hot, Caroline. I just thought it was weird."

"What's he look like?" Beth glances at the clock. When she sees it is after ten, she steps over to the tiny round table and closes her book.

"What time's your test?" Dawn watches her pack up her books and stuff them in a well-worn navy blue backpack.

"Eleven thirty," Beth answers. "But I need to take a shower."

"Longish brown hair. Green eyes. Square jaw."

Beth raises her eyes to meet Dawn's gaze as Caroline describes the guy. She purses her lips and tilts her head just enough that Dawn knows she is asking if Caroline is really interested in this guy. Dawn kind of shrugs and shakes her head.

"What's his name?" Beth stands up straight again. She stares at Caroline, notices the shine in her eyes. She might deny too much interest, but Caroline wears her heart in her eyes. Love at first sight meets Red Shoe Diaries, Beth thinks. She combs her fingers through her hair and sighs.

"Miles."

"I'm sorry?" Beth laughs and darts a glance at Dawn.

"Miles Wolfe." Caroline doesn't notice the silent communication between Beth and Dawn. "I thought he was sexy." She shakes her head as though snapping out of a daze and turns to set her orange juice glass in the stainless—looks pretty stained to Beth—steel sink. "Not just hot. But sort of mysterious."

"Ah." Beth nods. "Was he wearing a cloak? Carrying a dagger or something?"

"What?" Caroline sighs and looks at Beth over her shoulder. "What's that supposed to mean? He was interesting."

"*Miles*? Miles Wolfe. Sounds like something out of a British spy novel or something."

"Beth." Dawn attempts to step in and cool the debate before it begins. Beth ignores Dawn; she's used to the peacekeeper role her friend assumes. She's not afraid, and she's never been compliant or obedient. She doesn't plan to start any new behaviors anytime soon.

"What's a *Miles* doing at a bowling alley anyway? Should've been at a fox hunt or a wine tasting."

Caroline glances at Dawn—Beth knows she's aware of Dawn ready to step in, proverbial sword in hand to hold down the war—and laughs softly. Beth is pragmatic. She comes off as a bitch sometimes, and she knows it better than anyone. But she's been cursed with the vision of three people here, and she tends to see through the beginnings of things to the end and knows a good thing when she sees it. She knows a bad idea when she sees it too. Caroline isn't stupid, by any means, but she's a romantic and she's already had her ass kicked by love once. Not a good record for a twenty-one year old woman.

Wasn't just class rings and prom punch bowls either. Caroline's been down to hell and back already, and somewhere after getting to know her and befriending her, Beth had somehow become her caretaker. Self-appointed, yes, but still. Old habits die hard. An alcoholic mother and an absent father had taught Beth responsibility. Her responsibility gene doesn't know when *not* to function. In an apartment with two other college girls, Beth is more like a parent than a coed.

Caroline squeezes Beth's arm as she walks by, en route to the bedroom. "Love ya, Beth, but lighten up," she says with a small smile. "Not planning to run way with the guy. I just thought he was interesting."

THOUGH THE SUN IS OUT, IT'S COLD, AND Caroline steels herself for the cold rush of wind that waits just outside the glass-paned doors to ambush her the second she leaves the university library. Her maroon backpack slung up over her shoulder frees her hands, so she pulls her black leather gloves on and then shoves her gloved hands deep inside her coat pockets. She likes winter, but she's had enough of it for this go around. She's ready for spring. She and Dawn and Beth are all ready for spring, ready to go stir crazy cooped up in the apartment that is no bigger than a Fig Newton. Last night they'd entertained themselves by throwing popcorn at each other, to see who could hit an open mouth target. Dawn had won, taking them all by surprise, but Beth had dumped her bowl of popcorn over Dawn, just for laughs and then the rest of the night had involved cleaning up the mess, using the vacuum, watching *Mad About You*, and drinking Keystone beer.

With one last deep breath, Caroline pushes open the door and steps into the brisk winter afternoon. She's thinking about how much she hates canned beer, hell—she's not that big of a beer drinker at all to be honest—as she walks. She doesn't make eye contact with other students as they walk by, but she doesn't purposely avoid anyone's gaze either.

"Caroline?"

Her hair, long and loose, whips in her face when she stops walking and turns to see who has called her name. For a moment, it doesn't register. She doesn't know the guy hurrying the few steps from the library doors to catch up with her. When she does recognize him, she laughs softly at the absurdity of it.

"Miles." She licks her lips and then the wind stings them and she wishes she wouldn't have. Nervous energy can cause bad habits. She's familiar with a lot of them.

"Hi."

She doesn't remember his smile being so simple. Kind. He looks surprised to see her. Maybe he is. It's been a few weeks since the night he'd bought them a beer and double dipped, according to Beth. She might have expected him to look older or sinister, but maybe that's because she'd seen him in the unnatural, almost *dingy* light of the bowling alley and then sitting in the dark interior of his '92 Chevy Camaro. In broad daylight, sans Dawn and Beth, Miles Wolfe seems harmless and almost boyish, with that dimple just under his smile and happy to see her.

"Hi." She returns his smile. Now that she is standing still, the cold has caught up to her and crept inside her coat. "Were you in the library?"

"Guilty." He nods. He has a backpack tossed over his shoulder too. "Research paper."

She lifts her eyebrows but lets her eyelids close. Shakes her head a bit. She hates research papers. Given the choice, she'd rather go to the dentist than write a research paper. "Me too," she says on a sigh.

Cold air has snaked its way inside her blouse now. She can feel it against her neck and her chest. She pulls her hands from her pockets and folds her arms across her chest, attempting to fight off the cold. Without the beer crutch and the smoky haze of the bowling alley, she's lost as to what to say to him. She hasn't dated much since her senior year of high school. A couple of flings and a few things that didn't stick around long enough to qualify as flings, but she hasn't stood outside in front of the school library and talked to a guy in a long time. She stomps her heeled, booted feet to bring a little life back into them. Avoids meeting his eyes but sneaks a look at him when she thinks he's not looking. His hair is a gorgeous mix of sable and chocolate and even a touch of deep, dark red. She thinks there might be fewer than twenty red strands in it, but it is the perfect color with the thick shades of brown.

He catches her staring. She fights the urge to look away. "It's cold out here," he says the obvious and then laughs and sounds a bit nervous. It is cold, but hearing that tiny out of tune nerve in his voice warms her heart. She should get going. Do some studying before her next class. His eyes send a flash of heat over her face as he studies her. He pushes his hands deep into his pockets and hunches his shoulders and lowers his head for a moment.

Butterfly wings flutter against her stomach and then up against her heart. As if she is a swimmer, breaking the surface of water, she gasps for air and then looks away quickly. Watches other students come and go. Wishes she were at the apartment. Warm. Comfortable. Wishes he would say something. Kind of cool that he happened to see her again. She doesn't want to let this go so easily this time.

He lifts his head just a bit. Looks at her from the corner of his eye.

"You wanna go get some coffee or something?" The sheepish smile touches her. Kind of slams into her, actually. Again, she feels breathless. What if he just wants to talk to her about Dawn, though? She starts to answer him, but the words don't want to come. He might be interested in Dawn. He might think he can get something going with both of them. She studies his eyes when he stands up straight and stares at her expectantly. His eyes are so green, there's no room for duplicity there. Besides, what difference does it make? She is intrigued by him. Why not go and have a cup of coffee and talk to him? Get to know him.

"Sure." She figures her smile is as uncertain as his was. Except she doesn't have that damned cute dimple to knock the corner of hers up a fraction of an inch higher on one side. She hadn't noticed the dimple the first night, not even when he'd kissed her. She wonders what it would feel like to kiss him there. To touch the tip of her tongue to his dimple. To feel his lips smiling under hers.

"Do you wanna walk?" he asks with a shrug. "Stay on campus?"

It's still cold. She still can't feel her toes. But she wonders, as they walk side by side, if that has more to do with walking on air than the temperature.

RAPUNZEL

THREE

June, 2008

Springfield, IL

Caroline's eyes are still closed when she senses she is not alone in the room. She lays quietly, hoping that whoever is in the room with her did not notice her body stiffen with alarm when she sensed another presence. She lays with her back to the door, the one that was dead bolted from the outside. Slits open her left eye, the one half buried in her pillow. Searches, without moving, the room bathed in pale moonlight and streetlight together.

Miles? Miles is standing at the window, his back to her. She can see maybe a quarter of his face as he stares through the glass to the night beyond and sees something Caroline can only wonder about. Without a sound or movement, she studies him, his slumped shoulders and the sliver of his face that is visible to her. His body says defeat; his face is a mask she can't quite recognize. It's not innocence. There're too many lines carved in his aging skin to call his expression one of innocence or even innocence lost.

Sorrow. Spotlighted in moonlight, in her dark room, he is a black and white still life that she would entitle Sorrow. She wonders if this, if her accident, has caused him this much grief and aged him and branded him a haunted man. If they are husband and wife, it seems an accident, injuries of this magnitude could definitely sock him in the gut and take his zest for life away. It's not so much that she can't remember him or their life together that makes her question the paint he wears at the moment. It's simply that she doesn't understand why she is spending her recovery locked away in a prison he has tried to disguise as a simple, harmless bedroom.

Suddenly consumed with the possibility that he has spent more than one night standing in her room, staring out her window or watching her sleep, she pushes herself to sit up. To let him know that she is awake. Even though she wears knit boxers and a simple t-shirt that covers every curve on her rather angular, scrawny body—she couldn't have been this thin before, has to be the result of the accident and injuries and stress—she is careful to keep the sheet and comforter pulled up to her waist.

"What're you doing?" Her hoarse whisper doesn't jolt him. He stands still as time in that perfect, horrible moment just before tragedy steps in and nails your ass to the wall.

"Thinking." His voice is a little gruff, a little quiet. He turns toward her, leans a shoulder on the window trim and stares at her. He still wears the pants he wore earlier this evening. Dark and casual. His dark colored shirt is untucked, the top three buttons open to reveal a t-shirt beneath it.

"What about?"

Something, tonight, is different. She doesn't know if it's the moonlight that sucks the color out of the room and renders it neutral. Or if it's the uncharacteristic stubble that darkens Miles' jaw, in an already darkened room. Or if it's the weariness he wears as if carries the world on his shoulders and he is simply exhausted. At the moment, she does not see a man who holds her captive in a strange room. He's just a man who's seen better days.

In the absence of color and light and sound, she feels as if they are equals. Maybe they *were* once lovers. Husband and wife. She shifts, uncomfortable with her thoughts rather than the way he is watching her.

"About you," he finally says. The deep breath he sucks in and blows out is tinged with frustration and sadness.

"What about me?" Of course she wonders. What the hell is he thinking about, about her? She'd like to think about it too; she'd sure as hell like to remember more than the flashes she's gotten that go so fast she ends up with only sensations—pain, fear, dread—instead of memories.

Hands in his pockets, he lowers his head as if to rest his chin on his chest. The silence is long and lengthy and sits beside her on her bed, like a date trying to charm his way under the sheets. When he finally raises his chin, he turns back to the window, takes a deep breath, and shrugs, as if he is talking to himself and answering himself with a 'why not?'

"Do you wanna take a walk?" He turns back to her.

"Do I—? What?" She glances around, wondering what time it is. There are no clocks in her room. Not sure what clocks could have to do with memories that might harm her —unless she used to repair watches and iced a guy with a watch tool or was crushed beneath a grandfather clock and lost her memories as time weighed her down—she wonders why the hell Miles can't at least give her a simple alarm clock. Or a watch, for God's sake. "What time is it, Miles? Jesus, I don't even have a clock in here—"

Her voice had risen steadily, the familiar fear and anger growing inside of her. Miles holds his hands up in surrender and steps toward the bed. "It's twenty after two. And I'll get you a clock." He stops, still a few feet from her bed and swallows hard and repeats, "I'll get you a clock, Caroline."

Not sure how to take his gesture, his sudden move to placate her, she looks away from his probing eyes. Licks her lips and wishes for Chapstick. Figuring it's risky to ask for two things in one night, she instead focuses on his asking her if she wanted to take a walk.

"You want to go on a walk? At two-thirty in the morning?"

"Why not?" He shrugs. "Dawn's here. In the room next door to Max—"

"Why—" Again the anger seethes, front and center. Again, Miles steps toward her, a look of apology on his face.

"Please," he says softly. He's never sounded so real as he does here tonight. "Could we just walk for a while? And not fight?"

She curls her fingers into tight fists, to keep them from reaching out to him. They'd wanted badly to reach out and stroke his jaw. Feel the rough stubble and the softness of his lips.

"Did we fight a lot?" Her voice is husky, thick with memories that don't quite reach her heart or her mind.

"Not in the beginning." He reaches to rub the back of his neck, a pained look on his face. He doesn't like that they fought. Or he doesn't like admitting it.

"But." She doesn't know why she's pushing this. Why push this one little thing, because his answer isn't going to shed any miraculous light on anything. Why not get up and get dressed and go for a walk. She wonders absently if she could smell the honeysuckle outside, if she were to go out now and walk in the moonlight.

"But." He sighs and nods.

"In the end..."

"We did." He purses his lips and looks down at her and raises an eyebrow in question. "Walk with me?"

THE SMELL OF HONEYSUCKLE *IS* IN THE AIR WHEN she follows Miles out the front door. Though the temperature had spiked at ninety-six today, it's almost chilly now. The cool air against her bare skin is a comforting whisper. She moves slowly off the front porch, flexes her leg muscles tenderly. In the moonlight, her pale legs look silver and less pasty than they do in the sunlight. She'd slipped a pair of gray drawstring shorts on when Miles had left the room. Left the same t-shirt on and then stepped into her running shoes. The shoes someone else had bought her, she assumes. The white Nikes with little blue swishes look brand new, and she has no recollection of buying them.

Maybe Dawn picked them out. The thought comes from out of nowhere and then suddenly it's *right* there and she almost trips over it, and Miles lays a hand on her arm to steady her. She jumps back, yanks her arm away from him, although she'd felt no dominance or power in is touch. He looks away but not before she sees his eyes flash with hurt. If it hurts him so much that she reacts to him this way, why doesn't he understand how she feels, being treated as a prisoner?

"Max jumped off the high dive today," he tells her proudly. He flits a glance at her, but his eyes continue to roam the gray and black night. She nods and swallows hard, wonders if she's ever watched her son at swim lessons.

"Do you go with him?" she asks softly.

"Sometimes." He gives her a nod. "With work, I can't always take—"

She nods and then shakes her head and looks the other way, dismissing his words. He can't always take Max to lessons, so *Dawn* does. That's what he was going to say. She doesn't want to hear it. She doesn't want to hear the woman's name right now.

"Tell me something." She licks her lips. Folds her arms across her chest as they move slowly through the yard. They walk slower than she needs to for her leg. They're moving cautiously to avoid falling back into earlier. To the harsh words they can't seem to help exchanging.

"What?" He stops and turns to her.

"I—I don't know." She lowers her eyes when he stares at her. Hates that he studies her so openly. Had it always been like this? Him studying her face, her trying to turn away? "Just talk to me."

He purses his lips and nods absently. She feels the heat dissipate when he turns his head and watches a car creep by on the road out front. It's an odd time to be out, she thinks. Then again, it's *their* yard, *their* lives, which are so odd at the moment. It might be perfectly normal for that car to be out at this early morning hour. Somewhere someone is working third shift in a factory. Walking the halls of a hospital. Dancing hip to hip to pounding music in a nightclub. Maybe it's only this tiny part of the world that is on hold right now.

"Your favorite color is lavender," he says with a shrug. "You had this lavender blouse you used to wear. When we were in college." He looks at her again, meets her eyes and looks away quickly. "You were so gorgeous in that blouse."

Lavender seems wrong. It doesn't set right with her. It's a pretty color, but it doesn't seem like it should be her favorite. Then again, maybe clear blue is her favorite color right now, because it is the sky just beyond the window that teases her in her luxurious prison cell.

"We went to college together?" she asks, instead of worrying about lavender.

"We met when you were a senior."

She covers her teeth with the tip of her tongue and tries to remember. Tries to see Miles in college. Tries to see herself in college. She groans and shakes her head. Black wall. No memory. Just a black wall in her mind. A slippery black wall that she can't scale.

“Caroline, it’ll come to you.” He means well. But the gentleness in his voice rakes down her back like sharp fingernails.

“Don’t,” she snaps. “Don’t pity me. Don’t tell me it’ll come.” She loosens her folded arms and throws her hands in the air. “When? When, Miles? How long have I been like this? How long?”

He flinches at the anger in her voice. Is this hard on him? Or is he thinking about their fights? How often did they fight? Why did they fight?

“The accident was about eight,” he shrugs and presses his lips together, loses the battle with himself and continues, “Eight...nine months ago.”

Eight? Nine months ago? She opens her mouth to answer him, but his words have robbed her of her breath. She can’t breathe. Oh God. She touches her neck. She can’t breathe. Her lungs burn. They’re going to explode. She sobs and digs her fingernails into the skin on her neck. “Eight months? I’ve been locked in that fucking room for eight months?”

The tears that thicken her voice take the anger from her words. Still she claws desperately at her neck. Tears wet her face. “You’ve had me locked in that fucking cell for eight months?”

“Don’t say that.” His voice is clipped.

“Don’t—? But. You lock that door every night. It’s a deadbolt—"

He turns to her. The cold anger in his eyes makes her take a step back. "You know I don't like it when you talk that way. You don't say that word in front of me."

She takes another step back. "Fuck?" Her laugh is harsh and bent around the edges, barely disguising the pain that shreds her insides. "You're angry with me for saying fuck? And you've kept me a prisoner in that house for the past eight or nine months?"

"No." He almost yells. Almost. His voice is tight and clipped with anger. Nearly quivers with control. He's packing old and new rage right now, but she's not afraid of him. "No. I have not kept you a prisoner here. You're recovering from a serious accident. You've had everything you've—"

"That doesn't change that you have a deadbolt on my fucking door, Miles!" She can't hold her anger in. Her face is wet with tears. Her blood is hot as her heart pounds in her chest. "I don't care if you had specialists fly in from Germany or Switzerland to help me. You've had me locked in that Goddamned room for—"

She sucks in a hard breath as his hand clamps over her mouth. She'd been so intent on getting it out, getting that burning anger out, that she hadn't paid attention to him moving to stand closer to her. He's strong. The arms that circle her and pin hers to her side are made of steel. She fights, tries to wiggle out of his hold, but she can't.

"I didn't hold you prisoner for eight months. You were in the hospital, in a coma for six months. You've been here since March."

The words are like a sedative. Instantly still. She throws her head back on his shoulder and cries silently. The feeling of equality she'd had earlier in her room is gone. Once again, Miles is her captor, and she is helpless.

He leads her back to the house. She's weak, and she leans heavily on him. It makes her sick to lean on him, and when they reach the front porch, she puts her hand out. Leans to steady herself on the step. Her stomach tips. She coughs. Gags. She's going to throw up. Miles' hand is on her back. She wishes she had the strength to move. To get away from his touch. Sweat dampens the hair on her neckline. Her knees are weak and the sidewalk under her feet feels like quicksand.

She looks up, wishing for the courage to tell him to get away from her. Dawn watches them from the bay window in the living room.

~

THUNDER EXPLODES AROUND HER. JARS HER. SHE can feel it shake her deep in the bones. The rain, slow to come, now beats the grass in a steady rhythm. The wind, cool itself, angles cold splatters of rain against her bare legs. Knowing Dawn might think she is crazy and Max would worry about her, she fights the urge to climb down from the porch and stand in the rain. The rain might wash away this non-person she's become, and maybe when the storm moved on, she would be left with the woman she used to be.

True to his word, Miles had put a clock in her room. A digital alarm clock, on the small cherry nightstand beside her bed. He'd also brought her a calendar, laid it on her dresser, open to the month of June. Never mind that the clock is only a clock, not a radio and the calendar has no notes about preschool play dates or lunches with friends. She'd gotten up just after seven, even after not sleeping through most of the night.

She rubs her arms now, to smooth out the goose bumps on her skin. They have nothing to do with the cool rain. Miles had come back inside her room and put the clock and calendar there. Apparently she'd slept some, because she doesn't remember him coming into her room again. Dawn had brought her a cup of coffee and a muffin not long after she'd gotten dressed. She'd hardly touched either; her stomach was still sour after last night. When Miles had come to her door, just after ten, to ask if she wanted to sit outside, she'd jumped at the chance. She'd have gone happily with the devil just then if it meant sitting outside for a while.

The screen door makes a small squeak, as it is pushed open, but Caroline does not look to see who has come out on the porch. If it is Dawn or Miles, she doesn't care. If it is Max, she thinks she'd like him to sit with her on the swing and count the seconds between crashes of thunder and streaks of lightning.

One Mississippi. Two Mississippi. Laughing. Loud and happy. Thunder booming and chanting the count and laughing.

"Are you okay?"

Because she wonders if Dawn is a watchdog, waiting for her to exhibit signs of craziness, Caroline forces herself to be still when she hears her voice. The jump is inside her, but she contains it. She watches the rain for a moment and then finally looks to her right and sees Dawn a few feet from the swing. Looking at her with a mix of sadness and anxiety all over her face, the way Max used to wear his baby fruit and vegetables all over his face when he sat in his highchair and she pretended his spoon was an airplane flying to his mouth.

The thought flows naturally through her mind, but it leaves her chilled as it slips away. Max. Max as a baby. Had she really remembered that? Or has her mind taken to making things up in an attempt to soothe her and tell her she isn't crazy? Caroline looks away from Dawn again, sure the woman can read the mix of annoyance and confusion and frustration on her face. What does she do? Call Miles after she and Caroline have a conversation? Write it down? Does she journal? Is their verbatim conversation Miles' reading pleasure in the evening? If so, it's light reading, because conversation between herself and Dawn has been sparse.

"I'm fine," she answers calmly. She holds her breath. Wonders if Dawn has come to take her back inside. Back to the *room.* The *fucking room* with the deadbolt that locks from the outside.

"Last night..."

Caroline looks up in alarm. Dawn's brown eyes are huge in her pale face. Something has stripped off the healthy tan of her face, the one that makes Caroline crave sunshine. Dawn waits for Caroline to answer. Caroline gives her only silence. Dawn shoves her hands into the pockets of her denim shorts. She stares at Caroline, with eyes haunted by some unknown demon. Caroline pushes back an inch or two, into the corner of the swing, when Dawn moves hesitantly, to sit with her.

"What happened? Last night?" Dawn nearly swallows her own whisper.

Caroline clenches her teeth in time to catch her words. 'Go to hell.' A woman who stands by and lets a man *lock* his wife in a room and monitor her every action is not a friend. Stands by. Caroline snorts and looks away. Stands by, hell. Dawn is living the life she is supposed to believe was once hers. Talking to Miles every day. Spending time with her son. Reading to her son—

"What happened?" Dawn repeats. She leans forward and starts to reach for Caroline. To touch her. Caroline stares at her coldly and watches her hand fall between them, to rest on the wooden slats of the swing. "Did you remember something?"

"Should I have remembered something?" Caroline asks her. She looks over Dawn's shoulder, wondering what Max is doing. Dawn jerks her head around to see what Caroline is looking at.

"I heard you screaming—"

"I wasn't screaming—"

"You were angry—"

"I was yelling." Caroline shrugs. "Where's Max?"

"Fell asleep watching The Doodlebugs." Dawn licks her lips. "I carried him up to his room and laid him on his bed."

Caroline smacks her lips and gives Dawn a curt nod. "Do you have any idea." She takes a deep breath and lets it out slowly. Calm. Stay clam, for God's sake, or Miles might show up with a strait jacket and march you back to the room. "Do you have any idea what it's like to be told he's my son? And to see you with him like this?"

Dawn only stares at her.

"Do you?" Caroline pushes.

Dawn's eyes are wet with tears she does not try to hide. "Do you know what it's like to watch your best friend wake up in the same nightmare she went to sleep to a year ago?"

The words slam her in the chest. A little bit under her heart. Hard enough to hurt. She winces and raises her eyes to study the wooden ceiling of the porch. Closes her eyes when she feels Dawn's heavy, suffocating stare.

"You're not my friend, Dawn." She forces the words out. Anger is her shield, her talisman. Push and hold her off. Solitude is her only friend right now. She trusts no one. Not even herself. "If you were my friend, you would help me. Not him. You would help me."

Caroline opens her eyes and drags them from the ceiling overhead to the blonde who sits beside her. Face streaked with tears and eyeliner and mascara. Dawn cries out loud and then presses her fist to her mouth.

"It's not my choice, Caroline." She pushes her hair back from her face and shakes her head. "This isn't my choice."

CINDERELLA

FOUR

1994

Springfield, IL

"You're going out with him?" Beth finally raises her head from her trigonometry book and looks closely at Caroline. "Really?"

"Really." Caroline rolls her eyes. She's been flopped across Dawn's bed for the past half hour, talking to Beth about Miles Wolfe. She's said three times now that she and Miles are going out this coming Saturday night. Apparently Beth has finally chosen to hear her.

Beth tips her head a bit—thinking, Caroline knows she's thinking—and taps her pencil against her notebook. "Space Rats are playing the first weekend of March," she says absently. "At the bar."

The bar is actually Fitzgerald's, a college bar where the three of them have spent the majority of their college life. Space

Rats is a local grunge band that Beth claims is the new hot streak. She claims the lead singer is hotter than Jon Bon Jovi, which is saying something, because Beth loves the icons.

"Car." Beth sighs. Caroline sighs louder. Lecture time. She draws herself up to sit, crosses her legs and sinks her teeth into her bottom lip, waiting for Beth to begin. So she can tune out and wait for Beth to finish.

"This going to take long? Because I have to read some—"

"Shut up." Beth giggles. "Are you sure?"

"What's not to be sure of? It's just a date. Dinner and a movie."

Beth flops backwards on Caroline's bed and stretches. She is long and lean. Sexy, but unapproachable. She doesn't date much, to Caroline's knowledge. Spends the night away from the apartment now and then, so Caroline assumes she sees *someone* now and then. Never anything serious.

"I don't think I like him." Beth turns to her right side, stacks her hands, as if folded in prayer, under her cheek and stares at her.

"Beth, you don't even know him."

"But he hit on you and Dawn."

Caroline winces and glances at the bedroom door, as if she's expecting Dawn to swoop in and catch them talking about her. "Did she say something? Does she want to go out with him?"

"Dawn?" Beth shakes her head against her hand. "No, no.

Nothing like that. I just think it's wrong that he kissed both of you that night at the bowling alley."

"Beth, it was a kiss. Barely there. It's not like he had his tongue jammed down anyone's throat."

"But it doesn't seem weird to you?"

"No." Caroline shrugs. "You worry too much."

"When did he ask you out?"

Caroline launches Dawn's pillow at Beth. "When we were getting coffee the other day."

"I take it you told me that already?" Beth laughs and pushes Dawn's pillow off to the floor.

"Three times." Caroline lays back, head at the foot of Dawn's twin bed. The room is cramped, no doubt about it. Three twin beds tucked inside. A dresser that she and Dawn share. Beth got dibs on the closet. Caroline can't imagine it any other way. She'll be lost after graduation, when she moves wherever it is her life will take her. There's comfort in waking to the sounds of her two best friends breathing and sleeping peacefully. Except when one of them has a cold, she thinks. A small smile pushes at the corners of her mouth.

"What's he like?"

"He's quiet," Caroline answers immediately. She'd been hoping Beth would ask. Because she's been thinking about him all day. All day yesterday. And she needs to talk about him. To *gush* about him with a girlfriend. And she wants Beth to like him. Beth has been her backbone for the past three years, when she has gone soft or sad. Beth is a part of her, and she needs her approval as much or more than she would need her parents' approval.

"Quiet how?"

"Just. I don't know." Caroline shakes her head. "Economical. With words. Doesn't say more than needs to be said. He's calm. His eyes say so much. He can be calm, but his eyes are alive when he talks about what he's interested in ."

"What's he interested in?"

"Music," Caroline says for a start.

"Shit. You hooked up with a musician—"

"And art." If Caroline could reach the pillow on her own bed, she'd snag it and throw it at Beth. "Baseball. Science."

"Science?" Beth props herself up on her elbow. "Miles, the science geek."

"Beth." Caroline sits up again. "Don't. Please?"

"Don't what?"

"Don't make up your mind before you meet him. I want you to like him."

Beth nods. They hear the door to the apartment open and slam closed. Dawn's home. And she must be pissed. "Caroline, I want to like him," Beth says softly. "But I do like you. I don't wanna see you get hurt."

"I know—" Caroline looks up when Dawn appears in the bedroom doorway. "Hey. Dawn, what's wrong? You look like hell."

She does. Her hair is disheveled and tangled. Dried tear tracks decorate her pale face. Her fingers curl so tight around the small plastic bag in her hand, her knuckles are white. Caroline notices it is an Osco bag. Convenience store. Drug store.

"Are you sick?"

"I was at Trevor's place," Dawn mumbles.

"What's wrong?" Beth sits up and pats the bed beside her. Dawn takes two steps and sinks to the bed, plastic bag still clutched tightly in her hand.

"Guys," Dawn begins and then folds. She buries her face in her hands and cries quietly.

"Dawnie." Caroline moves with the stealth of a cat, to kneel on the floor in front of Dawn. Beth scoots sideways to sit closer to her. "What happened?"

Caroline touches Dawn's hand. Tries to uncurl the fingers locked tight around the bag.

"I think..." Dawn tries to take a breath, but she's still crying and her nose is stuffy. Caroline pries Dawn's fingers loose and opens the bag.

"Oh Dawn." Beth touches her hand to Dawn's back and rubs so slow and gentle, Dawn is hardly aware of the touch. EPT. The box is unopened.

"What about Trevor?" Caroline asks. She sets the box on the bed, beside Dawn, and then rests her hands on Dawn's knees. "You don't know yet. What about Trevor? Why are you crying?"

"I think I am." Dawn rubs her eyes. "We're just friends. It just happened one night. And now I think—He went out with this girl the other night. Fourth date. He told me he's in love with her. Thinks she walks on water."

Dawn sucks in a sob to hold it back. The quiet in the room is stifling. Beth still rubs Dawn's back. Caroline squeezes her knees.

"I can't do this to him," Dawn whispers and shakes her head.

"Wait," Caroline says firmly. "Why do you think you're pregnant?"

"I'm two weeks late."

"Have you done a test?"

"Not yet," Dawn admits.

"Then let's do one," Caroline suggests. She climbs to her feet and reaches out a hand to Dawn.

"Let's?" Dawn repeats.

"Me and Beth." Caroline nods. "All for one, one for all."

"You don't have to watch me pee on a stick." Dawn almost laughs.

"Watched you pee in that alley last weekend." Beth shrugs.

"I was drunk."

"Weren't we all?" Beth stands and takes Dawn's other hand.

"Okay, okay," Dawn groans. She pulls her hands away and stands and then rubs her eyes. "Okay. Gimme a minute."

"Open the door when you're done."

"Or what?" Dawn asks as she picks up the box from the bed.

"We'll break the door down," Caroline answers sweetly.

"You and what army?"

"Flimsy door," Beth says with a smile.

Dawn's hands shake as she rips the box open.

"No matter what," Caroline says when Dawn steps into the bathroom, "we're here."

The words set Dawn into more tears. Beth elbows Caroline and mutters 'good job.' Dawn laughs and cries and moves her lips around the words 'thank you' and then closes the door in their faces.

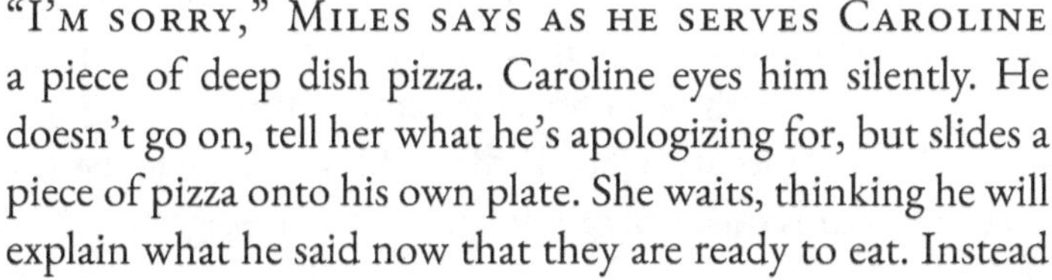

"I'M SORRY," MILES SAYS AS HE SERVES CAROLINE a piece of deep dish pizza. Caroline eyes him silently. He doesn't go on, tell her what he's apologizing for, but slides a piece of pizza onto his own plate. She waits, thinking he will explain what he said now that they are ready to eat. Instead he takes a drink from his pilsner glass and looks around the restaurant.

"Sorry?" She shakes her head and shrugs. "What're you sorry for?"

"For bringing you here," he mutters. He meets her eyes and smiles that quiet, sheepish smile she's come to like. She spends a half a second looking at his dimple, thinking about kissing that dimple and then gives herself a mental shake and looks up at him again.

"Why?"

"You deserve better," he says simply. "Should've done something fancy. For our first date."

Caroline picks up her bottle—she hates drinking beer out of a glass—takes a long drink, and looks around the restaurant, the same way Miles had just done.

"Why? Why do I deserve better than this?" She considers her jeans, her boots, the red sweater she wears. Her hair is long and loose over her shoulders. She has a touch of makeup on. All in all, she's not a bad package, and she knows that, but she's not a queen either. "I like pizza."

Miles laughs with her and maybe at himself and nods. "I do too." He shakes parmesan over his slice. "But I'd like to take you somewhere nice. Dinner. A bottle of wine."

Caroline is pretty sure the warmth she's feeling in her stomach that radiates to her fingertips has nothing to do with the beer or the comfortable temperature in the pizza joint. Any doubts are zapped when Miles reaches across the table and skims the back of her hand with his fingers.

She presses her lips together and raises her eyebrows. Smiles. "We could always do a second date."

When she turns her hand over on the table, Miles strokes his finger gently over her palm. "I'd like that."

His eyes, right now, are such a deep green Caroline feels as if she is being sucked into a forest where she and Miles are alone, together. She chews nervously on her lip and then realizes she's forgetting to breathe. Seems like her last breath was sometime around him saying bottle of wine. She laughs and breathes all at once and wishes she could kick herself for acting like a nervous teenager. This is a date. An actual date, not him buying her a beer at the bowling alley or a cup of coffee, after meeting up with her on campus between classes. This is a date. Dates mean goodnight kisses.

Struck by that thought, Caroline has to drag her eyes away from his lips. She wants to kiss him. She really wants to kiss him. Feel his lips on hers, on her face, on her neck. Press her body against his, to see if he's hard and lean—that's what he looks like—or if he's warm but sturdy.

She takes a deep breath again, but tries to disguise it. Doesn't want Miles to know she's suddenly a wreck inside. Kissing him. Thinking about Dawn, and the way he'd kissed her that first night. About Beth and her stubborn distrust of him. She doesn't know what to think.

Get to know him better, she tells herself. *Talk* to him and get to know him. Then make Beth get to know him and she'll like him.

"Did you get your research paper written?" Her question kills the lengthy silence that hovers over them. For a moment, he looks lost and then he grins. She thinks that grin must have saved his ass a time or two when he was in grade school, maybe even high school.

"Almost done with the first draft," he tells her.

"And what are you writing about?" She takes a bite of the pizza, careful not to burn herself with the cheese that inevitably strings from the slice and touches her lip and burns her.

"Multinational corporations in third world countries."

"Political science?"

He nods. Caroline notices that he seems excited that she was able to put his research topic with a field of study. "I'm studying some political science and some business courses."

"And do you like them?" she asks. He's got that gleam in his eyes right now, the one that seems to turn on when he's fired up about something. "Which classes do you prefer?"

"I do like them, actually." He takes a long drink of his beer and considers her next question. "I don't know that I like either better. My father's family owns a steel mill. I'm taking the business courses to take over the office for my father."

"And the political science classes because the steel mill is already a multinational corporation."

He answers with a small smile and a slight nod. "What about you?"

"What about me?"

He wears a crème colored turtleneck sweater. His skin is just enough of a color to look good with the crème sweater, but not tan enough to look painted on. His dark hair is on the longish side, the rich color perfect with the sweater. He's the exact opposite of Shane. Shane. Fair skinned. Close cropped blonde hair and dark blue eyes. She'd loved his eyes—

"What paper are you working on?"

"History. I'm studying the Federalist Papers."

"Really?" He purses his lips and nods. "Do you like it? History?"

She thinks for a moment. In the big scheme of things, she does like history. But she still doesn't have a clear cut view of her future, what she wants to be when she grows up. She's declared communications as her major, but she thinks that is college lingo for no fucking clue. She's considered advertising or marketing. She's considered teaching. Hell, after her senior year and the hell with Shane Beck, archeology sounded good. A dig on the far side of the world, where she'd never have to think about here. About home. About him.

"I like history," she answers Miles. "But I don't love it."

"What do you love?" he asks without hesitation.

He watches her intensely. She can't answer him. She can't put her heart out here on the table, the way he is studying her. She'd only mentioned to Beth and Dawn once or twice that she'd like to study law and either continue with law school or find a career in law enforcement. True, they'd both supported her and applauded her and for whatever reason, they both seem to believe she is capable of either choice she would make. But she is afraid to tell Miles that much about herself. Because what if she would fail? What would he think of her then?

"I don't know yet," she finally answers. "Still thinking about it."

"Okay," he says and nods. "Fair enough."

They pass the evening away with pizza and beer and storytelling. Caroline thinks she could easily slide back into the corner of the booth, hold her beer, and listen to him talk all night. She loves his voice, and twice he's made her laugh to the point of tears. But he doesn't let her just listen. He wants to hear her stories too. For the first time since Shane, Caroline finds herself opening to someone—a guy—and sharing more than a half hour of sweaty, mind blowing sex. It scares the hell out of her.

RAPUNZEL

FIVE

June, 2008

Springfield, IL

Caroline walks the house like a ghost. She passes through rooms as easily as if she hovers above the ground and moves through walls. Not a single room touches her, makes her mind tingle with an almost memory. She could just as easily be at a cozy bed and breakfast in the country. With a young boy and a man and another woman. As if she occupies one room and another *family* vacations in another suite.

She stops short, hand still on the doorframe, when she sees Dawn curled in the corner of a sofa. She takes a quick glance around to orient herself. Living room? Family room? Hell, if she knows. There's no TV. Just a sofa—a chocolate brown leather sofa. A turquoise and brown wingback chair with a matching ottoman. Closet door. Lots of bookshelves, lots of books. She's torn. Maybe looking at the spines of the books would make her remember something. And yet, to get to the bookshelves, she has to step into the room and make her presence known. She doesn't want to.

Before she can make up her mind, Dawn turns her head slightly. She sees her, but she makes no move to acknowledge her. Though their eyes meet, Caroline feels as if Dawn is looking at seventeen scenes of life before she sees her face. She'd caught Dawn in a pensive moment, and though she wonders what is on the woman's mind, she steps back to leave her alone.

"You can go," Dawn says softly.

"What?" Caroline looks back at her over her shoulder.

"You can go." Dawn stands up and crosses the room. Her bare feet make no sound on the dark, hardwood floor. She moves to stand further away from Caroline, rather than near her.

"Go where?"

"Just go." Dawn shrugs. She turns her back to Caroline and wanders farther into the room. She stands in shadows now in the far corner of the room. "Miles went out of town. He'll be gone through Sunday."

Go? Go where? For a walk? For a drive? The grocery store? A mall? Escape her prison? Wherever the hell she goes, she won't get far. She has no money—no spending cash, at least not to her knowledge. She has no identification. She has no safe haven to run to, at least not one that she can remember.

"And what? You're telling me to go?" Caroline steps into the room. The books, full of so many words, offer a hushed sort of silence she's always associated with churches and libraries. The silence calms her, but she still doesn't know where Dawn thinks she might go.

"Haven't you wanted to get out? Get away from him?" Dawn asks. She turns to watch Caroline, as she glances at books and reads titles, almost absently. "You hate that he locks you in that room."

Caroline turns to look at Dawn. "Am I wrong to hate being *locked* in that room?" Frustrated, she throws her hands up, palms to the ceiling and shrugs. "I never said—"

Dawn nods and looks away. "You did," she says quietly.

Caroline licks her lips and shakes her head. "Where would I go?" She stands awkwardly under Dawn's heavy gaze, waiting for the other woman to say something. When she doesn't, Caroline steps around her and walks slowly to the other side of the room. She feels Dawn's eyes on her still, but the hush of the books is now so loud she's not sure she would hear Dawn if the woman did speak.

Caroline wanders back behind the desk and trails her fingers over the surface. It now stands between her and apparent freedom, according to Dawn, if only she had a place to go. The desk is spotless. No dust. No paper clip out of place. No file folder askew on the calendar. The black Dell flat screen monitor is dark. No evidence to be found about who sits in this chair and uses this computer.

When the silence in the room becomes impossibly loud to bear, Caroline turns back to look at Dawn. The other woman is gone; Caroline is alone in the room. A chill climbs her spine, like tiny little spikes hitching into her vertebrae one by one. Miles is gone through Sunday. She glances back at the calendar. There are no notations on it.

No meetings. No dentist appointments. It's as if this is a dummy house. No one really lives here. It's a set on a movie stage. These walls hold no memories, no family laughter or secrets.

She hurries—as much as she can—to the hall when she hears Dawn on the stairs.

"Max?" she asks when Dawn looks at her in askance.

"With Miles."

"Where did they go?" Caroline asks. Dawn pauses near the top of the staircase. She swallows hard, as if she's about to tell Caroline something life altering. "Dawn, I just asked where they went."

"To see Miles' parents," Dawn answers. "His sister and her family are there. He and Max went to visit."

"Where does his sister live?"

"Baltimore."

"Where are we?"

"Springfield." Dawn runs her fingers through her hair. "Illinois."

"And Miles' parents? Where do they live?"

"Chicago."

Caroline nods. Dawn still stands near the top of the staircase. She hesitates. Looks uncertain. She studies her manicure, rather than look Caroline in the eye. "Thanks," Caroline finally says, because this is the most information she's gotten out of anyone since her life went black. Dawn gives her a quick nod and then dashes the rest of the way up the stairs and disappears into a room on the second floor. Caroline leans heavily on the doorframe of the small library.

Miles had stopped locking her door through the day earlier this week. When she hadn't ventured out on her own on the first day of freedom, Miles had gone to her and asked her to feel welcome walking the house and the yard. He'd reminded her of her limitations, telling her she still needed plenty of rest and that she needed to be mindful of her injuries, some still healing, so she wouldn't do any further damage. Caroline had wanted to tell him to go to hell, but she didn't want to end up locked in the room again, so she kept her mouth shut and her thoughts to herself.

The house has given her no clues, and she has wandered it several times in the past few days. She finds it hard to believe she'd lived here, despite that tiny snatch of a memory she'd had a few weeks ago, of Miles painting the window trim. She can't look at the island in the kitchen and remember fixing dinner there. She does not see herself and Miles in the breakfast nook sharing coffee and the morning paper. She doesn't hear Max giggling at cartoons in the living room. It's as if the walls have been given a fresh coat of paint and all of her memories have been smothered.

She stirs out of her thoughts when Dawn comes bounding back down the stairs. She wears flip-flops now, and she carries a small duffel over her shoulder. A small black duffel and a small brown leather purse. She realizes Caroline is still standing in the doorway of the library and stops dead in her tracks. Guilt paints her face in a harsh light.

"Where are you going?" Caroline asks. She stands up straight and takes a step away from the door.

"I gotta get outta here for a few days," Dawn says softly. "I'm gonna go home."

Home? Dawn has a home? Other than these hallowed halls? Does she have a family? A child?

"You're going to leave me here?" Afraid to ask a personal question, because she is afraid of where the answer may take her, she jumps on the fact that up until three or four days ago, she was locked in a bedroom and left to go crazy, all alone. Now suddenly, Miles and Max are gone and Dawn is leaving too. What had she done to pass the test for freedom?

What will she do now? Alone? Really alone?

"You'll be okay." Dawn takes the last two steps quickly and all but runs for the entry hall.

"What would Miles say?" Caroline asks quietly.

Again, Dawn comes to a complete halt about a foot from the door. She draws herself up to stand tall and turns back to Caroline. "What did you say?"

"What would Miles say? If he knew you'd left me here alone?"

Caroline moves slowly toward Dawn. She doesn't blink. Her shoulders and her back are made of steel. But her heart is pushed up into her throat and her stomach is up where her heart should be. She doesn't want to be alone. She doesn't *know* what the hell happened to her to put her in a coma. For all she knows, someone might have come inside this home and beat the hell out of her.

She's scared.

Dawn's doe-eyed innocence touches Caroline when they stand toe to toe. She has beautiful eyes. Rich chocolatey brown, though right now they are lighter. The color of rum. Thick black lashes and dark eyeliner. The eyeliner is smeared. Dawn has been crying.

"Maybe you're not gonna run," Dawn whispers, "But I am."

CINDERELLA

SIX

1994

Bloomington-Normal, IL

He'd kissed her, and she'd felt the jolt singe her lips and her stomach, all the way down to her toes. Miles Wolfe hadn't simply kissed her, he'd devoured her, but in a very genteel sort of way. He'd slipped one hand down over her waist, cupped a hip and drew her *just* against him. No pressure. Enough to feel the presence of his body but not enough to feel him solid against her. He'd tangled the fingers of his other hand in her hair, careful not to hurt her, and cupped her head in his hand and sipped from her lower lip and sucked it into his mouth and finally, he'd plunged his tongue inside her mouth and kissed her until she was breathless.

They had stood outside her apartment, heedless of any cars that had driven by. She still doesn't know if any had, and if they did, who they were. Dawn had been inside, but she'd never crossed Caroline's mind as she and Miles stood together on the tiny cement stoop. Caroline had been in love once, the childish sort of love that has more arrow than heart, and she thinks she's done it all with at least one guy, if not a few since Shane. But she's never been kissed as thoroughly as Miles Wolfe kissed her earlier tonight.

When she'd come inside and watched him walk back to his car, she'd had to lean on the door frame to catch her breath. To float back into her body. Her knees were weak, but she felt as if she were walking on air when she'd gone to the bedroom, stripping clothes off as she went. But when she'd crawled into bed—Dawn asleep over an open text book, in the next bed over—she'd felt the burn. The need. He'd kissed her and drained her, as a vampire might drain a body. But he'd left her wanting more.

Now, several hours later, she wakes suddenly and lays in the dark. Her heart pounds with a physical memory of the nightmare she's just had. Dawn is still asleep; the sound of her breathing should give her comfort, but tonight it doesn't. She turns her head to the left, looking for Beth. The room is the dark shade of gray, just before daylight, but it looks as if Beth's bed is still made, has not been slept in.

She wonders where Beth is, as she tries to slow her breathing. To calm herself. To make the nightmare go away. To make the memories behind the nightmares go away. She hears horrible, loud wailing. Suddenly, she's afraid she's making that sound—the wailing—and she closes her mouth and then covers it with both hands. She still hears it, so she knows it is in her head. She won't wake Dawn. One night she'd cried in her sleep, and Dawn had come and laid by her and asked her what was wrong. They'd been roommates before then, after that night, they were friends.

Still, Caroline hates to talk about it. She hates to think about it. She isn't crying out loud, but her hands over her mouth are wet. She wipes at her face to find it sticky with tears.

How does a date and a long kiss goodnight bring a nightmare about the past?

"Are you okay?"

She nods without answering Dawn. Without looking at Dawn.

"Did you have that dream again?" Dawn asks.

Caroline hitches in a small breath. "Was I crying? Did I wake you up?"

"You were saying his name," Dawn answers.

Caroline turns her head to look at Dawn in the dark room. She's laying on her stomach, with her arms stacked under her pillow. Watching her.

"I was saying Shane?" Caroline whispers.

Dawn nods, burying her chin in her pillow. "Want me to get you some milk?"

"Do we have any that isn't sour?"

Dawn laughs softly. "You haven't had this dream for a while."

"I know." Caroline nods. Wanting to get away from it, away from Shane, she rolls over to her side and looks at Dawn. "I thought you were going out tonight."

"I did." Dawn grins. "I went out with Danny Hayes."

"Well. Why were you home when I got home? You were already sleeping."

"I don't know. Danny and I went to a movie. Came back here. He left around eleven thirty."

"What's he like?"

"He's fun," Dawn answers with a smile. "I like him."

"Are you gonna go out with him again?"

"I don't know." Dawn flips over to lay on her back. "I want to. But I don't know."

"He didn't say he'd call you?"

"Well, yeah, he did. But." Dawn shrugs. "I don't know."

"You're gun shy."

"What?" Dawn rolls her head to look at Caroline.

"Since you thought you were pregnant, you've been a little gun shy about going out. Having fun."

"Guess it was a wakeup call," Dawn says simply. "I don't know, Caroline. I like him. I'd like to get things right this time."

“Good.” Caroline smiles. Her heartbeat is almost back to normal. Shane Beck is almost gone. Again.

“What about you?” Dawn nearly flips over to her side, suddenly all energy. “You had a date with Miles! How was it?”

“It was great.”

“That’s it?” Dawn sighs. “It was great?”

“Well, we went out for pizza. Took a walk around campus. Talked. We talked a lot. About our families. And about school. What we want—"

“Did you tell him you wanted to change your major? Study—"

“No.”

“Are you gonna?”

“Tell him?”

“Change your major?”

“I don’t know.”

“Did you tell him about Shane?”

“No.”

“Did he kiss any other women while you were with him?”

Caroline’s laugh is rich and deep. “No.” She looks again at Dawn. She can make out Dawn’s dark form in the room, just a shade darker than the air around her. Dawn’s eyes sparkle against the monochrome background. “Does it bother you?”

"I don't wanna go out with Miles," Dawn says honestly. "I'm excited for you."

"Are you? Because Beth is freaked out, can't stand him. Like he's the next John Wayne Gacy because he kissed you and I both that first night."

"Um, we're not John Wayne Gacy's type." Dawn clears her throat. "Ted Bundy."

"Shut up." Caroline laughs again. "You know what I mean."

"And you know Beth," Dawn reminds her. "It's just how she is. She's concerned about you. She'll be the same way with Danny, until she meets him."

"Oh? You are going out with him again?"

"I don't know!" Dawn laughs and groans. "Lemme alone."

"Where is Beth tonight?"

"She went to a party."

"Alone?"

"No. She had a date. Some mysterious guy. She never did tell me who he was."

"And we're not supposed to worry about her?"

Dawn props herself up on her elbow and sighs. "Beth can take care of herself, Caroline. She'll be fine."

"You're right."

Dawn flops over on her stomach again. She turns her head the other way. Caroline watches her wiggle around until she's comfortable. Caroline takes a deep breath, silent, and pushes Shane from her mind as she exhales. She's okay now. Without having to delve back into any of it, she's okay now.

"Dawn?"

"Mmm?"

"Thanks."

RAPUNZEL

SEVEN

June, 2008

Springfield, IL

Caroline stares at Dawn uncertainly. She takes a step back. Another. Dawn heaves a sigh and groans softly. Caroline shakes her head and steps back again.

"What?" Caroline asks quietly. "What? You're gonna run? What do you mean? What are you running from?'

Dawn shakes her head. Frustrated? Disgusted? At Caroline? At herself? She pushes the heels of her hands into her eyes and then drops her hands and lets the duffel and the purse slide off her shoulders and down her arms.

Caroline stares at the bag on the floor, rather than look at Dawn.

"I just need some time, Caroline." Dawn's voice is tight, packed with emotion Caroline can't identify.

"I don't wanna be alone," Caroline whispers. "Please? Just stay until he comes back?"

"You don't understand," Dawn mumbles.

"Then make me understand." Caroline enunciates each word clearly and precisely. She backs up until her heels hit the bottom stair and then she drops slowly to sit there and watch Dawn. To make sure the woman doesn't disappear.

"Danny's dead, Caroline," Dawn says, but her voice breaks. She covers her face with her hands and then drags her fingers down over her skin, stretching her eye sockets until they look misshapen and grotesque. "Danny's dead, and I need to grieve. To get through—"

She doesn't know who Danny is. He's someone important; she can see that from the look on Dawn's face. But she doesn't remember him. She's so sick of not remembering. Of closing her eyes and trying to find some connection to the past. Of remembering presidents and Dairy Queen blizzards and the lyrics to songs that pop into her head now and then and *not* remembering herself. Her life.

Dawn stares at her. Silent tears slide over her face. "You don't remember him."

Caroline barely moves her head. "I'm sorry. I don't."

Dawn laughs, but the sound is harsh and bitter. "Of course you don't."

"Help me," Caroline says quietly. "Help me remember."

"I can't."

"Why not?"

"Miles and Dr. Reed think—"

Caroline combs her hair back from her face with her fingers and then covers her ears with her hands. "Damn Miles and Dr. Reed. You keep telling me you're my friend. Help me remember."

"Dammit, Caroline, I can't," Dawn yells. "I can't help you—"

"What do you mean you can't help me? Did you lie to me? About being friends? The whole thing about college roommates? Was that a lie? For him?"

"It wasn't a lie," Dawn cries. She hurries to squat in front of Caroline and takes her hands in hers and squeezes them tight. "I am not lying to you. We were roommates, Caroline. You and me and Beth. We were the Three Musketeers."

"Beth?" Caroline sobs. "God, who's Beth? No more, Dawn. No more people I forgot."

"See?" Dawn whispers. She cups her hand around Caroline's chin and holds Caroline still so she can look in her eyes. "I can't do this to you. I can't show you this life that you can't remember. I don't wanna hurt you."

Caroline pries Dawn's fingers from her chin and holds her hand. "I need to know. I need to know who I am, Dawn."

"He'll tell you."

"He won't tell me." Caroline drags her hand up, fingers still threaded through Dawn's, to wipe at her eyes. "Maybe he thinks he's saving me, but he won't tell me. And I need to know."

"Danny was my husband," Dawn says quietly.

"Your husband? Danny was your husband?"

Dawn nods. She takes a deep breath and presses her lips together. "We got married the summer after you and Miles did—"

Music. Caroline hears music. She looks around the room, wondering what she is hearing. Where the music is coming from.

Dawn pulls herself together and stands. Caroline watches in disbelief as she moves back to her purse on the floor and squats down. Unzips it. Pulls out her cell phone.

"I'm sorry," Dawn whispers. "I'm so sorry."

Miles. Miles had called Dawn before she could tell her anything more about Danny. Or Beth. Or herself. Miles had unlocked the door, invited her to be welcome in this house that is supposedly hers, *left town*, and then called her jailer to check in just in time to stop Dawn from running away or giving her any answers. In truth, all Dawn had done was muddy the already dirty water.

Caroline had left Dawn to the phone call. She'd turned her back on the woman, on her *friend*, even when Dawn wore an expression that Caroline recognized on a face still foreign to her. Regret. Dawn's face had twisted with regret as Caroline had turned her back to her and walked away.

She'd roamed the house again, half of her praying Dawn wouldn't go. Half of her wishing Dawn would leave her alone. She doesn't remember being alone, being *independent.* She thinks she could handle the basics of being alone, the physical care, even cooking. But she's not sure she's emotionally stable. Mentally stable. Pretty sure she's not, in fact, because she's not a whole person, is she? She's walking around with half her mind, with only a few months of memories in her mind, when she should have several years' worth. Can a person function with half a mind? She's not sure. She knows she'd have a hell of a time carrying on with life, if she was missing half her body. Right now, this doesn't seem to be different.

She could probably drive. But as she'd said to Dawn earlier, where would she go? She has no identification. Hard to when she has no identity. A locked room, however horrible it is, seems preferable to a night on the street.

Why hadn't Miles told her he was leaving? Why would he just up and take Max and go out of town for days without telling her? Is that the way he'd operated when they'd been married? If so, she figures that might have been one of their recurring fights. It bothers her that he hadn't talked to her before he'd left. And *that* really bothers her, that she cares that he just up and left. She's not sure what she thinks about anything right now, but abandonment ranks right up there at the top, at the moment.

As darkness falls, chills march over her skin. She has no idea where Dawn is. The black Explorer Dawn drives is still outside the garage, so she knows Dawn has not left. She didn't run. Caroline wonders why she didn't. Wonders why she wanted to, what she was running from.

She climbs the steps to go back to her room. The house is big in daylight. In the darkness, it looms around her like a living thing. A living thing watching her. She pauses at the second floor landing and listens. For what, she doesn't know. The sound of breathing? Would she be certain it was Dawn? Or would it be the house, breathing, with her caught inside it? The hall is near dark, a heavy gray, with four rectangles of black aligning the walls, two on each side. The first of the rooms belongs to Max. She'd spent hours in this room today, surrounded by the scent of her son, by his toys and his artwork and his clothes. She'd opened his closet, looked at and touched his clothes, wishing for memories. Answers. She'd sat at his red and green Playskool desk and looked at pictures rendered in Crayola and Prang. Smiled at the horse he'd drawn and then cried at the picture he'd drawn of her in a small red car. It said Mommy. She'd found no answers, let alone comfort.

That's not my mommy. Caroline catches her breath and eyes the dark hall suspiciously. Why had Max said that? Why would Max look at her, eyes wide with fear, and say she wasn't his Mommy? Miles had not given her an answer when she'd demanded one.

The door next to Max's bedroom, she assumes, is a guest room. It is where Dawn sleeps. Unless Dawn is now a permanent resident here. She has to feel more at home here than Caroline does. Caroline had glanced into the room but when she'd seen the duffel bag—the one Dawn had carried downstairs earlier—in the wooden rocker, she'd passed the door quickly. Across the hall, there was a bathroom, also full of Max's belongings. Crayola soaps and kid shampoo. A basketball hoop stuck to the shower with suction cups, the Nerf ball stuffed down in a toy boat, parked on the side of the tub. The little boy atmosphere touched her, but only with sadness, not memories.

The last room was the master bedroom. She'd stood in the doorway earlier, after the run in with Dawn, just after Dawn had introduced two more strangers into her life, and prayed to glue enough courage together inside to step over the threshold, into the room. In the waning daylight, she'd watched shadows and dust gather in the far corner of the room. *Felt* her stomach squeeze and flop as she'd considered entering Miles' room. *Miles's room.* But if she was Miles' wife and they'd lived here together before her accident, the room was hers too.

She had to know. It was a little bit like staring into a jungle, teetering there in the doorway. Finally, she'd plunged further into the room. If Miles was well on his way to Chicago, she had time to wander this room. To learn this room. To look for herself in the deep green walls and the warm green and gold comforter over the bed.

King size bed. She'd stood at the foot of the bed for what felt like hours, but had only been minutes, because she hadn't spent an hour inside the *room.* The bed was modest for what she might have expected. Bronze bars at the head of the bed. Pillows in gold, green, and crème shams piled artfully in front of the bars. Caroline had stood, transfixed by those bars, for the longest moment. Wondering if she'd curled her hands around those bars while she and Miles made love. Wondering if they had conceived Max here in this bed or if he'd been a baby made in some cozy vacation getaway.

She'd pulled herself away from the bed, trying hard to forget the bars—the *feel* of the cold bars in the palms of her hands—and moved slowly around the room. She'd trailed her fingers over the nightstand—she assumes by her side of the bed. Nothing on it. No picture frames. No clock. No telephone. No dust. Around to the oil painting of wild flowers and further still to the oak armoire in the corner. She'd pulled the doors open boldly, half expecting Dawn to breeze in at any moment and chastise her for snooping.

Guilt had tugged at her as she touched sweaters and knit tops that apparently had belonged to her at some point. She'd picked one up, a black cashmere sweater and unfolded it and held it up to her body. Probably the right size. Whatever clothes she had now, those upstairs in the *room*, apparently were being brought to her from this room.

She'd pulled open the skinny drawers in the top of the armoire and stared in amazement at the jewelry there. Nothing over the top. Nothing that screamed 'safe' in her mind. But enough, to someone who had no memory of wearing them. She'd even taken a ring from the drawer and slid it on the ring finger of her right hand. Princess cut diamond. Princess cut alexandrite.

Alexandrite. She'd jumped and tugged the ring off and set back in its place, when she realized she had no idea how the hell she knew what Alexandrite was. With a glance over her shoulder, certain she was being watched, she'd pushed the drawer shut and then closed the doors of the armoire. Still alone in the room, heart jumping a staccato rhythm, she'd continued her journey. To his side of the room. A chest of drawers. She'd fingered the knob on the top drawer. Considered pulling it open to take a look.

Heart still racing, she'd backed away from it and taken one more look at his side of the room. Had to be his side. There was a digital alarm clock on the nightstand. A small lamp, with a crème-colored shade, and a framed snapshot of Max. A smiling, freckle-faced Max, holding a fishing pole.

Struck by the thought of Max with a fishing pole, wondering who had taken him fishing, had it been *Miles?*—she'd forfeited the rest of the trip around the master bedroom and rushed out of the room.

Now, in the darkness, the room calls to her. Teases her with the possibility of answers. What if there were pictures there? What if Miles had pictures in the closet? Or in his nightstand? Would he have a picture of her before the accident? Surely, somewhere there were pictures. She groans softly and damns herself for not latching onto that photo album Miles had brought her the day he'd told her she was his wife.

She'd been so disconcerted with Dawn's presence that she hadn't bothered to look. So overwhelmed by the thought of *having* a son, she hadn't opened the damned book to look at the pictures.

Not tonight. She hadn't been able to handle that room earlier, when it was still light outside. She sure as hell couldn't walk in there and flip a light on and dig through someone else's belongings—even if they had been *hers*, they were now someone else's—to see if she could find a map or a footnote to her past.

Instead she lifts her head and looks up the next flight of stairs. The third floor. The *room*. What had that room been before the accident? Before she'd been released from the hospital and locked away there? She sighs, rests her hand on the banister and sidles up the first two steps. The ache in her leg is prominent now. Probably because she'd been roaming all day. Certainly nothing strenuous, and yet more exercise than she's apparently had in eight or nine months.

Her footsteps down the long hallway are the only sound she hears. Where is Dawn? Who the hell is Dawn, and what is her story? Caroline passes a closed door—she'd looked inside the room earlier. Probably a spare room, could be a guest bedroom. At the moment, it is empty, but for an office chair in the corner.

Another door, this one open. Again, she'd looked in this room earlier. Storage. Boxes and dust.

Her stomach twists when she reaches the door. Her door. The brass deadbolt shines just a bit in the darkness. She swallows hard, wishes she'd looked for a light switch down the hall, and reaches for the doorknob. Her hand slips on the knob, but she twists it hard and pulls it open. She reaches inside quickly and flips the light switch.

Deep, calming breath when the overhead light floods the room. It is the same. Funny how right now she needs to see this room and see that it is the same. Within eight hours, her world has grown from one room to one house, and she's overwhelmed. This room is familiar. She steps inside, but she leans against the door to make sure it doesn't close. It won't. It's not on a spring; it's a regular bedroom door. But she leans on it just the same.

'Your favorite color was lavender' As lies go, it's not damaging. But it's a lie, all the same. She doesn't know how she knows it, but as she looks around the room, at the lavender walls that already seem to be moving—closing in on her as they do every time she enters—she knows lavender is not her favorite color and never was. No, it's not as if

Miles was out to hurt her with this lie, and yet, *why* did he say that? What harm would there be in telling her if her favorite color was green or red?

She can't stay here. She can't sleep in this room. Not tonight. What if she lays down and the door is closed and it locks? What if the damned thing locks? What if Dawn locks her in? She can't stand another night locked up in this room.

She considers Max's room, but she can't seek comfort from her son when she doesn't *remember* him. The sofa. She could sleep on the sofa in the library, where she'd found Dawn earlier. Or she could sleep on the sofa in the family room. Turn the TV on and stare at people with make believe problems that probably used to entertain her and now make her wish for a life that simple.

Slowly, she moves away from the door. Two steps toward the bed. She glances back at the door. Another step. Quickly, she grabs a pillow from the bed, yanks the navy comforter from the bed, and hurries back to the door. She's acting stupid. There's no one here but her and Dawn. Whatever else Dawn might be, she's not a deranged psychopath who's going to lock her in here and attack her at midnight.

Still, she can't bring herself to turn the light off. Her steps are brisk as she moves back down the hall to the stairs and back down past the second floor and then there she is, at the foot of the stairs where she and Dawn had talked earlier. Where Dawn had dumped Danny and Beth at her feet, and where they'd left them—because she still doesn't know who the hell they are. She takes a deep breath and then holds it, listening. For what, she doesn't know. A car? The door slamming closed upstairs? Dawn following her?

She wonders what time it is as she tiptoes into the library. She reaches the sofa and leans over the end of it to turn on the floor lamp. Soft light warms the room, but it doesn't reach her. Alone. She's not sure she can stand being alone in this house, when she hasn't been alone in at least eight months.

Restless, she puts the pillow and comforter down and then wanders back out to the hall. She stops when she hears someone in the kitchen. Heart pounding again, she makes her way through the family room to the arch way of the kitchen. Not Miles.

Dawn looks up when Caroline slumps against the arch. Her laugh is cold and bitter.

"You don't believe me, do you?"

"About what?" Caroline asks softly. Her heart is still jumping. She lays her hand flat on her chest and wills herself to calm down.

"That Miles went to Chicago." Dawn is chopping onions and green and red peppers.

"What are you doing?" Caroline watches Dawn's swift, efficient movements. She raises her eyes to the clock on the wall. "It's after ten. What are you doing?"

"He went to Chicago. You can call his fucking cell phone and ask him, if you don't believe me."

"Why would you think I don't believe you?"

"You were expecting to walk in here and see him. Not me."

Caroline presses her lips together, but she has nothing to say. She can't argue. Slowly, like a dog who's been kicked one too many times, she makes her way across the tiled kitchen floor and pulls herself up to sit on a stool at the counter. Dawn continues to chop the vegetables, stopping now and then to wipe her eyes. Caroline wonders if her eyes are watering because of the onions or if she is crying again.

"Put yourself in my place," Caroline whispers. Dawn's hands stop, mid chop. She lifts only her eyes to look at Caroline.

"You're kidding, right?"

"I don't know you," Caroline ignores her. "I don't know Miles. I don't know Max. I don't know myself. How do I trust someone I don't know?"

"I told you to run."

"Where would I go?" Caroline shakes her head.

"Anywhere you go is a step up from here," Dawn answers. She tosses down the butcher knife and half cries, half groans and reaches for an open bottle of beer.

"Then why are you here?"

"I'm here for you, Caroline."

"To what end?"

Dawn chews on her lower lip and stares at Caroline boldly. "You called me. And you begged me to help you. And all fucking hell broke loose and here I am, nine months later, trying to help you." She turns her back to Caroline and checks the skillet on the stove and then turns back for the vegetables on the cutting board. "Only you're not my

Caroline anymore, and I don't know how to help you and I don't know how to get away either." When she finishes, she's again turned her back to Caroline, and her anger has bled out, and her voice is see through and helpless.

Caroline slides off the stool and steps around the counter. She touches Dawn's arm and searches the other woman's face when she finally looks at her. "Get away from what?"

"Hell."

CINDERELLA

EIGHT

1994

Bloomington-Normal, IL

Caroline glares at Beth, silently demanding her to shut up. Beth, aware of Caroline's discomfort, leans forward in her chair and picks up her martini. She rests her elbow on the table, ignores Caroline and zeroes in on Miles. She's been focused on Miles all night, all but ignoring her own date.

Tests. She'd been testing Miles all evening, instead of sitting back and enjoying dinner. It's the first time she and Dawn and Beth have gone out for dinner, all with a date, that didn't include hot wings and plastic beer cups. Caroline wants to kick herself for thinking that Beth would behave.

She's run Miles through a long political discussion. Pushed him to lean one way or the other, but Miles had pushed back. He'd talked to Beth, he seemed to enjoy the conversation, but he hadn't given in and discussed his own political views. When she'd finally given up that tack, Beth had started in with questions about school and career plans. Again, Miles had handled them with aplomb and discussed his business classes with Beth as if he were recruiting her.

Caroline excuses herself, turns her face to Miles distractedly for a kiss before she gets up, and walks on steady legs to the ladies' room. She knows someone is following her. She hopes like hell it is Dawn, because right now, love Beth or not, she's ready for a fight.

"Hey." Dawn steps into the restroom behind her. The lounge—decorated in rose and gold damask, even the walls are covered in ornate silk and damask—is empty. Caroline drops heavily to a loveseat and buries her face in her hands.

"Tell me again why I like her?"

"Because she did your statistics assignments a couple of years ago," Dawn says simply. Caroline glances up at Dawn and laughs, as she dabs at her eyes. "And she fixes her own spaghetti sauce—"

"She taught you to do that." Caroline shakes her head. "Don't need her for that."

Dawn offers Caroline a smile of understanding. "Caroline, she cares about you."

"She's butchering him."

"She's testing him."

"Why doesn't she like him?" Caroline asks quietly. She runs her fingers through her long blonde curls. Curls. Acrylic nails. She'd gone in debt to her parents for this date. It had been that important to her. A night out with her two best friends and a guy whom she likes and thinks maybe could be the guy. She wears a short black skirt with a red blouse. Her hair falls in loose curls over her shoulders and her nail tips are the color of blood. Dawn had been with her all day; she'd splurged too. And again, Caroline knows she doesn't measure up to Dawn. That she never could. But she does for Miles. Miles appreciates *her*. Beth had taken a look at the two of them, in their short skirts and spiked heels and whistled and asked them how much for a little fun. They'd all laughed over their cheap wine and wondered how they would work it if all three of them got lucky after dinner.

"It's not that she doesn't like him," Dawn tells her. "She's just worried about you."

"Is it because of that first night?" Caroline asks, ignoring Dawn's answer. "Is it because he kissed you and me? Does that bother you, Dawn? Am I stupid that it doesn't bother me?"

"No." Dawn moves to sit beside Caroline. "No. You're not stupid, and it doesn't bother me. And I don't think that's what bothers her. She's just very concerned about you—"

"Why? What is it she doesn't like about him?" Caroline insists Dawn answer her. "Is it his name? Does she have a problem with the name Miles?"

"Car." Dawn sighs. "It's not Miles. It's not his name. Beth is careful. Beth is careful, and she doesn't want to see either one of us get hurt."

"I don't see her badgering Danny."

"Danny's different."

"What?" Caroline snaps. She stands up and stares down at Dawn, eyes wide with anger. "Danny's different? So it is Miles?"

The woosh of air as the door pushes open interrupts them.

"Thought I heard a pow wow in here." Beth flashes them a grin. "Let's go out for a drink—" Beth's words grind to a halt when the tension in the room zings her. "What?"

Dawn takes a deep breath and stands. Caroline turns her back to Beth.

"Talking about me?" Beth asks softly. "Do I have the right to know what I did?"

Caroline laughs. "Like you don't know."

"I don't," Beth answers. "Mind telling me?"

Caroline turns back to Beth. "You're not my mother." She takes a step toward her. "You're sure as hell not my father. Get the hell off his back—"

"I haven't been on his back." Beth's answer is simple and straightforward. "He and I have talked. A lot—"

"Because you're badgering him—"

"He doesn't care." Beth throws her hands up in defeat. "It's debating, Caroline. He's very intelligent. That's fun."

"If I believed you, I'd be thrilled." Caroline shrugs. "But I don't."

"He's okay," Beth says reluctantly. "I didn't think I'd like him, but he's okay."

Caroline nods and steps closer to Beth. Dawn watches silently from the corner of the lounge. "He's okay, and Danny's great."

"I never said that."

"But is it true?"

"Danny's different."

"Why is Danny different?"

"Because Danny's girlfriend hasn't had the shit kicked out of her like you have."

Caroline closes her eyes before the tears can betray her. "So you're ripping on Miles...because I'm unstable?"

"Caroline." Beth reaches for her, but Caroline pushes past her and yanks open the door, leaving Beth and Dawn alone.

"Did you like her?" Caroline refuses to look at him. They sit side by side on the tiny deck behind his apartment. He lives here alone. Somewhere in the back of her mind, it knocks around that Miles is a college student living alone in an apartment. But right now it doesn't matter.

She shivers and hugs her arms around herself, as she stares up at the sky. Two stars. She sees only two stars in this little patch of sky.

"Beth." Miles clarifies.

She nods, still without looking at him.

"I did."

"Are you lying?"

"Of course I'm not lying."

Suddenly she feels his arm around her shoulders, and he tugs her close to him. She snuggles against his chest, grateful for the warmth and the gesture. Even here with Miles, which is where she wants to be, she feels alone. She's angry with Beth. Hurt and angry and not inclined to get over it very soon.

"She's just protective of you," Miles tells her. "I like that. I like that you have someone else to care about you like that."

"She was a bitch." Caroline's voice is flat.

Miles looks down at her and touches his lips to the tip of her nose. "I'm not afraid of her."

"But I wanted you guys to hit it off," she whispers. "You're both important to me."

"And we will," Miles assures her. "It's okay, Caroline. Just give it a little time."

She sighs and nods. Closes her eyes as his fingers creep up her inner thigh, under the hem of her skirt. When he brushes his lips over hers, she sighs and opens her legs just a bit. Just enough. Moans quietly when she feels a ghostlike stroke over her center.

"Miles."

"Not tonight." He slides his hand back down her thigh.

"What?" She opens her eyes. Watches him adjust his jeans

and then stand and walk a few feet away before offering her a grin.

“I can’t tonight.”

“Looks to me like you could right now,” she answers. She looks up to meet his eyes.

“You’ve had too much to drink—"

“Miles—"

“You had a glass of wine before I picked you up. Two drinks at dinner. And three more at the club.”

“I’m not drunk.”

“I wanna wait,” he says quietly. “Until the whole night is about you and me.”

RAPUNZEL

NINE

June, 2008

Springfield, IL

"What happened to Danny?" Caroline asks. Dawn looks up from the sautéed vegetables she is scooping over a serving of rice.

"Are you hungry?" she asks Caroline. "Do you want some?"

It's after ten, but she is hungry. She gives Dawn a quick nod. Dawn continues with the food, but does not answer her question about Danny. Frustrated, Caroline tugs open the refrigerator. She studies the drawing on the freezer door. Skipper and Max.

'Leave me, Caroline, if that's what you want. But you won't get Max.'

She closes her eyes and rubs her forehead.

"Hey, I don't think it's a good idea for you to drink alcohol yet," Dawn calls, her back to Caroline, as she sets their plates on the table. "Miles would be pissed if I let you have—"

Caroline takes a bottle of water from the refrigerator, pushes the door shut and stares at Dawn, enough anger inside that she has to be wearing it.

"What's wrong?" Dawn asks quickly. "You look like hell."

'Leave me, Caroline, if that's what you want.'

"If you let me have a beer?" Caroline twists her water bottle open. "If you let me have a beer, Miles would be pissed?" She laughs softly. "It's okay, Dawn. I don't want a beer, and I don't give a damn what Miles would say."

Dawn swallows hard. "No, it's not like that." She shakes her head. "It's just. I mean. The head injuries and stuff—"

"I don't want a beer," Caroline repeats.

"Are you okay?" Dawn asks her again. "You're white as a ghost—"

"I am a ghost, Dawn." Caroline pushes past her and takes her plate from the table.

"Where are you going?"

"Anywhere but here." Caroline looks at Dawn over her shoulder.

"One night," Dawn says softly. Tears slide over her face, but she doesn't even seem to notice. "You were crying. I woke up, and I heard you crying in your sleep." She clears her throat, seems to realize she is crying now and rubs her fingertips over her face. "We didn't know each other well. School had just started."

Caroline stares at her, hungry for details, for some bit of truth in a past she does not recognize, but weary of lies. *'Your favorite color was lavender.'*

Dawn shrugs and meets Caroline's eyes but quickly looks away. Not because she's telling a lie. Caroline senses that. She looks away because the quiet in the kitchen echoes with the words that had fallen between them earlier, at the foot of the stairs. Friends, now strangers, uncomfortable with this raw intimacy.

"I went to you. To your bed. And I laid down by you and put my arm around you. And you just cried. You didn't talk. Not that night. But you trusted me. Just to be there with you. You trusted me."

The plate in Caroline's hands is heavy, the bottom hot against her fingers.

"The next morning, we woke up together. And we joked about it. Waking up together meant sleeping together. We said it was the best night we'd had since we'd been at school." Dawn sighs. "And then it was like it never happened."

Caroline opens her mouth to answer her. She can't. She doesn't know what to say.

"About a month later," Dawn continues, "We were studying. You were reading 'Hedda Gabbler.' You had to write an essay on it. I was studying for a biology test."

Dawn waits. Caroline nods, asking silently for her to go on.

"You started talking. You told me why you cry sometimes in your sleep."

"What did I say?" Caroline asks quietly.

Dawn pulls a chair out and sits at the table. "I feel like I'm playing Russian Roulette. I don't know how much I can say without hurting you—"

"I need to know."

"You've been through so much." Dawn swallows her words. "I don't wanna push you over the edge."

Caroline sits down at the table. "What did I say to you that night?"

Dawn takes a long drink of her beer. "Nightmares."

"What kind of nightmares?"

"Do you know the name Shane Beck?"

"Should I?" Caroline shakes her head.

"He was your first love."

Caroline drops her fork and sits back in her chair.

"Is that who the nightmares were about? Shane Beck?"

Dawn nods her head toward Caroline's plate. "You should eat. You haven't eaten much today."

"Dawn, please don't put me off. Were the nightmares about him? This Shane Beck?"

"You said you guys were crazy about each other." Dawn plays with her rice, makes patterns in it with her fork. "He was a baseball star. His mom wanted him to go to college.

He was going to be a doctor. His dad wanted him to play baseball. He got drafted."

"To the majors?"

"Reds' farm team," Dawn says simply. "Played first base. Broke his high school record for stolen bases when he was a junior."

Caroline nods. She picks up her water bottle because she needs to do something with her fingers. She's afraid. She's afraid of what Dawn is going to say next.

"His parents had money. You said they lived in a gorgeous house, and Shane drove a brand new truck. His mom hated you."

Caroline lifts her chin just a bit, to acknowledge that she'd heard Dawn, to urge her to continue.

"You got pregnant." Dawn is so quiet, Caroline has to lean forward to hear her. "You were a senior. Seventeen. Pregnant."

"He left me?" Caroline guesses.

"You said he wanted to keep the baby. Get married and keep the baby and he said he'd go to work."

"But?"

"His mother stepped in."

"And?"

"She went to work on Shane. Made him doubt you. Made him think maybe it wasn't his baby."

"Was it his baby?"

"You told me it was."

"What happened?"

"She came to see you. When you were at home alone. Your parents were at work. She gave you a check for five thousand dollars, but you had to promise to leave Shane alone. She gave you this song and dance about how Shane was too good, how his future was too bright for him to be trapped in a loveless marriage. That neither of you was ready to be a parent. She asked you to abort the baby. Said she'd drive you to the clinic herself. And she'd never tell your parents. If you'd get rid of the baby and leave Shane alone."

"Jesus." Caroline rubs her eyes so hard she sees a kaleidoscope of colors.

"She said Shane had changed his mind. He didn't want to be with you. Didn't want your baby."

"I did it, didn't I?" Caroline nods. "I took her money, and I had an abortion."

"She drove you to the clinic. Paid your medical bills. Drove you home. She was walking you into your house when Shane pulled into the driveway. When he saw you with his mother, he knew what you'd done."

Caroline wipes her nose with the back of her hand. "I killed a baby. For money."

"No," Dawn says quickly. "You didn't take her money. When you saw Shane...when he saw you. He knew. You said it was like you watched him die inside. Like a light inside him went out. You tore her check up, but it was too late. You'd had the abortion, and Shane thought you'd decided you didn't want him or the baby."

"What did he do?"

"I don't know." Dawn shakes her head. "I don't know. I think the last you knew, he'd gone to medical school."

"He didn't play baseball."

"No."

Caroline sits in silence, wondering if the dread she'd been carrying around for the past months had more to do with who she was than what had happened to her. Maybe she'd deserved it.

"Did Miles know?"

"You told him when it got serious between you two."

"And he didn't hate me?"

"You were a kid," Dawn says softly. "And you don't know, Caroline. Maybe it was the right thing."

"How is that the right thing?"

"If you and Shane had stayed together," Dawn reaches toward her and lays her hand over the back of Caroline's, "you wouldn't have met Miles. Without Miles, you wouldn't have Max."

Caroline stares at Dawn's hand over hers for a long moment before she turns her hand over and gently squeezes Dawn's fingers. "Was I a good mom to him? To Max?"

Dawn's smile is genuine. "You're head over heels for that kid, and he's crazy about you."

“Not now.” Caroline’s voice is gruff.

“He’s just scared.”

Caroline licks her lips. It’s hard to sit now, in her own company, knowing what she’d done. At the moment, nothing else matters. Not Miles. Not the locked door. Not the years between seventeen and now—suddenly, she feels damned old—nothing matters except that she’s just learned she’d aborted a child. A child apparently wanted very much by his father.

“Do you have children?” She breaks the silence that hangs over the table like a chandelier.

Dawn pulls her hand away as the last of the smiles over Max fade away. She stands and carries her forgotten plate to the sink. “No.”

CINDERELLA

TEN

1994

Springfield, IL

"C'mon," Beth whines. She throws her arm over Caroline's shoulder and gives her a grin. "It's my birthday. Go with me."

Caroline twists around Beth to squint at the alarm clock, as she stumbles from the bathroom back to her bed. "Beth. It's six o'clock in the morning." She groans and rubs her eyes with her fingertips. "What the hell did you just say?" Beth laughs softly as Caroline slips away from her and crawls back into bed. "Last time I get up to go to the bathroom when you're around. What? Were you laying there, awake, waiting to ambush me?"

"Will you? Go with me?" Beth asks and perches on the side of Caroline's bed. Caroline, laying on her stomach, turns her head to the left, looking for Dawn. She looks back at Beth when she finds Dawn's bed empty.

"Go with you where?"

"Spa." Beth senses Caroline is going to grumble and say no, so she drops to her knees beside the bed and lays her face on Caroline's pillow. They are practically nose to nose. "Please. Just for a facial. Manicure. I wanna get my hair colored. I need moral support."

"Why?"

"What?"

Caroline lifts her head and blinks and finally sees Beth's face clearly, in the gray morning light. "Why does this mean so much to you?"

"Because it's my birthday!" Beth answers with a grin.

"Nope." Caroline shakes her head. "Birthdays have never done much for you before."

"But this is my twenty-first," Beth argues.

Caroline studies her friend closely. *Something* is making her eyes light up and putting color in her cheeks, but Caroline doesn't believe it's a birthday, be it her twenty first or not. "Nope. Come clean or I won't go."

"What do you mean come clean?" Beth laughs. "C'mon—"

"What's going on?" Caroline asks with a small smile. "Did you meet somebody?"

"No." Beth sighs and sits back, resting her butt on her feet. "No. It's not a guy."

"Then what?"

"Um." She licks her lips and cocks her head to stare at Caroline for a moment. "Well, I'm not sure about this yet, but I think I might have a job offer."

"What?" Caroline sits up. She grabs her pillow and pulls it into her lap. "What kind of job offer? From who?"

"Well, I'm not sure—"

"Not sure yet, yada yada yada." Caroline nods and motions her hand in a circle as if to keep the conversation going. "Got that. But what job offer? Spill."

"Mike knows someone at NASA—"

"NASA!??" Caroline jumps off the bed and dances around Beth. She reaches down for Beth's hands and yanks her up from the floor. "NASA? What the hell? Beth, that's incredible!"

"Yeah, I know." Beth stands up in front of Caroline, her hands still in Caroline's. "I keep telling myself to wait. To be cautious. But—"

"But NASA??" Caroline laughs. "Holy shit, how do you be cautious about that? This is what you've been working for since you were like nine."

Beth blushes and ducks her head a bit.

"Oh no, no no no." Caroline shakes her head. "Don't you be embarrassed. This is great! Where the hell's Dawn? We need to celebrate. When will you know for sure? When will Mike—" Caroline stops, as if she sees a red light. "Wait. Mike." She arches an eyebrow at Beth. "Who's Mike?"

"Mr. McGarret."

"Mr. McGarret," Caroline repeats. "Mike. Is Mr. McGarret. And Mr. McGarret is your physics professor? Is that right?"

"Caroline," Beth says softly. "No. Please don't think that. It's not like that—"

"Hey." Caroline shakes her head and pulls her hand away from Beth's. She cups Beth's chin in her hand and leans over to kiss her cheek. "It's like you've worked your ass off in his class. And you deserve this."

Beth sinks her teeth into her lower lip and stares bravely at Caroline, even when her eyes are suddenly bright with tears. "Thank you," she whispers. "Just for knowing that."

"I know that," Caroline answers simply, "because I know you."

"I wish Dawn was here."

"Me too," Caroline agrees. "She'll be pissed that she missed this."

"Well," Beth shrugs, "And her nails look like shit. She's due for a manicure."

Caroline barks a laugh. "What time we doing this?" She glances at the clock again.

"Go back to bed for a while." Beth smiles. "We can go later this morning."

Caroline flops back down on her bed, but she turns over to her back when Beth climbs back into her own bed. "I've got a better idea."

"What?"

"Fix me breakfast."

"If I get to be an aeronautical engineer at NASA, I won't be cooking anymore."

"Well, and I won't be living with you anymore," Caroline points out. "But right now, I am living here and you're an excellent cook, so I think you should fix me breakfast."

"Pop tart?" Beth asks as she climbs out of bed.

"Toasted, please," Caroline answers and closes her eyes as Beth disappears from the room.

"Hey, Caroline?"

"Hmm?"

"Did you get a chance to read my paper?"

"I did." Caroline sits up and nods when Beth peeks her head around the doorway. "I marked a few things, but mostly, I think it's great."

"You're sure?" Beth asks uncertainly. "I mean, don't go easy on me. You're much better with the whole writing side—"

"Oh trust me," Caroline says with a grin as she gets up and joins Beth in the kitchen. "I'd hammer you, if I thought I needed to." They laugh, but Caroline sees the mix of fear and nerves in Beth's eyes. "I'm serious, Beth. It's an A paper. You'll be fine."

Beth lets out a big sigh, and Caroline knows it is relief. Beth, for all of her math and science knowledge, gets very uptight when it comes to writing and researching. Dawn falls both ways, so the three of them tend to back each other up or help each other out with assignments that send them all running for cover.

“Thanks.”

“You’re welcome.” Caroline stretches and yawns. “Wonder if Dawn’s missing Danny Boy.”

Beth shoots her a knowing look and then raises her eyebrow. “If you went home for the weekend, would you miss Miles?”

Caroline tries to consider Beth’s question—at least consider it for a *moment*—but she grins and shrugs and finally nods. “Yeah, I would.”

“Have you slept with him yet?”

“No.”

Beth stops in the act of pulling the carton of eggs and a bag of shredded cheese from the refrigerator. She eyes Caroline suspiciously.

“I swear I haven’t slept with him yet,” Caroline says sincerely. She holds her fingers up, as if to say ‘scout’s honor.’

“Why not?”

“He says he wants to wait.”

“Wait for what?” Beth asks, now suspicious of Miles rather than Caroline.

“Oh come on.” Caroline groans. “Now you’re gonna rip on him because he wants to wait and make it special?”

“Not ripping,” Beth answers. “I’m just surprised.”

"Well there's been a few nights, I'd like to rip on him," Caroline says quietly. She pours them each a glass of orange juice. "Good thing Dawn's not here for breakfast. We're out of Mountain Dew."

"Why would you want to rip on him?"

"Because he keeps stopping!" Caroline laughs. "I feel like I'm back in high school. Making out. Being careful not to go too far—"

"Yeah, right. That was you—"

"Shut up." Caroline laughs.

"Car? You in love with him?"

Caroline takes a deep breath and raises her eyebrows. "I don't know, Beth." She shrugs and smiles. "When I'm with him, everything else just melts away. When I'm not with him, everything else is in the way."

Beth studies Caroline a moment longer and then turns back to the avocado colored stove. "I hate this thing," she mumbles as she reaches for the skillet on the counter. "I'm glad for you."

"What?" Caroline asks quickly. She moves to stand beside Beth.

"I want you to be happy." Beth refuses to take her eyes from the egg she cracks over the skillet. "If he makes you happy, then I like him."

Caroline flashes Beth a big smile. "Thank you. I needed to hear you say that."

RAPUNZEL

ELEVEN

June, 2008

Springfield, IL

Dread sits like a rock in the pit of Caroline's stomach. She stretches, lying on her back on the sofa and stares at the window above. There's no moonlight; she lays in relative darkness. The quiet is absolute. The central air is on, and she was cold when she'd first laid down. But now she's hot, and she's kicked the navy and forest green plaid blanket off and as if she doesn't have more important things to think about, she's wondering where the blanket is from. There are no tags. She doesn't know if it is made by Ralph Lauren. She doesn't know if she's ever wrapped it around herself and pulled Max into her lap and snuggled with him, inside the blanket, to watch The Fox and The Hound. She doesn't know if she and Miles ever lay beneath the blanket, spooned together as lovers do.

Then again it's easier to wonder about something trivial like the blanket. Easier to ignore that *feeling* in her gut if she's worrying about the blanket. About the furniture in this room. About the house. She hasn't slept yet. Time doesn't move too quickly in this house, so she assumes it can't be much past one in the morning. She isn't bothered by the fact that there's no clock in the library. The door is unlocked and wide open. That is what matters. If she *wanted* to, she could get up and tiptoe down the hall to the kitchen and look at the clock on the wall or the digital display on the microwave.

She groans softly and rubs her stomach. Her skin is hot to the touch. The dread is different tonight. It's worse—like it has sharper edges or something—but it's different. It's not about Miles. Nothing at all about Miles. It's not really about Shane Beck and what she'd done with his baby. She hates herself for that, but hate is hate. This is dread. Fear.

Dawn. She can't be any more specific than that. It's something about Dawn. Something about Dawn is making her feel sicker by the moment. They'd been having a conversation. An okay conversation and Dawn had actually *told* her something about herself, to help, she thinks. She has no clear memories of Dawn, but she can feel the tug in her gut, now and then. She *knows* this woman, even if she doesn't *remember* her. Maybe if they had a few more quiet, normal conversations, she would find a pathway back to life before this storm. At the very least, maybe Caroline could feel comfortable with Dawn, establish a connection with someone, whether she be from the past or the present. She hates this drifting she's doing. She needs an anchor.

She hadn't realized it, but apparently she'd been hoping Dawn would be her anchor. Because *now*, after the scene in the kitchen, she feels more alone than she has since she woke up the first time in the sterile confines of the hospital. She doesn't know exactly what she'd been hoping for, but disappointment pushes heavily on the dread in her stomach.

'Do you have children?'

'No.'

It wasn't the word no that had cut Caroline loose and set her drifting again. It was the look on Dawn's face. The way she'd stood and walked away from Caroline.

It's crazy, of course, to think this way. But then again, what is Caroline Wolfe if she is not crazy at the moment? A crazy woman with no past and no hope of stumbling out of the dark present. Caroline can't rid herself of the thought, of the *guilt*, that Dawn does not have children. Why in the hell should she feel this way? Did she do something to Dawn? To take away her hopes of having children? Or is this a normal feeling? Finding out that she'd aborted a baby and learning in the next breath that her *friend* does not have children might make anyone feel a twinge of guilt, right? Surely that's enough to make anyone feel a little uncomfortable. And besides, who said Dawn *wanted* children? Dawn hadn't said so. Then again, Dawn's face had turned to stone when Caroline had asked.

Is it normal? She wonders again. Hell if she knows, because she doesn't know what the hell normal people feel. Groaning quietly again, she sits up on the couch and stares at the window from the new angle. It's dark. She can't see anything, not really even the reflection of the room behind her.

"Can't sleep?"

She jumps when she hears Dawn's voice and then swallows hard and turns to look at the woman standing in the doorway.

"No," she finally answers. Too tired to struggle for something to say to Dawn, she turns back to the window and wishes she were alone. Hell, wishes are a dime a dozen. Why not wish herself back in the past by ten or twelve months?

"Me neither."

The house creaks and settles. The sounds no longer scare Caroline. She just wishes she could settle here too.

"I've been having dreams," Dawn whispers. Caroline looks over her shoulder and watches Dawn move slowly toward the couch. There's not enough light to see her face. She can only make out a darker form moving cautiously through the room.

"Look, Dawn," Caroline swallows hard, but forces herself to go on, "I was wrong to ask you to stay."

"About Danny." Dawn perches on the end of the couch and leans forward to cover her face with her hands.

"You don't have to stay," Caroline continues, "if you want to go."

"I miss you." Dawn drops her hands and lifts her head to look at Caroline. Her voice breaks just a little, and her breathing is slightly uneven. “I miss the way we used to be able to say anything to each other.”

Caroline winces as Dawn’s words grab her by the neck and dig in. Dawn is crying. Caroline forces herself to look away. To look at the window, which is really no more than a black rectangle right now.

“If you could say anything to me right now,” Caroline says so low she wonders if Dawn can hear her, “what would it be?”

Dawn’s breathing changes again. “Doesn’t matter.” Her voice is thick. “I can—"

“What would you say to me? Just say it.”

“I’d tell you how bad it hurts. Every day. To wake up without Danny.”

“Tell me,” Caroline urges her. “Tell me how bad it hurts.”

“I love him.” Dawn swipes at her eyes. “God, I loved him so much.”

“You guys were happy?”

“We were happy,” Dawn answers softly. “But we were sad too.”

Caroline stares at Dawn expecting her to explain what she said, but she doesn’t. Finally the sound of Dawn’s quiet crying chills Caroline, until she scoots down the couch and puts her arms around Dawn and pulls her tight against her. Dawn rests her head on Caroline’s shoulder. Her tears wet Caroline’s shirt.

"I want to remember, Dawn," Caroline whispers against her hair. "I want to remember. But I don't. I'm scared."

"I need you back, Car." Dawn huffs a deep breath and tries to sit up. Caroline still holds her. "I need you back, or I need to get the hell outta here. If you're gone, I need to go and never look back."

"I may never be that person again. I may not be the same Caroline you knew."

Dawn draws back a bit now. "You won't be." Dawn's husky voice rakes chills over Caroline's bare arms. "But I'm not the same Dawn you used to know."

THE MORNING IS GRAY, AS IF NIGHT WILL NOT relinquish its hold on time. Caroline has laid awake long enough to watch the inky black fade into steel gray and then freeze. Even the clouds are a dirty gray, heavy, with the threat of rain.

The rock in her stomach last night is gone, melted away by Dawn's words. Dawn's sadness. Instead she is simply weary, as she leaves the library and the blanket and pillow behind. Coffee. Coffee will not change the world. It won't color the sky blue. But she wants it, *needs* it just the same.

'Did you sleep down here again?'

The voice is so real, she looks behind her. Heart in her throat. *Miles.* Alone in the hallway, she sees Miles with his hands on his hips and his head cocked and his face twisted with a look of impatience or anger.

'I couldn't sleep. Didn't want to wake you up.'

The hall is different though. It's this one. It's this narrow passageway from the front of the house to the back, to the kitchen, but it's different. Caroline sags against the wall. *Pictures. A framed family picture. Miles, Max, and a woman. A blonde woman she does not recognize.* She closes her eyes, desperate to bring the memory into focus. *Three picture frames, a big one and two smaller frames flanking it on the sides.*

'I'm tired of my wife choosing not to sleep with me!' The anger in the memory voice pulls her attention away from the picture frames. From the family pictures.

'Miles, please don't do this—'

'Get the library cleaned up. Put your stuff away before Max sees it.'

'I'm not choosing not to sleep with you. I'm not sleeping, Miles. I don't—'

Caroline gasps, realizing she's been holding her breath, as Miles' eyes flash with anger. She cringes and covers her ears, as Miles yanks the middle picture frame from the wall and sends it crashing to the floor. She cries out, in the memory and now, and shrinks away from him. And the noise.

'Get the Goddamned library cleaned up.'

The memory fades as Caroline slides down the wall to sit on the floor. Her breath hitches as the hallway comes back into focus. Plain walls. Plain beige walls. In the memory, they were darker. Like the color of sand. The pictures. There had been pictures on the wall, where she now leans. She stares at her hands, now trembling in her lap.

She takes a deep breath to blow out the demons in her lungs. She swallows hard and stares at the blank wall opposite her. Where are those pictures? What other pictures have been taken down? What the *hell* had happened here? What had sucked the color, the life out of this house and left the people who live here soulless and empty?

Dawn. Where is Dawn? Wouldn't she know? Wouldn't Dawn know if there had been pictures on the walls in this house? Wouldn't Dawn know, if she was her best friend, whether or not Miles had been violent? She can see his face frozen in a mask of rage as his fingers gripped the frame and threw it to the floor. If they were as close as Dawn says they were, as close as Caroline felt to her last night when Dawn cried in her arms, wouldn't she have told Dawn if there were problems in her marriage?

She climbs to her feet, her legs shaky as she makes her way to the kitchen. It's the longest memory she's had. Since. Since whenever. She doesn't know when she stopped remembering. When she stopped being Caroline Wolfe. The kitchen is empty. A little disappointed, she yanks open random cabinets, looking for coffee. Her hands still tremble, but not as much as her stomach does. Disappointed. She'd needed Dawn to be here, *right now*, so she could confront her about this memory.

Confront? Why would she confront her best friend about a memory of her husband? Caroline hangs her head and buries her face in her hands. Confront. Even after the talk last night, after Dawn had given her a memory, after Dawn had cried in her arms, her first instinct is to protect herself. At all costs. From everyone. Even from Dawn.

"Caroline?"

Caroline jumps and hits her head on the corner of the cabinet door just above her. She groans and rubs the spot with gentle fingertips, rather than turning to look at Dawn.

"Are you okay?"

She can't answer. She can't make her voice work, because she doesn't know. She doesn't know if she's okay. She doesn't *know* anything. She nods and tries to say yes, but she's crying and she knows Dawn didn't get what she'd said.

"Caroline? What's wrong?"

She senses Dawn move closer to her. She doesn't want her to touch her. She's just not ready yet. Not ready, in broad daylight, to look Dawn in the eye and buy the bill of goods she's trying so hard to sell. And she knows she will flinch if Dawn touches her. She reaches up to push the cabinet door closed and takes a deep breath and turns to Dawn, as tall and strong as she can be. Today, she's not tall or strong and she reads that and Dawn's concern in her brown eyes.

"What happened?"

Caroline shakes her head and lowers her gaze to Dawn's stomach and then her shorts and her legs and finally to the floor. Dawn's legs are lean and tan; her toenails are bright pink, like cotton candy. Caroline swallows hard, but the suspicion, the fear gets stuck sideways in her throat. When she tries to speak, her mouth is so full of emotion she simply shakes her head again and turns to look at the French doors.

Outside. She should get a cup of coffee and go outside. See if the monotonous gray of the day could settle her enough that looking at this woman, this friend of hers, does not spook her.

"Is there coffee?" she finally asks Dawn. Her voice is a rough whisper, like the dark feelings inside her press any melody out of it.

"Miles didn't want you to have too much caff—"

"To hell with Miles, Dawn," Caroline growls. "Jesus Christ, this is you telling me this? Who had the three Mountain Dews a day, starting with one first thing every morning?" This time her voice explodes out of her. She's silent now shocked by that guttural voice. Wonders if her head is going to start spinning and if maybe Dawn should call a priest.

She sighs and puts herself back together for a moment, a hastily put together puzzle, like a child shoved the wrong pieces together in a hurry to finish her. "I'm sorry," she says softly. She raises only her eyes to look at Dawn, surprised to see her crying. "I'm sorry. Just please stop telling me what I can and can not do, according to Miles. I just want coffee."

"Caroline," Dawn half whispers, half sobs. "Oh my God." Caroline tries to step away from Dawn as she takes a few awkward steps toward her. She bumps the counter at her back and sends up a silent prayer that Dawn will come no closer. Not yet.

"What?"

"You—I—Mountain Dew." Dawn laughs softly. She rubs her eyes, tries to dry the tears on her fingers. Her pale eyeliner smudges a bit. "What you just said..."

"I don't know what I said," Caroline admits. She shakes her head again. "I want coffee."

"You said—"

"You drank three Mountain Dews a day and started first thing in the morning."

Dawn nods and raises her eyebrows. This time Caroline moves sideways to step away from her.

"You remembered something."

Caroline holds her right hand up as if to hold Dawn at bay. "I don't know."

"You did. Because I did that. In college, I drank three Mountain Dews a day and it drove Beth crazy that I drank soda for breakfast."

Caroline shakes her head. "I'm sorry, Dawn."

"But I didn't tell you that—"

"I know you didn't tell me that," Caroline answers. She rests her elbows on the island and then lowers her face to her hands. "But it doesn't mean anything."

"What do you mean?" Dawn says softly. She steps closer to Caroline, but she stops, careful to leave a buffer between them. "What do you mean it doesn't mean anything?"

"I've just..."

Dawn turns away from her. A tight fist squeezes in Caroline's chest and holds her next breath. She opens her mouth, but with her breath trapped inside her, she can't find her voice. She's not sure what she would say anyway. At the moment, she doesn't want Dawn's company. She wants coffee. She wants to be alone. She *needs* to be alone.

"You've been remembering things, haven't you?"

Caroline is mesmerized by Dawn's movements. She opens the cabinet next to the refrigerator and takes out a container of coffee. She glances over her shoulder at Caroline, but neither of them speak. Dawn shrugs and goes back to making coffee. Caroline watches Dawn's hands. Long, elegant fingers with short, manicured nails. She stands up straight and flattens her palms on the counter. Studies her own fingers. Average. Nothing special about them. Her nails are cut short, as they have been since she woke up in the hospital. She wonders who had cut them for her then, before she'd been able to groom and take care of herself.

"Were you—" She clears her throat and starts again, "Were you here? When I was in the hospital?"

Dawn doesn't say anything, but Caroline sees her curt nod. Maybe Dawn had taken care of her, trimming her nails and brushing her hair.

"Are you remembering things?" Dawn asks again. The coffee maker is going. With nothing to do with her hands now, she turns and leans back on the cabinet behind her and folds her arms across her chest.

"I've had," Caroline shrugs and licks her lips, "I've had flashes of memories. But not many." She squints hard when her eyes burn with tears. "They don't add up to anything." She takes a deep breath and meets Dawn's eyes. "I can't piece anything together."

Dawn stares at her silently. Finally she nods and lets her hands fall to her sides. "You still don't trust me."

Caroline looks away quickly, afraid of the guilt that climbs her throat like acid. Her face burns with shame. On the surface, it seems like Dawn has tried to help her. But she just isn't *sure* what to think. Of *anyone.* She looks back when she hears Dawn pull open a drawer. Watches silently as Dawn takes a set of keys from the drawer.

"These are to the Lexus. Parked in the garage." Dawn looks pointedly at Caroline. "If you go, don't look back."

"What? Where are you—? Dawn?"

Dawn stops in the kitchen doorway, but she doesn't turn to look at Caroline. "If I don't have you or your trust, I have nothing left."

CINDERELLA

TWELVE

1994

Bloomington-Normal, IL

"Wait," Caroline says and leans toward Beth as they settle into Beth's '92 Beretta.

"What?" Beth giggles as Caroline's fingertips graze her cheek. "What're you doing? People are gonna think we're making out."

"Wanna give 'em a show?" Caroline laughs. "Close your eyes."

"Caroline!"

"Shut up." Caroline playfully pushes Beth's shoulder. "Your eyes are gorgeous. I love that makeup."

"Yeah?"

"You gonna stay with it? I've seen you wear makeup like two times since I've known you."

"You like it?"

"Beth, it's incredible," Caroline answers. "You're gorgeous without it, but this is amazing. And the hair color is perfect." Caroline lifts her hand and runs her fingers through Beth's hair. She leans forward and studies the caramel highlights.

Beth presses her lips together and nods. "Thanks."

"I wish Dawn was here," Caroline says for the tenth time.

"Me too." Beth bats Caroline's hand away and reaches toward her. "Look at this! I can't believe you did it!"

Caroline smiles a bit sheepishly as Beth plays with the ends of her short hair. She'd sat down in the chair and asked for something different. She hadn't looked once, while her stylist had worked. Not even when Beth had oohed or awed over it. She'd sat down with long, carefree hair and when the stylist had turned her around to show her the finished look, she had a sexy, tousled bob. She'd seen inches of her blonde hair on the floor and for a moment, she'd wanted to cry. Instead she'd stood and leaned closer to see herself better in the mirror. Gone was the young girl who'd loved and lost and made the mistakes of a woman in an immature, teen body. Here was Caroline Evans, independent woman.

"Do you like it?" she whispers now.

"It's incredible," Beth answers. "Your cheekbones, God, you look like a completely different person."

Caroline flattens her hands on her thighs and studies her nails, painted in rich Burgundy Frost.

“Different? How?”

“Sophisticated and sexy,” Beth tells her. “What’s Miles gonna say?”

Caroline grabs Beth’s hand and squeezes it. “Do you think he’ll like it?”

“I don’t know what’s not to like.” Beth shakes her head. “Unless he had a thing for long hair.”

“I hope he doesn’t have a thing for long hair.” Caroline winces. “I needed this, Beth. I needed a change.”

“Hey, you don’t have to convince me.” Beth sits back and reaches to start the car. “I love it. Dawn’s gonna love it.”

“Damn her for not being here.” Caroline runs her fingers through her hair, still shocked when the silky threads fall so soon to her neck.

“You have plans with Miles?” Beth asks.

“Not ‘til later. Going to a movie at nine.”

Beth glances at her watch. “Wanna get something to eat before we go home?”

“Sure.”

“Caroline?”

“Hmm?” Caroline turns to look at Beth as she merges the car into traffic.

“You know how I said that it wasn’t like that with Mike?”

"Yeah?"

"It's not," Beth says quickly. "But I want it to be."

"You've got a thing for Mike McGarret?"

"It's not really a thing."

"Okay," Caroline says softly. "What is it?"

Beth starts to answer her, but she stops before any words make it to her lips. "I like him. I mean—"

"Beth." Caroline touches her shoulder. "It's okay. I'm not gonna laugh."

"I'm not afraid you're going to laugh." Beth's gaze roams the interior of the car and back out to the road in front of her, without making eye contact with Caroline.

"Then what?"

"I'm afraid you're gonna judge me."

"Why? Since when do friends judge each other?"

"I don't even know what I want from him," Beth admits. "I just like him. I love spending time with him."

"Are you attracted to him?"

"I don't know," Beth whispers. "I am, I think. But."

"But what?"

"But I'm scared to throw that into the mix. I like him. I don't wanna lose this fun friendship over mediocre sex."

"How do you know it would be mediocre sex?"

"Just what if it was?"

“What if it’s incredible?”

“He’s older.”

“So that means he’d be mediocre?”

“No.” Beth laughs. “New concern. He’s just older.”

“How old?”

“Thirty-eight.”

Caroline considers this and then shrugs. “Is he married?”

“Divorced.”

“Have you been with him?”

“No.” Beth shoots Caroline a glance. She looks sad. “I just. What if this is all me? He’s trying to get me this job. Maybe he feels sorry for me—"

“Why the hell would anyone feel sorry for you?” Caroline asks with a frown. “You’re smart. You’re disciplined. You work your ass off. You’re gorgeous—"

“Broken family.”

“Big deal.” Caroline shrugs. “That’s in now, Beth. You know that.”

“I’m just scared.” Beth turns her head and blurts her admission to the window.

“Are you afraid of how it would work out with you guys? Or are you afraid that if you got involved with him people would say you slept your way to NASA?”

“Both.”

"Everyone that knows you knows you wouldn't compromise yourself that way."

"And what about people that don't know me?"

"Since when do you care what they say?"

Beth glances at Caroline and smiles. "Thank you, Caroline. I needed that."

CAROLINE STARES AT MILES, DYING FOR HIM TO say something. He'd picked her up nearly an hour ago, and aside from a slight smile and a nod, he hadn't even acknowledged that she'd cut her hair. So much more than that, really. The hair cut had been a huge step in shedding her former self. Miles has no way of knowing that, and she knows if they continue seeing each other, she's going to have to tell him why something so simple should mean so much to her. Right now, though, she'd just like a word. Even 'nice' at this point would be okay.

Miles studies her quietly over his empty dinner plate and her half eaten rice and chimichanga. The corner of his mouth curves upward just a bit, but still he says nothing. Unable to stand it any longer, she laughs out loud and leans over the table. She closes her fingers around his wrist. "Well? Are you going to say anything or not? You're killing me."

He flashes her a grin, finally, but he continues to study her quietly.

"C'mon." She tilts her head a bit. "What? You hate it?"

"No," he says and shakes his head. "Of course I don't hate it."

"But you don't love it?" She cringes. Her fingers go cold around his wrist, but before she can let go, he covers them with his other hand.

"I'm thinking," he answers.

"And?"

"It's very sexy."

She wonders if he realizes he's rubbing his thumb over hers. "Sexy?"

"Well, I was shocked at first. I dropped you off last night, and you had all this long, soft blonde hair. And then the next time I see you, it's all gone." He laughs, but he narrows his eyes at her. She feels like he's drinking her in. "I have to admit, it hurt. I loved the long hair. Like a princess. Could've seen you with a tiara and all that long hair."

"But?" she whispers.

"I like this." He nods. "It's very sophisticated. Bold and sexy."

She lifts an eyebrow and wiggles a bit in her chair. The hands that touch hers now have roamed her body once or twice, but they've never gotten intimately acquainted yet and it's killing her. "Yeah?" She grins. "Enough to make you want me?"

"Oh, I want you." His voice is low and clipped, like it's painful to want her the way he does. "You're just a different kind of fantasy now."

“Miles.” The mood is broken now. She pulls her hand away from his and drops back in her chair. It’s hardly the place for this kind of conversation, but she can’t help the sting of his words. “I don’t wanna be your fantasy.”

“I didn’t mean it literally,” he answers. “Trust me.”

“Why are we waiting?” She picks up her beer bottle and takes a healthy swallow when she realizes she’d said that out loud. Miles arches an eyebrow, but he doesn’t answer her.

CINDERELLA

THIRTEEN

June, 2008

Present Day

Springfield, IL

Caroline knows *how* to drive a car. That part of her memory is intact. She can add and spell and read and drive, if she wants to. Doesn't make a damned bit of sense to her that she remembers that stuff but can't remember her son or her husband. Then again, she thinks as she plops down in the patio chair on the deck, it makes perfect sense. She could go on this way forever. She could live sufficiently on her own. But she would no longer live as Caroline Wolfe. Caroline Wolfe has been wiped from her mind.

Not *completely* wiped away, she reminds herself. There's no one offering much help at the moment, but there's something inside that seems damned determined that she's going to remember. Going to be a hell of a long ride and whatever's inside her is driving painstakingly slow. But she is remembering things.

The air around her is so heavy with heat and humidity; it's as if it is a physical entity, holding her steadfast in the chair. Still, she sips the hot coffee like it is the drink of gods and she is immortal. The memories that have teased her, that have been circling around her but have yet to truly land inside her, are still vague. But at this moment, on the patio, with the oversized blue stoneware mug in hand, she is at home. Something inside her has shifted, and she knows that at one time, she did indeed call this house—this prison—home.

She's just not certain that it was ever a happy home.

Damn Dawn for leaving her this morning. She needs to talk to her. She needs to talk to *someone*. She can't say that Dawn is her first choice, simply her only choice at the moment. She trusts no one, not even—*especially*—herself. How in the hell can Dawn think she will just tie up a gift of blind trust and hand it to her with a pretty bow?

Dawn's never been in this situation before, she reminds herself. *She can't possibly understand the fear or the desperation the unknown brings.*

Caroline leans back in the chair. Her mug is on the patio table, but the fingers of her right hand curl around it possessively. The hot stoneware calms her, even when her hair sticks with sweat to the back of her neck.

She'd had an abortion. *Dawn says* she'd had an abortion. As a teenager. She'd been desperately in love with someone, gotten pregnant and then aborted his child. The fact that she hadn't taken money for it gives her little comfort. She'd aborted a child.

How had she aborted a child and then several years later given birth to a child and, according to Dawn, fallen head over heels in love with him? How had she been a good mother if she'd been lugging around that kind of guilt? The kind that comes with taking an innocent life? How had she been a good mother to Max if she *hadn't* been lugging around that kind of guilt? How can a woman abort one child and love another?

She drops her chin to her chest and rubs the fingers of her left hand over her forehead. She doesn't know. She doesn't know if women can do that. If she did that. If she'd been capable of getting rid of a baby simply because her boyfriend's mother had pushed her to do it. If she'd been thrilled to learn she was pregnant with Max. She doesn't know. And that's the hell of it.

What if Dawn is lying? The skin on the back of her neck crawls. Someone is behind her. Someone—*Miles?*—is behind her. Watching her. She lifts her head slowly and lets her eyes sweep the landscape in front of her. No one around.

What's wrong, Car?

It's Beth.

What about Beth?

Oh my God—

Caroline, confused by the random memory, jumps up so fast her chair tips backwards. Hot coffee sloshes over her hand as she turns around expecting to see Miles standing behind her. Watching her. *Always watching her. Like he doesn't trust her.* Caroline gasps a tight breath of air, as upset by the thought of Miles not trusting her as she is by the burning sensation in her hand and the unnerving feeling of being watched.

Clutching her hand to her stomach, skin stinging from the contact of her other hand, she raises her eyes to study the windows of the house. What if he's in there? What if he's in there watching her right now? He'd come home while she was out here, and now maybe he's in there somewhere, hiding, and watching her.

What if he'd never really been gone at all?

"Jesus, Caroline, get a grip," she mumbles. She takes a deep breath and reaches to set the chair upright. She ignores the angry red splotch on her hand. Doesn't matter. Doesn't matter if Miles is inside right now. Doesn't even matter if he'd been here the whole time, hiding and watching her. She's done nothing wrong.

She picks up her coffee mug, surprised to see her hand trembling. Wrong? She takes a step toward the door but stops herself and looks around again. Everything is as it should be. Why should she worry that she might have done something wrong? *Something to anger Miles?* If he's her husband, they are equals. It's not as if she's a child and she might do something to get into trouble with a parent or some other authority figure.

Another deep breath to steady herself. Finally, she goes back inside the kitchen and rinses her mug out. Runs cool water on her hand and wonders if cool water soothes burns or if she is supposed to put butter on it. The water seems to help. The clock ticking on the kitchen wall is so loud, it rubs Caroline's last nerve. Like in the movies, when all noise falls away, except a steady tick tock that counts down to the moment when all hell will break loose.

Unnerved again, she leaves the kitchen quickly and hand in a white knuckle grip on the rail of the stairs, hurries as fast as her still mending body will allow her, back to her room. A shower. She wants a quick shower and then maybe she'll go back outside. Take a walk. What the hell? She could find the keys and go for a drive.

She digs through the top dresser drawer and finds lavender lace panties with a matching bra. Her favorite color has never been lavender. It's not important, but it's true. She's never been a lavender or a pink kind of girl. Why is Miles lying to her about something so simple? And if he's lying to her about something this simple, what other things might he lie about?

With a glance back at her bedroom door, open as far as it will go, Caroline takes a step toward her bathroom. The bathroom with a shower and a sink and a toilet. But no mirror. She hates that Miles will not give her a mirror. She's not *asked* for one after that day she'd first seen herself, after the bandages had come off. But what difference does it make now? She's seen her face, and she doesn't recognize it. What harm would there be in hanging a mirror in the bathroom now?

She stops outside the bathroom and looks back at her door. What if he comes home? While she's in the shower? What if when she gets out of the shower, that door is closed and locked again? Damn Dawn for leaving her like this.

There are other bathrooms in the house. She could shower in another bathroom. One with a mirror. One where there's no deadbolt on the outside of the door. With a sigh of relief, she moves back across the room. Of course that's what she'll do. Simple. She has to find clothes first. Doesn't want to step out of the shower and have only the underwear to put on. In the second drawer down, she finds a white tank and from the bottom drawer, she pulls a pair of khaki shorts.

Her gaze falls on the gold wedding band laying on the dresser.

'It's gorgeous, Miles. I love it.'

'If giving you a ring like this means making love like this every night, I'll put one on each finger of your hands.'

'We can't make love like this every night. Everyone'll call me Cowboy Jane.'

'Am I hurting you? I can stop.'

They'd been laughing, teasing, up until now. But the teasing stops, and Miles studies her with concern in his eyes.

'Don't stop.' She splays her hands over his face, framing his mouth in her fingers, and pulls him back down to kiss him. Soft, wet kisses. The candlelight flickers and catches a cut in the diamond on her finger. 'Don't ever stop loving me like this, Miles.'

Shaken by the memory, Caroline is surprised to find herself reaching to pick the ring up. She pushes it gently onto her ring finger. Tries to call the memory back. Any memory back as the ring settles into place. There is a groove on her finger, a mark, from wearing a ring for many years. Is this the one? Is this the ring that marked her finger? She rushes out of her bedroom then, intent on the shower and getting out of the house for a while.

She hesitates outside the bathroom door. The house is silent. She didn't even check to make sure the doors are all locked. And yet, she knows there is no danger to her outside the house. Any threat to her at this time in her life comes from within these walls. Feeling stupid, she steps into the bathroom, turns on the shower water and strips down to nothing. A quick shower. She can handle a quick shower.

Except there's a mirror in this bathroom. And she wants to see herself. She pushes the door closed and locks it from the inside, but a jolt of nerves tightens her stomach. She takes a deep breath and turns to the face in the mirror.

If character and personality make a person beautiful, she is nothing to look at. She is nothing inside and it reflects back to her in the mirror. She steps back from the mirror and sees more of herself. There is a scar on her upper arm. Starts in her chest, above her right breast and extends into her right arm. Straight cut, maybe four or five inches long. She can't see the rest of herself in the mirror, but she stretches and twists to see her body. To catalog the scars. There's another one on her stomach. To the right of her belly button. On her left knee.

Scars give pirates character. So maybe she has character. But she doesn't know who the hell that character inside her is. Steam billows around her, so she eventually gives up the study of her arms and legs and climbs into the shower. The ring on her finger is loose and it twists and turns and once, it almost slides off. What would Miles do, she wonders, if she lost this ring? The shower, the shampoo, the soap—none of it teases any memories to life. Anxious now to get out of the house, she shuts the water off quickly and towels herself dry, now ignoring the scars. Her long legs are skinny and scrawny looking. Pasty white. Like someone dead or dying. She supposes for a long time she might have been dying and even though she's walking and talking now, she feels dead.

Lavender panties over her angular hipbones. Lavender bra. The shorts. Tank. She finds lotion in the cabinet beneath the sink and slathers it over her arms and legs, wishing she'd have found it before she dressed. There's a comb in the top drawer, so she stands up straight to run it through her hair, wondering how she used to style it. What she looked like when she and Miles had met.

She needs a style now. She needs some makeup. Some sun. A little vanity to fill in the gaps and make her at least *look* like someone. She could go get some makeup. Get in the Lexus and drive—*to the mall?*—and get makeup and maybe some new clothes. Get rid of the lavender stuff. It's so far from her favorite color right now, she hates it.

As she pulls the comb gently through her chin length hair, she leans forward to study her face in the mirror. There's a tiny, faint scar under her right eye. What the hell had happened to her right side? Looks like she'd done the hokey pokey on a train track and left her right side in a bit too long. The scar gives her the creeps. She lifts her gaze just enough to look herself in the eye.

Blue eyes, but not the ice blue that can cut right through a person. Big, warm blue eyes. Lips pressed hard together, as if they might unleash a cry of anguish if they open. And then she hears it. A fist on flesh. And a cry of pain. She sees blood. She sees way too damned much blood for it to be a simple fistfight.

Despite the heat and the steam in the bathroom, Caroline is chilled. She watches in the mirror as the blood drains from her face and leaves her so pale, she thinks she can see through her own face.

The blue eyes she has been remembering are her own.

Caroline is outside when she hears the car door. She doesn't have a watch on—*probably doesn't have a watch*—but she doesn't think it took Dawn a full ten minutes to get here after she'd called her. Choked on fear and sadness—mostly fear—Caroline had rushed from the bathroom down to the kitchen and the black cordless GE and called Dawn.

Right now, she sits at the patio table, the same table she'd been sitting at earlier when she'd sloshed coffee and burned her hand. She waits at the table for Dawn to find her. She's swallowed the fear for the moment. She'd called Dawn. In a moment of panic, she'd called Dawn. Without thinking, she'd grabbed the phone and called Dawn. She'd simply said "Please come back." And Dawn had promised she'd be right there. And now Dawn is here. Walking through the house looking for her.

Caroline doesn't know Dawn's phone number. She's been sitting here, since making that phone call, wondering how the hell she'd known Dawn's number. At the moment, she's blank. She doesn't know any phone numbers, not even her own, and especially not Dawn's.

"Caroline?" Dawn's voice. Caroline hears the French doors behind her close, but she doesn't turn to look at Dawn. The answers—*the questions*—she needs to know are buried somewhere inside her. Why is she remembering some things and not everything? She needs to see a doctor. Her choice of doctor, not someone on Miles' payroll.

"Caroline?" Dawn huffs as she squats down beside Caroline's chair. "What happened? Are you okay?"

Still reeling from the jagged memories that come to her like lost pieces of random puzzles, Caroline turns to Dawn. Though the woman is right beside her, Caroline hardly sees her. She still sees the blue eyes in the mirror, the phone in her hand, calling Dawn.

"What happened?" Dawn asks again.

Caroline wraps her cold fingers around Dawn's hands and looks her in the eye. "I need you—"

"Okay." Dawn nods. Her eyes are wide with panic. Caroline feels her chest squeeze uncomfortably tight. "I'm here. Tell me. Tell me what happened."

Caroline shakes her head and opens her mouth to speak. She can't find the words to tell Dawn what she thinks. She doesn't know what she's thinking. What she feels. She doesn't know where to start, how to make Dawn understand the confusion inside her.

"No," Caroline says softly. "It's not like that." She sighs and shakes her head again.

"What?" Dawn looks down at their hands, at Caroline's hands closed over her own. "Why do you have that on?"

"What?" Caroline lets her gaze slide from Dawn's face down to their hands. To the wedding band on her finger. "Oh. I just." She shrugs. "Picked it up for a minute and put it on."

Dawn nods, clearly waiting for Caroline to go on.

"Dawn, I need you to be patient with me," Caroline mumbles. "You can't know what this is like—"

"Then tell me," Dawn answers. "Tell me what you're thinking. What's going on inside your head."

"I'm scared." Caroline draws her hands away from Dawn and stands up.

"Of me?" Dawn asks as she stands and watches Caroline pace away from the table.

"Of you." Caroline clears her throat. "Of Miles."

Dawn's lips form a silent O. She takes a deep breath but still says nothing.

"Should I be scared?" Caroline whispers.

"Not of me," Dawn answers without hesitation.

Caroline nods and turns away from Dawn. "As much as I need to know," she says quietly, "I have to figure it out for myself."

"What do you mean?" Dawn takes a step toward her.

“I’m not even sure I believe the one thing you told me,” Caroline whispers. “And that has nothing to do with Miles.”

Dawn raises her eyebrows. She looks affronted to be accused of lying or feeding Caroline false memories. “Why would I lie to you about that? What would I gain from that?”

Caroline shakes her head. Her lips quirk up in a humorless smile. “It’s not that you would gain anything from it. Just hard to want to believe that about yourself.”

“Fair enough.” Dawn licks her lips. “Are you remembering things?”

“Just flashes. These flashes that make no sense. Even if I put them all together, it’s all a mess. Things that don’t go together at all.”

“Do you remember me?” Dawn asks softly.

Caroline struggles to swallow her guilt. “Not on a conscious level, no.” She looks away when the hurt paints Dawn’s face. “I know I know you, Dawn. I feel it. I called you today. After...after I called you. I’ve been sitting out here since I called you wondering how in the hell I knew your phone number.”

“We used to talk every day.” Dawn dabs at the corners of her eyes with her fingertips. “Sometimes fifteen two second conversations. Sometimes two calls, each lasting an hour or longer. We shopped. Did lunch. Went out for drinks. Talked about everything.”

“Did that stop because of what happened to me?” Caroline asks. “Or did something happen between us before that?”

"We were closer than sisters, Car," Dawn answers. "Things happen. We went through a few rough times, but we always talked through everything."

"Was it a rough time? Before what happened to me?"

Dawn gives up the fight against the tears and lets them slide over her face.

"Do you remember it? Is that why you're pushing this?"

CINDERELLA

FOURTEEN

1994

Bloomington-Normal, IL

“Look,” Beth says on the ragged edges of a deep breath. “Don’t get mad, okay? But there’s something I need to say to you. ‘Kay? Can I be honest?”

Caroline’s gaze drops to the beer can in Beth’s hand, and she wonders how many she’s had. She has that look in her eye, and her words are falling together in the way they sometimes do when Beth’s had too much to drink. It’s not often, but Caroline has seen Beth tipsy a few times and flat out drunk once, and right now, other than that serious, predator like gleam in her eye, Caroline thinks Beth is tipsy.

“I hate when someone has to ask me if she can be honest with me before she says something,” Caroline answers softly. She sits at the tiny kitchen table in their apartment, legs drawn up against her chest, her arms circling her knees.

Her beer —number three—is on the table in front of her. Judging from the look on Beth's face and the sudden nervousness in her stomach, beer number three will be the last for her. "Scares me, Beth."

Beth raises her eyebrows—in thought or apology? Caroline is not sure—and angles her can so she can peer into it. "*Can* I be honest?"

Caroline presses her lips together and turns to look at Dawn. The end of their college careers is quickly approaching. In just a few short weeks they will all don the black cap and gown and march in the long line of students seeking their diplomas, the right to call themselves graduates. Mostly Caroline has looked forward to this time in her life. In fact, she's been more excited about it recently. She's always been certain that she and Dawn and Beth will remain close, even after they graduate and spread out and find their own way in life. And now she has Miles. There are no definite plans for the future, but she and Miles have talked and dreamed for hours at a time about what their life together will be like. The house they'll own and the children they'll have. Thinking about having a baby with Miles has almost eased the guilt Caroline has dragged with her everywhere since aborting her first child. Like if she loves a new baby enough, her first one will feel it and know that she regrets her decision every day. That she loved him too.

But she wonders, now, if this isn't some kind of sitcom happy ending that she's had in her mind, but Beth and maybe Dawn don't see it. Maybe Beth wants to sever the ties with graduation. Maybe she thinks cutting the cord is the only way the three of them will make it in the real world.

Caroline tucks a loose strand of hair behind her ear, still taken aback by how short it is. She nods and breathes deeply through her nose and without looking at Beth says, "Sure, Bethie. Be honest."

"I don't like him."

Caroline remains stoic on the outside. But she hates that one of her best friends does not like the man she's in love with. It's almost as bad as if one of her parents didn't like him, and they do. Her parents think Miles is hard-working, intelligent, charming and perfect for her. So why does Beth have to be so stubborn?

"You have to give him a chance, Beth—"

"I have given him a chance, Caroline," Beth reminds her. Suddenly she sounds stone cold sober, though when Caroline takes a glance at her, she sees that fire is still in her eyes. "I've been around him a lot lately. Enough to know that I don't like him."

"You made up your mind about him before you met him," Caroline argues. "Just because he kissed Dawn and me both at the bowling alley."

"Nope." Beth shakes her head. "Nope, that's not really it, Car. I know other guys that might try that. I know guys who would die to sleep with the three of us here together. I've had guys ask me if we'd be interested." Beth sighs and drags her fingers back through her hair. "It's not that he did it. It's that he felt he had the right to do it. That he took it without asking. As if he's entitled to whatever he wants."

Caroline rolls her eyes and shakes her head.

"I'm worried about you, Caroline."

"Why are you worried about me?" Caroline lowers her legs and flattens her hands on the table to stand up. Beth lays her hand over Caroline's.

"He's changing you. You're far too much woman for a guy like that."

"What?" Caroline snaps. She turns to Dawn again. "Do you think that too?"

Dawn opens her mouth, but she says nothing. She's never been as outspoken as Beth.

"He's making you less, Caroline," Beth whispers. "You are this amazing woman. And you can be or do anything you want, and this guy—this fucking knight in shining armor charges in—and makes you believe you're a little lost girl and you need to be rescued."

Caroline laughs sarcastically and drops back down in her chair. "So. Because I'm in love with someone, because I'm involved in a serious relationship, you think my life is going to go to hell?"

"I think he's not who he says he is," Beth says urgently. She nods and strokes Caroline's fingers. "He's—"

"I think you're jealous." Caroline pulls her hand out from under Beth's. "I have Miles. And Dawn is with Danny. And I think you're jealous." She stands up and stares at Beth with all the anger she can garner. "Pretty sad way to treat a friend, Beth."

Beth shakes her head silently and looks at Dawn for help. Caroline looks at Dawn again, waiting for her to say something. Beth groans and sighs and pushes her chair back to stand when Dawn presses her lips together and refuses to say anything.

"I'm not jealous, Car," Beth says simply. "I just love you. I don't wanna see you get hurt."

Caroline turns her back to them and dumps the remains of beer number three in the sink. "What about Dawn and Danny?"

"Danny wants me to be myself first," Dawn whispers. "And his girlfriend second."

Caroline sucks in a sharp breath. Miles hates it when she talks about a career, in anything but an abstract way. He doesn't argue, never says he doesn't want her to work. He just nuzzles her close and kisses her and steers her back to talking about all the mornings they will wake up together and the nights they will make love and the world they'll show their children. Does dreaming about a future together as a couple, as a family have to mean that he wants to make her less than who she is?

"So what does that mean?" Caroline clears her throat and looks over her shoulder at Beth.

"What?"

"What's it mean? For us? To hell with me?"

"Caroline, I just said I—"

"No, seriously, Beth." Caroline turns back to them, but she keeps her eyes on Beth. "We graduate in a couple of weeks.

So is that it for us? You don't like Miles, so screw you, see ya later?"

"No." Beth throws her hands up in surrender. "Of course not. I'm just telling you I don't like him. I had to say it. As your friend, I had to say it. He's not good enough for you, Car."

"I'm in love with him, Beth." Caroline draws herself up to her full height, but her words are small and quiet.

Beth's mouth works to say something, but instead she shakes her head. Caroline notices the tears in her eyes before she looks away. "You've never said that before."

"Been busy thinking about it," Caroline answers with a small shrug.

"Ah, God, Car." Beth scrubs her face with her hands and then drags her fingers back through her hair. "I'm sorry. I just want you to be happy—"

"I am happy," Caroline insists. She brushes at the tears on her face. "You know me, Beth. Don't you think I've been happy? Since I started seeing him?"

Beth sighs and looks at Dawn. "Maybe happy, Caroline, but different." She reaches toward Caroline, but lets her hand drop to her side before she actually touches her. "You're not the Caroline I met, and I hate to lose that woman as a friend."

"That's kind of unfair," Caroline says quietly. "Don't you think?"

"Beth doesn't wanna see you barefoot and pregnant and seven kids and stuck in a rut in the house while Miles is out entertaining or being successful or doing whatever it is Miles is gonna do."

"But if that's what I want, if that's what would make me happy, shouldn't I have that chance?" Caroline asks them both, though she looks at Dawn. She laughs softly, tears still on her face, when she sees the look of horror on Dawn's face. "That's not what I want, guys. C'mon, you know that. I'm not gonna be a barefoot pregnant, baby-making machine for Miles. But I'm in love with him. I want to spend my life with him. I want to have his children."

"But what about law school? What about Miles being succcssful and gonc and treating you like it's your place to raise his children and keep his house?"

"Who said Miles sees me that way?" Caroline blows out a breath of frustration. "He's never said he doesn't want me to work. He's never said he wants ten kids. He's never had anything negative to say about women working. Why would you think that, Beth?"

"How many law schools have you applied to?" Beth asks.

"What—?" Caroline jerks her head back as if Beth slapped her. "Why does that—? Seriously, Beth? God, I got caught up in this. I got caught up in the romance of being with the perfect man. I never thought I'd find this again. Never thought I could feel this way with someone. Not after Shane." Caroline drops back into her chair by the table. She looks from Dawn up to Beth. "This is different, Beth. This is so much more. This is it. This is real."

Beth sighs and averts her eyes from Caroline's heavy stare. "And what about law school?"

Caroline raises her eyebrows.

“Do you still wanna go?” Dawn pushes gently.

“If I don’t, that means I’m less of a woman? And that it’s all Miles’ fault?”

“Caroline—"

“No, wait. Is that what you’re saying? Because if it is, that’s you making me less—"

“Look,” Dawn scoots to the edge of her chair and reaches to cover Caroline’s hands with her own, “I know what you mean. I know how you feel. Getting lost in how wonderful he makes you feel.” Dawn’s eyes are bright with unshed tears. “That’s how I feel about Danny.”

Caroline lowers her gaze to Dawn’s hands over hers, rather than look her in the eye.

“But I’m sending out resumes. I’m looking for a job, Car. I wanna make something of myself. I wanna be someone. I want Danny to be proud of me—"

“I’ll do it,” Caroline says in a cool, clipped tone, “when I’m ready. And it’s not Miles holding me back. It’s me being happy and living in the moment. And I have to wonder how long you guys have had this ambush planned, which makes me feel pretty shitty.”

“We didn’t ambush you—"

“You didn’t?” Caroline laughs sarcastically. “You got rid of Miles for the night. You plied me with alcohol. And then you unload on me about how you don’t like the man I want to spend my life with.”

"This is a girls' night, Caroline," Beth whispers. "Even married women have them now and then. Dawn and I are your friends. We're concerned about you."

The three of them are quiet for several moments. Caroline wants to ask Dawn to remove the knives from her back, because she can't reach them. Finally she sighs and walks out of the kitchen. "Caroline—" Beth calls after her.

"Lemme alone, Beth," Caroline answers from the bedroom. "I don't feel like talking anymore." Caroline crawls into bed, wondering how she's going to tell Miles that Beth broke her heart. Miles isn't crazy about Beth anyway. She might be mad at Beth right now, but she doesn't want to stir the pot and create any more animosity between them.

RAPUNZEL

FIFTEEN

June, 2008

Springfield, IL

Caroline presses her lips together, realizing that something had happened between herself and Dawn, before the accident. She doesn't remember anything specific, but Dawn's answer leaves her feeling chilled.

"No," she finally answers. "I don't remember anything from before the accident. I mean—" She cuts herself off with a growl of frustration.

"Just talk, Caroline," Dawn whispers. "There's no hurry. Please. Just talk to me."

Caroline drags her fingers back through her hair and paces the patio, unable to look at Dawn. The woman's face is haggard and tired, as if she's ninety years old and she's lived through hell. A chill chases up Caroline's spine. Dawn isn't ninety years old. Not by a long shot. She's simply lived through hell.

"I don't remember. It's not like a black hole before the accident. It's not like I remember everything up 'til the morning before the accident and then it all goes blank." Caroline turns and looks at Dawn.

Dawn nods. "What's it like then? What do you see? In your head, what do you see?"

"This," Caroline says and throws her hands up in a sweeping gesture to encompass the house and the yard and Dawn. "This, like it's the first time I've seen any of it. I don't remember you. I don't remember buying this house with Miles. I don't remember college. I don't remember math class in eighth grade." She purses her lips and blows out a sigh of exhaustion.

"Except out of the blue, I do remember something," she continues, "but not enough to make any sense. I feel like I'm going crazy, Dawn. I'm scared."

Dawn nods, but she doesn't say anything. Caroline watches her as she takes her turn pacing back and forth in front of the French doors. Finally, worn out from watching her, Caroline slinks back to the table and drops into a chair.

"Say something," she finally hisses. "Stop the pacing and say something."

Dawn's laugh is sharp and humorless. She leans on the glass door at her back and stares at Caroline. "What am I supposed to say? You don't trust me. If I try to help you remember, you think I'm lying to you. Feeding you memories, like I have something to gain from that. If I don't help you, you think I'm holding things back from you purposely."

Chagrined, Caroline looks away from Dawn's angry eyes.

"Do me a favor?" Dawn says quietly.

"What?"

"Take the ring off."

Caroline looks back at her, surprised at her request. "What?"

"Your wedding ring. Take it off."

Caroline slides the ring off and lays it on the glass topped patio table. "Why?"

"I just..." Dawn shudders and pushes herself away from the door. She moves slowly to the table and sits down across from Caroline.

"Miles told me we used to fight a lot."

Dawn gives her a tiny nod in response.

"Why? What did we fight about?"

"I'm not gonna do this," Dawn answers. She shakes her head. "I'm not gonna tell you the truth, only to have you rip me apart the next day because it was something you didn't wanna hear."

"I need your help," Caroline cries. Her voice breaks. She falls back in her chair and stares helplessly at Dawn. "I need you to help me get back to who I am, Dawn. Something's not right here. Something is off in this house, and I need you to help me figure it out."

"I can't—"

"Are you closer to Miles than you are to me? Have you been in this house helping me? Or guarding me for him?"

"I hate the son-of-a-bitch," Dawn snaps. Fire lights her eyes. "God help me, I have hated him for years, Caroline."

Caroline raises her eyebrows, surprised at the vehemence in Dawn's voice. She believes she hates Miles. But she doesn't know why. "So you've been here for me?"

"Of course I've been here for you." Dawn's anger drains and her voice softens to little more than a whisper. "I told you that we've been through hell together, Caroline. You've done so much for me through the years. I would do anything for you—"

"What?"

Dawn shakes her head. "What do you mean?"

"What have I done for you?"

"You've always been my safe place to land," Dawn answers, eyes drawn to a nick in the glass table top. "You and Beth talked me through a pregnancy scare in college. You sat with me, the night after my mom died. Sat up with me and held me hand. You—"

"When did your mom die?"

"Four years after we graduated from college." Dawn raises her eyes to look at Caroline but quickly looks away. "Breast cancer."

"I'm sorry." Caroline nods and clears her throat. "What about my parents, Dawn?"

"Your dad passed away the year before my mom. Your mom...in 2001."

Even though she doesn't remember them, just hearing that her parents are gone makes Caroline feel alone and abandoned.

"Danny and I..."

"What?" Caroline leans forward, as if by sheer closeness she can force the words from Dawn.

"We tried for years," Dawn swallows hard, "to have a baby." Caroline watches the woman struggle to get control over herself. Tears fall anyway, but Dawn doesn't try to wipe them away. "Doctors said there was no physical reason we couldn't conceive."

"You never got pregnant?"

"Yeah, we did." Dawn finally takes a swipe at her face, smearing eyeliner under her bloodshot eyes. "Premature labor. I was only five months along. She didn't make it."

"Why?" Caroline asks softly. "You're young and healthy. Why did you go into labor so early?"

"I dunno," Dawn mumbles. "No one could ever tell me. Danny was dead before we could ever try again."

"I'm so sorry." Caroline touches Dawn's hand gently. She watches Dawn's eyes, half consumed with the need to comfort her and half afraid to touch her.

"You were with me. With us." Dawn turns her hand over and squeezes Caroline's hand. "At the hospital. You were with us, until it got really bad. And then you just waited. Right outside the door, you waited. When Danny went for you...to get you...in the hall, he was crying and then you were sobbing. I heard you both."

"Jesus." Caroline closes her eyes. "I'm sorry, Dawn."

Dawn takes a deep breath. "You've been like a sister to me, Caroline." She lowers her eyes to their hands. "I wouldn't do anything to hurt you."

"How did Danny die?"

"He was a fireman," Dawn answers. She clears her throat and finds a little control over her emotions. "Killed on the job."

Caroline thinks about this for a moment. She doesn't remember Danny, but Dawn's answer doesn't set right with her. "Do you have anyone? Brothers or sisters? Your father?"

"No." Dawn shrugs. "Just me."

"Did you love him?"

"Danny?"

Caroline nods.

"A little bit more every day."

Silence creeps in around them. Caroline is hot, but she doesn't want to move the conversation and risk a complete break down in communication.

"What're you remembering?" Dawn's voice is gruff. Caroline knows it is sheer will holding some raw emotion inside her.

"Nothing right now—"

"No." Dawn kicks off her flip flops and pulls her legs up to rest her feet on the chair. "What things have you remembered?"

"Just these flashes," Caroline says, frustrated all over again. "Earlier, I was going to take a shower. And I saw my ring on the dresser. I had a flash of making love with Miles. He said he would buy me rings like that all the time if it meant we made love like that all the time."

Dawn takes a deep breath, as if she is readying herself to speak, but she stays silent and holds the poker face.

"One day, I was outside. With Max." Caroline looks around the yard. "It was one of the first days he let me outside. I was just sitting out here and I looked up at the house and I was just thinking about how Miles had painted the window trim and then it hit me that I was thinking that. But I couldn't pull anything back to the surface."

Dawn nods.

"Why do you hate him?"

"Because he's never treated you well," Dawn answers without hesitation. "Beth was right about him."

"What did Beth say about him?"

"She didn't like him from the word go."

"Where is Beth?" Caroline whispers after a slight hesitation. She doesn't really want to know. Not after the chip of a memory she'd had about the phone call about her.

"What else?" Dawn ignores her. "What else have you remembered?"

"Did he ever hit me?"

Dawn stares at Caroline in silence.

"Just tell me," Caroline pleads. "If we were as close as you say we were, then you would know. You might be the only person besides Miles who knows the truth about what went on in this house, Dawn."

"He did." Dawn nods. She presses her fingertips to her lips, as if she is trying to shove the words back inside.

"Was it bad?"

Dawn groans and shoves her chair back to stand up. "Sometimes it was bad. Sometimes it was horrible. Since you married him—"

Caroline waits, but Dawn doesn't seem inclined to go on. "Since I married him, what?"

Dawn shakes her head. "You fought back." She squints and laughs, but it is a sad laugh. "I think you surprised him. You fought back. You guys fought one night. So bad. He usually...

"What? Dammit, Dawn, what?" Caroline sits on the edge of her seat.

"He usually hit you where no one would see." Dawn

deflates into her chair again. “Where he thought no one would see it.”

“But I showed you?”

“I don’t know if you showed me everything, but you showed me a lot,” Dawn whispers. “One night, he hit you in the face. I think it just got so out of hand between both of you. You hit him back. Without thinking, you swung on him. He had to have six stitches.”

“That scar on his face?”

Dawn shakes her head. “No. I’m not sure how that happened, but I think you threw something at him.”

“Oh my God.”

“I think he thought...” Dawn pauses and glances at Caroline, “I think he thought that you were the damsel in distress type. Which is what pissed Beth off about him. You are a fighter, Caroline. You’re tough. You’re independent. Too smart to let a man like Miles control you.”

“This morning,” Caroline begins, but she breaks off, lost in the memory again. “I was coming down the hall. And I heard his voice. It was like he was here. He was angry because I hadn’t slept in the bedroom with him.”

Dawn nods. “He got angry over anything, Caroline.”

“There were pictures in the hallway. In my memory. There were pictures.”

Again Dawn nods.

“Where are they now?”

"He took them all down." Dawn avoids Caroline's intense stare. "After your accident, he took all the pictures down. Redecorated."

"Remodeled. To put in a third story prison."

"Yes." Dawn's eyes find the nick in the patio table again.

"He wiped the slate clean and he locked me in a room and he told you not to talk to me." Caroline states matter-of-factly. Dawn answers with a tiny nod. "Why?"

CINDERELLA

SIXTEEN

1994

Springfield, IL

Caroline does not notice the city speed by outside the car windows. Miles navigates the highway with ease, now and then poking her with conversation, but more often than not letting her ride alone with her thoughts. She is thinking about Beth. And though she has been careful not to say much to Miles about the confrontation a couple of weeks ago, she knows he's picked up on the vibes. He knows her well enough to know when she is upset about something, and he has to have noticed that Beth is never around when he comes to the apartment.

"Where are we going?" she asks when she finally realizes Bloomington-Normal is miles behind them in the rearview mirror. "I thought we were having dinner."

"We are," he says with a nod. "It's a surprise."

The look in his eyes makes her melt. She puts her hand out to cover his when he reaches toward her. She hates that Beth doesn't get this. That Beth can't see this side of Miles. He's so romantic and sexy, sometimes when she lies awake at night, she has to pinch herself to make sure she—*this* —is all real.

"Close your eyes," Miles suggests. "I'll wake you when we get there."

"Where's there?" She grins.

"Surprise."

"C'mon, tell me! I wanna know what you've got planned."

"Nope." He squeezes her fingers and then lets go of her hand. "This is a surprise for you."

She sighs and lays her head back against the seat. "I hate surprises," she says softly.

"No you don't," he answers with a laugh. "You look like a little girl on her way to a surprise birthday party, all giddy with excitement."

"My birthday is in November."

"I know. This isn't a birthday party."

"What is it then?"

"I'm not telling!" He laughs again. "Go to sleep, woman, or I'm going to throw you down and tickle you until you can't breathe when we get there."

"And there....would be..." She turns toward him in her seat and raises her eyebrows, inviting him to spill the surprise.

"Did I tell you I dreamt about you the other night?"

"Don't try to change the subject." She shakes her head. "Where are you taking me? We're a long way from Bloomington, aren't we?"

"You were pregnant."

"Miles, graduation is Sunday. Where are you going? We have to be—" Caroline cocks her head and fights the smile that plays at her lips. "Pregnant?"

"Mm-hmm."

"Was it—? Were we—? I mean—"

"We were married, and you were pregnant," he explains. "I had my hands on your belly. I could feel our baby move."

"Oh my God," she whispers. She looks away, gives herself enough time to blink the tears out of her eyes.

"I want you to have my baby, Caroline," he tells her.

"But—" She glances at him but quickly looks away again. She'd told him about Shane. About the baby. She'd told him everything, the same as she'd said to Dawn one night long ago, when their friendship had evolved into sisterhood. Miles had held her, soothed her and let her cry over the loss she'd been stupid enough to bring upon herself. She'd asked his forgiveness that night, for the abortion, for hurting Shane, for being weak. Miles had touched her face, stroked his thumbs over the tears on her face, and told her he loved her and that he had nothing to forgive. He understood that she'd been young and scared and impressionable and admitted that he probably would have done the same in her place.

"We'll never forget your first child." He reaches across the seat again and touches her hand. "We won't. I promise. But I want to have a child with you."

"Have you ever—" Caroline stops and takes a deep breath. "Been around someone who's had a baby? Have you felt a baby move like that?"

Miles looks at her, clearly surprised by her question. "My sister has kids, but no, I never touched her stomach or felt the babies move."

"I wonder what it feels like," she says softly. "I didn't carry long enough to know."

"We'll find out together," he assures her. "And yes, I know it's graduation weekend. We'll be back in plenty of time."

"Like when?"

"Like tomorrow sometime."

"Where are you taking me?"

He laughs and pulls her across the seat. She unhooks her seatbelt and slides over to sit close to him. He groans quietly when she presses her lips to his neck and slides her hand down over his chest and his stomach. She wants to touch him. Right now. A giggle pushes up from her stomach as she remembers teasing Shane when he was driving, climbing into his lap and rubbing against him until he had to pull over behind someone's garage and take her there, against the steering wheel. She'd had a rounded bruise on her lower back for days. But it had been worth it.

"What the hell—?" He laughs and bites off his words as her fingers inch over his fly.

"Shhh." She nibbles her way up his neck to his ear, fingers still stroking over his zipper.

"Jesus, Caroline," he groans in a way that suggests he's enjoying her attention. She knows he is; she feels him grow hard beneath her fingertips.

"I want you," she whispers and then she tugs at his earlobe with her teeth.

"We've waited this long." He closes his hand over hers and stills her fingers. "I'm sure not going to make love to you for the first time against the steering wheel of a car."

"Don't you ever wanna just fuck me, Miles? You're killing me with this waiting and being romantic and wanting the perfect moment."

"Caroline, I love you." He lifts her hand from his lap and cuts clear green eyes to stare at her. "I don't wanna fuck you, and I don't care for that word."

She laughs softly and ducks her head to rest it on his shoulder. "I'm sorry. I'm just so tired of waiting."

She stays close to him, for the rest of the drive. It's uncomfortable, hanging over the edge of her bucket seat. Illegal, since she is not wearing her seatbelt, and yet, she stays close to him. He takes a Springfield exit, which surprises her, but she has no idea where he's going or what he's got planned, so she says nothing.

He parks the car in front of a gorgeous old house on a downtown street in Springfield. Tucked away neatly so as to be framed by tree limbs is a sign identifying the house as a bed and breakfast.

"Miles?" Instantly alert, she jumps out of her side of the car and hurries to meet him as he rounds the front of it. "What're we doing?"

"We're going out for dinner," he tells her.

"Here?"

"No." He smiles. "We're having dinner at The Chesapeake and then we're going to stay here tonight. And then I'll drive you back to Bloomington tomorrow, and we'll have plenty of time before graduation."

She opens her mouth to answer him, but she can think of nothing to say.

"I didn't pack for dinner," she tells him finally. She laughs and throws her arms around him. "You didn't tell me we were doing this. I didn't pack—"

"I brought you something," he says softly.

"You brought me something? You packed for me?" She raises her eyebrows in surprise.

"No, I didn't pack for you. I bought you a new dress."

"Oh my God!" She smacks her lips against his cheek. "Miles, this is so romantic!"

"And you wanted to get nasty in the front seat of the car." He grins and slides his arms around her waist.

"Well, that can be fun too." She giggles. "I love you."

The new dress and the room at the bed and breakfast and dinner with Miles, the man she's in love with, put Beth far from her mind. Nothing matters at the moment, but the wine she drinks, the lavender silk dress she wears, and the man across the table who can not take his eyes from her.

When they leave The Chesapeake, Miles puts his arm around her and pulls her tight against him. She moans softly as his fingers slide up her side and brush her breast. It's a beautiful night, and the stars and the wine make her drunk with happiness. She can't put it in words at the moment for Miles, but she finally understands that she had to live through the hurt she'd dealt Shane, she'd had to lose her first child to find this perfect life with Miles Wolfe. Happiness is not without sacrifice or loss.

At the bed and breakfast, she stands on the small balcony outside their room and stares at the stars as if she expects them to move. She sighs and leans into him when Miles moves to stand close behind her. He is hard against her middle, where he rubs against her. Knowing now that the time is right, she turns to him and combs her fingers up over the back of his neck and into his hair. He kisses her and the stars seem to move above them, and then suddenly he is pushing her back. Again. Breaking the kiss.

"Miles, please," she whispers, eyes still closed. "Make love to me."

"There's something I want to talk to you about first," he answers. She opens her eyes to find him on his knee in front of her. He is holding a star in his hand, offering it to her.

"Miles?" The wine has gone to her head, and she reaches back to hold the railing of the balcony and steady herself.

"Will you marry me, Caroline?" He takes her hand and slides the star over her ring finger. More stars dance in his eyes as he stares up at her, waiting for her answer.

"Wh—" She blinks and stares at him, needing him to repeat what he'd just said. "Did you—? What's—" She lifts her hand and realizes it is not a star on her finger, but a diamond. A huge princess cut diamond in a simple gold band, reflecting the starlight back at her.

"Marry me?" he says again. "Marry me, Caroline. I'll make you happy."

She smiles. He *will* make her happy. She will never find the same happiness with anyone else that she knows she will find with Miles.

"Yes."

RAPUNZEL

SEVENTEEN

June, 2008

Springfield, IL

"It started right after you married him," Dawn tells Caroline. "It wasn't fighting, not at first. It was abuse. Uncalled for. The first time he hit you because he came home from his office, and he wanted a beer. There was no Red Stripe in the fridge. It pissed him off. You were telling him just to drink a Miller Lite. There was plenty of it. Danny and I drank Miller Lite, so you guys always had it in the fridge."

"So he hit me?"

"He sucker punched you. The next day, you showed me the bruise on your stomach. It wasn't perfectly round. I could see the exact outline of his knuckles in your skin."

"What did you do? What did you say to me?"

"I begged you to get out. I never said much when you were dating him. Not like Beth did. I saw what happened with you two, and I was so afraid to speak my mind." Dawn does not fight the tears that slide off her face, nor does she try to hide them. "I wish a hundred times over I would've said something back then."

"Would I have listened to you?" Caroline whispers.

"No." Dawn swallows a throat full of emotion and avoids Caroline's intense stare.

"Then it's not your fault."

"I should have tried to stop you." Dawn shakes her head. "We wouldn't be where we are today if we could've gotten you away from Miles."

Caroline is exhausted, and yet she feels each minute melting away, as time ticks closer to the hour of Miles' homecoming. There is so much she needs to know, *to remember*, and so little time to freely track the clues that together will be the life of Caroline Wolfe.

"What happened between me and Beth?" She hates to ask this question. More than any other, she hates this question and she dreads Dawn's answer.

"She, um," Dawn begins, but she cuts herself off. Her eyelids slide closed as more tears trail over her face, taking with them her eyeliner and her mascara. "She told you one night. Just before graduation. She didn't like him. She said she was worried about you, about Miles making you less of a woman. Taking away your independence and your self-respect."

"And I got mad. Right?"

"You did." Dawn shrugs. "I probably would have too. You felt like we ambushed you. Neither of us meant it that way. We just didn't want to see you—" Again Dawn interrupts herself. "This. We didn't want to see this."

"So that's it then? Beth and I had words, and so we graduated and parted company and she's living happily ever after somewhere without me? One of us found happiness. Right?"

"Beth." Dawn purses her lips and glances at Caroline. Caroline shakes her head when Dawn looks away quickly. She doesn't want to know. 'I take it back!' she wants to scream. 'Don't tell me. Don't tell me about Beth. Let me believe—"Bethie was killed in a car accident a few days after graduation."

Caroline shivers as ice sweeps up her spine. She'd known this was coming. She doesn't remember Beth any more than she remembers Dawn, but somehow she'd known this was coming. "What happened?"

"She'd been drinking. A lot. Parties. There were so many parties. And she was drunk, and she got in her car and lost control on a back road, coming back to the apartment after a party." Dawn rubs her hands over her face and takes a deep breath. "She rolled the car. Three times. Wasn't wearing a seatbelt." She lets her hands drop and fall to her lap. Her eyes are glued to the fence at the far side of Caroline's yard, but Caroline imagines she does not see the fence, but Beth's car.

"Beth didn't drink that much," Caroline says quietly,

shaking her head. "I don't believe she'd get drunk in the first place, much less get behind the wheel of her car."

Caroline's words are answered with a heavy, pregnant silence. When she realizes minutes have passed and Dawn has not said anything, she turns to look at Dawn. "What?" She shakes her head and shrugs.

"Beth didn't drink very much," Dawn answers quietly. "But after that night she confronted you and you accused her of being jealous, she started drinking more."

"We never fixed things?"

"You did." Dawn lowers her legs to put her bare feet on the patio and pushes her chair back. "But it wasn't the same between you two after that."

"So it's my fault."

"No." Dawn stands and wanders the patio again, as if she is a caged animal desperate to find the wild.

"I'm sorry, Dawn. Sorry for what you've lost. Because of me."

Dawn doesn't answer her. Caroline's stomach growls, but she ignores it. She has no time for food. She needs information, *memories*, more than food.

"Is that how it is?" Dawn finally breaks the relative silence. Beyond them, the world still turns on its axis and Caroline's neighbors make typical noises with their motorcycles and stereos.

"What do you mean?" Caroline looks up at Dawn when the woman draws near to her again.

"The memories. They just come and go that quick?"

"What memories?" Caroline lifts an eyebrow and stares at Dawn impatiently.

"The thing with Beth. You just sat here very calmly and told me that Beth didn't drink much. *Like you know her, like you remembered her.* And now you don't even remember having that memory."

Caroline clicks her tongue against the roof of her mouth and then nods and flies out of her chair, hands over her mouth. "That's how it is." She sounds sarcastic, even to herself, but she doesn't care. She's suffocating. It's like black stuff is climbing her throat and she's going to choke on it, and yet, she needs to swallow it because it is the essence of who she is and she has to have it, *she has to digest it*, for any chance of remembering what happened.

"What's wrong?" Dawn lays her hand on Caroline's shoulder. Caroline's first instinct is to swipe the hand away. She doesn't want to be touched. She doesn't want this stranger to touch her. But she can't afford to alienate Dawn now.

"I don't know how to do this," she sobs. "I don't know how to piece this together, but I know I have to figure this out. I have to figure this out, before he comes back, because if I don't—"

He's going to kill me.

She doesn't know where the thought comes from, but there it is. In her mind. Huge, like the Hollywood sign. Fighting is one thing. Abuse, violence, it's a cycle that seldom disappears in such a relationship. Caroline assumes many women probably live their entire married lives in that cycle. Perhaps she might have been one of them. Before. But now, suddenly and certainly, she knows Miles is going to kill her. She just doesn't know why.

"Can I ask you something?" She sighs and lowers her head, until her chin rests on her chest. "Please. Tell me the truth."

"Of course I will." Dawn's fingers squeeze gently on her shoulder.

"Is Max my son?"

"Yes," Dawn answers immediately. She digs her fingers into Caroline's shoulder and spins her around to face her. "I was with you. I was there with you,when you had him, Caroline. Miles and I were right there with you. It was the most incredible thing I've ever seen."

Caroline nods.

"I don't know what Miles did with the pictures, Caroline. I don't know. He's bound and determined you won't remember anything outside of what he wants you to know." Dawn's hands are now on Caroline's upper arms, squeezing, shaking, as if she is trying to shake sense into her. "But I have pictures. I have pictures of our lives together as friends, and I will give you every one of them to help you."

"Thank you."

Dawn sniffles and wipes at her eyes with the back of her hands. "Why?'

"Why what?"

"Why would you ask if Max is your son?"

Caroline's mouth forms words—they vie for her voice to climb from her mouth. Finally, she meets Dawn's eyes and shrugs. "Why did he say that then? When the doctor took my bandages off, why did Max say I'm not his mommy?"

BEAUTY & THE BEAST

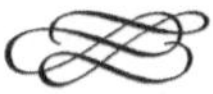

EIGHTEEN

1995

Springfield, IL

Miles gets angry with her when she talks about Beth. She wants him to understand how much Beth had meant to her, but he doesn't get it. He tells her that they hadn't known each other long enough to have the sort of bond that childhood friends have. She tries to explain—seems like she's defending her grief for Beth almost every day—that she and Beth and Dawn had been like sisters. The last time he'd come home from work and found her sitting silently on the patio, a glass of wine at hand and surmised that she'd been thinking about Beth (Of course she was thinking about Beth. She'd thought about Beth almost every day since the accident. The beginning of her married life has been beleaguered by the loss of one of her roommates) he'd forbidden her to talk, *let alone think*, about Beth Summers. He'd said he was tired of his wife moping around the house, missing a damned lesbian drunk who'd barely gotten through college and hadn't known how to handle the real world and had opted out through suicide via car accident.

Caroline had stared at him in stunned silence. She'd never heard anything so vile and hateful come out of her husband's mouth. That he would say this about a woman he had known and claimed to like, a woman Caroline had thought of as a sister, infuriated her.

"Go to hell, she'd said simply. She'd picked up her keys and walked out of the house. Her insides shook as she drove down Wabash to pick up the highway. She should have gone to Dawn. Who better to miss Beth with than the woman who'd suffered her same loss? But she didn't. She didn't want to tell Dawn what Miles had said about their friend.

She'd driven aimlessly and focused on deep breathing to calm herself. She loved Miles, but she would never forget Beth. She would never allow Miles to take away her grief, her love for Beth Summers. She hadn't been certain what she would find when she got home that evening. For over an hour, she'd cruised around aimlessly to drive the demons out of her mind. They'd had arguments before, but never one that had wedged a wall of silence or miles between them.

Miles had apologized when she'd come home. Quietly and sincerely, he'd said he was sorry for what he'd said about Beth, promised her that he hadn't meant any of it, and explained that he just hated seeing Caroline so depressed. Caroline had been quick to forgive him, but she'd told him in no uncertain terms that she wouldn't sweep Beth away with old college texts and exam papers.

Today she sits again on the patio. Thinking of her wedding. Of the bittersweet way she and Dawn had stuck together, as if they'd been joined at the hip. The way they'd shared memories and stories and they'd laughed and they'd cried and together, quietly, they'd missed Beth. She and Miles had first talked about a December wedding, but after the accident, Caroline had asked him for more time. She couldn't plan a wedding when her friend had just died.

Instead they'd married in June, earlier this year. The day had started with a light rain shower, but it had gradually cleared off and the sun had peeked out and dusted them with summer. And now Dawn and Danny are planning their wedding. Caroline is thrilled for Dawn. She'd known that they would get married; everyone had known Dawn and Danny were a sure thing. The guessing game came in how long they would wait until they tied the knot.

Danny had asked Caroline to go with him to pick out Dawn's ring. Caroline had been torn, wanting to be with Danny for that moment, though she'd never have actually picked out Dawn's ring. Danny was in love with her; he would recognize the ring as soon as he saw it. But Caroline had wanted Dawn's engagement to be a surprise for her, something for Dawn to call her about in the middle of the night, giggling and crying and saying "Caroline, I'm getting married." She'd wanted that moment for Dawn, because she'd called Dawn from the bed and breakfast after Miles had proposed to her, after he'd made love to her.

Caroline had gone with Danny in the end. By that time, she'd known anyway that he was going to propose to her. She hadn't said a word either. Danny had looked at four rings and the fifth was the one. The One. She'd known it as soon as the balding sales man had handed it to Danny that it was The One, but she'd kept her mouth shut. Danny had stared at the ring—a pear shaped solitaire in a white gold setting—for several long, quiet minutes. He'd worn a small smile when he looked up at her.

"This is Dawn's," he'd said with a nod. Caroline had only smiled to agree with him. She'd asked him he give her no details about how he planned to propose. She wanted to hear it all from Dawn. He'd kissed her on the cheek that day, when they parted company in front of the jewelry store, and thanked her.

There is something pure and innocent and yet enduring in Dawn and Danny's relationship. As happy as Caroline is in her marriage, there is something intangible between Dawn and Danny that Caroline has never seen before. She's happy for Dawn. She wishes Beth could be at the wedding.

"I'm home," Miles calls. The front door closes behind him. In the office, Caroline shuts down her computer and watches the hallway for his shadow outside the door. Their house is beautiful, but it's big and old and dark and most likely, Caroline will not see his shadow. Sometimes the house is big and dark enough to be depressing. It's why she goes out often, to the mall, the library, cafes for lunches, whatever she can come up with as an excuse to get out. She'd even put out some feelers on a job, and today she'd had a call from a woman, asking if she was the Caroline Wolfe who tutored. Caroline had never tutored before in her life, other than the help she'd given Beth or Dawn on one subject while they'd repaid with help in a subject she didn't care for. But as a college graduate, she'd assumed she could handle tutoring grade school, even high school students.

The woman was the mother of a thirteen year old boy who had trouble with reading comprehension. Apparently he was a whiz in math, but his reading skills were lacking. Caroline had her first session with Andrew Schaeffer tomorrow after school.

"Hi." She offers Miles a smile when he appears in the office doorway. "How was your day?"

"Much better now," he answers and moves into the room. He leans over the desk and she lifts herself off her chair and their lips meet above the computer monitor. "Yours?"

"The same."

"Let's go out for dinner," he suggests. His tie is loosened, tugged to the side, as if he'd done it with one hand as he drove with the other. The sleeves of his white dress shirt are rolled up, exposing sinewy forearms. Caroline's eyes travel over his hands. She loves his hands on her body.

"I made dinner." She kisses the corner of his mouth. "But we can put it in the refrigerator if you want to go out."

He smiles as her lips trail up over his cheekbone.

"What did you make?"

"Chicken. Baked potatoes. Salad. A little dessert." With that, she raises an eyebrow seductively.

"Let's stay in." His eyes burn through her. "And start with dessert."

"Nope." She backs away from him and steps out from behind the desk. "No starting with dessert, Miles Wolfe. The chicken is ready. Let's eat first."

"You'd rather have chicken than me?" He looks puppy dog sad, but he sets his briefcase down on the desk and follows her out of the office.

"We need sustenance," she tells him. "Dessert is a seven course meal tonight."

"How about an appetizer?" He tries, snaking an arm out and looping it around her waist. "Right here."

She laughs as his fingers deftly fly over the buttons of her blouse. Lays her head against the wall as he pushes her bra up and cups her breasts in his hands. "You should be a model. You would kill men with this body."

"Don't want any man looking at me but you." She sinks her fingers into his hair as he leans over and brushes his lips over the pale swell of her breast. "Oh. Hey. I got a call today from a woman who wants a tutor for her son. He has trouble with reading comprehension."

Miles flicks his tongue over the center of her breast, but draws away and stands up straight to look at her. "Since when do you tutor?"

She shrugs. "I need to do something. To get out of the house now and then. I was at the library the other day, and it just hit me that I could tutor. Help someone else and get out of the house." She pushes herself away from the wall and starts buttoning her blouse. "C'mon. Have a beer while I put dinner on the table."

"I like that you're at home when I get home."

"Well, I won't be doing this all day, every day." She leads him into the kitchen and picks up a hot pad. "I just need to do something, Miles. I feel like I could waste away here in this huge house. What if I melted away upstairs? On the third floor and it took you two weeks to find me?"

Miles' laugh is short and forced. "I just don't like this idea. My wife doesn't need a job."

"I told you, it's not about money. It's me needing to get out and be around people now and then."

"I'll think about it." Miles tugs the refrigerator door open. "I thought you said we had beer."

Caroline pulls the oven door open and takes a glance at the chicken. It's done, and it needs to come out of the oven now. "We do. Hang on a second."

Miles groans and mutters under his breath as he waits for her. She pulls the broiler pan out of the oven and sets it on the stovetop. Without looking at him, she grabs the potatoes off the oven rack and sets them next to the broiler pan. His eyes are cold when she turns to him and joins him in front of the refrigerator.

"Right there." She laughs softly and reaches into the cold. As her fingers snag a longneck, she turns to look at him over her shoulder. "I know you'd rather have Red—"

The cold look in his eyes has turned to fire. Shocked by the look of—anger? hatred?—on his face, Caroline does not see his fist coming until it connects with her stomach. The force of his hit knocks her backward, and she hits her head on the closed freezer door. Coughing, she doubles over and crosses her arms over her stomach.

"Miles, what the hell—"

"You don't suggest to me that I drink anything other than what I want to drink." His voice is lethally sharp, as he grabs a handful of her blouse and hauls her up to stand before him. "And you don't suggest that this is good enough. And you'll tutor someone when I goddamned good and well tell you you'll tutor someone."

RAPUNZEL

NINETEEN

June, 2008

Springfield, IL

Caroline does not know how much time has passed since she got up this morning. Since the blue-eyed memory in the mirror had shaken her so badly she'd called Dawn. Since Dawn had joined her on the patio. She's afraid it's passing too quickly. She has so much to learn, to *remember*, and her head is pounding. Miles will be home tomorrow.

The sun has come out and it is baking her skin, burning the part in her hair, and her shirt sticks to her with sweat. She stands in silent expectation, watching Dawn watch her. Why had Max said she was not his mommy? Why has this question rendered Dawn speechless when they had been making progress?

"Why did he say that, Dawn?" Caroline whispers.

“The accident,” Dawn finally breathes these words, but she stops, as if those words alone can explain it all.

“What about it?” Caroline pushes, gently at first, but then louder, “What about the accident? Don’t hold back from me, Dawn. I don’t have enough time—"

“He used the accident,” Dawn says, staring at Caroline with dead eyes. “He used it as a chance to change you.”

“Change me,” Caroline repeats.

“Dr. Montell is a plastic surgeon.” Dawn licks her lips and tilts her head a bit, obviously wondering if Caroline knows to whom she is referring.

“The doctor who took my bandages off was a plastic surgeon.” Caroline nods.

“Yes.”

“So I had facial injuries in the accident.” Caroline hears the throb of hope in her voice. She is glad only Dawn is here to witness her desperation.

“No.”

“I don’t understand what you’re saying, Dawn. What’re you saying? What do you mean?”

“Exactly what I said,” Dawn answers, still almost dreamlike or zombie like. “He used the accident as a chance to remake you. With your head injuries, he knew there was a good chance that you wouldn’t remember things. He wanted to change you—"

“So I wouldn’t remember myself. And wouldn’t remember what kind of marriage I was in.”

Dawn lifts a shoulder but says nothing.

"You swear to me. You swear to me that Max is my son. I don't know what game Miles is playing, but I know I need you on my side. I can't—"

"I swear." Dawn's whispered words are cold enough to burn Caroline and chill her at the same time.

Dread makes Caroline's stomach turn. She doesn't remember swallowing it, but she doesn't remember much of anything. Something just rocked the boat with Dawn. It's like Caroline reached inside her and flipped a switch from warm and friendly to withdrawn.

Frustrated and overheated from the sun, Caroline rubs the back of her neck. She sighs and nods her head toward the house. "I'm gonna go inside for a while. Get something to drink."

"'K."

"C'mon." Caroline takes Dawn's hand and leads her inside. The cool air chases a chill up her spine. She glances at the clock on the kitchen wall. It's after one in the afternoon. "Are you hungry?"

Dawn shakes her head silently, watching as Caroline pulls the refrigerator door open and begins to rummage for something to eat.

"Do I like corned beef?" Caroline asks without looking back at Dawn. When Dawn doesn't answer, Caroline looks back over her shoulder to find her staring at her with a distant look in her eyes. "Dawn?"

"Huh?" Dawn snaps out of her thoughts and zeroes in on Caroline. "I'm sorry. What'd you say?"

"Do I like corned beef?"

"No. Miles does," she answers, sounding normal now. Caroline studies her for a moment longer and then turns back to the refrigerator. "You like chicken salad."

"I do?" Caroline eyes the refrigerator contents and decides she's not up to fixing chicken salad, even if she has the necessary ingredients. "What about chipotle turkey?" She stands up straight and examines the package of lunch meat in her hand.

"You have some?" Dawn sounds excited. She sidles up beside Caroline and looks over her shoulder. "Oh man."

"Want some?" Caroline asks. She turns her head a fraction of an inch. She and Dawn are nearly nose to nose. Dawn's gaze slides over her face, moving quickly over her eyes. For all practical purposes, Caroline might have been born yesterday. But she can still read guilt when she sees it.

"Yeah," Dawn says softly. "Sounds good."

"Tell me about Max."

Dawn watches Caroline go through the motions of making sandwiches, noticing that Caroline fixes them just as the two of them would always eat them. Right down to the vertical cut to slice them in half. They'd both always cut vertically so they had half of the top crust on each sandwich. Caroline catches Dawn watching her when she looks up.

"You slept with him, didn't you?" she asks boldly. What besides infidelity with your best friend's husband would engender that kind of guilt? Avoidance? Caroline figures she might as well blurt it out now, because she has no feeling for Miles, except fear and she needs to deal with Dawn one on one. No need for skeletons of truth or secrets creeping up around them while they try to forge a game plan against Miles.

The look on Dawn's face speaks, though her lips stay together in silence. Caroline takes a deep breath and nods and turns back to the refrigerator.

"What do you want to drink?"

"Wait." Dawn pushes the sandwich away from her and shakes her head. "You ask me that and then you follow it up with 'what do you want to drink?' What the hell?"

"What more is there to say?"

"I didn't say anything!" Dawn snaps.

"Your eyes gave it away." Caroline shrugs.

"Caroline, wait. It's not like that—"

"Dawn," Caroline turns back to her and forgets that their sandwiches wait and the refrigerator door is open. There is nothing at this moment but she and Dawn and her own need to *know* the details of the story, the same way Dawn and Miles know them. "I don't care what it was like. Not now."

"But—"

"I don't have time for that," Caroline whispers. "He's going to be back. And I still don't know what the hell is going on here. I need to know then before I care about now." Caroline knows somewhere deep inside she should be hurt that her best friend had climbed into bed with her husband. And yet, really, what did it matter? She'd been in a coma, as good as gone to both of them. Hell, for all she knew, it had been an attempt for both of them to find comfort.

"What do you need to know for?" Dawn clears her throat. "Are you going to leave him?"

"I don't know what I'm going to do," Caroline answers. "I just know I need to know about what he took away from me. I need those memories, Dawn. They're who I am."

Dawn sits on a barstool at the counter and avoids Caroline's eyes. "When Max plays Checkers, he likes to be black. And he loves to be kinged." Dawn looks up at Caroline. Her eyes are bright with tears. "His favorite game, though, is Aggravation. Likes to be the blue marbles."

Caroline nods. She breaks the eye contact and looks down at the sandwich she still hasn't touched. This hurts. She could give a damn that Dawn slept with Miles, but it hurts like hell to think of another woman mothering her son.

"What about outside? What's he like to do outside? Can he ride a bike?" Keep her talking. As much as it hurts, Caroline needs to keep Dawn talking about Max so she can ease her back to talking about Miles.

"With help," Dawn answers. "If I run along behind him, and he thinks I'm holding onto the bike, he'll ride."

Caroline drops her sandwich on her plate and looks away from Dawn. So much for keeping Dawn talking. She doesn't think she can stomach another word about Max.

"You said..." Caroline hesitates. She feels Dawn watching her, but she takes a deep breath before continuing. "You said you have pictures."

"I do," Dawn says quickly. "At my house."

Caroline wants to ask Dawn to take her there. To the pictures. To a house that might provide more memories than her own. But her lips won't move and the words won't form and her voice seems to be broken.

"Do you wanna go there? To my house?"

Caroline nods. "What about Miles? What if he calls?"

"He'll call my cell."

Caroline stands and takes her plate to the sink. She tosses the sandwich into the garbage can in the cabinet under the sink.

"I never meant to hurt you," Dawn whispers, while Caroline stands with her back to her. Caroline's shoulders tighten, and she raises her head but she does not look at Dawn. "Danny was gone—"

"Dawn, please." Caroline shakes her head. "Not now."

"I need to make this right with you." Dawn rushes to stand beside Caroline and lunges at her when Caroline tries to move away from her. "I hate—"

"If you need to make this right, show me who I was. And show me who he is. I need to know who he is, Dawn, because if I don't, he's going to kill me."

Caroline expects Dawn to roll her eyes and comment on her

whisper, heavy with drama. When she doesn't, the chill that climbs Caroline's spine is razor sharp.

RAPUNZEL

TWENTY

June, 2008

Springfield, IL

Nothing about the ride to Dawn's house drowns Caroline in memories. She does not feel a tug on her heart as she climbs up into the black Explorer, just a twinge of pain in her thigh. She doesn't look at the yard as Dawn's slender fingers hold the wheel and remember working in it. She doesn't look at any neighbor's houses and suddenly remember the people behind the brick.

Worse, she doesn't look at the McDonald's four blocks away, into town, and remember taking Max there for a Happy Meal. There's nothing inside her that is familiar. At the moment, her chest is so tight with worry over Miles, that there is no room for anything else. What if Miles finds out Dawn has taken her from the house? What if Miles knows that Dawn is going to show her pictures? Of herself?

Of a life she used to live? What will he do? She's not afraid of his fists. Dawn has already told her she fights back. She's seen the scar on Miles' face that she apparently put there.

But she is afraid of Miles. If feelings are colors, when she thinks about Miles, she is red and black. Uneasy and fearful. Red and black, like images of blood and death. What the hell will he do to her, what the hell has he done to her to make her fear him, when she does not fear his fists?

Caroline's stomach clenches when Dawn's cell phone rings. Without a word, Dawn reaches to turn the radio down and then picks up her phone. Caroline looks out her side window, trying to ignore the phone call. Wishing she could ignore the phone call, but desperate to know what Miles is saying.

It is a short conversation, but Dawn seems relaxed. She's slept with Miles. What if she doesn't hate him? What if she's in love with him? What if it's all a set up? What the hell is the game for? If they want to be together—

Dawn laughs and says she'll return the call later and then she hangs up. Before Caroline can ask her anything, Dawn shakes her head. "It wasn't Miles. It was a friend."

Caroline stares at Dawn and tries to make herself believe her. She nods, but she can't. Suddenly the idea that maybe Dawn is working with Miles to set her up is all that she can think about.

"Amy Evans. Her husband worked with Danny."

Caroline doesn't answer her.

"You don't believe me." Dawn's words are so quiet,

Caroline almost doesn't hear her over the sound of the tires on the pavement. "Here."

Caroline turns her head to look at Dawn. Dawn's hand is outstretched toward her, cell phone in hand.

"See for yourself."

Caroline fights to keep her hands in her lap. If Dawn is telling the truth, Caroline's doubt will knock them backwards five or six steps. But if she's lying, Caroline might be walking blindly into a trap.

"You don't believe me. I can see it in your eyes, Caroline. Just take the Goddamned phone and look at my received calls."

Caroline sighs and takes the phone from Dawn's hand. She'll call her bluff. She flips the phone open and pushes the button that will take her to received calls. Cell phones she can handle. Knowing what she likes to read is beyond her.

The number is one she doesn't immediately recognize. Knowing that Dawn is watching her, she pushes the select button again to get the details on the last call. Amy Evans.

"I'm sorry." Caroline drops the phone on the seat next to her and slouches down in her seat. She feels like she might vomit. The guilt and the fear inside her tug relentlessly at her stomach.

"Why do you think I'm lying to you?"

Caroline closes her eyes and rests her head on the seat. "I said I was sorry."

"Danny was the nicest man I have ever known. He was

strong, but he was gentle. Very giving. He always wanted to do the right thing. He liked—"

"Why are you telling me this?" Caroline asks with a frown.

"Because you need to understand that Danny was the polar opposite of Miles. They could not have been any more different."

"And?" Caroline opens her eyes to stare at Dawn. "What? You obviously made the better choice in husbands? Except yours is dead now—"

"My husband is dead because your husband killed him—"

"Pull over." Caroline sits forward quickly.

"What?" Dawn looks around. They are on a residential street, a few blocks from her house. She eyes the rearview mirror. There is a Mustang Cobra ten feet behind them.

"Pull over."

"What're you gonna do? Walk home—"

"Pull the damned truck over, Dawn." Caroline cups her hand over her mouth. Dawn eases to the curb, but Caroline pushes the door open and twists in her seat before Dawn is stopped. She hangs out the door to vomit. There isn't much in her stomach, just the coffee. But it rushes up her throat violently. She wrestles with the seatbelt and finally pops the release. Dawn climbs out of her side of the truck and hurries around to help Caroline.

"I'm sorry," Dawn says as Caroline leans a hand against the Explorer. *Get your fucking hand off the car. I just waxed it, Caroline.* "I'm sorry. I shouldn't have said that."

"Is it true?" Caroline leans into her arm now, ducks her head against her bicep. She doesn't want to look at Dawn. She hates this not knowing anything and depending on someone—anyone—else to turn the lights on for her.

"I shouldn't have said that."

"Is. It. True?"

"C'mon." Dawn glances over her shoulder and looks around the quiet neighborhood. There are two adolescent boys three or four houses down who are watching them unapologetically. "Let's get out of here. My house is just a few blocks away."

"Is it true?"

Dawn slips her arm around Caroline's waist, but Caroline does not move.

"I'm not getting in the damned truck until you tell me if it's true."

"I don't know, Car." The anger in Dawn's answer is weakened by the tears that fill her eyes. "I don't know."

"Is it possible?" Caroline finally looks up at her.

Dawn nods her head silently and looks away from Caroline's hungry stare. Caroline draws herself up to her full height, ready to badger Dawn with more questions.

"Please." Dawn rubs her forehead and avoids Caroline's eyes. "Please, get in the truck. And let's go?"

Caroline gets back into the vehicle without further argument. When Dawn climbs back in on her side, she turns the radio off. The rest of the drive is silent, though

Caroline can almost hear the tension tightening up between them.

Dawn's house is an average sized brick bungalow on a big corner lot. Caroline stands in the driveway and studies the house, waiting for a spark of recognition to burn her. There's nothing, though, so she turns her head and looks at the houses across the street, the flowers in front of the houses, and the bikes and skateboards parked in the yards and driveways.

"How long did you and..." Caroline can't say his name. "How long have you lived here?"

"Eight years. You came with me to look at the house. Danny was working. You and I grabbed coffee, and then we went to Walmart. You needed laundry detergent. We met the realtor here around nine. We loved the house. It was the seventh or eighth we'd all looked at. You and I would scout them out, and then if we liked one, I'd tell Danny about it and he and I would come back."

"I envy you," Caroline mumbles as her eyes come back to rest on the house.

"You envy me." Dawn's voice is harsh, and Caroline knows without asking that she is thinking about Danny.

"The details. Your whole life is in the details."

Dawn sighs and purses her lips. "Danny and Max used to sit on the swing."

"Why was Max here?"

"You would all come. You were here a lot. For dinner. For

drinks. For games." Dawn shrugs. "Danny was crazy about Max."

"How did Max take it? When Danny—when Danny died?"

"He was sad," Dawn answers. She studies the driveway and grinds the toe of her shoe into a tiny hole in the pavement. "But I don't know that he really understands that Danny is gone."

Dawn turns and walks up the driveway. Caroline looks back over her shoulder one more time, half expecting to see Miles parked at the curb watching her. There is no one in the street. She glances at the street sign—Oak and Nineteenth. She'd lived a lot of her life here on Oak and Nineteenth, she guesses. And she remembers none of it.

Dawn is gone when she looks back toward the house. Caroline doesn't panic. Instead she follows the driveway up to the side of the house and finds the back door open. She tugs the screen door open and steps inside, hoping to be assaulted with memories but feeling nothing. She steps through a tidy laundry room—how much laundry can Dawn have to do, if she lives alone—and into a homey kitchen. The apple green counters are spotless, the small round wooden table also cleared of everything.

"How often are you with me?" Caroline asks Dawn, who is standing by the sink and looking out the window. She looks to be lost in thought, but she doesn't startle at Caroline's voice.

"I told you we were best friends. We were together all the time—"

"No." Caroline shakes her head and steps further into the room. "I mean after the accident. How often were you there?"

Dawn shrugs. "I spent a lot of nights up at the hospital. When you were released, I just packed a bag and moved into your house for a while."

Caroline crosses her arms over her chest. She is out of her element. The house had become familiar after days of being kept there, but she has felt small and afraid since leaving the house with Dawn. Part of her wants to go back. To lock herself inside the house and feel safe.

Except she wouldn't feel safe there anymore when Miles came home.

Before she can ask Dawn about pictures, she notices a few tacked up on the refrigerator with magnets. Drawn to them, but afraid of the letdown she will feel when she does not recognize anyone in them, she moves slowly toward the refrigerator.

There is a drawing, obviously done by Max. A man in a fireman's hat. Tears burn her eyes. She is crying for a man she doesn't remember. *For Danny. Love Max.* A professional 5x7 of Max, in jeans and a denim jacket, seated on a bale of hay, the colors of autumn alive in the trees around him. His hair looks freshly cut. Caroline wonders if she'd just had it done for the picture.

She studies a snapshot on the freezer door. The picture is old. The top left corner is curled a bit. Three college girls. She recognizes Dawn. In black jeans and a v-neck sweater. The other two, Caroline does not know, but she assumes they are herself and Beth. Both of them in faded jeans and sweatshirts. Hair a mess. Eyes bloodshot. Smiles to die for.

"That was taken at the end of final exams week. When we were juniors." Dawn has moved to stand close to her. "A girl who lived in the apartment next to us took it. We went out that night."

Caroline nods, but she doesn't say anything. She can't. Because she doesn't know which one she is, and it seems pathetic that she should have to ask, so she doesn't.

"This is you, Car." Dawn points to the girl in the middle, with the red ISU sweatshirt on. "And that's Beth."

Caroline presses her lips together and breathes deeply through her nose. "Do you have any idea what it's like to see yourself, but not recognize yourself?"

"No," Dawn whispers. "I don't."

"Why did he do this, Dawn?" Caroline shakes her head. "Why? If he loved me, why would he take this away from me?"

"There's a lot of different kinds of love, Caroline." Dawn turns away. "They aren't all good."

"Did he ever love me the right way?"

When Dawn doesn't answer her, Caroline turns to look at her. She stands in a shadowed corner of the kitchen, her face a blank mask. White teeth sink into a full lower lip. Eyelids close slowly. In that instant, Caroline knows she is right not to trust Dawn. She has no idea what it is, but Dawn is keeping something from her. The woman has supposedly brought her here to help her remember, but there is no good reason for Dawn to spoon feed her certain memories and pass on others.

The smallest bit of peace Caroline had garnered through the long day with Dawn shatters at her feet. What if Miles is here? What if Miles had instructed Dawn to bring Caroline here—

"No. Miles never loved you the right way." Dawn's words draw Caroline out of her heightening fear.

BEAUTY & THE BEAST

TWENTY-ONE

1995

Springfield, IL

Caroline watches Michael Pederson as his pencil moves hesitantly over the page of easy multiplication tables. She has been tutoring the boy for nearly a month. He is a reserved eight year old, with a cowlick at the part of his brown hair and one front tooth still missing after being knocked out while playing baseball. Though he's a smart kid, he seems to have trouble with conventional learning and testing. Caroline gives him extra help in math and reading. She likes the boy, she likes his mother, and really, aren't math and reading what it's all about in the lower grades? She likes feeling just a little bit important, knowing that if she can help Michael with his reading *now*, he will do well in so many other subjects as he gets older.

Miles had told her again that he did not want her to tutor

anyone. He didn't want her to be outside the home, doing anything to earn money.

Her answer, *'I'll do it if I want to, Miles,'* had earned her another fist. Again, he'd hit her in the abdominal area, and Caroline had realized that he would be careful to hit her where no one would notice.

"You go to hell, Miles."

She still can't quite believe she'd stood up to him. Not after he'd hit her twice in as many nights. She'd dug her fingers into his upper arms, squeezed and then shoved as hard as she could. Probably she'd only caught him off-guard, but he'd stumbled backwards, hard enough to hit the dresser in their bedroom. The mirror had rattled, and Miles had cocked an eyebrow and stared at her, either in shock or maybe he had been thinking about where to hit her next.

"You go to hell," she'd repeated. "I'll do what I want to do. You're my husband. Not my master."

"One and the same," he'd said as he'd taken a step toward her again.

The doorbell rang then, stopping him in his tracks. The house was big. If she'd have yelled for help, whoever was on the porch wouldn't have heard her. She'd kept her mouth shut, daring him to take one more step toward her, to raise his hand to her again.

"I don't see that the decision involves you, if I'm at home when you get home at night," she'd said quietly.

"This isn't over." His calm words were heavy with his intended threat.

"It is over," she'd answered as she left the bedroom. She half expected him to follow her, maybe grab her by her hair, but he hadn't. He'd simply put on his social face and slipped past her to answer the door.

"Hey." Dawn had offered Miles a quick smile and then slipped past him to the kitchen where Caroline was swallowing a couple of Advil.

"Hey." Caroline painted a smile on her face. "I ordered the pizza a few minutes ago."

Caroline glances at her watch now. It is nearing four. She doesn't want to rush Michael, but if he doesn't finish soon, she may not be home before Miles. She isn't afraid of him, exactly, but she doesn't really care to push him. Her stomach is now a patchwork quilt, in various shades of deep purple and faded blue and even a bit of green and yellow. Her lower back is sore, maybe from the way she'd fallen against the wall the other day when Miles had pushed her and yelled to make a point about what he didn't want for dinner. Or maybe it was simply sore from tensing up each time he hit her.

"I'm finished," Michael says and hands her the paper. His eyes are big and brown, and they watch her anxiously as she quickly checks his answers.

"Very good, Michael!" She marks the paper with a star and hands it back to him. "You got them all right. I think you should take that one home and show it to Mom and Dad."

"I did them right?"

"Every last one of them."

The grin on his face as he packs up his backpack makes Caroline decide that she made the right decision, no matter what Miles said.

"Hey Michael," she says after he tells her goodbye.

He turns back to look at her. She feels a pang inside, thinking about the baby she'd aborted. Wishing for just a second that this boy was hers. Wishing that she had a child at home to go to and put her arms around.

"Don't forget to read your Nate the Great book, okay?"

"Do I have to do a report on it?" He wrinkles his nose up, but the thought of doing a book report seems to bring a sparkle to his eyes.

"Do you want to?"

He shrugs, but he smiles.

"Sure. If you want to." She nods and glances at her watch again. She is cutting it close. Chances are Miles will be home when she gets there. What'll it be tonight? A sucker punch in her stomach? Or a shove against the wall, maybe a punch in her kidneys? The first time he'd hit here there, it had driven her to her knees. She'd lingered there, not afraid to get up, but wondering how in the hell her life had come to this.

Beth had been right. Beth had somehow known that Caroline was making a mistake.

"A page?" Michael asks her now.

"Just the front side of a page." Caroline smiles. "Just tell me what the story is about."

"Complete sentences?" This time Michael frowns, as if complete sentences are the enemy.

"Of course, complete sentences, Michael Pederson."

He grins and nods. "Okay. Goodbye, Caroline."

Though it's after four and Miles is probably on his way home right now, the urgency to get home has passed. She is drained, and what she really wants to do now is to sit and stare at the walls and not think about anything. Not about Michael or complete sentences or Miles and the way he'd changed from Prince Charming to a snake after they'd gotten married. Not about how she never knew which Miles to expect. Sometimes he was the old Miles, the one she'd fallen in love with. Fun and giving and passionate. Sometimes he treated her like a princess. But she wasn't sure it was enough to make up for the times he used her as a punching bag.

The thought is heavy inside her. Settles on her shoulders and pushes her into the chair at the six top table at the back of the library. No one pays her any attention, as the backs of her legs hit the chair and a weary sigh escapes her lips. No one can know the way her head is about to explode with her sudden realization. Since Miles had raised a hand to her, she's hated that they *fight*. Suddenly though, just now, it hits her. She is a battered wife. Miles Wolfe has changed her from a strong, independent woman—the woman Beth Summers had tried to reason with a couple of years ago—to a battered wife who takes the blows and turns her head and slowly becomes less and less until one day she might wake up as nothing.

She feels like she is glowing or fluorescent, and everyone should be watching her when she gets up and hurriedly tosses her pen and file folder back into her bag. She zips it so quickly she catches her finger in it and then yelps and sucks on the tip of it for a moment. Still no one looks at her. She shoves her chair in a bit too hard and makes her way across the reference department.

A part of her wants to make a commotion. Enough of a commotion to draw every eye in the room. A part of her needs these people here to *see* her, to *witness* all that she is as she leaves, because it's so very possible that when she next comes here, there will be another piece of her missing.

Never physical. There is never physical evidence that she is one of them. One of the battered wives. There is never a bruise on her eye, and she never has a split lip. But surely, each time it happens, a part of her soul fades and sooner or later, she will be a walking shadow and then surely, *someone* will notice and...And what? Rescue her?

Caroline laughs out loud, and she is startled at the harsh sound. She is in the parking lot now, and she pulls her keys from her pocket and unlocks the door of her Sonata and tosses her bag inside. Rescue her. How pathetic that she has become someone to cower in the corner and wish that someone would rescue her from Miles' anger and her marriage.

Four twenty-five. Miles has to be home by now. It's a wonder he has not called her cell phone. It's on vibrate, but Caroline is so in tune with the phone, with Miles, that she always hears it and feels it vibrate. He has not called.

She pulls out of the parking lot. The radio is off. The silence is so loud, it thunders in her head. But music or talk radio will grate on her nerves. She drives with her left hand. The fingers of her right hand dig into the taut muscles at the back of her neck. The light at Maine is red. She can make a right turn on red. She can zip on through this light and hurry home and say she's sorry. She can grovel and hope that Miles is in a forgiving or inattentive mood.

Her foot taps the brake pedal and her left hand steers the car directly into the lane for traffic going straight. She waits impatiently behind the navy Chevy Ventura and when the light turns to green, she goes straight and crosses Maine and does not even glance in the direction of home.

It is chilly, and she wishes for a jacket as she parks her car on the narrow, one lane road in the cemetery. She gives an almost imperceptible shrug as she folds her arms over her chest and makes her way across graves dating back to the 1800's. It doesn't matter now. She is chilled bone deep, and a jacket will not warm her.

Beth is buried in Rockford, Illinois, where she lived before she'd gone to Illinois State in Normal. Obviously Caroline can't get in the car and drive to Beth's grave whenever she misses her, so she'd started going to local cemeteries and walking the small paths, letting her eye wander over the gravestones while her mind wandered over the short-lived friendship she'd had with Beth.

Caroline stops at a huge gravestone carved as a guardian angel. She stares at the letters in the stone, but she isn't thinking about the person buried here. The last hour—the truth of the last hour—lays over her shoulders like a mantle.

Self-pity and sadness war with shame and hatred inside her. And still she can't say it. She can't say out loud that Beth was right.

RAPUNZEL

TWENTY-TWO

June, 2008

Springfield, IL

Dawn stares silently at Caroline. There is nothing in her eyes to suggest that she is lying or holding something back, and yet for Caroline nothing is everything. A chill tiptoes up her spine and makes the hair on the back of her neck stand. She feels Miles everywhere, almost more so here at Dawn's house, than she had at the home she apparently lives in with Miles.

"I wish you would just tell me," Caroline mumbles. She is out of her element. Away from her prison, she has become a nobody. She does not carry a purse; Dawn has the key to Caroline's house on her key chain and at the moment—the moment when Caroline most needs an ID—she does not have one or if she does, she does not know where it is. Her hands feel superfluous, so she shoves them into the pockets of her shorts. When, a moment later, that becomes uncomfortable, she pulls them out and stares at her fingers as if they belong to someone else.

Her breath comes in short, choppy gasps, and she feels sweat, like ice, on her back and her neck. Desperate for answers, for a *hand*, she looks up at Dawn again. Dawn does not seem to notice Caroline's sudden distress.

"Can you please just tell me?" Caroline tries again.

"Tell you what?" Dawn answers, as if she's just realized Caroline is talking to her.

"What's going on. Just sit down with me and tell me what's going on and who I am and—"

"What's the point of my filling in the gaps for you, Caroline? When I talk about the past, it's like I'm telling you about a book I read. None of it touches you. You don't relate to any of it." Dawn raises her hand to brush her hair off her face. Caroline notices that she is trembling. "You accuse me of lying. Of making things up."

"Maybe we'd all be better off if you just made something up, and I went back to the lavender room and you stayed here and life moved on."

"You've lived under glass since you met him." Dawn swallows the last of her words, but Caroline hears her. "Right now, it's just a smaller pedestal and a smaller looking glass."

"What the hell does that mean?" Caroline snaps.

"What the hell do you think it means?" Dawn steps toward Caroline. Anger takes her voice up a notch, and her eyes burn with something that looks like hate.

"I don't know what it means," Caroline answers. She shakes her head and steps back from Dawn. She turns and rests her hands on the countertop. She wonders if she and Dawn prepared meals together at this counter. If they sipped from wine glasses or drank cold bottled beer while they worked together to make a meal for their families. If she could only rewind and get back to a moment like that. "I don't know what it means," she repeats, "but I can tell you what it sounds like."

"What?" Dawn's voice is still taut with anger.

"It sounds like you're jealous—"

"Go to hell."

Caroline glances at her over her shoulder. Dawn turns to leave the kitchen, but Caroline isn't ready to take a break.

"He kissed you. Didn't he?"

"What?" Dawn stops in the short hallway to the family room. She does not look back at Caroline. Rather, she hunches her shoulders, as if she is readying herself to carry Caroline's accusations.

"When we first met him." Caroline's lips are moving, but she doesn't know where the words are coming from. "We were at the bowling alley on campus. And he kissed us both...I ended up going out with him..."

Dawn's shoulders raise and then Caroline hears her blow out a sigh and she sags against the wall. Twists so she is leaning her back on the wall, but she keeps her eyes on her feet.

"Why can't you look at me?" Caroline pushes. "You were jealous that I—"

"Jealous? What was there to be jealous of, Caroline? An overbearing ass who jerked you around from the word go. A guy that talked you down whenever you talked about law school. A jerk who hated Beth and treated her like she was a nobody from the day he met her. An ass who used his fists on you, whenever he wanted to. A disgusting son-of-a-bitch who seduced your best friend, after she lost her baby. And her hus—"

"Alright." Caroline nods. "I get it." She presses her lips together and then lets her eyes roam the kitchen in an attempt to not look at Dawn. "I get it."

"No, you don't. Not really." Dawn clears her throat. Still leaning against the wall, she lifts her hands and presses her fingertips to her eyes. She is crying. "You can't really get it until you really remember it."

"Then make me remember it."

"I can't." Dawn stands up straight and turns to look at Caroline.

"This is getting us nowhere!" Caroline shouts. "Dammit, Dawn, I *need* you! I need you to be my memory—"

"I can't!" Dawn smacks her hand against the wall. "I can't, because I don't know what happened. I don't know what the hell happened to blow it wide open, Caroline. I don't know. I don't know." Her words get lost in quiet sobs. She turns away again, as if she is embarrassed for Caroline to see her fall apart.

"What do you mean you don't know?" Caroline's words are whispers, but she knows Dawn had to hear the ragged edge of need in them.

"I don't know what happened! I don't know why you left. Why you took off the way you did. I don't know what had you so Goddamned scared that you jumped in the car and left—"

"I left?" Caroline says quietly. "I left? I left Miles? What about Max? Did I leave Max?"

Dawn cries and drags her hands back through her hair. She falls gently to the wall again and slides down to the floor. "I dunno. I don't—"

"Dawn, if I left Max, it doesn't matter." Caroline's stomach twists. Nothing matters if she left Miles and left her son with him. Miles can do with her what he wants, because she will never forgive herself for leaving Max with someone like Miles.

"No—"

"Just take me back." Caroline shrugs. The fear is gone. Everything inside her is gone. To kill her first baby and then leave Max to Miles. The truth rises up inside her. She deserves any hell Miles can put her through.

"You're gonna let him win now?" Dawn says from the floor. Caroline looks down and meets her gaze when she hears what sounds like a laugh.

"Is this funny?"

"You're just gonna go back to the house and give in. And let Miles slowly kill you. Drain you." Dawn licks her lips. Her face is streaked with mascara. Caroline is so caught up in self-loathing that Dawn's tears don't touch her.

"Maybe it's what I get."

Dawn nods. "Maybe it is," she mumbles. Her eyes burn a hole through Caroline. "You're gonna leave him all over again. If you let Miles beat you, you're leaving Max all over again."

'Leave me, Caroline, if that's what you want. But you won't get Max.'

Caroline cringes when she hears Miles' voice in her head. She groans and shakes her head.

"Go away, Miles."

"What did you say?"

"I keep hearing Miles. In my head. I keep hearing him talking to me."

"What's he saying?"

"You name it." Caroline laughs and cries at the same time. "Threats. I keep hearing him threaten me. He told me to leave if I wanted. But he said I'd never get Max."

"Look." Dawn rests her head against the wall and closes her eyes. "When I said you left...I didn't mean you left him. That you'd packed up and left him."

"What did you mean?"

"It may have been your intention. I don't know. I'm not lying. I don't know what blew up and started this whole mess we're in right now."

"But what did you mean?"

"You guys were fighting. When I got there that night...you had called me. You were frantic. Begged me to come." Dawn bites her lip. "Frantic. I didn't want to go. I didn't want to see you."

"Why?" Caroline whispers, hurt now by Dawn's admission. She lowers herself to her knees in front of her. "Why wouldn't you want to see me?"

Dawn opens her eyes and stares at Caroline for several long silent moments. "I'd lost my baby. My husband." She hesitates, but she doesn't look away. "It all felt connected to you. Everything I lost, somehow inside me it was all connected to you."

"You blamed me. For your loss."

"No, not blame." Dawn frowns as if she is searching for the right word. "I didn't blame you. But I couldn't get away from it when I was around you." She finally lowers her eyes and stares at Caroline's hands, clasped, as if in prayer, in her lap.

"I'm sorry."

"Everything about my life was normal. High school. Parties. Friends. Jobs. Even college. Hanging out with you and Beth. Going to classes. Thinking I was pregnant then and having my two best friends there with me. Meeting Danny. It was all normal, Caroline."

"Until..."

"Until Miles. Everything was normal until Miles. You started dating Miles. And you changed—"

"Changed? How did I change?"

"He put enough doubt between you and Bethie, that she killed herself. He tried so hard to pull you and I apart. He took you away." Dawn narrows her eyes, as if she is seeing Miles in the distance, changing the landscape of her life. "Stripped away the parts of you that made you who you are. Beat you—"

"You said I fought back," Caroline mumbles. She is grasping at straws, because shame teases the back of her throat. The thought of being a battered wife does not set well, and she doesn't even know the woman she used to be.

"You did." Dawn shrugs. "But who should live like that, Caroline?" When Caroline looks up, Dawn is watching her. "Who should have to live like that?"

Caroline sniffles and sighs. She is so tired. There is a dull, steady ache in her leg. Wouldn't Miles love to know he was right, too much and she would overdo it? Still recovering from the accident—

"That night. When I called you...and I was upset—"

"Hysterical," Dawn corrects her.

"That was the night of the accident, wasn't it?"

Dawn nods.

"Then thank God I didn't have Max."

"You were—" Dawn shakes her head, again grasping for the right word, "You were out of control. Frantic when you called me, but you were seething when I got there. Screaming at him. Maybe if I hadn't shown up when I did, you would've killed him."

"Why? Why was I so angry?"

"I don't know."

Caroline studies Dawn's face for several moments before deciding to believe her.

"When you called. You begged me to come. When I said no, you cried. You begged. Said it was life or death, and I had to come and I had to help. You had to talk to me about something. Couldn't do it over the phone. Couldn't wait for another time."

"If I—" Caroline sighs. She can't say it.

"If you what?"

"If I...if he—God," she whispers. "I hate that this is what I've become."

"If you what?" Dawn repeats.

"If he beat me. If he beat me, like you say he did—"

"Damn you. Damn you, Caroline. Don't do this. Don't make me talk and then second guess every damned word I say. Don't do this to me. I don't deserve any of this shit. You dragged me into your nightmare, and you still won't let me out. Either you believe me or you walk—"

"Wow." Caroline laughs humorlessly. She tastes the salt in the corner of her lips. "Just a bad choice of words." She raises her eyebrows. "Hard to admit something like this about yourself."

Dawn waits for her to go on.

"I know he hit me. I remember some of it."

Caroline takes a deep breath and then waits until the tightness in her throat eases. She flexes her fingers when Dawn touches the back of her hand. Silently, their fingers intertwine and Caroline finds the strength to go on.

"Did I call you a lot?"

She shakes her head before Dawn can answer her.

"Upset. Did I call you to cry on you when he did it?"

"No." Dawn squeezes her hand. "You always told me, I think. But no. You didn't call me to cry on me. You held your own with him. I don't think he got the better of you too often."

Caroline wants to take this road. What happened when he did get the better of her? Maybe the scar on her chest and arm had something to do with him getting the better of her. She wants to have this conversation. But there are another two or three threads of conversation lying on the floor around them and she thinks they are more important at the moment.

"So. I called you. And I begged you to come. Because I had to talk to you."

"Yeah. I don't think he was home when you called me. I think after you hung up and before I got there, he came home. And I don't know what happened, but when I knocked on your door, I could hear you screaming—"

"What?"

"You were screaming—"

"What was I saying?"

"I tried the door. It was unlocked. I stepped inside. You were hammering your fists on him. On his chest. Screaming that he was a liar. That everything was a lie, and that you hated him."

"What did I mean by that, Dawn?"

"I don't know. He grabbed you by your upper arms and threw you off him. I really don't even know if it had registered with either of you that I was there. That I was seeing what was going on. You hit the floor. Scrambled to get up, like you knew he would kick you. Attack you. He grabbed your arm. Your wrist. Told you to shut up. That he wanted dinner, and he never wanted to hear any of it again."

Caroline closes her eyes and tries to summon the memories. There is nothing. Just emptiness.

"You yanked away from him again and ran for the kitchen. He went after you. You grabbed the keys and ran out the door. Miles was following you out the door, when I heard Max."

"Oh God."

"He was in his room, but he'd heard the fight. I don't know how much he heard. I don't know if he knows what set you off. But he'd heard enough to be upset. He was crying. I went upstairs. Heard your car start. Miles screaming at you to come back. Max was curled up on his bed. He didn't want me. He wanted you."

Caroline presses her lips together, but she still sobs. She can't hold it in, and she is cold and alone on the floor of

Dawn's kitchen. Even with Dawn's hands both holding her own now.

"Miles came back inside. He was in the kitchen. So calm. It was like..." Dawn shakes her head and then shrugs. "It was like nothing had happened. He was making dinner. He was making some homemade ravioli dish for himself and Max. I tiptoed down the steps. I wanted to leave. Thought I could slip out before he realized I was there."

"You left Max?"

"You didn't make it a quarter of a mile up Eighth street. You hadn't been gone ten minutes. Miles heard me on the steps. Cut me off before I got to the front door. Said you were angry with him because you'd found out that he and I slept together. And the only way you would've found that out was if I'd told you."

"You didn't."

"No, I didn't. I don't know if you found out or not. I don't know. But it was a good way for Miles to blame me. To shift the responsibility."

"What happened?"

"He backhanded me. He'd told me..." Dawn stops talking and ducks her head. Caroline waits, but when Dawn doesn't seem likely to continue, Caroline lifts her hand and reaches out to cup Dawn's chin.

"He'd told you what?"

"He said he'd kill me if you ever found out we'd slept together."

“You believed him?” Caroline asks softly. Not as a challenge. As confirmation. Dawn saw the threat before the accident. Maybe Caroline did and maybe she didn’t. But she feels it now.

“I did.”

“What happened after he hit you?”

“Sirens. I could hear them in the distance. He hit me hard enough that it could have been in my head. But then I could make it out, the sounds of sirens. And then the phone rang. He didn’t want to turn his back to me, but he did. I ran. I was out the door before he picked the phone up.”

Caroline nods.

“I saw it. Before he even called me. I saw your car. Wrapped around a tree. A tree in the park...by the street. The car was totaled, but I knew. I knew it was you.”

Caroline forces herself to breathe calmly.

“The firemen were cutting you out.” Dawn pulls her hands away from Caroline and vigorously rubs her own upper arms. “There were cops everywhere. Four cars. There were four cars. And a firetruck and an ambulance. And they were cutting you out of the car.

“I stopped. I couldn’t have kept driving, even if I’d wanted to. I stopped and got out and I was just standing there with the crowd that had already gathered. You know how people love a tragedy.”

“Puts life in perspective,” Caroline mumbles.

"The cops got your information from your plates. Called Miles. He called me. I let my phone ring forever. Someone in the crowd finally told me to answer my phone already." Dawn shakes her head. "I knew without looking that it was him. I took it from my pocket and threw it down and stepped on it. Twisted my foot on it, like I was putting a cigarette out."

Dawn's eyes seem to take inventory of Caroline's face.

"I thought you were dead. I thought you—I thought you were like Beth. Dead. And so I was gonna go. I was gonna get as far away from your memory and Miles as I could. Start over." Dawn lets the tears flow unchecked. "And then they peeled your door off the car. It was like a big can opener taking the top off a can. And then...and then they lifted you out and put you on stretcher. You were a mess. You were like a rag doll, and I thought you were dead. I wanted to leave. But I couldn't move. I couldn't pick up my feet to go. I couldn't. I couldn't leave you."

Caroline swallows hard. Her throat aches. Speechless, she waits for Dawn to recount the details of what should have been her death.

"You were soaked with blood. It was dark out, and there was so much blood, I couldn't see anything but the blood. All of the lights were flashing and they kept lighting up your face. Blue and red. I've never been so scared in my life.

Just like Beth. I kept thinking how it was so weird that it would all end this way. With you dead, just like Beth. And me, without Danny. And I had to get away. I kept thinking how Miles would come after me and kill me, because if you'd found out about him and I, and you were upset about it, then it was my fault you were dead."

"I didn't, Dawn." Caroline leans back on the wall behind her. "I didn't know."

"I heard a paramedic say they had a pulse. I kept wondering if that was what Beth looked like. Every time the lights flashed over your face, I'd see you and then I'd see Beth and I thought I was losing my mind. And then they said you had a pulse. And I heard this sound. It was like someone was torturing a dog. Horrible sound. It was horrible. It was me —it was horrible—it was me. I was so scared, Caroline. Afraid to lose you. Afraid it was my fault."

"None of it was your fault." Caroline says matter-of-factly. "I know that much, Dawn."

"They put you in the ambulance, and I just kept thinking you would die. Before you got to the hospital. Didn't think you could live if you'd lost all that blood and I didn't want you to die alone. And Miles wasn't there yet. He was with Max. Had to find someone to take Max, since I hadn't answered when he called me. And so. So I got in the ambulance with you. I got in with you. The paramedics thought I was psycho. Tried to give me a shot. A sedative."

Dawn's words slow and her teeth begin to chatter.

"I tried to pull myself together. So I could be with you. I didn't want the shot. I didn't want anybody messing with me, because I had to be there for you. I held your hand. All the way to the hospital, with the siren screaming out there, I held your hand. I begged you to come back to me. Begged you to open your eyes. To talk to me. You didn't. I thought you were dead, but the paramedics were monitoring your heartbeat. They made me let you go. When we got to the hospital. They made me stay in the waiting room, while they rushed you into an exam room. You were still bleeding, and they took you away...and."

"What?" Caroline's voice is flat, as if she is back on the gurney, bleeding out, empty of emotion.

"I was alone. I couldn't call anyone. I was alone, and I knew you were going to die in the ER. And I was sitting there waiting. Waiting to hear that. Waiting for Miles to come for me. People in the waiting room were looking at me like I was a freak. An ax-murderer or something.

"I had your blood on me. On my shirt. And my hands. I had your blood on my hands."

BEAUTY & THE BEAST

TWENTY-THREE

2003

Springfield, IL

"It doesn't change anything," Caroline mumbles. She keeps her eyes on the carrots and the knife she continues to use on them. As if her hands are not connected to her brain and her train of thought, she continues to chop the vegetables quickly, like Emeril or Martha Stewart might do. "Does it?"

Dawn stands at the far counter, rinsing strawberries in the sink. She turns her head to look at Caroline over her shoulder. "What doesn't change anything?"

"Fighting back." Caroline answers, eyes still on the hand that wields the knife and efficiently chops the carrots into nearly razor thin slices for a salad. "It doesn't change anything that I fight him."

The hand stills. Caroline stares at the long, slender fingers and the pearl ring on the middle finger and the French manicure on the nail tips. It is her hand. It has to be her hand, because Miles insists that she wears only a French manicure. She is never allowed color. She is never allowed to let her fingernails go. Once, Miles had backhanded her across the mouth for picking the nail tips off her fingers. She'd claimed the flu to anyone in the outside world, who'd asked why she didn't leave her house for a week. The swelling in her lip went down after two days, but the bruise lingered. She remained sequestered—imprisoned—in the house until the purplish blue mark faded to a sour yellow. One that she could cover with makeup.

She glances up now, with only her eyes, to see Dawn standing at the counter with her. Dawn dries her hands on a dish towel. A dish towel with the word Tuesday embroidered in it. Dawn's home is sunny and warm and homey. Dawn's home never fails to make Caroline feel safe and happy. Caroline's eyes abandon the study of her hand and instead stare fixedly at the dish towel. Miles would never allow her to have dish towels with the days of the week embroidered on them. Her dish towels are all solid red. Seven of them. Seven solid red dish towels and a small scrubbing sponge that she is to dispose of every night. That she is never to leave in plain sight after she has cleaned the kitchen for the day or evening.

"I'm still a battered wife." She doesn't realize she is going to speak, until she hears her own voice saying these ugly words. "It doesn't matter if I can fight back, because I'm still a battered wife."

Fueled by sudden anger at her place in life, she raises her eyes to meet Dawn's gaze. Thank God she sees no pity. She could not handle pity.

"Leave him, Caroline." Dawn does not mince words. Caroline remembers a day a few years back when Beth had announced that she did not like Miles. When Dawn had stood silently and still managed to align herself with Beth's way of thinking. "You are strong enough to pack up and leave him and get free—"

"I can't." Caroline shakes her head.

"You can. You just stood here and told me you can fight back. You have to fight back, Car. Get away from him. Danny and I will do anything we can to help you—"

"I can't," Caroline repeats. "I'm pregnant."

Dawn's eyes go wide with shock, but before she can answer, they hear the screech of the screen door. Caroline wills her body to relax, even though she is scared to death it is Miles. He knows that she is pregnant, but he has told her he doesn't want her to tell anyone until she is at least four months along.

"Awfully quiet in here," Danny calls as he yanks the refrigerator door open. He grabs two Miller Lites and then turns back to Dawn and Caroline. Caroline's eyes dance over Dawn's face and Danny's face and come to a halt on the beer bottles. Why can Miles drink Miller Lite here, even when Dawn makes a point of having Red Stripe here for him? Why can he drink Miller Lite here, but slap her around at home if she does not keep his favorite beer stocked?

"I'm tired," Dawn finally answers. She tries to smile around a yawn. "I've been working outside all day, remember?" Caroline wonders how much Danny knows about her and Miles. Dawn had mowed and trimmed their yard earlier, but Caroline knows she is not particularly tired. She is making lame conversation to ease the tension and send Danny back outside to Miles.

"I know." Danny drops a kiss on the tip of Dawn's nose. Caroline looks away. In the nine years they have been together, Miles has never playfully kissed Caroline anywhere. "The grill's ready, so let me know when you're ready for me to put the steaks on."

Dawn nods absently. Caroline wonders again how much Danny knows about her marriage. It's not as if she doesn't trust him. She knows he will not say anything to Miles. But it makes her feel weird to think other people might *know*.

Shame.

Caroline sets the knife on the counter and steps back as Danny disappears behind her and the screen door screeches again and then bangs closed.

"What?" Dawn asks softly. She glances at the knife. "What's the matter?"

Caroline raises her eyebrows. In another world, her words about being pregnant would have been met with shrieks of happiness from her best friend. Or maybe she would have announced it over dessert while the rest of them had a glass of wine and she sipped ginger ale. In another world, Miles and Danny would be outside having an animated conversation about the race for the pennant in major league baseball. And she and Dawn would be hurrying to finish making dinner so they could sit outside and soak up the late afternoon sun while they listened to Miles and Danny and threw in their own two cents.

Instead they are inside and Caroline is consumed with thoughts about how she must groom herself as Miles says and how she must keep in her home only what Miles will allow her to keep in her home—seven red dish towels and ten thick black bath towels and only Red Stripe beer and jazz music—

Shame floods the back of her throat. She tries to swallow it away, but a wave of nausea nearly flattens her.

She is a battered wife, and if she has stayed in this hellish marriage this long, perhaps she deserves no better. But now she's pregnant. She is pregnant. She has a bond with Miles now, a bond much deeper than wedding vows and wedding lies, and for a moment, she stands completely still and wonders how the hell she had been so stupid to let herself conceive a child with the monster she sleeps with.

"Does he know?" Dawn avoids Caroline's eyes. Because she feels it too. They are best friends. They should be celebrating Caroline's first pregnancy. Instead they tread through waters of regret.

Unable to summon so much as a yes, Caroline simply nods.

"I was on the pill for a few years. And then he up and decided it was time to have a baby." Caroline watches her fingers curl around the knife again. Her voice is quiet but steady. She doesn't often cry about Miles and the way he treats her. There is no point. Beth and Dawn had tried to warn her, and she'd gotten angry at Beth and had never resolved that anger before Beth died. It would be unfair of her to cry on Dawn's shoulder now, about the life she's found herself trapped in. "He gets the mail every day. Goes through it before I see it. Each time I had a package with my prescription, he made me watch him punch each pill out. And flush them down the toilet."

She stops talking and looks at Dawn for a moment. She doesn't know if she needs a breather or if maybe she's listening to make sure Miles is not at the screen door, about to come inside to use the restroom or grab another beer, either of which Caroline knows would be an excuse to make sure she is not telling secrets.

"I don't know why he did that. I didn't argue with him. When he said it was time for a baby." Caroline shrugs. "At the time, I thought it would be nice to have a baby."

"Unconditional love."

"Something like that."

"When are you due?"

"Took several years to get pregnant. By the time I realized I didn't want a baby, that having a baby with him would be a huge mistake, I relaxed a little bit. It took us so long to get pregnant, I thought maybe it wasn't going to happen." Caroline's fingers move from the knife to the cutting board. She lifts it and scrapes the carrot slices into a salad bowl. "I'm due in August."

Dawn is quiet for such a long time, Caroline assumes the conversation is over.

"Can I ask you something?"

Caroline looks up at Dawn hesitantly. "What?"

"How can you stand to be with him like that? How can you let him touch you?"

Caroline picks up the knife when she hears the door behind her again. She takes a deep breath and forces her body to relax. Miles approaches from behind her and slips his arm around her waist. She makes her lips curve upward when he kisses her neck just below her ear.

She is glad that he has come inside just now. He's saved her from answering Dawn's question. She doesn't know how she lets him touch her. She doesn't always *let* him. Sometimes their lovemaking is violent and painful, and as he moves over her, she pounds her fists against him to make him stop. Sometimes she simply closes her eyes and waits for him to finish.

But sometimes, she glimpses the Miles she'd fallen in love with. She treasures those times and lets him touch her and send her over the edge with pleasure.

She looks up at Miles now and touches her lips to his cheek. Because she does not cry, because she has trained her body to relax around him, he does not know that she and Dawn have been discussing the pregnancy.

Miles walks down the hall. Caroline is relieved that Dawn has gone back to the strawberry shortcake she is making for dessert.

The baby she carries has tied her to Miles in a way that the diamond on her finger and the vows she spoke and the last name she now goes by can never do. She just hopes that the baby was conceived in one of the few tender moments she's shared with her husband.

RAPUNZEL

TWENTY-FOUR

June, 2008

Springfield, IL

It is sobering to hear the details of what could have been her death. Caroline sits in silence in Dawn's kitchen, which is beginning to grow dim in the faded afternoon light. She does not want to think about the accident. She doesn't remember calling Dawn and begging her to come to the house, fighting with Miles or leaving. She doesn't remember driving off in the car or losing control.

She doesn't want to dwell on Dawn's memories of the accident. Of the thought of her car totaled by a collision with a tree. Of Dawn watching as the paramedics cut her out of the wreckage and placed her rag doll body on the stretcher.

And yet, in the silence that follows Dawn's emotional confession, Dawn's memories of the accident are all that she can think of. She sits on the floor—half in the kitchen, half in the hallway—her head resting on the wall behind her. Eyes closed, she sees the car and the flashing lights and her rag doll self on the stretcher. Unable to stand the pictures anymore, she opens her eyes.

The fading sunlight throws ominous shadows over the room. Dawn sits a foot away from her, legs drawn up and her forehead resting on her knees. The house makes the noises that her parents used to tell her were a house settling, but Caroline knows now that it was a lie. This house, as well as the house she shared with Miles, is haunted. With memories of a ghost and the monster who drove her to near death.

"How bad was it?" Her voice is gruff and loud in the oppressive silence.

Looking suddenly pale and gaunt, sitting in the shadows of the small hall between the kitchen and the living room, Dawn stares at Caroline for several seconds before she answers.

"Did you know I was voted most likely to succeed, when I was a senior in high school?" She laughs, but it is a cold sound, and it doesn't reach her eyes. "Wonder what they'd think of me now."

"I know you won the state spelling bee when you were in sixth grade," Caroline answers quietly.

Dawn nods. "You know, you feel like you can't trust me. To tell you the truth."

"It's not you. It's me." Caroline shrugs. "I know that I

know you. I feel it. But looking at you, I can't remember anything—"

"But you do remember things," Dawn interrupts her. "Every now and then, you remember something and you deliver it to me like it's completely normal and I'm supposed to sit here and believe that two seconds ago you remembered me telling you that I won the spelling bee when I was in sixth grade, but that you're looking at me and you don't remember being in my wedding or sitting with me when my mom died."

Dawn's hidden accusation hurts. Caroline sits up straight and feels a pinch in her left thigh. Not the spot that has been medically corrected. She squirms a bit. There is something in her pocket that is pushing into her leg. She stretches and pushes her hand into her pocket. Dawn turns away when Caroline pulls out her wedding ring. She doesn't really remember shoving it in her pocket earlier, but she'd been preoccupied so it doesn't surprise her.

"Why would I lie?" she finally asks Dawn.

"I don't think you're lying. It's just unnerving."

Caroline hears a car door slam outside the house.

"It's unnerving to look at you. You're not the same woman you used to be. You don't look the same. You don't remember me. Us. You don't remember the big things. The little things. And then whammy. You say something about what you do remember and it's a jolt, because when I look at you and don't see the Caroline I know, I wanna know how the hell you know something that we shared."

"Damned if I do and damned if I don't."

"Your injuries weren't that bad," Dawn finally answers Caroline's original question. "Well. They were bad. But."

"But?"

"You weren't brain dead. No Dr. Frankenstein came to put you back together."

"No, just to take me apart," Caroline mumbles.

Dawn acknowledges her point with a small nod.

"You had a concussion. I mean...you were in a coma, but the doctors kept saying that was good. That it gave your body a chance to heal."

"There's no medical reason I can't remember anything?"

"No. They say your memory loss is just from the trauma of what happened."

"What else?"

"Broken bones. Some internal bleeding. Your spleen was damaged. Broken ribs. Punctured left lung. Three broken fingers on your right hand. Broken leg."

"And nothing on my face? No cuts?"

"Yeah, you had cuts. One in your hairline that was pretty bad. But...you would've recovered...with a couple of small scars. Your hair would've covered the worst of it."

"So there was no reason for plastic surgery?"

"Not for you. You were never vain. I don't think a couple of scars would've bothered you."

"Did he tell you he did it so I wouldn't remember?"

Dawn nods. "I thought he didn't want you to remember that we'd slept together."

"But now you think something different?"

"I don't know what I think anymore."

Caroline sighs. Her leg hurts. She's exhausted. She hasn't seen the pictures yet, only the ones on Dawn's refrigerator. A picture of a boy who is supposedly her son and a picture of a woman she may never recognize, with her college roommates. Roommates she remembers in her gut, rather than her head.

She wants to go home. She's so tired, the thought of that house—*the lavender room*—as home doesn't really bother her. What bothers her is the thought of Miles coming back tomorrow. The energy it will take for her to pretend that she isn't remembering bits and pieces. That the jigsaw puzzle her brain is making of her past life isn't turning into a nightmare. She will have to be careful not to make Miles any more suspicious than he already is.

Footsteps on the front porch jerk them both to action. Dawn jumps and quickly, gracefully climbs to her feet. Caroline, though going through vigorous physical therapy, just after she awoke and was moved to the lavender room, is not fully recovered and understands her limits now, as she struggles to get up. Over the hammering in her chest, she hears someone walking around on Dawn's front porch. No knocking. Just someone walking around.

Dawn touches her finger to her lips and motions for Caroline to stay where she is, hidden from sight, where there are no windows. Caroline holds her breath and watches Dawn slip through the kitchen to the back door. She almost calls after her. Is she going outside? Why would she go outside? Why would she just walk right into—what? What is she walking into? Just because there are footsteps on the porch, just because someone might be on the porch, does not mean it is Miles.

What if it is Miles? What if he's not out of town? What if this had been a test? What if he had told Dawn to bring Caroline here—

"I think it was just the mailman," Dawn whispers when she appears in the hall again. "No cars out there, but mine. I locked the backdoor, but Caroline, maybe we should get back to your house."

Caroline notices that Dawn says it as if she expects Caroline to argue. Suddenly so exhausted she can't even speak, she simply nods. Dawn hurries to grab her purse from the kitchen counter. Caroline sees a flash of memory. Sunshine and strawberries and herself, standing at the counter. She feels the sudden tension in her body, and she reaches for a barstool to steady herself.

"Are you okay?" Dawn looks up suddenly. She has the strap of her purse thrown over her shoulder and her keys in her right hand.

"I'm fine," Caroline lies.

Dawn studies her face, as if she is trying to determine if she is telling the truth.

"We were standing right here. Fixing dinner. When you told me you were pregnant with Max."

Caroline nods. "I know."

"You remember that?"

Caroline nods. "I just...yeah. Just now."

"Do you remember what I asked you?"

Caroline's stomach pitches, and she glances around wondering where the bathroom is. Wondering if instinct will kick in and she'll find it before she gets sick.

"I asked you how you could let him touch you." Dawn presses her lips together. "You never answered me."

"Well." Caroline raises her eyebrows. "I guess maybe now I can ask you the same thing."

RAPUNZEL

TWENTY-FIVE

June, 2008

Springfield, IL

The ride home is quiet, but it is an unsettling kind of quiet that screams for something to be said. Drained, Caroline can't think of anything to say, and even though the quiet leaves huge gaps in her mind for Miles' voice to come to her, she doesn't want to talk. Not to Miles. Not to Dawn.

It is still summer, so they drive in daylight, albeit daylight with the sunshine filtered now through the later afternoon hours. The thought of darkness settling in around the house pushes her heart to pound like a horse's hoof beats as it races around a track. It feels weird in her chest, but she doesn't acknowledge it. She doesn't want to move and draw Dawn's attention. She doesn't want Dawn to channel Miles and say how upset he would be if he knew how she had tired herself out today.

While she was gone, Caroline hadn't thought much about the house. And yet, now that Dawn pulls her Explorer to a halt in front of it, Caroline is amazed to see that it is just an old, three-story brick house. She isn't sure what she expected to find, but there is something dark and scary about the house that makes it hard for her to breathe.

They walk side by side to the porch, but neither of them speaks. Caroline watches the house suspiciously, as if it will suddenly become black brick or maybe the door will open and Miles will appear before them, all-knowing.

That's what bothers her. She knows it is not the house. There are no demons inside the house that await her. None other than her own, anyway. It is Miles that she fears. Not his fists. But there is something dark and sinister about him that makes her afraid to go back inside this house. She is free right now, free to walk away and never look back.

Except that Miles has Max. She knows in her gut that Miles has never hurt Max. But she does not want a man like Miles raising the boy.

Besides. He would find her. No matter where she might go, Miles would find her effortlessly. She knows that about him. He would find her, and he would kill her.

"Do you know the name Michael Ramsay?" Caroline stops walking. She stares at the house, paying particular attention to the windows, where someone could be hiding and watching them approach the house. Where Miles could be watching.

"Should I?" Dawn slows but keeps walking. She stops finally and looks back at Caroline. Her face is ashen, but Caroline has seen the change in pallor settling in all afternoon. It is not the stranger's name that has drained the color from her friend.

Dawn is a friend. Caroline knows that now. It bothers her that knowing the woman has been a friend does not automatically make her want to invest all of her trust. Why wouldn't she trust a friend? A friend as close as Dawn has been.

"No." Caroline shakes her head. Michael Ramsay. Why had she suddenly had that name in her mind? "I don't know why I asked you that."

"You don't know him?"

"I don't know," Caroline answers. She glances at the house again. Completely unnerved by the sensation of the windows of the house being eyes for some unseen evil, Caroline rushes toward the porch. She trips, but Dawn catches her hand before she can stumble too far and fall.

"Be careful."

"I have to get inside." Somehow being inside, even if the house is haunted, seems better. Being surrounded by it seems less frightening than feeling it stare at her. Knowing that it is cataloging every move she makes. Maybe she can hide within its shadows.

Dawn unlocks the front door. The house is still, just as they had left it. Empty walls. No pictures. No memories vie for her attention. Just the empty foyer and the staircase that sweeps up to the lavender room.

She takes a deep breath and turns to face Dawn. A slight tremble touches her. She does not want to be alone here. And yet, Dawn is exhausted. After all of the loss Dawn has suffered through Caroline, she can't ask her to stay. She can't ask her to give more of herself, when she is beginning to fade from sight now.

"Your friend that called…" Caroline licks her lips and stares at the floor near Dawn's feet. Maybe Dawn has made new friends and would prefer to spend her time with them. "Do you—"

"I'll stay," Dawn says quietly. Caroline wants to be brave, to argue and say that she doesn't need Dawn. She wants to breathe some sort of life back into Dawn, but she can't do any of the above.

"I'm sorry—" Maybe she should thank her. But she can't. She hates that she needs someone with her, and she hates to be a burden to someone who so obviously has needs of her own.

Dawn shakes her head. "Look." She swallows hard. "Maybe you and I will never be what we used to be…"

"Dawn—"

"Not after all that's happened," Dawn shrugs and continues, "but, I care about you and I care about Max."

Caroline nods. The house, the air in the house, seems to press in around her, making her feel claustrophobic even though she stands in the open foyer at the base of the stairs.

"If Miles never called you again, where would you go?"

Rather than answer her, Dawn glances at her watch. She pulls her cell phone out of her purse and looks at the display.

"Speaking of Miles, it's kind of odd that he hasn't called."

Caroline recognizes the unease in Dawn's voice. It is the same unease she has been swallowing all day.

"Does he go out of town often?"

"He used to. Before the accident."

Caroline wants to ask Dawn if it's possible that Miles did not go out of town. If it's possible that he might be right here watching them. Testing them. She doesn't though. Miles may have been abusive, but she is making him out to be some sinister madman, someone maybe Batman and Robin need to defeat in order to save her. She doesn't want to voice her irrational fears and make Dawn think she's going crazy.

"We have to tell him we were gone."

Dawn shakes her head. "No."

"We have to. Just in case."

Dawn doesn't ask 'just in case what?' Caroline wonders if she holds the same suspicions.

"We can't tell him you were at my house."

What if he already knows? Caroline wants to ask. But it is easier not to say the words out loud.

"Can we just tell him we went for a ride?"

Neither of them wants to talk about the fact that if Miles knows they were not at his house, that he might know they were at Dawn's house.

"Yeah. Okay," Dawn agrees. "We went for a drive around town, just so you could get out for a while."

They can't say anything about hoping to jog Caroline's memory.

"Does your leg hurt?" Dawn asks as she follows Caroline into the kitchen. Caroline knows it is useless to argue, so she simply nods. She watches when Dawn puts her purse down on the counter and opens the cabinet by the wall oven. Dawn picks up the aspirin, opens it, shakes two out and hands them to Caroline.

"There's a whirlpool tub in the master bath," she tells Caroline. "You could relax for a while. See if it makes your leg feel any better."

Caroline crunches down on the 'no' that fights to get out of her mouth. Dawn has just handed her another opportunity for trust. If she slaps it aside, she will hurt her at the very least. Drive Dawn away and find herself alone at the most.

Caroline gets a bottle of water from the refrigerator and washes the aspirin down with a swallow. "That sounds good." It does sound good. If only she could relax and not picture Dawn downstairs, on the phone with Miles, assuring him that Caroline may be remembering things but that she does not remember...what? What does she not remember?

"But?" Dawn asks when Caroline does not move.

"Just," Caroline sighs and blows her bangs off her face. "Just trying to remember..."

"Michael Ramsay." Dawn leans against the counter at her back. "Was that a memory? Or—"

"Or what?" Caroline asks. What else could it be? She's been locked in this damned house for months and in a coma for months before that. She's not sure how Michael Ramsay could be a part of this new life, unless he was a doctor or nurse who attended to her.

"I don't know." Dawn frowns. "A name you've seen since the accident?"

Caroline smiles sadly. "Haven't seen much of anything since the accident, Dawn."

"I don't remember a Michael Ramsay."

Caroline feels as if she is a dead man walking as she follows Dawn up the stairs.

"Hey. How about if I read for a while?" Dawn seems to sense her uneasiness. "I could hang out in the bedroom and read. In case you need me."

Caroline nods, grateful that Dawn will be nearby. In case she needs her. In case Miles calls.

They go on up to the third floor, where Dawn waits as Caroline gathers clean panties and athletic shorts to slip into. Remembering the diamond ring in her pocket, she takes it out and sets it on the dresser.

"I went with Danny," she whispers. Dawn looks up quickly, her eyes sharp and focused. "When he bought your ring."

Dawn raises her eyebrows. She looks down at the ring on her finger.

"You helped him pick it out?"

"No." Caroline stares at the rock on the dresser and then looks at Dawn's ring. It is smaller, and yet probably more stunning. "I went with him. But he knew it when he saw it. That one was yours."

Dawn swallows hard and looks away. "He never told me."

"I asked him not to. I wanted to be surprised by all of it. For you."

Awkward silence joins them in the doorway. None of the unease of earlier, just that awkward silence that hovers when someone has said something that maybe they should not have said.

Finally, eyes still anywhere but on Caroline's face, Dawn nods. She turns and starts back down the steps. Caroline follows, glancing behind her as she slowly makes her way down. She thinks the door next to the lavender room should be closed. Wasn't it closed this morning? When she'd first come downstairs? She can't remember now.

"Dawn." She stops, halfway down the stairs.

"Yeah?"

"What is that room? The one next to the lavender room?"

Dawn walks back up the four steps to be even with Caroline. She follows Caroline's gaze.

"It was Miles' office."

"I thought the office was downstairs."

Dawn nods. "But that was Miles' private office."

BEAUTY & THE BEAST

TWENTY-SIX

2007

Springfield, IL

Caroline tries to remember, as Dawn cries with pain, what Dawn did for her. What did Dawn do to comfort her when she was in labor with Max? She'd rubbed her back, held her hand, laughed and cried and talked with her. Dawn had done all the right things. Dawn had known what it would take to ease Caroline through Max's birth. In fact, Dawn had been so good to her, she doesn't really remember Miles even being there.

None of that matters though. Nothing she can do for Dawn will make her feel better. Dawn is seven centimeters dilated and four months too early to be delivering this baby. Doctors had tried to stop the contractions. The first time they had started, two days ago, Danny had rushed Dawn to the hospital. Caroline had been unable to meet them there. She'd been at home, in bed with Miles, who refused to let her answer the phone. The call had come in after midnight, and even after hearing Danny's voice and knowing the reason for the call—*the emergency*—Miles held her there and told her there was nothing she could do anyway. He hadn't been hateful, exactly. Just adamant that the doctors would slow Dawn's labor and get everything under control.

And they had. Dawn had been admitted, given nifedipine—a drug to stop contractions—intravenously, and the contractions had stopped after a few hours. She had been released later the next morning and told to stay off her feet. Danny had called back to let Caroline know that they were home, that Dawn was resting comfortably, although not happy about being put on bed rest in the fifth month of her pregnancy. Caroline had answered the call in the kitchen, and Miles was nowhere to be seen. But even so, she'd stepped out onto the patio to talk to Danny. Tried to apologize for not coming, but how did you do that really? How did one apologize for being under the thumb of someone else and not being *allowed* to leave the house and meet a loved one at the hospital during an emergency? Luckily, Danny seemed to understand and blew away her apology on a soft, nervous laugh. Caroline had been relieved to be off the hook, and yet, it had made her wonder just how much Dawn had told Danny about the punches and fists and bruises that had marred her body from the time she'd been married.

And now, here they are, the following day and Dawn is in preterm labor and the nifedipine is not working. The baby is coming, and Dawn knows it, and though the doctors assure her that it is *possible* to save the baby, Dawn knows it is not *probable*. Caroline wonders if she is helping her best friend through the birth of her baby, or if she is keeping vigil at what will be a death bed.

"Why my baby, Caroline?" Dawn whispers.

"She's okay, Dawn," Caroline answers. She squeezes Dawn's hand hard and leans over the bed. "She's going to be okay. She's a tough little girl, just like her mama."

"She?" Dawn's smile is more of a grimace, a twist of her lips, as tears wash her cheeks.

"Gotta believe, Dawnie, gotta believe," Caroline says with a nod. "She's gonna be beautiful. Blond hair and big brown eyes. Just like you, Dawn. She's gonna be just like you."

"It's too soon." Dawn shakes her head. "She's not going to make it, Caroline."

"You listen to me." Caroline brushes Dawn's hair off her forehead. "Your baby is going to be fine. We're going to make this work, Dawn. Me and Danny, we're right here. And you're going to deliver a beautiful baby girl, okay?"

Dawn nods, but she cries out and squeezes Caroline's hand hard enough to bruise it. Another contraction. Caroline watches the nurse watch the screen that gives them a visual on the baby's heart rate.

The baby is in distress. The nurse glances at Caroline for a moment, and then looks at first Danny and then Dawn.

"I'm going to bring Doctor Reese in for a moment," she says without further explanation. Doctor Reese is an exceptionally tall woman, and Caroline thinks that by her height, by the way she fills the room, that she should have the answers. She should be able to fix everything and deliver Dawn and Danny's baby.

Caroline moves closer to Dawn as the doctor checks her. She remembers the discomfort of labor and the birth, she reads it all in Dawns' face, and yet, Caroline knows Max's birth had been so very easy, compared to this. Caroline leans close and presses her lips to Dawn's forehead, and then studies their intertwined hands. Dawn's knuckles are white, Caroline's hand is red from the blood Dawn has trapped there, under the skin.

"Dawn." Doctor Reese stands up straight and snaps off the latex gloves. Caroline doesn't know why but she associates the motion and the accompanying sound with death. Violent death. Probably the overabundance of cop shows on TV now. Cop shows that glamorize death and violence and the offenders.

Dawn looks up at her doctor but squeezes her eyes shut as another contraction seizes her.

"Your baby is losing oxygen," the doctor says in a quiet, calm voice. "We need to take it now."

"What do you mean?" Danny asks. Caroline's heart goes out to him. His eyes are bloodshot, the circles around them dark and deep. He looks like a junkie who has gone hours without a hit. His brown hair sticks up at all angles, from where he has raked his fingers through it, in repeated acts of helplessness.

"We need to do a C-section. The baby can't handle any more—"

"Okay," Dawn answers, even though the doctor is talking to Danny. "Please. Do whatever you have to do. Save the baby."

"Dawn," Danny groans. Caroline feels a surge of helplessness threaten to smother her. Dawn will want to save the baby at all costs. Danny does not want to lose his wife *and* his child.

"Danny, if we're going to do this, we gotta move now."

Danny glances at Dawn. Caroline is moved by the love between them. Dawn wants her baby to live, and Danny loves Dawn enough to give her anything. Caroline squeezes Dawn's hand again, kisses her cheek, and then gives Danny a quick hug. More than anything, she would like to stay there in Danny's arms, both giving strength and taking comfort. Yet, Danny has no comfort to give and no time and Caroline rushes out of the birthing room. Knowing, even though she'd demanded that Dawn believe, that Dawn was going to lose her baby.

Her cell phone vibrates against her leg four times as she paces the waiting room. She knows without checking the caller ID that it is Miles. At the moment, she feels nothing at all for Miles and she has nothing to say to him. Never mind that her best friend is losing her baby right now, if she were to answer, Miles would demand that she come home now. For whatever ignorant reason, he would demand that she leave Dawn and Danny to their grief and come home and tend to him. He has often reminded her that her place is with her husband and her son. Now is not the time for a scene, so Caroline leaves her phone—*which isn't even supposed to be on*—in her pocket.

She does not know how much time has passed when Danny comes for her. And yet she knows, the moment she sees him, that it is not good. She opens her arms to him and takes him to her body and presses her arms tight around him, wishing somehow she could make it better. Hurting for him and for Dawn.

"Danny," she whispers. "Is Dawn okay?"

"She's in recovery," he answers. He shakes his head against her shoulder and then takes a deep breath and lifts his head and looks away.

"I'm so sorry." Sorry does not begin to cover how she feels. She watches Danny, even though she doesn't want to watch him in his grief, and she wonders for just a moment if he begrudges her her own child. What if Dawn and Danny both feel that way? That Caroline should not have been able to have a child, especially since she is trapped in a loveless marriage, with a man who claims to be her master, rather than her mate.

It's not a loveless marriage though. Loveless, maybe, as in possession or fixations. Not hate though. She has never felt that Miles hates her. It might be so much easier if he did. She has never hated Miles, though she has wished time and again that she could. Maybe she will never love Miles the way she once did, but he had given her Max. She can't hate the man who gave her a son.

Danny nods and sighs and then closes his eyes and rubs them.

"Danny. Do you wanna go home and shower? Get some sleep?"

"No." He shakes his head and groans out loud and then opens his eyes to look at her. "No. I need to be with Dawn."

Caroline nods. She had not expected him to say anything different. Her phone vibrates again. She wonders what Miles is thinking. She has never bowed down to him and his demands, and yet, she doesn't *try* to set him off, either.

"Why don't you go home and get some rest?" Danny rubs his hand over his face. He pops his neck and blinks hard and then looks back toward the door he'd come in.

"Can I see Dawn for a sec? Do you mind?"

"'course not," he answers quietly.

Caroline fishes her cell phone out of her pocket as they walk back down the hall to the birthing unit. She flips her phone open, notices that she has messages, and then pushes the button to turn it off. She will deal with Miles later.

They stop at the door to the recovery room. Caroline looks up at Danny and feels the sadness in his eyes boor into her.

"Dawn named her..." Danny's voice is gruff. Caroline winces as he struggles to get the words out. "Dawn named her Marah. Marah Caroline."

Caroline's knees feel weak. The tears on her face are warm, but it feels good to let them fall. It feels good to cry for her best friend's loss. She purses her lips, and draws a quick, short breath through her nose and tries to speak.

"I'm so sorry, Danny."

He nods, and he hugs her and she shakes as this grown man cries out loud, in her arms. She waits patiently for him to find his strength, wondering what sort of broken woman she will find in the recovery room. Dawn had waited so long for this baby, and now instead of cribs and pink receiving blankets and the warmth of her baby asleep in her arms, she will have a small, cold stone with the name Marah Caroline cut into it. Slipping her fingers into the grooves of those letters, no matter how smooth they might become, would never be the same as brushing her fingers over her baby's soft skin.

Caroline wants to be strong for Dawn, but she unravels the second she sees her. She looks so small and so lost in the hospital bed. So pale, Caroline almost wonders where the hospital garb ends and Dawn begins. The only bit of color Caroline sees is Dawn's eyes. The brown eyes she knows so well, and the red lines that tell the story of loss.

"Car—"

Caroline rushes to Dawn's side and lowers the bed rail and carefully, so carefully, she climbs into the bed and lies down beside her. Dawn burrows her head into Caroline's shoulder and cries.

RAPUNZEL

TWENTY-SEVEN

June, 2008

Springfield, IL

Caroline admits to herself, as she towels off, that soaking in the whirlpool tub had been relaxing. Her leg still hurts, but not like it did earlier. She is shaken, though, by the onslaught of memories that had come to her while she soaked, stretched out in the tub, head back and eyes closed. For the first time since the accident, she'd had an entire scene as a memory. Not bits and pieces, but the whole scene of Dawn losing her baby.

She is shaken by the solid memory—by the remembering itself—and by the raw emotion that still fills her. By Dawn's fear that had erupted from her and flowed into Caroline, perhaps where their fingers had intertwined and Dawn had held on so tightly, Caroline's blood had stopped flowing. By the grief that had overwhelmed her when Danny had come to her, and she'd known without a word that the baby had not survived the Cesarean delivery. By the awe and the honor, when Danny had told her Dawn named the baby Marah Caroline.

The urge to comfort and protect, when she'd seen Dawn lying—so still and pale—in the recovery room.

Just one solid memory, and yet it is enough for Caroline to know now, without a doubt, that she and Dawn had once been like sisters. She's keen enough to know there were things that had come between them before the accident, but she knows now that Dawn is on her side.

And yet, there is still a quiver of distrust in her stomach as she dresses in soft, athletic shorts and a plain white t-shirt. She chances a look in the mirror and wonders why, if she knows that Dawn has not lied about how close they were, she still feels that distrust.

Dawn has not lied about how close they were. But maybe Dawn has lied by omission. Something happened before the accident. Caroline had assumed that Dawn had slept with Miles *after* the accident. Now that she knows they were together before the accident, she wonders what else she has made assumptions about that might prove to be wrong.

True to her word, *again*, Caroline can't help but think, Dawn is sprawled across the bed—the bed Caroline has shared with Miles—with a book in her hand. She is not reading, though. The book is propped open, and Dawn's eyes stare at the exposed page, but Caroline *knows* she is not reading.

Dawn looks up when Caroline flips the bathroom light off. A rush of—*jealousy?*—hits Caroline, when she thinks of

Dawn in bed with Miles. Had they made love right here? In Caroline's bed? *Why? Why, if Dawn hated Miles, had she made love to him?*

"Feel any better?" Dawn asks softly. She lets the book drop to the bed, without marking her page. A spy novel. Dawn had always been a mystery reader. Caroline wonders when she switched to espionage and action.

Caroline licks her lips and tips her head a bit to the side. She doesn't know if she feels better—physically, maybe—but her head is still spinning with the questions and the fragmented memories and the need and suspicion. She doesn't know how she feels, so she doesn't give Dawn a real answer. Instead she wanders around the room on unsteady legs.

"When you lost her," she begins, and she doesn't see Dawn sit up to pay attention, but she hears the movement on the bed and she knows Dawn is listening, "I was with you. Miles called me nine times. Left me six messages. Ordering me home. My phone was on vibrate. I knew he was calling. When I was with you in the birthing room, I knew he was calling me." Caroline chews absently on her lower lip. She stops in front of the dresser and stares into the mirror. The woman who stares back at her is a stranger, but for the moment, she knows the woman in the background intimately.

"When they took you to the OR, to do the Cesarean, I went to the waiting room. He called again." Caroline meets Dawn's eyes in the mirror. "I didn't care. I knew he would beat the hell out of me when I got home. For not being home. For ignoring his calls." She shrugs. "It didn't matter. I needed to be there. With you. And Danny."

For a moment, Dawn looks as if she wants to say something, but she takes a sharp, quick breath and waits for Caroline to continue.

"I stayed with you. As long as I could. After...You were so fragile. You looked so fragile, and I was so afraid that if I left you, you would just break and you would be gone and I might never find you again. Maybe I should have left." She raises her eyebrows and looks away from Dawn's eyes, in the mirror, when Dawn shakes her head. "Danny was there. I should have left and given you and Danny that time together."

Dawn shakes her head again. "I needed you."

"Miles told me I overstepped." Caroline sighs. "He met me at the door, and he tore me apart. His words were sometimes worse than his fists. I ignored him. Again. I went to the kitchen, and I started fixing coffee. I don't think I knew what I wanted. I was restless. I wanted to do something for you, but even I knew at that time, I couldn't. I couldn't do anything. But I had to move. I had to do something. So I fixed coffee. And I got a cup out of the cabinet, and all the while he was telling me how stupid I was. He didn't yell. He didn't yell very often. He was dead calm, and he was telling me I was stupid, and that you didn't need me. You needed your husband, and maybe if Danny had taken control of the situation earlier, maybe you wouldn't have lost his child."

Caroline turns away from the mirror to look at the real Dawn. Maybe she is cried out, because while Caroline talks about the night she lost her baby, she is dry-eyed. Her eyes are bright and sharp.

"I was furious. I was so angry with him. It was one thing for him to do it to me. But I wasn't about to let him say something like that about you. Not about you and Danny. I had just seen the truest and deepest of love, and Miles was belittling that, and I was furious. I didn't think. I just reacted. I picked up the cup, and I turned and I threw it. I threw it at him."

Dawn nods, but still she says nothing.

"Hit him in the face and busted his lip open. I think it shocked him. I walked out of the room, and he grabbed me when I walked by him. Told me to get him a wet washrag and some ice. I told him to go to hell, and I left him standing there. He drove himself to the hospital for stitches." Caroline looks around the room. "I came up and showered. And went to bed."

"You didn't tell me that," Dawn says quietly. "You told me you'd fought, and that you'd hit him with the cup and cut him. But you didn't tell me it was about me and Danny."

Caroline stares at Dawn, again wondering how someone so in love with her husband could have willingly gone to bed with a man who respected nothing but himself. Suddenly exhausted all over again, she turns and shuffles to the door.

"Do you remember—"

Caroline shakes her head. "No."

Doesn't matter what Dawn is going to ask her. She remembers Dawn losing her baby. She remembers Danny, even what he looks like and the sound of his voice. And she remembers the way her body had gone taut with anger when she'd thrown the coffee cup at Miles.

She remembers the sounds of a struggle and blue eyes looking back at her in the mirror. She remembers inane things that matter to no one.

She doesn't remember any of the gaps in between.

But somehow she knows there is something sinister lurking just behind the shadows in this house.

RAPUNZEL

TWENTY-EIGHT

June, 2008

Springfield, IL

Caroline awakens to the sensation of being watched. Slowly, she opens her eyes to find herself in the lavender room. Panic washes over her, but she remains calm. Instinctually she knows that somewhere in her past, she'd trained her body to remain calm under Miles' heavy eye. Moments of silence tick by, until the numbers on her digital clock morph and a minute has passed. She hears no one breathing. No one whispering.

Closing her eyes again, she turns her head to the other side of the bed. Slitting one eye open, she sees nothing but the lavender walls and the door to the bedroom wide open. Relieved to see there is no one there, she sighs and sits up, and startles when she sees Max at the foot of her bed.

She lets out a small yelp which makes Max jump and turn to the door.

"Max, wait," she calls. He stops and looks back at her over his shoulder.

"When did you get back?" she asks him. She feels groggy, almost as if she's been drugged. There had been no drugs, of course. After the whirlpool bath and the talk with Dawn, she'd wandered the house aimlessly for what felt like days, and then finally climbed the stairs to this room and collapsed. Sleep had brought shadowy images, ones that Caroline could not make out and still, upon waking, can not decipher.

"Just a little bit ago," Max answers in a small voice.

"Did you have fun?"

It saddens her that she has no idea what to say to this boy. She is desperate to have him here, to talk to him and to attempt to make a connection, whether it is old or new. But at the same time, she doesn't know what to say. She finds herself almost afraid of him.

He nods and smiles, but his eyes seem to accuse her of something, and Caroline is struck with guilt. Does Max remember the things she can't? Sure, he's young, but children tend to remember things. It might be something he represses, something he won't remember until he's nineteen years old and away at college and suddenly he remembers that his father beat his mother, until one night she'd snapped and ran out and ended up taking out a tree with her car.

Or is the guilt just Caroline's imagination running away with her? Maybe all that she has learned from Dawn the past couple of days is weighing so heavily on her that she's projecting it onto Max and feeling guilty where there is no fault.

Perceived guilt or true feeling, there is fault. Miles may be the one who lifts his fists first, but Caroline is just as guilty as he is for any damage Max suffers.

"I missed you," she says softly and she is relieved to realize this is true. She did miss Max. Last night, she'd walked through his room again and sat down on his bed and let her mind go. No pushing or prodding for memories. She hadn't remembered anything, except the sweet little boy on his knees in the lavender room putting the puzzle together. The little boy outside playing with his dog. The little boy she hopes to get to know better.

"I missed you too," he answers.

"Max!"

She jumps when she hears Miles' voice. Luckily, he is calling from downstairs, so Miles does not see her. However, Max does. The smile on his face melts and paints a look of unease across his features.

"Your lunch is ready!"

Lunch? Caroline raises her eyebrows and turns to look again at her clock. It is nearing twelve, noon. She'd slept for a solid ten hours, and she is still tired. She wonders if Miles had come up here to look at her. Goosebumps break out on her skin. She shivers and realizes Max is still watching her.

"Are you hungry?" he says hopefully.

She nods, though she's not hungry. Her stomach feels heavy and full.

"I'm going to take a quick shower, and then I'll be down, okay?"

This time, Max flashes her a genuine smile. She sits for a moment, after he is gone. Why had she come back up here? Why had she chosen to sleep in this room?

'We could make it a library.'

'We don't need a library, Caroline. When would you have the time to read? You're already out of the house four days a week, and you're outside with Max at night. What about the house? When is the last time you cleaned it?'

"Hi."

The voice startles her yet again, but she remains still. Miles' cool green eyes chase away his own voice from her memory.

"Hi."

He doesn't look huge and overbearing and evil, the way her memory has built him up in her mind since he's been gone. Rather, he looks average and worn and a bit sad. He wears brown pants, she wonders why he wouldn't wear shorts when it is hot outside, and a loose fitting button up shirt. It is the middle of summer, and he is ghostly pale. In fact, he looks sick.

"You must have been tired." His words are said with a small smile. Caroline stretches, starts to lift her hands over her head, but stops when she realizes she might call attention to her body. She does not want his hands on her.

"I guess I was." She nods. "Dawn and I went for a ride yesterday." Full disclosure. Make the confession up front, but distort the truth just a little.

"Really?" He steps into her room. "Where?"

Caroline sighs. She has never been an actress, and yet she is now in the role of a lifetime.

"I don't know." She shrugs. "Just around, I guess. I was a little stir crazy here. It was nice to get out for a bit, but it did wear me out."

"Did you remember anything?" He sounds hopeful, but his eyes are flat. He doesn't want her to piece the past back together. It serves him well, broken.

"Not really."

"But something?" he asks quickly. When she looks up at him, she finds him smiling, but again, his eyes are lifeless. She wonders if she told him exactly the things she's remembered so far, if his eyes would change. Would they show fear or anger?

"I remembered that I like chicken salad sandwiches and that we used to watch TV together on Wednesday nights." That came out of the blue, but she sees from the look on his face that she is right.

It takes all of her will power to stay where she is, when he sits on the edge of her bed. She takes a deep breath, through her nose, hoping Miles won't notice.

"Who's downstairs?" she asks him when she hears Max giggling.

"Dawn. She fixed Max his favorite lunch."

“Which is what?” Caroline fights hard to stop the hot flare of jealousy. How long has Dawn been up? What has Dawn said to Miles and Max while she was up here sleeping so deeply, she might have been dead for all they knew?

“Peanut butter and jelly and Bugles and a glass of milk.”

“Bugles?” she repeats. She used to eat Bugles, she remembers. She and her dad would play like they were playing the bugle, or they would put them over their fingertips as if they were long, witchy fingernails. Her mom used to roll her eyes at them.

Miles is suddenly so close she can feel his breath on her face. When she looks up, she is staring into his eyes. Sad, soulful eyes. She in unnerved, but before she can draw back away from him, his fingers slide up her neck and into her hair and his lips brush gently over hers.

“Miles—" she whispers but he kisses her again. A soft, lingering kiss. The air is cold on her wet lips when he pulls away from her.

“I’ve missed you, Caroline.” He stares at her, as if he swallowing her up, memorizing her. “I’ve missed you so much.”

For a moment she has the feeling he doesn’t mean that he’d missed her during the short time he’d been gone. That he means he’s missed her since the coma, and the accident. The violence.

“Miles, I’m not ready—"

“I know you’re not,” he says with a nod. “You don’t remember me. I understand that.”

She watches him stand up and when he turns to leave her room, she climbs out of bed.

"You'll never be ready when you remember either." He sounds sad, but he doesn't look at her. "You'll never want to make love to the bastard I've become to you."

Caroline stares after him, completely thrown by his last comment.

She does remember the bastard he was, and she doesn't want his hands on her. She doesn't want the intimacy with him. All that she wants is to take Max and get the hell away from him.

Except that his kiss today was so gentle. Tender. Tender, like the man she'd first met.

It isn't his kiss that makes her double over and vomit when she strips down to get in the shower. Not his kiss, but the way her body had reacted.

BEAUTY & THE BEAST

TWENTY-NINE

2005

Springfield, IL

"What're you thinking about?"

Caroline lays her head back on the swing and closes her eyes. The heat of the day has fallen away and a gentle breeze dusts her bare limbs. Indian Summer is upon them, but the forecast is calling for crisp autumn temperatures to creep up on them within the next day or two. Caroline is ready for the change. It is hot, but not necessarily hot enough to turn the air on in the house. And yet, with cleaning out the rooms on the third floor and her hopes to paint and redecorate, it is hotter than hell through the day.

The beer bottle she is drinking from dangles from her fingers. She lifts it and takes another drink.

"What?" she says with a tired laugh. "My thoughts aren't even worth a penny to you?"

She knows as she says it that she is likely to set him off. It has been a quiet, peaceful evening. Max is in bed now, but earlier they had all gone for a walk together, Max in his stroller. Miles has been quiet, not the stewing and brooding quiet, but comfortably quiet. She's not sure why she would take the gamble now, and say something that could likely add another bruise to her body. But she doesn't regret the words. Miles might beat the hell out of her on a regular basis, but he has never taken away the core of who she is.

"How about a quarter?"

She cracks an eye open to look at him and laughs when she sees the goofy grin on his face. "Can you afford that?"

"Of course I can, for you."

"Okay."

Still, she isn't inclined to talk. She is thinking about Beth, and Beth has never been a good subject between them.

"So? What are you thinking about?" He leans toward her. "Something serious, because you have that line between your eyebrows."

She moans softly when his fingertip trances the worry line between her eyebrows.

"Just thinking about Beth."

Now is when he'll blow up. Throw her off the swing, maybe. She wouldn't put it past him, after the night he'd "forgotten" he had a knife in his hand and taken a swing at her. The blade of the hunting knife—she'd never known why Miles had a collection of hunting knives and guns, when he was not a hunter—had slashed through her skin.

In her chest and on into her arm. He'd been apologetic—as never before—and grabbed Max, who was too small to understand what was going on, and rushed her to the hospital for stitches. He'd begged her forgiveness, which she'd granted, but she'd never believed it had been an accident. He preferred his fists when it came to hurting her, but Caroline didn't believe that he would hesitate to use a knife or any other handy tool on her again.

Punishment. Threat. Bodily harm. He'd never plunge a knife so far inside her, he couldn't bring her back to torture her more. She knows he would never go that far, but she doubts there are boundaries in his mind when it comes to punishing or threatening her.

"What about Beth?" he asks her quietly.

"I still don't understand how she died."

"Honey, drunk drivers kill themselves and other people all the time." His voice is patient, but his answer still irritates her.

She shakes her head. "You never knew Beth the way Dawn and I did. She just didn't drink that much."

"Everyone gets drunk now and then, whether they drink a lot or not. She had a lot on her mind. She was probably still stung about you two, and she was celebrating graduation. I'm sure she drank too much. It probably didn't even take that much."

"Don't you think it's odd that they didn't do an autopsy?"

Miles considers her question carefully. "Yeah. I guess that is odd. I'd think they'd have wanted to know what her blood alcohol level was."

Caroline nods. "You know what I keep wondering?"

"What?"

"What if someone drugged her?"

"You mean like a date rape drug?" Miles looks at her sharply.

"Yeah."

"I don't think she'd have been able to get to her car to drive."

"Something that takes a little time to have an effect?"

"I don't know, Car," Miles says softly. He shakes his head. "I don't know anything about drugs."

"I guess I just can't accept how she died." Caroline shrugs and sits up straight. The swing stops its gentle sway as she sits forward and plants her feet firmly on the porch floor. "Even now, I still feel guilty about it. And I miss her."

She buries her face in her hands and then sighs in pleasure as Miles slides his hands over her back and begins to work at the tension in her shoulders. There is no sound for what seems an eternity as Miles squeezes and rubs the pain away. She doesn't fight him when he slips his hand under her shirt tail and around to her stomach.

"Do you think we can make love out here? On the swing?"

"I think it would hurt my knees," she giggles.

"Yeah? What'dya say we try it?"

"Easy for you to say. You won't be the one with black and blue knees."

Caroline winces inwardly. Black and blue. There is always something on her body that is black and blue, and now is not the time to draw Miles' mind to it.

"I love you, Caroline Wolfe."

Expecting him to be angry, Caroline is caught off guard by his words. She sits up straight again and turns to straddle his lap. At least black and blue knees would be easier to explain, should anyone ask.

RAPUNZEL

THIRTY

June, 2008

Springfield, IL

The sun is bright enough to give her a headache, and the late afternoon air is thick against her skin. With a hand up over her eyes to block the sun, she watches Miles and Max toss a football back and forth. Skipper, unimpressed with the football, lays in a heap under the nearest shade tree, eyes closed, tail twitching now and then.

Dawn had gone home earlier, when Caroline had come downstairs. Miles had pretended to read the paper, but Caroline had known he was watching them, deciding what might have passed between them while he was gone. Though she and Dawn had gained ground, Caroline had not had to act as if she felt funny around Dawn. Waking up past noon and hearing her son giggle with the woman had grabbed her up and dropped her in another reality. One where it seemed entirely possible that Dawn and Miles were together, raising the child she had given birth to.

There was no place for Caroline in that reality. Stomach churning, though she'd just been ill earlier, Caroline had poured herself a glass of juice and sipped at it. Dawn had stood from the table, where she sat with Miles and Max, *her* family, dropped a kiss on Max's head and said goodbye to Miles. She'd turned stiffly to Caroline and opened her mouth—to say something other than the "see ya, Caroline" that had popped out—(Caroline could see it in her eyes that she wanted to say more) and then she was gone.

Miles had insisted on fixing breakfast for Caroline. The thought of grease or syrup on her stomach made her feel even worse. When Miles had reminded her that she needed to eat to keep her strength for recovering from the accident, she'd agreed to eat a chicken sandwich and a small salad. Caroline had almost felt normal, almost *relaxed*, while she ate. Miles and Max sat with her at the kitchen table. At first she'd had to fight the deluge of memories of the past couple of days with Dawn, all the words that had been said between them that could not be shared with Miles. But Max had been chatty, and he'd told them both about the movie his Grandmother had taken him to, while he and Miles had been away. Caroline wondered briefly about her mother-in-law. What would this woman say if she knew her son had abused her from the time they had gotten married? What would her *own* mother say?

After Caroline had eaten and Miles had cleaned the kitchen, insisting that she sit and rest, the three of them had gone outside. Miles suggested a walk, which had sounded wonderful to Caroline. The heat had yet to hit her, and she was still hungry for fresh air. Max had asked if he could ride his bike while they walked. It had been a long walk, but Caroline didn't feel bad now. The only thing that bothered her now was that Miles had reached out and taken her hand as they walked. His fingers had gently intertwined with hers and touched the back of her hand in soft, whispery strokes.

First the kiss earlier in the lavender room. And then the hand holding. Granted, Miles had not forced himself on her, but she didn't like the way things were going. She certainly didn't like the way her body wanted to react whenever he touched her. He was still a good-looking man, although she is sure he's aged since she first met him. There is something so downtrodden about him right now that appeals to her, as if he's finally understood what he's done to her all these years and he feels genuine regret. Maybe that's what is calling to her, maybe that's what is sparking that tingle low in her belly whenever his fingers trail over her skin. Or maybe, despite the violence, they'd had an explosive sex life and her body remembers what her mind and heart won't.

Whatever the case, there is still a whisper inside her that gets a little louder each day. She has to get away from Miles Wolfe, dead or alive.

As Caroline watches the men in the life she doesn't remember, she wonders yet again what is going on with Miles and Dawn. Is it just as Dawn says? Does Miles have Dawn under his thumb with his threat over them sleeping together? Is Dawn honestly here for her and scared for her life at the same time? Caroline can believe that; it's not a stretch of her imagination whatsoever to believe that Dawn might really fear for her life.

And yet, it's not a stretch of her imagination either, for her to picture Max asleep in his bed this morning—she still doesn't know exactly what time Miles and Max had come home—and Dawn and Miles making love in the master bedroom or the living room or on the swing on the front porch.

At this thought, Caroline turns her head and looks around. The grass has gone from a lush green to the dried out almost colorless brown that late summer and no rain always brings. The brick house is vivid against the dead grass and the deep blue sky. Caroline glances up toward her window, the window of the lavender room.

Her eyes are drawn away, though, and instead she focuses on the window next to it. The window of the room next to hers. The room Dawn had said had at one time been Miles' office.

Michael Ramsay.

Caroline cringes at the thought and the headache it brings. Who in the hell is Michael Ramsay?

Cold chills flush over her, the kind she gets when it's ninety-nine degrees outside and she gets into a blazing hot car and turns the air on. Uncomfortable. Almost enough to make her sick.

The shadowy images of her dream sharpen suddenly in her mind. The window. The door. Caroline had been walking in the yard, looking up at *that* window or starting down the stairs, looking at *that* door over and over and over in her dreams.

RAPUNZEL

THIRTY-ONE

July, 2008

Springfield, IL

Caroline nudges the porch floor with her toe, and the swing sways gently. There is no breeze today, and the thick August humidity blankets her and Dawn. The rhythmic screech of the swing is the only sound. Neither Caroline nor Dawn has the energy to say much.

Caroline studies her legs. Still a pasty white, even after she has been allowed to come outside. She can't stand the oppressive heat, and the sun hurts so much, it feels as if the top of her head might blow off. Had she been one to lie outside and soak up the sun? She can't imagine it now, and yet, she is so tired of looking different. Of looking sickly and pale and fragile.

"What're you doing?" Dawn asks when Caroline stands up.

Caroline sits on the steps of the porch and stretches her legs out in front of her.

"I need some color," she finally answers Dawn.

"By this time of the summer, you're normally darker than me."

Caroline looks up as Dawn joins her on the steps.

"I can't imagine. I hate this heat, and the sun just kills me." She squints up at the sky, but looks away quickly.

"Maybe it's from the accident," Dawn suggests.

"Maybe it's from being kept inside for nearly a year."

"You could do a tanning bed—"

Caroline laughs before she knows she is going to say anything. "And watch Miles have a rage stroke?" The memory is vivid in her mind. Miles never wanted her to be in the sun, much less in a tanning bed. He had always insisted that her skin was beautiful, that she had the perfect peaches and cream complexion of a fairytale princess. She'd tanned one time in a sun bed and rather than sporting a healthy glow, she'd been black and blue for the following week or two. It had never been worth it to her, to argue that one however, she'd told him flat out that he would not keep her inside. She was outside all the time in tank tops and swimsuits playing with Max or working in the yard.

"He didn't like that, did he?" Dawn frowns. "I'd forgotten that."

Caroline sighs and finger combs her hair away from her face.

"Why don't we do a spa day, Caroline?"

"What?"

"You and me. Let's take a day and do facials and pedicures and manicures. Get our hair done."

She almost says that she doesn't want to, because she suddenly remembers how Miles always insisted she do those things. Not for the relaxation, but because his wife needed a certain look. And yet, Caroline has always liked pampering herself, and in spite of Miles' directives, she has always been proud and neat and the thought of doing something about her appearance, her *character* appeals to her.

"Okay."

Dawn smiles her first true smile of the day. They have not seen each other for a few days. Caroline has been at the house alone or with Max for most of those two days. She's enjoyed being with him, playing games and reading to him. As with Dawn, she doesn't specifically remember Max, but she's begun to feel in her heart and soul that he belongs to her.

Miles had taken them out for dinner the night before. Just the three of them. They'd sat outside on the patio of a mom and pop restaurant Miles said they used to come to often. Caroline had been surprised. From what she knew of Miles at the moment, she would have expected him to frequent fancier, upscale restaurants.

He'd kissed her goodnight. He'd been kissing her goodnight now since he and Max had come home. Just soft, chaste kisses. But last night, his lips had lingered over hers and his hands had settled on her waist, and he pulled just enough to rub her middle against his. It had scared her. One of these nights, he was going to push her. Either insist in his irritatingly matter-of-fact way that he had the right to touch her because he was her husband or force himself on her the way he'd done so many times in the past. She wasn't ready for either scenario.

"Do you know where he moved it to?" she asks Dawn now.

"Moved what to?" Dawn stretches her legs out too. Caroline is struck again by what a pretty woman she is and the fear that maybe she and Miles are lovers.

But why? Why would they do that to her? If Miles wants Dawn, why not just divorce her and do what he wants? It hurt to think that Dawn, her *best friend* would do that to her, but she wouldn't care if Miles found someone else.

"Do you know where he moved his office?"

Dawn turns and gives Caroline her full attention. "No. Why?"

Caroline groans and shakes her head. "I don't know. God, maybe it's nothing, but there's something about that room that's driving me crazy."

"The room by...your room?"

Caroline nods. "You said it was Miles' office."

"It was."

"I keep having dreams about that room."

"What do you mean? Why don't you just ask Miles?"

"Dreams. I'm outside, and someone is in that room

watching me. I just keep seeing that window." Caroline shivers.

"You think someone is in there now spying on you?"

"No." Caroline sits up straight and bends her legs again. She rests her elbows on her knees. "It's something from before."

"Someone was watching you before the accident?"

"I don't know if someone was ever really watching me. There's just something about that room that's really bothering me."

"Can I ask you something?" Dawn's question is spoken so quietly, Caroline knows she is about to drop a bomb.

"What?"

"Have you and Miles made love? Since the accident? Since you...woke up..."

Caroline studies Dawn's face, wondering why in the hell Dawn would ask her that. Jealousy? Does Dawn want Miles for her own?

"How many times did you sleep with him, Dawn?"

"One night."

Dawn purses her lips and raises her eyebrows.

"Because sometimes you guys seem pretty cozy together."

"Thanks, Caroline," Dawn whispers. "It's nice to know you believe in me."

"You've already told me you slept with him once. What's to

believe in? You cross that kind of line once, I'd think you could cross it often."

"Danny and I tried for so long to have a baby." She doesn't look at Caroline. "And then when I finally did get pregnant..."

Caroline lays her hand on Dawn's arm, but Dawn shakes her touch off. She stares straight ahead, but Caroline can see the tears on her face.

"We lost our baby..." Dawn shrugs, as if she is saying it isn't important, but Caroline knows how important it really is. "I was so low, Car. I just wanted to die. Danny was working one night. He was at the firehouse. Miles came by. Said you'd asked him to check on me before he went home. I hated him, Caroline. I'd hated him for so long. I hated how he was such a bastard to you, and I hated that he could still turn on the charm and make people like him."

Caroline wants to say something, but the things she wants to say would only hurt Dawn so she remains quiet.

"He was getting ready to leave. Hugged me goodbye. And I asked him to stay. Just...I just asked him to stay for a drink. I don't know. I guess I thought I could fix him dinner, just so I wouldn't have to be alone. I hated being alone. I always thought I could hear Marah crying, and I thought I was going insane. I actually caught myself going to her nursery a couple of times to pick her up. And then I'd remember."

"Did he come on to you?"

"Yes. But he would tell you I came on to him."

"To save his ass," Caroline mumbles with a shrug.

Dawn nods her agreement. “We had a glass of wine. If you questioned him, he would tell you that my offering him a glass of wine was my way of saying I wanted to be with him that way. But he sat next to me on the sofa. He put his arm around me. Kept telling me it was okay to let go, that I could cry. He kissed me. One thing led to another.”

“Let me guess,” Caroline says softly. “As he kissed you and undressed you, he told you that he would give you a baby. And you could pretend it was Danny’s, and no one would ever have to know.”

“Was I that stupid to believe him?”

Caroline glances at Dawn and feels instantly trapped in her gaze.

“No. It just sounds like something Miles would say.”

“Sometimes,” Dawn whispers, “When you look at him, I’d swear you remember him. And you’re still in love with him.”

Caroline blows out a long, tired sigh and tries to compose herself. “Sometimes when I look at him, I *do* remember him. And I remember being in love with him. I remember being in love with him, despite all of it.”

“But?”

“But I also know that something happened. Something woke me up, Dawn, to who he really is.”

“What?”

Caroline shakes her head. “I don’t know. I don’t remember that.”

"I think you should leave him." Dawn stands up suddenly and keeps her back to Caroline. Again Caroline wonders about the true nature of Dawn and Miles' relationship.

"I know I need to leave him." Caroline's voice is steady, though her stomach is in knots. "But I need to know everything I can before I walk out the door. I need to remember everything first. So I have a chance to survive."

That's the trouble though. Caroline is pretty sure the answers are locked up in Miles' office, and now she doesn't even know where to find Miles' office.

"You still need to look at the pictures," Dawn reminds her. She turns around and looks down at her, and in that moment, Caroline feels the trust that's begun to develop between them.

"I know, but I feel better doing that when he's out of town."

"Does he have any plans to go out of town again?"

Caroline shrugs and tosses her hands up. "How the hell should I know? He didn't tell me the last time he went out of town."

"Right."

"And to answer your question," Caroline pushes herself up to stand beside Dawn, "No. I haven't been with him since the accident. I have no desire to be that close to him again."

Dawn nods and looks around the yard in front of them. It's just two in the afternoon, but Caroline knows Dawn feels that same suspicious feeling that Miles could pop out of nowhere and hear what they are saying.

"Did Danny ever know?"

"What?"

"When I first realized you'd slept with Miles, I assumed it was after Danny was gone. I assumed it was a natural thing for you two to do, since I was in a coma and Danny was dead." Caroline laughs, but the sound is hollow. "Did Danny ever know? That you were with Miles?"

"I never told him," Dawn whispers. "If that's what you're asking."

"Good." Caroline nods. "That kind of confession usually does more harm than good."

RAPUNZEL

THIRTY-TWO

July, 2008

Springfield, IL

Caroline studies the walls of the library one by one. Looking for what, she has no idea. It's not as if she expects to find a lever for a secret door. She stretches her legs out on the sofa and continues to stare at the walls. Miles is a business man. What sort of business he does she doesn't really know, but he is a business man and business men have files and papers and computers. All of Miles' things had been in that office upstairs, and now, after the accident, everything has been removed from that room.

The room—rather the windows and door of that room—seem to haunt her. She doesn't believe there are dead bodies locked away in the closet, and she doesn't believe that there are malevolent spirits there that are angry with her for whatever reason.

There is a rational explanation as to why that room is bothering her. But trying to remember has begun to feel a little like banging her head against a wall of bricks.

She's a little bit afraid to remember what she's forgotten. Seems like remembering that her husband beat her, that she fought him, that they had a violent marriage should be enough for one woman to handle. What more could there be?

Something.

All day she's been bombarded with bits and pieces of memory and none of them seem to fall together neatly. She's had flashes of memory involving Beth and Dawn and school and her parents and her childhood bedroom. She's been seeing a house, with huge orange flames leaping out of the roof and Max sitting on Dawn and Danny's porch swing. Even the flashes of memory involving Beth and Dawn and school aren't falling into place. She remembers going with Beth on a spa day, for Beth's birthday, she thinks. Getting their nails done and getting her hair cut. Beth telling her about a guy, but Caroline can't remember who the guy was and if Beth had a thing for him or if she worked with him. She's remembered Dawn's pregnancy scare, but from there her memory keeps jumping to that house with the flames.

Her head hurts. A dull throb had started just behind her eyes at least an hour ago. But she'd been so intent on pulling the memories into focus that she hadn't paid attention to the headache, and in fact, had probably made it worse. Is this natural? Yes, she'd been in a car accident and had been knocked unconscious. But according to Dawn, she didn't have any serious brain injury. She'd spent eight months in a coma, apparently letting her brain recover from the trauma, but there was supposedly no lasting damage. So why the hell couldn't she remember?

And the question that has suddenly become so huge that it takes her breath away each time she thinks it:

If she could look in a mirror and *see her own face*, would she remember everything? Had Miles won after all? Had he stripped her of her truest self, by taking away her physical self?

"Caroline."

Her heart jumps, but she is careful not to react to Miles' voice. She looks up at him as he steps into the library. It is late afternoon. Dawn has been gone for hours, and Max had played so hard outside he had fallen asleep after a snack. Sitting here in the library, pushing herself through mental exercises, hoping to get a grip on at least one of these memory fragments, Caroline has lot track of time.

"Are you alright? Why are you sitting in the dark?"

How can he be so solicitous now, when he'd nearly driven her to kill herself not quite a year ago? How can that compassionate face twist into such rage when he swings his fists at her? She is not the first woman to have fallen in love with a man like Miles. But she will not be another statistic. She will get away from him, and she'll take Max with her.

"I'm fine," she answers quietly. "Max fell asleep, so I came in here to relax. Guess I lost track of time."

Miles turns on the lamp behind her and sits beside her on the couch.

"I fixed dinner." He reaches for her hand and strokes his thumb over the back of her fingers. His green eyes search her face. She wonders if this will be the night. Will he push her? Will he rape her when she says no?

Solicitous or not, she knows that eventually Miles will swing at her again. Men like Miles don't change without a lot of counseling and sometimes, maybe never.

"Look, Miles," she pulls her hand away from him, "I know what you're trying to do...fixing dinner and taking me out and walking with me and..." She shakes her head, but she stops. Her throat aches with visions she can't remember and words she is afraid to say. It hurts her to admit that, even to herself. In her heart, she knows she has never been afraid of Miles. She's been angry with him, yes, and she has hated him fifteen ways from Sunday. But she's never been afraid of him.

Right now, she is afraid of him. Because he has the upper hand. She's at a distinct disadvantage right now, because he's cleared her card, and she knows nothing except what he is willing to tell her. She is unarmed and vulnerable.

"What am I trying to do, Caroline?"

She turns her head slightly as he traces his thumb along the line of her jaw.

"You've been very kind. Very patient. But I can't do this. I don't remember you well enough, and I'm not ready to make love to you."

A lie of sorts, but she knows he won't see through her. In truth, though she doesn't remember everything, she remembers well enough to know she *can't* make love to him.

"I'm not trying to pressure you." He drops his hand, but he keeps his eyes trained on her. "I just want to take care of you. I love you."

Somehow, Caroline believes him. He does love her, but she thinks love means something entirely different to him than it does to her. And most other people.

"Are you hungry?"

She's not, but she can't tell him that. Instead she answers with a small nod.

"Can I ask you something?"

"What?" She turns to look at him, curious as to what *he might ask her.*

"Do you remember Dawn?"

"Sort of."

He nods. "C'mon. Let's have dinner."

He walks with his arm around her and leads her to the kitchen. Caroline tries not to flinch when those same memories come to her as she walks down the hall to the kitchen. Miles screaming at her that she will clean the library and that she should be sleeping with him. The pictures hanging in the hallway. The walls, a different color.

It's so disconcerting, it's as if someone is pointing a remote control at her and constantly changing channels. As if there are other lives going on in her head that have nothing at all to do with her.

He pulls her chair out for her and pours her a glass of wine. She eyes it suspiciously and again wonders if he will rape her tonight. Of course she'll fight him, but she's not very strong right now. Miles is not a big man, but he is surprisingly strong.

"I'll get Max and be right back," he tells her.

She won't drink the wine. One glass might be enough to take her over the edge, if she hasn't touched alcohol in nearly a year. Especially in her condition. She thinks about pouring some out in the sink, but Miles would notice there is too much gone.

A minute later, he appears carrying Max on his back. Max rubs his eyes and rewards Caroline with a sleepy grin.

"Hey Buddy." She fingers the stem of her wine glass, just to make it look as if she intends to drink it.

"Max." The boy is suddenly solemn as Miles lets him down and directs him to his chair. Caroline glances at Miles to see a scowl on his face. Apparently she'd made a mistake in calling her son Buddy.

"Did you have a good nap?" She chooses to ignore her blunder and their reaction. From the way Max had gone quiet, she assumes Miles has read her the riot act for this before.

Max grins. "Dad, we played hide and go seek today."

"Who did?" Miles asks as he brings Caroline's dinner plate to the table. Grilled fish and steamed vegetables. Caroline has to admit it looks good.

Max glances at her and stumbles over his words. "Mom—me and her did. We played hide and seek outside."

Caroline presses her lips together. Her son can't call her Mommy. Because she doesn't look like Mommy. As much as it hurts her, she doesn't blame him. His world has been ripped at the seams, and he's much too young to understand or put it back together. Caroline *is* an adult, and *she* can't figure any of it out.

"Max, you say Mom and I played hide and seek," Miles corrects him, but Caroline thinks he is correcting his grammar, rather than making Max call her Mommy.

"It was fun. Skipper played too, but he got hot right away."

"Retired to his shade tree, did he?" Miles asks as he sets Max's and his own plate on the table. "And what're you doing tomorrow?"

Max looks at Caroline. She shakes her head when she sees Miles looking at her.

"I don't know." She wonders if she used to plan every day with Max, or if the two of them just got up and did things on the spur of the moment. She'd like to think she was a fun, spontaneous mom, but she suspects that Miles would not approve and that she was probably a very organized, plan ahead kind of mom.

"If you don't mind, Caroline, I'd like to take the day off work."

She hopes he doesn't see the way she cringes. The weekends are hard enough. Tiptoeing around the house, trying to avoid Miles is exhausting.

She stares at him, afraid to answer him. Afraid the wrong words will slip out, or that her tone will betray her.

“School will be starting soon—"

“School?”

“Max will be five next week,” Miles tells her.

Caroline looks at Max, who grins at the mention of his birthday. Her son will be five next week, and she’d had no idea. No one had given her the heads up about this. She had no memories of conceiving him or carrying him or giving birth to him.

“He’ll be starting kindergarten after Labor Day.” Miles takes a sip of his wine. “Mm...Perfect. Try your wine, Caroline, you’ll love it.”

Obediently, Caroline picks up her glass and tips it just enough for the wine to touch her lips. She pretends to swallow and licks her lips. The wine is good. Dry red, just as she likes it. And yet, she won’t drink it.

“Do you like it?” Miles asks. He smiles at her, and Caroline finds him cold that he is discussing wine after dropping the bomb that her son’s birthday is next week.

“It’s good.” She nods. Tonight is a night when he could hit her. She’s very aware of this as she sits at the table. Tonight he has that look in his eye, so she will sit quietly and not argue, because she would like to spare Max any more trauma.

“So Max will start kindergarten.”

“That’s incredible, Max,” she whispers and looks at him. “Are you excited?”

He nods, and his grin is ninety-nine percent excited and one percent scared.

"I'd like to spend the day with Max tomorrow. I thought we could go swimming, Max."

Caroline nods, but her mind is whirling. Miles wants to spend the day with Max. Not with the two of them. Wouldn't a normal family spend the day together? But they'd never been a normal family, had they? Not from the moment she'd said 'I do' had anything been normal.

Miles is taking Max for the day. As much as she loves being with Max, when Miles is gone, Caroline's palms sweat at the thought of going to Dawn's house. Seeing the pictures. Pictures of her son. Her baby. Pictures of herself, pregnant with this little boy.

"Is that okay with you?" Miles asks her. She knows he is just asking for Max's benefit. If she were to tell him no, that she had plans to take Max shopping for school supplies or to take him to the park or just to stay here and bake cupcakes with him, Miles would backhand her and possibly knock the wineglass over in the process. There would be blood, broken glass and spilled wine.

"It's fine," she answers, but she tries not to sound excited or relieved.

"What will you do all day?"

Why does he constantly ask her that? What is it that she might do that threatens him? Is it the pictures? Has it crossed his mind that Dawn might show her pictures of the past?

She shakes her head, but she remembers suddenly that Miles does not approve of idleness. He used to tell her there is always something she should be doing. He should never find her being lazy just as he had earlier before dinner.

“Actually, Dawn mentioned going to a spa. Getting our nails done. Facials.”

She takes a bite of the fish. It is spicy and actually quite good, but she is not hungry. Her stomach is twisted in knots, and eating is not going to help.

“That’s a great idea.”

He is still watching her closely, so she smiles and picks up her glass and takes a small sip of the wine.

RAPUNZEL

THIRTY-THREE

July, 2008

Springfield, IL

Nightmares get the best of her, so she is up before dawn.

At least, she assumes they are nightmares. She wishes for a robe, as she quickly shimmies into a t-shirt and a pair of sweatpants. Miles keeps the house cool, and usually she likes that, but right now she is freezing.

Which, she assumes, has more to do with the nightmares or whatever the visions are, than the actual temperature in the house. She hates being in this generic, lavender room, although she is nowhere near ready to go back to the master bedroom. In fact, she will never share a bed with Miles again. There are plenty of other rooms in the house. Maybe this one would be okay if she had her own belongings up here. More of her clothes. A robe. Books. Makeup. Pictures.

It is four-thirty when she opens her door and steps into the hallway.

A lock, she thinks as she pulls her door closed. This room might not be so bad if she could lock the door from the *inside.* She intends to go downstairs and make coffee. Since first waking up here in the lavender prison, she has come to crave the smell of coffee. The first drink. She is surprised Miles has it in the house. He does not drink coffee, and she knows he had once forbidden her. He had told her she would drink tea, as he did, or she would drink no hot beverage.

'You and Earl Grey can both go to hell. I'll drink what I want to drink.'

He'd grabbed her wrist and twisted it up behind her back, but he'd let go when she'd dropped his idiotic, dainty teapot and it shattered on the tile floor.

Caroline stops now, with one hand on the banister and looks at the closed door next to hers. She glances down the stairway. Miles is most likely in bed. He is usually up around six on a work day, but today, he might sleep a little later, since he is spending the day with Max.

There's nothing in the room. Before Miles had gone to Chicago, before Dawn had told her it had once been Miles' office, there had been nothing in that room. Nothing has magically appeared in there. And yet, she *has* to open the door.

She draws her hand away from the banister and takes a small step toward the door. The house is old, but Caroline has gotten used to the creaks and cracks it makes. Miles has to be as familiar, if not more familiar, with the noises of the house. If he is awake, he will hear her walking around up here.

She doesn't recognize her own hand as it reaches out to touch the doorknob. It is one of those old fashioned jeweled knobs, like a huge diamond. Cold to the touch. Caroline slowly twists it. A little bit at a time.

She stops to listen for a moment. Nothing. Not even the central air conditioning is running. The silence is like a heartbeat pounding in her ears. Her fingers, cold and sweaty now, turn the knob a little bit more.

Locked.

The door is locked.

Caroline lays her other hand against the wooden door itself. She takes a deep breath and wonders, just for a moment, if she's losing her mind. If this is all a game they are playing, Miles, Dawn and herself, them trying to push her over the edge. And yet, it doesn't make sense.

If Miles wants out of the marriage, he could divorce her. If he wants Dawn, he could divorce her and go to Dawn.

Or he could just kill her.

There is just no point in him creating this elaborate scheme to make her think she is losing her mind. Unless he's pure evil.

Caroline lets her hands fall away from the door. She needs coffee. Maybe the dreams are getting to her. The nightmares. The visions of that house, with the flames reaching for the black sky. The fire trucks. She has to be pulling real memories and stories together and making her own nightmares that much more vivid. It is surreal to be up, alone in this huge house, after the dreams like she's had.

Still careful not to wake Miles or Max, Caroline makes her way down the steps to the second floor. She almost goes on, but something stops her. Is Miles in bed? What if he was upstairs? In the room next to her own? What if he had spy equipment in that room, and he watched her all the time?

Paranoid. She shakes her head and shuffles a step down the hall. Toward the master bedroom. Too much noise. This time, she tiptoes. She glances into Max's room and sees him sprawled out on his stomach, one arm curled up under his pillow. She could go in and sit down in the rocker and watch him sleep. It would be peaceful and safe.

Safe.

Will she ever truly feel safe again? Never, inside this house.

Three more steps and she is at the door of the master bedroom. What will she do if the door is closed? She can't open it. What if it made noise? What if she woke Miles? He might think she is coming to him, to his bed. No. She won't open the door. But. What if he's not there? What if he's not in the master bed? Does that mean he's in that other room? Upstairs? Near where she sleeps?

And what if...she takes a deep breath. What if he's awake, just waiting for her to appear in his doorway? What if he's heard every step she's taken and he's waiting?

Doesn't matter. She has to know. She has to see him lying there, in his bed, asleep. Nothing matters right at this moment like seeing Miles in a vulnerable state.

The door is open. Caroline takes another breath, wraps her fingers around the door trim and leans just enough to peek into the room. Miles is spread out, taking up the whole bed, like a little kid. He is sound asleep, his hair mussed and almost endearing. Caroline fights a sudden need to go to him and brush his hair from his face. If she wakes him now, he will mistake her intentions.

For a moment, she sees herself in the bed. With him. She thinks it is just conjecture, a fantasy of sorts presented by her mind. But when Miles climbs over her body and straddles her and then wraps his hands around her neck, she realizes she is remembering. There were nights he'd tried to kill her. She doesn't know if she was too stupid to get that when he'd done it, but she sees it ever so clearly now.

Hands trembling, she tiptoes quickly away from the room and back to the stairs. On weak knees, she rushes down the last of the stairs and nearly loses her balance. She catches herself but not without a bit of commotion.

"Shit."

She hurries to the kitchen and with hands still shaking, she makes a pot of coffee and silently wills it to brew faster.

She'd thought she was safe from that ultimate betrayal. She'd assumed that though Miles had beat her and that it would never stop, that he'd never kill her. She was a play thing to him. A shiny, sexy play thing that he lusted after and loved the way a predator loved his prey.

When the coffee is ready, she pours herself a cup and drinks it black. Every day she spends in this house is a day too long. Means and opportunity. And a destination. She needs money. And she needs Miles to go on a business trip or on another visit to his parents' house. And she needs to grab her son and get the hell out.

"Good morning."

She jumps and turns to look at him. Hot coffee splashes over the rim of her cup. He is smiling, but he hurries to her when he sees that he's scared her.

"Did that burn you? Are you okay?" he asks her.

She nods and then shakes her head and tries to turn away from him when he takes her cup from her and sets it on the counter.

"I was dreaming of you," he tells her as he slides his arms around her and presses her against him. She feels the remainder of his dream against her, and she struggles not to shudder at his touch. His breath is hot in her ear. His hands slide under her t-shirt, and instantly she realizes her mistake. She had not put on her bra, she'd just thrown on whatever she could find to make coffee before she showered.

He draws back to look at her, and she forces a smile, which fades as he covers it with his own. She tastes his toothpaste as his tongue traces her lip. He hadn't pushed this last night, not even after getting her to drink half the glass of wine. Apparently he feels he needs to be rewarded for his gallantry.

Caroline squeezes her eyes shut and tells herself to think of something else. Take yourself away from it, she thinks.

His fingers are cold, but soft on her skin.

'What are you doing?'

Caroline, sitting comfortably at the kitchen table, feet up on the next chair, looks up at him. She glances at the paperback in her hands and then at the cup of coffee on the table.

'Reading. Waiting for Max—"

'My wife will not read trashy novels.'

Before she can move, he grabs a handful of her hair and pulls quick and sharp.

'It's not a trashy novel, Miles. It's Wuthering Heights.'

'There are dishes to do. And I tracked snow in on the tile last night. Get your ass up and mop it. If I catch you wasting time—'

Caroline swallows hard when his hands slide up to cup her breasts.

'Get your hands off me—'

Miles lets go of her hair, only to throw his hand across her face. She doesn't wince or cover her face in shame or fear.

'You made the mess in the foyer, you mop it up—'

"Stop it!" She shoves him backwards when he tries to stroke her breasts. "Get the hell away from me, and keep your hands off me, you son-of-a-bitch."

He stumbles backwards and the middle of his back collides with the island. She waits, ready for him to come back at her. Her whole body shakes violently. She can still feel his hands on her. His erection against her middle.

"I'm sorry."

She narrows her eyes at him, still ready to lash out if he steps toward her.

"Caroline, forgive me. I was dreaming about making love to you, and I heard you down here. I got carried away."

Caroline is desperate now to get upstairs. To the shower. To scrub her body where he touched her. But she is afraid to walk past him. To turn her back to him.

"Please?" he whispers. He slides down the island to the end, and then steps backward. "I'm sorry. I'll leave you alone. Just please forgive me?"

Still, she doesn't answer him. She watches without a word as he leaves the kitchen. When she hears him in the bathroom, she slumps against the counter and lets the trembling take over.

She reaches for the phone and knocks the cordless handset over. Nearly knocks it to the floor. Her fingers feel fat and useless as she dials Dawn's number.

She hangs up just before it rings. Dawn had told her she'd never come crying to her about anything Miles did to her. Damned if she'd start now.

Instead she takes her coffee and the phone and she goes outside to sit on the patio. She still needs the shower. And it is already sticky humid out here. But she can't lock her door, so she will wait until Miles is gone before she showers.

When he and Max come downstairs together, after seven, she is still on the patio. The pot of coffee is dry, and she is jittery. But she knows it's not from the coffee. She has to get out of this house.

"Max and I are going to start our day with breakfast," Miles tells her as he steps out onto the patio.

She nods. Max comes outside and approaches her hesitantly. She pulls herself together enough to give him a smile, but she fears it is a frightening smile, like a clown would wear.

"Have fun today, Max."

"Thanks." He reaches out, like he's going to touch her arm, but he lets his hand drop before he touches her. Max never touches her.

Miles tosses a piece of hard plastic on the table. She glances down and sees it is a credit card. Of course he wouldn't give her a debit card. She might clear his account and run.

"Get the works today."

She stares at him silently.

"I don't care to see my wife dressed in rags, looking like trash."

She fingers her empty coffee cup on the table. Imagines hurling it at him and hitting him in the head.

"Thank you, Miles." She smiles brightly. Max is watching her intently, as if he knows exactly what she is thinking.

BEAUTY & THE BEAST

THIRTY-FOUR

2007

Springfield, IL

Caroline's heart pounds as she rushes out of the office. Her stomach is in her throat, but she doesn't have time to slow down and let it settle. Max is in the living room watching *Blue's Clues*. She rushes down the stairs, calling to him as she goes. Asking him to pack a bag because they're going to take a little trip.

She needs to call Dawn. And then she needs to get her own things together and then she and Max are getting the hell out. Away from Miles. Somewhere in the back of her mind, she knows this isn't the way to do it. Miles is too damned smart. He'll find her. Even if she spent the next six months planning the perfect escape, he would find her.

Even so. She can't go another day under this roof with Miles Wolfe. Or whoever the hell he is.

Max trudges up the steps and watches as she jabs at the keypad on the cordless phone.

“Where are we going, Mommy?” he asks quietly.

“We’re gonna take a little trip,” she tells him. “You and me and maybe Dawnie. Okay? You wanna do that?”

“What about Daddy?”

“He’ll be here when we get back home, okay?” Caroline’s hand trembles as she presses the phone to her ear. “Can you pack a few things for Mommy? Just make sure you get your jammies and your toothbrush, okay? Mommy’s gonna pack some stuff really quick too.”

Max nods, but he still looks uncertain as he steps into his room and flips the light switch. Caroline watches him for a moment, as he pulls an overnight bag from under his bed. He’s too young to have any idea what’s going on, and yet, he seems to know something isn’t right.

“Hello?” Dawn sounds exhausted. Caroline hates to hear her so down, but she can’t worry about that right now.

“Dawn. It’s Caroline.” Her words tumble out in a breathless rush. “I need you—"

“It’s not a good time, Caroline.”

“Dawn, please? I really need you here. There’s something I need to talk to you about.”

“Just tell me now.”

“I can’t tell you over the phone,” Caroline argues. She glances at the alarm clock as she yanks her closet door open.

It's just after three in the afternoon. She is losing time. "Please, Dawn. It's really important."

"Caroline." Dawn sighs. She sounds frustrated. "I'm sorry, but I just don't wanna deal—"

"I need you. Now." Caroline's voice is hard and firm. She tamps down the desperation. She's never called Dawn and begged for help, never, even in all the times she and Miles have fought. "It's life or death. I am begging you to come. Max and I need your help."

Caroline throws jeans and blouses into a suitcase. Miles is not usually home until after four, most of the time not until after five. But she's scared. Caroline is scared that today will be a day when Miles shows up at home early. He always seems to know just when Caroline does not want him around.

"I'll be there in a few minutes."

Caroline clicks off the phone and tosses it on the bed. She zips up the suitcase and then sets it on the floor by the bed. Money. She needs money. She's got her ATM card and credit cards, but once Miles realizes she is gone, he'll freeze the accounts. Besides, if she used the cards, he could track her movements. No sense in making it that easy for him.

He keeps cash in the office. She hates the thought of going back upstairs. Of setting foot in that room. But she needs the cash to get started. She and Max need something to live on until she can get them set up somewhere and she can get a job. Something that will pay a bit more than the tutoring she's done.

As she steps into the hallway, she hears the back door open. Shit. Miles is home. It's like he *knows* what she's thinking, what she's doing at all times in this house. Fear makes her heartbeat ragged. She's got to get a hold of herself. Chances are, she'd only seen the tip of the iceberg upstairs, so she has to tread carefully.

Caroline stands at the top of the steps, listening to Miles in the kitchen. She hears his keys jingle as he hangs them on the rack just inside the back door. The sound of his briefcase gently hitting the counter. What does he carry in that briefcase? What the hell does he *do* for a living? Had anything he ever told her been the truth? Would she ever know?

"Caroline!" Miles appears at the bottom of the stairs. He smiles as if he is truly happy to see her. Images, memories drown her as she stares at him. The romantic nights they'd shared when they were dating. After they were married. Miles' face twisted in rage. Fists flying. Her body crashing against walls and the floor, Miles standing over her, as if he is daring her to get up and fight him.

Beth. Caroline feels her body begin to tremble.

Miles puts a foot on the bottom step. She can't let him come upstairs. A fight with him upstairs could end up with him pushing her down the steps. Broken neck. Head injuries. Might be just what he's looking for, but she won't give him that opportunity.

Caroline hurries down the steps and launches herself at him.

"Caroline?" Miles turns his head. She grabs hands full of his dress shirt. Fear is a fire burning in her stomach.

"You lying son-of-a-bitch!" Anger and hatred rival the fear. "You son-of-a-bitch!"

"What's wrong, Caroline?" Miles asks. He remains calm, which only adds to the whirlwind of fury and fear inside her.

"I hate you!"

"Why don't you calm down? Come into the kitchen. I'll fix you a drink, and we can talk about whatever it is you think I did."

"What I think you did?" She snaps and beats his chest with her fists. "What I think?"

"What's this all about? It's been a long day, Caroline. I'm not really in the mood for this—"

"This is about you and your lies."

"What lies?" He grabs her by the upper arms and shakes her.

"Beth was right about you—"

Without warning, he lets go of her arms and backhands her across the face. Used to the sudden blows, Caroline doesn't flinch. She feels blood trickle down her chin, but she doesn't wipe it away. Instead she thunders her fists on his chest again, but not in anger this time. She wants to hurt him. To hurt him as he's hurt her.

"I hate you. I hate this lie I've been living, Miles. Everything in our lives has been a lie!"

From the corner of her eye, Caroline sees the front door open. She'd forgotten she called Dawn. She shouldn't have done that. She should never have called Dawn and dragged her into this. What would Miles do to her?

Again, Miles grabs her by the arms and throws her backwards. Her tail bone hits the hardwood floor and pain shoots up through her back. Miles looms over her. She knows him now. She knows that he will not hesitate to kick her, even with Dawn standing right here watching. She knows he is capable of killing her. Forgetting the pain in her back, she scrambles to her feet.

Dawn. Caroline wants to yell for Dawn to leave. Miles' fingers close around Caroline's wrist. She groans when he yanks her arm up behind her back.

"I've had enough," he says calmly. "Stop acting so childish. I'm ready for dinner."

"Fuck you." The words are so quiet that Caroline barely hears them, even though they came from her mouth. Somehow, though, Miles hears her. The last time she'd said those words to him, he'd threatened to burn her with her curling iron. She pulls away from him and stumbles as she hurries from the foyer and to the kitchen.

Dawn is here. Dawn will stay with Max. If Miles comes after her, she knows Dawn will stay with Max. She grabs the keys from the key rack and flings the back door wide open.

Her hands shake as she pulls the car door closed and tries to jam the key into the ignition. Right hand struggling to start the car, she sees Miles coming toward her. Quickly she pushes the automatic lock down and finally gets the car started. Miles has finally lost his cool, and he's screaming at her, but she can't hear him with the windows up.

She puts the car in gear and floors the accelerator. Miles jumps out of the way as she flies out of the driveway and pulls out onto Eighth Street.

Her hands shake so she white knuckles the steering wheel. Stomach heaving, she takes several deep breaths, trying to calm herself. Miles wouldn't hesitate to hurt Dawn, but Caroline doubts he would do anything to her with Max there.

Get somewhere safe. Safe. And then call Dawn. They'll all leave him together.

Caroline's foot is heavy on the accelerator. She is doing eighty in a forty zone. Her mind races faster than the car. Miles. Beth. Miles' soft kisses and his hard fists. Beth had hated Miles.

A car horn snaps her out of the memories—

A little girl, running into the street, chasing a soccer ball—

Caroline swerves to miss the girl. Shaking all over again, knowing she is going to be sick, Caroline turns to see the girl, to make sure the little girl is okay. That she is in one piece. Still going eighty, Caroline's hands slip from the wheel—

Caroline hears the horrific crash of metal. She feels the collision, but she sees nothing as everything around her goes black...

RAPUNZEL

THIRTY-FIVE

July, 2008

Springfield, IL

Caroline's hands shake as she turns the pages of Dawn's photo albums. Maybe at the time, when she was in the hospital giving birth to Max, she had been irritated or embarrassed to have her picture taken. Now, though, she is grateful that Dawn had a camera and had recorded the moments that led up to the birth of her son. Dawn has pictures of her at all stages of her pregnancy, but those that mean the most are those taken the day he was born.

Dawn sits patiently while Caroline stares at the pictures of a stranger, with a swollen belly, in a hospital gown. The woman—Caroline does not recognize herself—wears a smile that belies the pain she must have been in and the abusive husband who poses with her as if they are the poster couple for happy marriages.

Caroline smooths her fingers over her jawbone in the pictures.

"Why would he take this away from me?" she whispers. She looks up when Dawn does not answer her.

"He started stripping you away the day you met him, Car."

"Was I that naïve?" Caroline wipes her eyes with her free hand.

"You were young. And you were in love."

"What kind of woman falls in love with a monster like that?" She doesn't expect an answer.

"Lots of women fall in love with men like that." Dawn purses her lips. She doesn't blink when Caroline looks at her again. "That's why the sons-of-bitches get away with it, Caroline."

"If you feel that way—" Caroline stops herself and looks back at the photo album. She is mesmerized by the blonde woman in the pictures. Even with the baby weight, she was pretty. It surprises her, because she feels unattractive now, as if the woman she had been was unacceptable, at most, and the woman she is now is scarred and ephemeral.

"If I feel that way, what?" Dawn asks.

Caroline shakes her head and continues to study the picture. Dawn leans forward and reaches toward Caroline. Her fingers gently cup Caroline's chin.

"It's hard to see in this picture, because of the weight gain, but you had an angular face and big eyes. High cheekbones." Dawn takes a quick breath through her nose, and Caroline realizes she is close to crying. "He took that away from you. Doctor Montell changed the bone structure of your face."

Caroline shivers.

"Jesus, Dawn, I married a Stefano." Though her stomach is churning, though her whole body shakes in fear and sorrow, though she speaks through tears, Caroline laughs. "I married a Stefano Demira."

Dawn shakes her head, but she has to laugh.

"Do you remember how we used to obsess over Days?" Caroline sags over the photo album, still open in her lap. Now her body convulses with laughter. She is about to break, and she and Dawn both know it.

"Do you remember how we used to obsess over Days?" Dawn turns the question back to her.

"I do." Caroline nods. She laughs and cries at the same time. "Beth would turn the TV up so loud, the neighbors down the block had to hear it too. You would sprawl out all over the living room floor—"

"And you always had to eat popcorn while we watched it, like it was Saturday night at the movies. Every afternoon, you ate popcorn. Buttery popcorn. And you never gained a pound."

"Oh please!" Caroline groans and sits up straight. She rubs her eyes and then takes a deep breath.

"Do you remember Beth?" Dawn asks softly. She can't seem to look at Caroline. Instead, she stares at Caroline's hand, still resting on the picture in the album.

"Not really," Caroline answers honestly. "It's like I feel her... I feel who she was to me. But no, I don't really remember her."

"But you did. Just for a second, you remembered her?"

Caroline nods. She takes another deep breath and then turns another page in the album. Finally, the woman in the pictures is holding a tiny bundle wrapped in blue.

"I'm sorry. I don't have any pictures of the actual birth." Dawn clears her throat.

Caroline traces the baby's face and wills herself to remember, but there is nothing. "It's okay." She shakes her head. "I just needed this."

"What were you going to ask me earlier?"

Caroline looks up at Dawn and chews on her lip for a moment. If she asks what is on her mind, it will likely start another argument and there is no time for arguments.

"Just ask."

"If you feel that way about Miles. If you think he's a son-of-a-bitch, why did you sleep with him?"

Dawn squirms a bit in her seat. She stares at the diamond wedding ring she still wears on her ring finger.

"I thought this didn't matter to you."

"It—I—It." Frustrated, Caroline stands up and steps away from Dawn. She paces the tiny room in the attic for a moment.

"If you hate him, why does it matter to you?"

Caroline turns and looks at Dawn, who still sits on the floor by the stack of photo albums. She cocks her head and studies the woman and realizes they are playing cat and mouse. Dawn doesn't seem to trust her any more than she trusts Dawn. Maybe the only way to push through the suspicion is to throw all her cards out on the table and let Dawn read them.

"He doesn't matter to me. It doesn't matter to me that he slept with someone else." Caroline stops to stand at the dormer window. She can't help herself. She has to look. Her eyes do a quick scan of the street, expecting to see Miles' car parked there. When will she shake this fear?

Not until she is away from him. She will have no peace until she and Max are safely away from him.

"Do you know what I mean?" she finally asks, when Dawn doesn't answer her.

"It matters that I slept with your husband. Even if we both hate him, it matters because I betrayed you."

Caroline turns her back to the window to face Dawn again.

"That's part of it."

Dawn shakes her head. She climbs to her feet, as if she needs to be at her full height to hear Caroline out.

"It's just that." Caroline swallows hard, "it's that I don't understand it. At least the person I am right now can't understand you sleeping with Miles. I know you hate him. I know you're as afraid of him as I am. I can feel that. It's just...there's a huge gap in this whole story for me. I don't know everything you and Miles know—"

“But I don’t know the whole story, either, Caroline. I don’t know what made you—"

“I know.” Caroline nods. “But you know this part. You know about sleeping with him. You know about whatever it was that came between you and me before the accident.”

“No, no, no! It’s not like that. It’s not like anything was wrong between you and me. I didn’t do it to get back at you. I didn’t do it to hurt you. There was nothing between us, Caroline.”

“Then how? How could you hate him and let him touch you that way?”

“How did you?”

Caroline opens her mouth to answer, but she doesn’t know what to say. “I didn’t.”

“He raped you?”

“Sometimes.”

“Look, it’s like I told you. I was alone. I was upset.” Dawn draws in a deep breath. “Depression.”

Caroline’s lips form a perfect O. “Post-partum depression.”

“It’s no excuse for what happened. But...I guess.”

Caroline takes a deep breath and turns around again to look out the window. She watches a little girl across the street ride her bike down the sidewalk.

“Look. It’s not going to come between us.” Her lips feel dry and chapped. She presses them together, breathes deeply again, and then continues. “You and Miles are not going to come between us, unless you want it to.”

Her words are met with such complete silence, Caroline thinks Dawn must have slipped out of the room while she has her back turned. Afraid to find the room empty behind her, and even more afraid to turn around and see unwanted emotions on Dawn's face, Caroline squats down and lowers her chin to her chest.

"Unless I—unless I—Caroline—what the hell?"

"I'm sorry," Caroline gushes. I'm sorry, but yes," she stands up and glances back over her shoulder. "yes, there is a part of me that is scared to death you're still sleeping with Miles and that you're in this big scheme together just to hurt me. To take Max and leave me like this—"

Caroline chances another look over her shoulder. She swipes at the tears on her face. Dawn raises her eyebrows, but she says nothing. Caroline watches her turn and walk out of the room. She takes a deep breath and then sinks back to the floor of the attic room. From outside, she hears kids calling to each other and laughing—maybe the little girl on the bike—but inside Dawn's house there is a sad, desperate hush, like a church just before the bell tolls to begin a funeral.

She assumes Dawn is gone, but she doesn't know where. Maybe while Caroline has been unconscious and a little bit dead, Dawn has made a new friend. Maybe Dawn is going to her new friend now for support. Maybe Dawn wants off the crazy train, and though Caroline is falling apart right now, all alone in Dawn's stuffy attic room, she can't blame her.

Caroline doesn't startle when Dawn comes back into the room a few moments later. Dawn approaches Caroline, arms folded over her chest, and squats down in front of her. Her pale face is streaked with tears and mascara.

"I have nothing left to give you," she says softly, "to prove to you that I am here for you. That I care about you. This is who I am now, Caroline. Lost, dead inside, and so exhausted there are days I have to bargain with myself to get out of bed. Just one more day. If I can just make it through one more day..."

Caroline swallows hard.

"But I swear to you...I promise you...whatever solemn vow you can take at face value...I hate the son-of-a-bitch you're married to, and I regret nothing more in my life than that one moment of weakness."

Dawn unfolds her arms. In her right hand, she holds a small, shiny gun. Caroline looks from the gun, up to Dawn's eyes, and back to the gun again.

"What are you doing?" she asks quickly. "What are you doing with a gun?"

"If he comes around here again." Dawn's voice is deceptively soft, but her eyes are huge, like glowing saucers, in her pale face. They burn with an intensity that Caroline has never seen. "If he comes over here again, late at night, to scare me...to threaten me that he'll kill me if I ever tell you what happened between us..." She stares solemnly at Caroline. "Ever again, Caroline. I'll kill him."

For a moment, just for a tiny moment, Caroline feels something inside loosen. Just a tiny bit of slack on the nerves that have been taut inside her since waking up from the coma and knowing, *feeling*, that something is wrong, something is *dead* wrong.

If Dawn killed Miles, she would be free. *If* Dawn killed Miles, *she* would be free. She. *Caroline.* As much as she wants to be free, she can't be free without Dawn.

"Dawn—" she starts to argue, but Dawn lunges at her. Her left hand shoots out and grabs her by the chin.

"Tell me. Go ahead. Tell me." Her fingers dig into Caroline's skin. Hard enough to dig into her bone. "You tell me I can't kill him, because you're in love with him. Tell me you can't live without him, and things are gonna work out—"

Caroline wraps her hands around Dawn's and tries to pull her fingers away, but Dawn doesn't budge.

"Tell me." Dawn's voice is an emotionless rasp now. Caroline can read the rage and the fear in her eyes. The fear. Caroline goes cold. Dawn is afraid of Caroline. "Tell me you and Miles are playing me for the fool—"

Caroline yanks Dawn's iron grip away from her face and squeezes her hand tightly in hers.

"If you kill him, you'll go to prison."

"I don't care." Dawn's voice is like steel. "I don't care what they do to me, as long as Miles Wolfe ends up dead."

"Prison, Dawn. If you go to prison, he wins."

"He already won, Caroline."

"You can start over—"

“I lost my baby. I know you don’t get that, because you *do* have Max. But I lost my child—"

“Dawn—"

“No.” Dawn shakes her head. “No, I don’t mean that to be harsh for you. I’m not attacking you. I’m telling you what’s in here.” She pulls their hands, still entwined, to lay over her chest. “There’s nothing left inside me. My baby is gone. And my husband is dead.”

“But Miles isn’t—"

“Danny’s gone.” Dawn repeats. “He took him from me.”

Caroline shivers. In the blazing hot attic, a chill climbs her spine.

“You said that. Before. You said that,” she rambles. Left hand still holding Dawn’s, she drops her head to her right hand and runs her fingers through her hair. “You said that before. You said that Miles killed Danny.”

Dawn shrinks into herself and cries. Caroline knows, on some level, she is Dawn’s best friend. Or she had been Dawn’s best friend at one time, and she should comfort her. She wonders briefly if she did comfort Dawn when Danny died. She remembers being there with her when she lost the baby. But she’s never had any memory of Dawn losing Danny and how or if those around her had closed rank and helped her back to her feet.

Her head is pounding. Beads of sweat trickle down her back, one by one, just enough to annoy her. The kids are still making noise outside, and Caroline knows it’s what kids do, but she needs silence. Memories are lurking, and

Caroline wants absolute silence and perfect concentration so she can pull them all together.

Michael Ramsay. Michael Ramsay.

Danny.

Miles wins. Miles won a long time ago.

“You said that before, Dawn. You said before that Miles killed Danny.” Caroline wipes tears and sweat off her face and then gives Dawn’s fingers a gentle squeeze. “Before. The last time we were here, you said that Miles had killed Danny.”

When Dawn looks up at her, the despair on her face turns Caroline inside out.

“I thought he died in the line of duty.” Caroline presses her lips together. She is trembling. Her mind is teetering on the edge of something huge. Those memories sneak in closer, and she feels them press against her, cold and uncomfortable. Her stomach is clenched hard in fear, and her throat is tight. “I thought Danny died fighting a fire, Dawn.”

“He did, Caroline.”

Caroline’s breath hitches again. The memories slither around her neck and tighten.

“The fire was arson,” Dawn tells her. Caroline’s jaw and neck ache, they are so tight. Her fingers are ice cold, and still, beads of sweat roll one by one down her back. The name Michael Ramsay is still stuck in her mind.

“But Danny—"

“Miles started that fire, Caroline.”

The heat and the humidity in the attic room are so thick, that Caroline wonders if she is having a heart attack trying to breathe, or if the ice cold pain that shoots through her chest is simply Dawn’s words meeting the darkest fears Caroline does not even remember.

“Do you—"

“If you ask me if I have proof, you can walk out now—"

“Do you know if I knew? Did I know that Miles killed him?”

SLEEPING BEAUTY

THIRTY-SIX

2008

Springfield, IL

Soft, gauzy light. Voices. Monotonous, quiet and soothing, but the longer she lays here and listens, the more distinct they become. Mostly one man and one woman. Still she does not recognize them. Trying to listen to the words, when she doesn't know who they are and doesn't particularly care what they are saying, makes her head hurt. Instead she is content to float in this soft light as someone's memories, vivid like movie images, play against her eyelids.

Gentle, but firm hands poke and prod occasionally. Now and then a sharp invasive light pierces the almost drunken state she hovers in, and almost always at the same time, another voice—this one is different, authoritative—speaks directly to her. She does not know the name by which the voice addresses her, but she knows by the tone, the intensity, that the person is speaking to her.

Can you hear me? That sharp, deep voice keeps asking. Blink if you can hear me. Caroline, blink if you hear me. She can hear him. But who is Caroline? Why is he calling her Caroline? Who is he, and why does he call her Caroline?

Blink if you can hear me. Squeeze my hand. Caroline, if you can hear me, squeeze my hand.

She can hear him. She hears him, and she feels his confident fingers trace over her hands and arms. She hears the other voices around her hush, and she senses them gather close to her. Watching. Like vultures, they watch her struggle to hear and understand. They watch her struggle to acclimate to her surroundings.

It's a fishbowl. She feels like she is swimming in a fishbowl. The water is comforting. She is warm and languid in this small and cozy fishbowl. Where people are watching her. People she does not know.

Caroline. Can you hear me?

She can hear him. She's not sure, though, that she wants to blink. She's not sure she wants to try to open her eyes. She did once, and the harsh flash of light that had zapped her eyes had sent her scrambling back to the comfort of the hazy way she has lived for so long.

The voices blend. Suddenly the voices blend into one loud, accusing voice. She cowers, deep in her haze, as the voice gets louder. Sweat pools on her lower back, both in her mind, and in real time. Her stomach turns when the voice suddenly stops. There is more to fear when the silence comes.

Caroline. That sharp voice again. Not the accusing voice. The sharp, insistent voice from now.

Caroline. Can you hear me?

You're losing her.

There is more to fear when the silence falls.

Caroline.

More to fear...

Can you hear me?

Silence...The central air has stopped running. Silence has fallen on the house. Her suitcase is open on her bed, clothes pitched at it are heaped half in and half out. As she walks from the closet to the bed, she glances out to the hallway. To the stairs.

The stairs that go to the third floor...the office...

Caroline? Can you hear me?

You're losing her. Louder this time. Harsh and angry.

More to fear...silence...The house is silent. The house is silent around her. A door slams...

You're losing her! The harsh voice.

Footsteps across the hardwood floor. The tap of a man's dress shoe and the sound of someone's weight on the first step.

Caroline? Can you hear me?

You're losing her...losing her...losing...losing...Same. Same voice. It's the same voice. That dreaded voice in these dreams is the same voice right here, where she hovers in this fishbowl. That man that owns that voice and the fists that have done so much damage is right here, watching her struggle to be invisible to him, in the fishbowl.

RAPUNZEL

THIRTY-SEVEN

August, 2008

Present Day

Springfield, IL

Though Caroline had felt that moment of relief when she saw the gun, she now feels wound much tighter. The memories hover just out of reach. Not the memories of Max. Not the memories of Beth and college and her parents and her life. But the memories of what was the start of her death. Something happened in Dawn's attic room. Something clicked and a few more puzzle pieces fell into place. But Caroline still can't see the whole picture, and the feeling of dread closes in around her like darkness in a casket.

Not dread. Imminent danger. The feeling of imminent danger. Caroline is dancing a very thin line, and her steps become more weighted with each move, and she fears she is going to topple off the high wire before she can see the other side of the tent. Dawn had clammed up, sealed her mouth like she'd used glue for lip gloss, when Caroline has asked her if she knew. If Caroline had known Dawn's suspicions about Danny's death.

Unless Dawn still didn't trust her, Caroline didn't understand her reaction. She'd asked Dawn several times throughout the day if *she* had known the fire was arson, but Dawn had either answered her with silence or changed the subject. Silence in the beginning and diversion tactics when they left the attic and headed out for their girls' day. Caroline had known she had to go home with a new manicure and pedicure and new clothes, or all hell would break loose. Miles would demand to know the minute by minute itinerary of what they had done, and while part of Caroline wanted to tell him exactly what they'd done and then pack her bag and walk out, that dread, the feeling of danger, had kept her obedient.

All hell had broken loose anyway, because Caroline had come home with a bright pink OPI color on her toenails and fingernails, *Strawberry Margarita*, rather than the simple French that had always been required. Thankfully, Max had been outside with Dawn when Miles had exploded in the kitchen and thrown the backhand that had missed her and cleared the counter of the canister set and a bottle of wine.

Rage had swelled so high inside her, she thought it might choke her. Who the hell did he think he was to control another living person this way? Who the hell had she been to fight the son-of-a-bitch and not leave? How had she ever loved him?

"You'll clean it up," he had told her in a quiet, tense voice. "And then you'll go upstairs and take that whoring color off."

"Go to hell."

She'd walked out of the kitchen, with a bottle of water in hand, and joined Dawn and Max outside. Hours later, after a shower, a game of Checkers with Max and reading for a while in the lavender room, she'd gone downstairs for a snack. The wine and the flour and sugar and tea bags had been cleaned up. No trace of the violent strike against her.

Now though, a week later, she is scared. She can fight him until the end of time, but she is not as strong now as she was before the accident. Distracted as she is by the memories that threaten to crash in around her and yet slither away each time she really tries to pull them in, Miles can and will catch her off guard one of these days. He has cool hatred and the strength to kill her with one blow. He knows that, and he has always known that. It is that knowledge and his restraint that scares the hell out of her.

She needs a plan, and she needs money. If she leaves him, she has to be able to burn her trail so he will never find her. And yet, she knows he will. Doesn't matter where she goes, Miles Wolfe will find her. And he'll kill her.

It's not what he will do to her that makes her cautious. It's what will happen to Max after she is gone that scares her. She doesn't truly believe that Miles would lay a hand on the boy, but what he might do could eventually be worse. Miles could teach Max that it is okay to treat a woman the way he treats her. Miles could teach, by example alone, that it is okay to respect no one besides oneself. Miles could teach, by example, hatred and arrogance as a way of life.

Caroline will do everything in her power to protect her son.

The only way she will get away from Miles is if she remembers. Miles is too shrewd to lose this game; she is a worthy opponent only if she remembers what Miles and her mind are trying so hard to keep from her.

Even then, he will find her. Caroline keeps thinking of all of the movies she has seen where a battered wife or girlfriend is trying so desperately to escape her abuser.

The only way Caroline will ever be free of the fear is if Miles Wolfe is dead.

And now her best friend has a gun.

"Caroline?"

She looks up from the book she had laid open on the desk in front of her. Miles stands uncertainly, half in and half out of the library door. She hadn't realized it was so late, and she wonders now if Max is still sleeping. He'd fallen asleep on the couch after watching a movie after lunch.

She has only a second to decide how to react to him. Antagonistic will get her nowhere. She needs to save the frustration and the rage for when she really needs it to fuel her, and she would bet her life on needing it one day soon.

"I didn't hear you come in," she says quietly. "Didn't realize it was that late."

Miles steps into the room and shrugs almost apologetically. "I'm a bit early, actually."

"Oh." She lets the book fall closed and then flinches inwardly, wondering what sort of fit Miles will throw when he sees the title. It is biblical fiction, and though she doesn't remember him ever berating her reading that particular genre, nothing would surprise her.

"I brought a pizza home." He slides his hands into the front pockets of his slacks and raises his eyebrows in invitation. "Are you hungry?"

Caroline feels a pang of sadness as she stares at him. She misses this Miles. The easy-going Miles who loved her before he started beating her. She sinks back in her chair, shocked at herself and her thoughts.

"Sausage and green pepper," he announces, still trying to convince her to join him.

"Was that my favorite?"

"No," he answers truthfully. He offers her a sheepish grin. "Your favorite is sausage, pepperoni and green pepper. I don't like pepperoni."

She wonders, as she smiles at him, if she is betraying Dawn's trust in her, just by talking to him like this. Is she betraying Dawn when all she really wants is answers? She's not in love with him. She's not going to fall back in love with him.

"I also picked up some cold Red Stripe."

She knows Red Stripe is his favorite beer, not hers. She actually remembers the first time he swung at her, when she didn't have Red Stripe in the refrigerator and she suggested he drink Miller Lite.

"We could sit out on the patio." The little shrug of his shoulders is almost endearing. Caroline lays her head back on the chair and closes her eyes for a moment. Easier to remind herself that he's playing her and he's not to be trusted when she's not looking at him and watching his performance.

She hears him take another step into the room, and she knows he is now close enough to see the book clearly. Maybe she should have chosen a smutty bodice ripper, just to anger him. And yet, what would that do? His fists will not bring her answers, only more questions.

What makes him so arrogant and unfeeling? How does he go from loving and gentle to cold and calculating in two seconds? What made her fight him, rather than cower before him or leave him? What had changed that made her fear for her life and begin packing to save herself and her son?

"What are you reading?" he asks. When she opens her eyes, he is standing directly in front of her. His nearness takes her by surprise. She watches his fingers skim over the cover of the book. They almost trace the letters in the title, *The Red Tent.* She dares a glance at his face and wonders if he is angry behind the calm mask he wears.

"I just started it, actually." She pushes the chair back and stands up. "Was Max sleeping?"

"No, he's watching TV."

"Well, I'm sure he'd like some pizza. He didn't eat much lunch."

Miles throws his arm over her shoulder and pulls her gently to him. Caroline hitches in a quick breath and tries to sallow the repulsion that climbs her throat.

"What was that for?" she asks when he kisses her cheek.

"I'm just happy."

"Happy about what?" She steps away from him and hurries down the hall, looking for Max, but she smiles back at Miles over her shoulder.

"That you're okay." His smile is small and playful.

She knows that under the calm surface, under that playful smile, Miles is seething with anger. She knows that he is angry with her for letting Max fall asleep on the couch, because the couch is for sitting, not sleeping. And she knows he is angry at her because Max is now awake and watching TV and she was in another room in the house and didn't know it.

"Me too." She smiles again but turns away from him. "Hey Max, are you hungry for some pizza?"

At some point tonight, Miles will punish her. It's sort of a memory that tells her this, but mostly, she knows it instinctively. According to Miles, she has been irresponsible. He'll wait until Max is asleep, and then he will act. And as always, she will fight back.

"Hey Max."

Caroline watches as Miles scoops her son up from the sofa and tosses him playfully over his shoulder. Max's shrill giggle fills the room. Why can't things always be as simple and happy as that giggle?

In the kitchen, Miles opens two beers and pours Max a cup of juice while she plates the pizza. Outside, it is warm, but not sticky hot, a welcome change. Skipper sits patiently at Max's feet, waiting for the inevitable drop. Miles laughs and reaches out to pet the dog.

"Did you talk to Dawn today?" he asks her after a few moments of silence. He asks her every day if she's talked to Dawn. She never lies, because she wonders if he has already checked in with Dawn. It's not that she doesn't trust Dawn; the gun had gone a long way toward gaining her trust. But Miles does not know about the gun, and she assumes he still believes Dawn to be his spy.

"She called earlier, but we didn't talk long."

"Why not?"

Caroline looks up at his sharp tone. She swallows the pizza in her mouth and answers him. "Max and I had just finished lunch. We were watching Lilo and Stitch. I told her I'd call her back."

"What's she doing these days?"

As if you don't know. Caroline presses her lips together to make sure the words don't really slip out.

"Looking for a job, I think."

"Danny had life insurance. She shouldn't need to work."

The cool way Miles tosses Danny's name out makes her grit her teeth. If Dawn is right, Miles is the reason Danny is dead. And not in some bizarre, accidental way. Miles killed Danny. If Dawn is right. Caroline's stomach clenches. She takes a quick, careful breath and shrugs.

"I don't think it has anything to do with money, Miles." She takes a drink of her beer, wishing she'd have brought a glass of water out with her. She's not crazy about Red Stripe, and she needs to be on her game to sit here and talk to Miles, especially in a conversation like this.

"What do you mean?"

"She's alone. She lost her baby. Her husband. She's probably bored."

"She can't be lonely. She has you."

"Not really the same, is it?" Caroline mumbles, although she knows when she says it that even before the accident, she was closer to Dawn than Miles.

"Do you remember?"

Again, she looks up sharply. "Remember what?"

"Danny's death? The fire?"

"I don't remember anything about Danny." She hates that she's being honest, because she really *wants* to remember Danny. She really *needs* to remember Danny. Remembering Danny might push her to unravel the rest of the memories knotted together in her mind.

"And the baby?"

Caroline raises her eyebrows. She does remember the baby. And she remembers comforting Danny in the waiting room. Maybe...maybe if she concentrates on that memory, she can put the rest of the memories together.

Careful not to let Miles know what she is thinking, she nods slowly. "I remember parts of that night."

"Do you?" Miles pretends to be happy, but Caroline senses that he's not.

"Just parts of it. Being with Dawn in the delivery room. The doctor saying she needed—" Caroline glances at Max and stops herself. "After. Sitting with Dawn in recovery."

Miles takes a moment before he answers her. She sneaks a sideways glance at him as he takes a healthy swallow of his beer. She's treading in dangerous waters now. Talking about memories with Miles and wondering how honest she should be with him. She can't let him know how much she remembers. It would be too much like handing over her one gun to the enemy in a gun fight.

"And you don't remember Danny?"

"Not really," she answers. He stares at her skeptically. "Some things I don't remember, but I feel. Does that make sense to you?"

Now he sets his beer down and cocks his head as he studies her. "No. What do you mean?"

He sounds interested, not angry.

"I don't know how to explain it," she answers honestly. "It's just that some things I don't remember, I sort of feel. Like instinct or something."

"And if you don't remember us," he says softly and leans toward her, "do you feel that we're right for each other?"

Caroline raises her eyebrows, but she nods. Apparently she's been a good actress in this marriage. She hopes she hasn't lost the talent.

Miles leans toward her again. This time she lets him kiss her and then takes a big drink of her beer to hide her distaste.

SLEEPING BEAUTY

THIRTY-EIGHT

2007

Springfield, IL

Michael Ramsay. 2117 Sterling Way. Bloomington, IL...

Dawn and Danny's house is decked out for the Fourth of July. Dawn's gone all out; red and blue garland is wrapped around the light post in the front yard. Small red and blue Christmas lights decorate the front porch, and blue luminaries line the driveway. Caroline can hear Danny and a few other guys in the backyard, and she envisions him manning the grill. Danny's barbeque is second to none. Parties at Dawn and Danny's are what life should be, what life had been for Caroline. Before. Before she'd married him.

Three year old Max runs down the driveway ahead of her and Miles. Caroline starts to call out to him, to warn him not to trip and fall, but she catches herself. Miles does not like it when she babies Max, and calling a warning to him now will surely turn a fun evening with friends into an appearance of Miles the-know-it-all, which would ruin everyone's night, not just hers.

The flash of despair fades quickly, as Caroline and Miles round the house and she sees Danny standing by the grill. He holds a barbeque fork in his right hand, a bottle of Miller Lite, in a St. Louis Cardinal sleeve (Miles hates those) in his left. He is listening to a story one of his friends from college is telling him, but his eyes are on the ribs he is grilling. She takes a deep breath and swallows the smoky smell and forgets that she is with Miles and that her life with Miles is miserable.

At Dawn and Danny's, she is home. Knowing Dawn will be in the kitchen, probably with the other women, Caroline sets down her picnic basket, grabs a cold beer from Dawn and Danny's cooler by the back door and goes inside. The three other women inside are wives of Danny's friends, all friendly, but Caroline notices the way Dawn's shoulder relax and her smile warms when she sees her.

Good friends and good times. It's what life is all about.

She and Dawn finish the salads and the cake inside and the other women go outside. When they go outside, Caroline immediately scans the backyard, searching for Miles. She's learned, since she's been married, to always be aware of his whereabouts. She knows better than to say anything about him or the situation she has found herself in. She will never be in the process of telling someone how horrible her marriage is, only to have Miles walk up behind her and overhear her. And yet, she is safest, and *feels* safest when she knows exactly where he is.

She finds him standing at the gate at the back of Dawn and Danny's yard. He is talking to Steve Maynard, one of Danny's friends from the fire station. They appear to be deep in conversation, which Caroline finds curious, but shrugs away because if Miles is deep in conversation with someone else, she is free to relax for a while.

He turns his head just then, as if he senses her looking at him. His eyes are cool. Even from the patio where she stands, Caroline can see the cool, assessing look in his eyes. He smiles, though and lifts his hand in a half wave. She smiles too and lifts her hand to wave back. But then she sees the glass tumbler in his other hand. Miles is drinking the hard stuff, and she knows by experience that he is meaner and sloppier when he drinks the hard stuff...

Michael Ramsay...

Michael Ramsay. 2117 Sterling Way. Bloomington, IL. 6'0". Blue eyes. Blonde hair.

Michael Ramsay...

...Even though the house is empty, she climbs the staircase slowly. Each footfall placed gingerly on each step, and still, on the third, fifth, sixth and ninth step, the creak is loud enough to send a chill up her spine. She's climbed these stairs so many times. Daily, for the past three weeks.

The door is always locked. It used to be open, but now, suddenly, Miles keeps the door to his office locked. She glances up, as she makes her way painstakingly up the steps. It is closed. The door is closed.

She should just go back down. Go back down. If she is downstairs in the kitchen or the library and he comes home, he will never catch her in his office. As long as she stays where she is, he can't catch her doing something he has wordlessly forbidden her to do.

Stay blind. She can't do it anymore. She can't be blind anymore.

The top step creaks, and that one is new to her. She wipes her sweaty palms on her shorts and glances back over her shoulder. Late afternoon sunlight dapples the wooden floor at the base of the stairs. Caroline is mesmerized by the patterns that play over the floor. Seconds tick by as she watches the sunlight and thinks that she can not be blind anymore.

From somewhere outside, a car squeals its tires, and Caroline jumps. She swallows hard, wills her heartbeat to slow down and then steps up toward the door. The door to his office. The door that used to be open and now suddenly is shut and locked. Only someone with something to hide would be so secretive.

But when had Miles found something to hide from her? She is his wife. What is he hiding from her?

Her hands touch the door, and she splays her palms over it, as she would if there was a fire in the house and she was testing to see if the fire was on the other side of the door. She lowers her hand and wraps her fingers around the old-fashioned jeweled knob.

She could go back downstairs. She could go back down and bake a cake. Draw something to put in Max's room, by the picture she'd drawn and framed of Thomas the Train. Clean something. If she goes back downstairs and finds *something* to do, and Miles comes home and sees her doing that *something*, everything will be okay. If he catches her in his office...

Something has changed. Something, in the last few weeks, has changed and now Miles has a secret to keep from her...

Unless he's always had the secret, but now for some reason, he thinks Caroline has stumbled onto it...

She has to know. With a deep breath, she twists and the knob turns in her hand...

Michael Ramsay. 6'0". Blonde hair. Green eyes....

RAPUNZEL

THIRTY-NINE

August, 2008

Springfield, IL

"Are you in love with him?"

Caroline pauses in the process of dusting the end table in the living room. Dawn is squatting down in the corner, dusting the baseboard. Miles' parents are coming for the weekend to see Max before he starts school. Caroline does not remember them, and yet she knows she does not like them. She feels that in every bone of her body. Even more than that, she knows *they* do not like *her.* They have never approved of Miles marrying her. Miles has not threatened her, but she feels it is best for everyone involved if the house is in perfect order, regardless that she is technically still recovering from a major trauma.

She glances at Dawn now and tries to read the expression on her face. They have developed a good relationship now.

The gun had been the cornerstone that they had begun to rebuild their trust on. Maybe for someone else, that would be a little like building on quicksand. For Caroline, and she'd thought for Dawn, it was as solid as bedrock.

"I mean—" Dawn presses her lips together and thinks for a minute. Caroline doesn't think the look on her face is one of anger or suspicion. But there is definitely worry.

"You mean I fell in love with him once, so is it possible that I'm falling in love with him again?"

"Well." Dawn sinks lower and lets her butt hit the floor. She looks up at Caroline and stares at her for several long seconds.

"Sometimes I see the man I fell in love with," Caroline admits. "Sometimes he'll say something to me and it's just... cute or funny....and I can see him. In my mind, I can see him, the way he was when we were dating."

"That scares me."

Caroline shakes her head and wonders how to explain to Dawn what she feels now. She's aware of the danger of protesting too much.

"It'd be a little like believing in Santa Claus after watching your parents put the presents out on Christmas Eve."

"You feel differently because you know he beat you?"

Caroline winces. No matter that she knows the truth, it will never be easy to *hear* those words about herself. She chews on her lower lip, aware of Dawn waiting for an answer and aware that the longer she waits to answer, the more Dawn could doubt her.

"I think it's more than that." The whispered words fall with the weight of a missile to the floor. Her heart races; sweat beads on her upper lip.

"What do you mean?" Dawn dumps her words quickly into the hushed living room. Caroline feels her eyes boring into her, willing her to answer. To explain. It's as if all of her life has come down to this moment, and even the dust motes hover expectantly in the weak afternoon sunlight coming through the window over the TV. While even the still life has stopped to wait expectantly for Caroline's answer, time has accelerated and Caroline's blood rushes through her body and her head pounds. It is imperative that she remember, and that she remember *right now*.

"I don't know," she mumbles. She shakes her head, as if trying to clear out the cluttering thoughts and really focus on the memory she knows is in there. "I don't know, Dawn. It's just right there, but I can't make myself get it. I can't remember."

"But there's something more."

"I don't know!" Caroline snaps. "Dammit, I don't know what is going on. There's something I know I have to remember, but it's blocked."

"Okay," Dawn says calmly. "It's okay, Caroline—"

"It's not okay!" Caroline stands up and stalks around the room. "It's not okay. I walk around this house and I'm never quite sure if I'm here now or then and I hear his voice and I remember the way we fought. I remember his rules, the way he made me live. I remember. And I know there's something else that I have to remember—"

“Getting upset isn’t going to help.”

Of course Dawn is right. But then again staying calm hasn’t helped her yet either. It’s not like she’s dying to remember something now and at two o’clock tomorrow morning she’ll roll over and wake up and the elusive memory will reveal itself to her. Not like she’s going to call Dawn at two in the morning and say oh yeah, I remembered.

“Michael Ramsay.”

“What?” Dawn’s fingers still curl around the dust rag she’s been wiping the baseboard with. “What about Michael Ramsay?”

Caroline shakes her head. “I dunno—"

“Focus, Caroline. You’ve mentioned that name several times. Who is he?”

“Michael Ramsay. 2117 Sterling Way.”

“That’s an address,” Dawn says quietly. She nods encouragement.

“2117 Sterling Way, Bloomington IL.”

“Bloomington?” Dawn frowns, obviously surprised.

“Bloomington.”

“Someone we knew from school?”

Caroline shakes her head. “I don’t know, Dawn. I just keep seeing his name. The address. It’s like...It’s—" Caroline looks up quickly as it dawns on her what she is seeing in her mind.

"What?" Dawn lunges at her. She reaches out and clasps her hands around Caroline's. "What is it, Caroline?"

"An ID. A driver's license. I keep seeing a driver's license with the name Michael Ramsay on it."

Dawn cocks her head and absorbs Caroline's words. "A driver's license."

Caroline nods and closes her eyes, the better to focus on the license in her mind. "Michael Ramsay. 2117 Sterling Way. Bloomington, IL. Blond hair—"

"Is there a picture? Can you see a picture?"

"I can't see it. It's like that part of it is just dark."

"Okay." Dawn squeezes Caroline's hands. "Okay. That's good."

"It's not enough—"

"It's good," Dawn repeats. Caroline tugs her hands away from Dawn's and runs her fingers through her hair. She groans and opens her eyes to look at Dawn.

"I can't stand this, Dawn." Caroline's breath catches. She rubs her forehead with her fingertips and tries to ease the knot of tears back down her throat.

"I know."

Dawn wraps her fingers around Caroline's wrists again and pulls her hands down. "It's okay. This is good. This is something solid."

"A piece of a memory? Is solid?

“But you’ve been trying to dig this Michael Ramsay out of your mind for days. Now we have a little more to go on.”

“What? You mean like driving to Bloomington?”

Dawn raises her eyebrows and shrugs. “We could. But I was thinking we could google him. Besides that, we can try to figure out why you have that memory—"

“You think so?” Caroline snorts sarcastically. “Maybe he’s important—"

“Stop it!” Dawn shakes Caroline gently. “Why are you remembering an ID with his information? Not because you had Early Civ with him sophomore year at ISU. Then you’d remember his name. Maybe his face. Why are you remembering an ID? A driver’s license?”

“I saw his license.”

“Exactly.”

Caroline sighs and drops back to sit on the couch. “I don’t get it. Where would I have seen—"

“Caroline?”

Caroline notices, as she looks up to see Miles stride into the room, that Dawn is pale. As if Miles’ sudden appearance unnerved her. Scared her. Dawn has not lived with Miles, and therefore has not trained herself not to visibly react to him.

“Is it five already?” she asks him calmly. Her heart had jumped when she’d heard his voice, but already, her mind is racing to explain the intense scene she can not hide.

"Just after." He nods and studies her face for a moment before turning to look at Dawn. "Everything okay?"

He doesn't sound suspicious. In fact, it sounds like he *cares.* Like he's any other husband who has just come from work to find his wife and her best friend deep in an upsetting emotional conversation.

Why can't it be that simple? She wonders even as she nods and begins the lie her mind has placed front and center.

"Fine." She raises her eyebrows and glances at Dawn. "I just remembered something that upset me. I think I had Dawn a little concerned."

"Really?" Miles steps further into the room. He slides his hands into the front pocket of his slacks. "What is it?"

Though she knows exactly what she is going to say, Caroline hesitates. As if talking about whatever she's remembered upsets her. She feels Dawn's eyes on her as she studies her hands, now folded in her lap, and she wonders what Dawn is thinking.

"The baby." Caroline swallows hard. It's not hard to pretend that this upsets her. In fact, she hates using the guilt over that baby, the guilt that belongs to her alone and has nothing to do with Miles Wolfe.

"Max?"

Caroline paces across the floor and chances a glance at him. He still wears the mask of the concerned husband, though now there is a touch of confusion too.

"Dawn's—"

"My baby," Caroline interrupts him before he can finish his sentence. She doesn't want to discuss Dawn's grief right here in front of her. "The baby I aborted before I met you."

She isn't gambling. She'd had a flash of telling him about the baby, after they'd made love one night before they were married. Dawn doesn't say anything, so she knows that she's safe with that memory. Miles had indeed known about her abortion.

Miles nods thoughtfully. "You remember Shane, then?" He studies his shoes, rather than look her in the eye. What is that about? Miles is usually aggressive with her, but lately, he's been handing her this uncertain act. It *is* an act, she tells herself now. Miles does not have a compassionate bone in his body. Well. Maybe for his son. But there is no compassion for Caroline. Only a twisted possessive love hate dichotomy.

She doesn't really remember Shane. She has just a vague impression of him, same as most other things in her life.

"Not really," she admits, because Miles knows enough about Shane to trip her up if she lies. "I just remember finding out I was pregnant. That...fear. Not knowing what to do."

"You aborted the baby." There was the cold, cunning Miles. Reminding her of the bad thing she had done when she was younger. Probably hoping to cast doubt on her current mothering skills. To keep her under his thumb.

Caroline nods. "I did." She wishes, suddenly, that she hadn't aborted Shane Beck's baby. Maybe she wouldn't be in this mess if she'd kept that baby. Maybe she'd be married to Shane, and she'd have more children—

More children. *Other* children. She can't possibly wish for a life with anyone else, because she has a child. Here and now, with this monster standing here before her, she has a child. She may not remember the bond they shared, but she won't wish him away for better, easier times.

"And Beth?" Miles asks. He is quiet again, playing the role of the caring husband.

Caroline shakes her head and shrugs. "What about Beth?"

"Do you remember her?"

"I remember—" She stops herself suddenly. She'd been about to say that she remembers Beth's death, although she doesn't remember *Beth.* But something inside had stopped her. Her head pounds, and she's suddenly trembling. She's afraid. Miles is watching her closely. She is afraid to look him in the eye, but she is afraid to look away. Like if she looks away, Miles will suspect her of *knowing* something.

What? What could she know, but not remember?

She swallows hard, pushing the hard lump of fear back down into her stomach. Under his intense gaze, she shakes her head.

"You remember what?"

"I don't remember her," she answers. "But I feel her. It's like I know her and I know I should remember her, but I don't."

He nods, as if her words make perfect sense to him.

"I think that you should go lie down."

Caroline, forgetting for a moment what it is like to be given orders, looks back at him in shock. “What?”

“You’re very pale, as if you don’t feel well. You’ve over done it with the cleaning. I think you need to rest.”

Rest. She wants to look at Dawn, but she doesn’t. Miles does not want her to rest. He wants her to vanish, so he can quiz Dawn and see if she can hold up under pressure and tell the same story.

“Miles, I’m fine. I just want the house to be nice for—"

“I said you need to lie down.”

She wants to tell him to go to hell. But she won’t. Not with Dawn standing here. They have argued in front of her before, but Miles has not hit her since the accident. This time, Caroline suspects, it might be different. Besides, it might be good to lie down and test her theory. Let Miles quiz Dawn. She and Dawn can compare notes later.

“Fine.” She gives him a curt nod and leaves the room without glancing at Dawn.

Shamed and angry to be shamed in front of her friend, Caroline climbs the stairs as gracefully as she can. How in God’s name had she ever lived this way? What sort of woman had she been that she would let a sociopath cow her into obedience?

On the second floor, she pauses and peeks into Max’s room. He is listening to a Cars story, on his Leapfrog. He looks up at her and smiles shyly.

“Doin’ okay?”

He nods.

"I'm going to lay down for a while," she tells him. "Dawnie and Dad are downstairs."

"Okay." His tiny voice sends a pang of regret through her as she climbs to the third floor. She pushes her door closed behind her and lets her eyes roam over the lavender room. How can she rest in this room? Her blood pressure automatically sky rockets when she steps inside the room. This room has been her prison.

Why should she allow him to imprison her?

She sits on the edge of the bed and takes a deep breath. Why hadn't she felt comfortable telling Miles that she remembers Beth's death? If she can pick and choose which memories to admit to having, why didn't she want to admit remembering the way Beth had died?

RAPUNZEL

FORTY

August, 2008

Springfield, IL

Skipper lays under a big shade tree, occasionally groaning or flopping his tail back and forth, as if to let Caroline and Max know that he's still breathing. The heat is too much for him. He doesn't want to get up and chase the ball Max had brought out to play with. Instead Skipper is being lazy, and Caroline and Max are throwing a Frisbee.

Sweat drips in her eyes, and Caroline thinks she should probably apply more sunscreen on Max. When he was just two, she'd taken him to a pool on an overcast day. Even with the sunscreen and the cloud cover, Max's ears and scalp had still burned a bit. Caroline felt bad enough, but Miles had torn her apart when he'd seen that his son was burnt. He'd come upstairs to ask her if she wanted wine with dinner, paring knife in hand from the carrots he was slicing. When Miles was feeling romantic, he enjoyed coming home early and cooking dinner. Playing soft jazz music while they ate dinner together. And sneaking quick, longing looks over the top of Max's head, as if he could not keep his eyes off her. This night had started out that way, but Miles had walked into the bathroom as Caroline was toweling Max off after a bath.

The tips of his ears were red. Caroline had dropped the towel and begun to rub lotion into Max's chubby arms and legs. She'd paid special attention to his ears, dabbing small amounts of aloe on the burnt skin. Miles had shocked her by grabbing her right shoulder and shoving her back so she was standing straight up and looking up at him.

"What, Miles?" she'd snapped. "Yes, he's a bit burnt. Yes, I put sunscreen on him. It happens." She'd turned away from him to reach down and pick up the towel. Miles had swung, this time with his right hand, which still held the knife. A flash of heat in her shoulder. And then the burn and the blood.

She'd looked down at the blood, now gushing from the cut in her arm. Just out of the tub herself, she was still nude. Miles had seemed fascinated with the sight of her blood running over her skin.

"Miles!" she'd shouted. "I need a bandage—"

"You need stitches, Caroline," he'd said calmly.

"Then I need some clothes." She stood rooted to the spot in the bathroom. If she went for her own clothes and dripped blood over the hardwood floor, Miles was likely to add to her injuries and then assign her the task of cleaning the mess later.

"Mommy." Max began to cry. The room nearly vibrated with tension, but Caroline knew Max was upset because of the blood.

"I'm sorry," Miles had said quietly. His apologies were never sincere, because there was always a reason—*an excuse*—tacked on the end of them. "You know better than to have him out in the sun that long."

"We were at the pool for an hour. The sun is not out. And he had half a bottle of sunscreen on—"

"Then buy him a hat, for God's sake."

The blood continued to fall. Caroline, weak at the knees, reached for a washrag to press to the throbbing wound. She would get nowhere arguing with a man too arrogant to give anyone else the opportunity for the last word..

"Max." Caroline runs backwards a few steps and catches the Frisbee. "Let's put more sunscreen on."

"Mo-om," Max groans. She laughs and tosses the Frisbee down on the picnic table they keep in their yard. She grabs the bottle of Coppertone for babies and squirts a healthy bit into her palm. "I'm not a baby, Mom."

Still with baby fat cheeks, Max glares at her with angry eyes as she rubs the lotion in on his arms and his face and over the tops of his ears. She will never skimp on sun screen. Seven stitches had taught her that lesson well.

Feeling someone's eyes on her, Caroline lifts her chin and looks up at the house. She and Max are the only ones home. Miles is still at the office, although there are days she would swear Miles comes home early and spies on them before even letting them know he's home.

From outside, looking at those windows that reflect the sunlight and make the house seem empty and cold, Caroline thinks the house looks haunted. She's never been particularly afraid when she's inside, not even when she's alone. But when she's outside, like right now, she could swear that the house is watching her. Watching and waiting.

She raises her eyes and looks up at the third floor windows. Miles' office. Someone is standing in the window watching her. It has to be Miles. Who the hell else would come into her home and go to Miles' office and then stand and blatantly stare at her, even after she's seen him? It's Miles. He must watch her a lot, for her to always have that feeling when she is outside in the yard. Caroline just wonders why. This is the man she married, for God's sake. She'd borne his child, and yet, he just seems to grow more and more mysterious.

RAPUNZEL

FORTY-ONE

August, 2008

Springfield, IL

Caroline actually remembers Miles' mother. It hits her so suddenly it knocks the breath out of her. She is upstairs, double checking that each of the rooms are clean, that the clutter is picked up and there is no dust in which Mrs. Wolfe can run her finger and leave a trail. As she plumps a throw pillow and tosses it back down in a wingback chair in the corner of the spare bedroom on the second floor, she hears a car pull up outside. She looks out the window. Miles' parents are driving an SUV, best guess something high dollar and pristine. His father emerges from the vehicle first. From the second story, Caroline can't get a good impression of him. He looks tall, and he carries himself with the same arrogance Caroline has long since seen in Miles. Dressed in gray trousers and a golf shirt, he looks cold and crisp, even in the late August humidity.

Mr. Wolfe opens the door for his wife. Caroline sucks in a breath so sharp it slices her lungs as Mrs. Wolfe steps out of the SUV. Her stomach clenches and suddenly the palms of her hands are wet with sweat. Hatred and fear swell inside her. From her black heels, over her black slacks and shiny silver blouse, up to her striking silver hair, the woman commands attention and fear. Especially from her daughter-in-law.

"Do you remember them?"

Caroline pushes her trembling hands into the pockets in her capris and turns to look at Dawn. She'd taken the time to dress a little nicer, in hopes of getting in their good graces. Thinking maybe if she was careful, this could be a pleasant visit. Up until this moment, she had not had any memories of Miles' parents at all.

"Yes," she whispers. "I remember his mother."

"You do?" Dawn sounds shocked, as if she had only asked automatically, without expecting an answer. "You remember his mother?"

"Oh God, Dawn, she's horrible," Caroline groans. She dips her chin to her chest and sighs. "How in the hell am I gonna get through this?"

"Hey." Dawn moves closer to her and rubs the back of her neck. "You can do it. I'm right here. We'll get through it together."

Caroline stiffens and lifts her head when she hears Miles call up at her from the main floor. Once again she's struck by how *normal* he sounds. How *average* this whole scene is and should be. Miles, out by the grill, turning the skewers so the steak and shrimp do not burn. Calling up to tell her his parents are here for dinner. Max, hurrying down the stairs to greet them. Caroline should be going downstairs to greet them also. But she can't. She can't make her feet work. Her legs feel like lead, and her feet are nailed to the spot. Her body trembles violently as she looks at Dawn and shakes her head.

"I can't. I can't, Dawn. I can't go down there."

"Car—" Dawn studies her face closely. "What is it? What?"

Caroline presses her lips together. "I don't—"

" Caroline!" Miles yells to her again.

"What is it? What do you remember about Mrs. Wolfe?"

Caroline squeezes her eyes shut. She remembers a million different instances, and yet, they could all be the same. Miles' mother had always treated her as if she were not good enough for her son. Like she might not be good enough to be the dirt beneath Miles' feet. The woman has never spoken to her with anything but contempt, and she has always been cold with Max. Max has never been allowed to sit in her lap. He has never been allowed to call her Grandma. It's always been Grandmother, and when he couldn't say that clearly, he was to call her Miss.

One year at Thanksgiving, Caroline was in the kitchen, checking an apple crisp she'd made. Miles liked apples. He'd told her once that his mom had always made apple pie. Knowing she could never make an apple pie that would touch his mother's, Caroline had attempted the crisp as a substitute. His mother had cornered her there in the kitchen, while Miles and his father were sipping wine and watching football in the living room.

"You are a conniving, whoring piece of trash," his mother had stated with the same calm tone that Miles used when delivering his harsh words and blows. "I know about the boys you slept with, and I know about the child you conceived and aborted, and I believe that child is better off without you. If you do not give my child a son, I will blame your inabilities on your previous life."

Caroline had stood frozen, stunned by the vicious words, delivered in the same tone that someone might use to relay the score of the game or the weather forecast.

"And furthermore, once you've given my son his own son, I will insist that he divorce you and move on."

"Caroline?" Miles appears in the doorway of the spare room now. He stares at her and Dawn curiously. Caroline meets his eyes and wonders if he'd known his mother had said such vicious things to her.

Miles appraises her with those steel eyes, and she knows. He has known all along, every cold, hateful thing she has ever said to Caroline. Of course he knows. He treats her the same way. It's obvious where Miles learned how to treat women.

Not women. People.

Caroline feels the room tilt a bit. She throws her arms out to her sides to steady herself. Dawn takes her by the arm and leads her to the same chair Caroline had just been standing by.

"Caroline's feeling a bit woozy," Dawn tells Miles. Caroline sits still, like stone, and waits to see what he will do. Will he come to her and offer comfort? Ask her what's wrong? If she needs a glass of water? Or will he *know* that she is sweating memories? Looks meant to kill and words of hate thrown in that damned dispassionate tone. The fists and the skin against skin and the night he'd nearly strangled her.

Michael Ramsay.

What would be worse? To have Miles walk toward her and squat down in front of her and take her hand? To have him *act* like a normal husband? Or to see him stare at her with those cold eyes and to see his the hatred, the *contempt* fall over his face as he pieces things together and realizes she was physically sick with fear and hate and sadness?

"My parents are here," he says quietly. "Dinner will be served in twenty minutes." He watches her to see if she is going to argue. "You will be downstairs in five. No excuses."

The words are in her head immediately. That she will be down when she damned well pleases. But there is something that stops her. She can't get the words to the tip of her tongue, and she can't make her mouth move. Fear sits in her mouth, ice cold and burning like an ice cube too big to swallow.

Dawn, still standing in front of Caroline, watches Miles retreat down the hall and finally down the stairs. When she is sure they are alone again, she kneels down in front of her.

"What is it? What are you remembering?"

"Every horrible, hateful word that woman has ever spoken to me."

Dawn shakes her head. “There’s something else.”

“I don’t know.”

“There’s something in your head right now that is scaring the hell out of you, Caroline.” Dawn glances back over her shoulder. “Your mother-in-law trashing you wouldn’t scare you like this. No one’s mother-in-law can scare them like this. You look like you were just face to face with the devil—"

“I don’t know, Dawn,” Caroline insists. Dawn’s right. She knows that. There’s something locked in her head that she can’t get to, no matter how hard she tries. What she does know is now is not the time to push it. If she isn’t downstairs in five minutes—*four now*—Miles will come back up and drag her down by her hair. If he doesn’t hit her now, he will later. He probably already will, just because it’s obvious she’s remembered how much she hates his mother.

“We need to put this all—"

“Not now.” Caroline shakes her head.

“Car—"

“Dawn, I know, but not now.” Caroline swallows hard. “Not now. If I don’t get down there and act normal, he’ll beat the hell out of me, and he might not wait until you guys are all gone.”

“Okay.” Dawn springs up to stand and Caroline remembers the days when she was as limber and flexible and free as Dawn. The thought brings guilt, and Caroline fights it. Dawn might be free flying right now, but it sure as hell isn’t by choice.

A violent shiver rips through Caroline. She feels Dawn watching her closely.

"I'm okay," she whispers. "I'm okay. Just stay with me."

"Won't leave your side," Dawn answers and Caroline knows without a doubt that Dawn has never left her side. For all the suspicions she'd had in those first days, Caroline knows now that Dawn would do anything for her.

Earlier that day, Caroline and Dawn had tossed salads and sliced fruit and chilled white wine, all in hopes that Caroline could stay one step ahead through the evening. Even subconsciously, she had known it would be a nightmare. Now there is nothing to do but go downstairs and hold on tight.

Max is in the living room with Miles' father. The TV is off, and Max is reading. Caroline is partly proud that her four year old son can read and partly horrified that her inlaws might try to snatch him from her and send him to boarding school until he is eighteen. Miles' mother has said often that there is no education here that would be fitting for her grandson.

Caroline greets her father-in-law when he glances up at her. He smiles and says hello. Because the situation dictates, he gets up and moves, without hurry, toward her. Her body goes rigid when he hugs her in that chaste, cold way rich people hug. They are rich. Caroline suddenly remembers that Miles family has unfathomable amounts of money. She remembers the way Miles had backhanded her when she'd asked if the money was all from the steel business his father owned. She'd thought it was a legitimate question, but she'd never asked again.

Steeling herself for the first up close sight of her mother-in-law since the accident, Caroline moves on through the arched doorway to the kitchen. It is empty, and Caroline breathes a huge sigh of relief.

"Looking for me?" The voice is cool and flecked with amusement. The woman had heard Caroline's relief, apparently stepping into the room behind her and Dawn, after coming from the restroom.

"Amanda," Caroline says softly. She wonders if her smile looks as generic as it feels.

"Caroline." The woman hugs her just as dutifully and coldly as her husband had. "It's good to see you. You're lucky to be alive."

The words alone are innocuous, but something dark lies just beneath them. Caroline is aware of this, but she knows Dawn can't know what she's thinking.

"So I'm told."

"You look incredible." Amanda's eyes rove over Caroline's new face. Caroline steps back when Amanda lifts her hand and traces her fingertip over her cheekbone. She wonders briefly if she is more appealing to her now. Has Miles changed her appearance as a way to please his mother?

Caroline clears her throat. "Would you like a glass of chardonnay?"

"Please." Amanda gives her a curt nod. Caroline's hand shakes, and white wine splashes into the glass. Unsightly. If Miles had seen that, he'd have had a word for her. Wondering where he is, Caroline glances up at the French doors and sees that he is outside, standing at the grill, with his back to the door.

"I understand you're having trouble remembering things."

Caroline hands her the glass and then folds her arms across her chest. Defensive position, she knows. Amanda eyes her arms in distaste.

"The doctors have said there's no physical reason for the amnesia."

"Whatever could cause it then?" Amanda asks politely. She takes a sip of the wine.

"The trauma, I guess."

"The trauma," Amanda repeats and then adds, "of the accident?"

The threat is delivered without words, but Caroline feels it creep up her spine and slither into her nerves. Her knees go weak. Dawn clears her throat and steers Caroline toward the bar.

"Sit down," she urges her, ignoring Amanda completely. "You're very pale."

Caroline sits down, grateful to Dawn.

"Dawn." Amanda turns her attention to Dawn, with all the cunning of a snake about to devour its prey. "How are you doing? I'm sure Danny's death must have been very hard for you."

"I'm fine, thank you," Dawn answers, clearly not intending to play into Amanda's hands.

"Was the fire ruled arson? I know there was some concern."

"Yes, it was."

Dawn turns her back to them and pulls the refrigerator door open. She begins taking the dinner salads and the fruits from shelves and setting them out on the bar.

"Are you staying for dinner, Dear?" Amanda asks suddenly.

"Yes, I am."

"Miles said you've been a big help to him since Caroline has been incapacitated."

Caroline looks up quickly. Amanda's perfectly shaped brows are arched, waiting to see if Dawn takes the bait. So Amanda knows that Miles slept with Dawn. Caroline files that away to consider later.

"Caroline is far from incapacitated now, Mrs. Wolfe," Dawn tells her. "As you can see. The doctors have said she'll make a full recovery."

"Except, perhaps, for her memory."

"I think she'll remember what's important."

Caroline almost smiles. Dawn is at bat for her right now. It is the first time, since she saw the gun, that she feels any hope.

"Do you remember your life before Miles?" Amanda asks, turning her attention back to Caroline.

Before she can answer, the door behind her opens and Miles carries the skewers in on a large tray. Caroline stares at the tray when Miles sets it on the counter in front of her. The large chunks of steak and onion and mushroom turn her stomach. But her eyes are drawn to the tips of the skewers, so sharp and pointy.

Dawn opens a beer and takes a long drink. Caroline watches her stare defiantly at Miles, waiting for him to berate her for drinking cheap beer on a night he believes is special and conducive to fine wine and jazz. When Miles does look at Dawn, Caroline does not look away. She wonders, not for the first time, what it had been like for the two of them to make love. If it had been frenzied and passionate and even vulgar, as it sometimes was with Miles, when they'd fought or when their anger was palpable. Or had it been slow and gentle lovemaking? Had Miles pinched Dawn and left bruises or had he caressed her lovingly? Had he kissed her neck or had he left bite marks on her skin? Had she cried? And if she had, did he press his lips to her tears to take them away or had he covered her face with a pillow so he would not have to see them?

Which Miles Wolfe had Dawn slept with? Part of Caroline desperately wishes it had been the brutal man who got off on inflicting pain. She didn't want to think that this man who was so stingy with the sweet words and gentle touches might have given them so freely to another woman.

And yet, how could she be so cruel to wish that violence on Dawn?

Caroline sweeps her gaze down over Dawn's body. Looking for bruises that would be long gone or imagining her husband's hands and mouth on her, bringing her pleasure, she's not sure. The thought of Miles's hands on her, making her come, is almost more disturbing than thinking of him biting her and drawing blood.

Dawn breaks the stare with Miles and turns to look at her so suddenly, she catches her inspection. And knows. Dawn knows immediately what she is thinking. Caroline can tell from the way the defiance folds itself a million times and slips away, out of sight, and Dawn is left stripped and vulnerable. Guilty and full of regrets.

"Excuse me," Caroline says quietly. She manages to stand and slip out of the room without Miles or Amanda realizing what has just passed.

Miles comes to get her a few moments later. She is in her bathroom, the one off her room, the lavender room.

"Are you okay?" he asks, again assuming the role of the concerned husband.

"I'm fine."

"Why are you feeling so badly today?"

She has brushed her teeth already. They feel smooth as she runs her tongue over them and considers her answer.

"Just nervous, I think. Seeing your parents."

"Really?" He frowns. "Why would you be nervous about that? We're celebrating"

"I know. We got the cake, right? Did Dawn and I remember to pick up Max's cake?" She knows they did. She and Dawn had picked up last minute groceries and a chocolate layer cake that was meant to celebrate Max's birthday and his beginning of kindergarten.

"We're celebrating you too, you know."

"No, I don't know." Caroline pushes Miles slightly so he will move. "Why would we be celebrating me?"

"Because you're here," he answers with a sheepish smile. "Because you survived a horrible accident, and you're here and you're going to be okay. And I love you."

The last words are like nails on a chalk board. Unable to make her mouth form the words, Caroline simply smiles and raises her eyebrows.

"Caroline." Miles reaches for her as she tries to slip away from him.

"What?"

"Will you ever?"

Caroline's heart catches in her chest and then beats harder when he slides his hands over her hips. Gently, he pulls her closer, close enough that she feels him against her middle.

"Will I ever what?"

"Love me again."

Unsure of what he is asking, Caroline turns her head away and closes her eyes. Love him again? Pretend to be happy with him again in this farce of a marriage? Or make love to him again? Submit herself to him and let him do what he wants?

She can't. She can't pretend to love him, let alone share an intimate relationship with him again.

"I don't know, Miles." She shakes her head. "I don't know. I'm just not ready to think about it."

"I know I've hurt you in the past. I want that to change—"

"You don't want that to change, Miles. You're still doing it."

"I'll get help."

He has never suggested that he might *need* help, never mind that he might get it. Caroline stares into his eyes and wonders what is inside him to make him such a tangled mess of man. He won't get help, she tells herself.

He'll kill you before he gets help.

"Dinner's ready, Miles."

"Can I kiss you?"

They are suddenly pressed tightly against each other, and his fingers encircle her upper arms. She has visions of him shoving her back on her bed and raping her and then buttoning his slacks to go back downstairs and pretend that life here is normal. The only problem is she can see him pushing one kiss to taking the rest of what he wants just as easily as she can picture him getting angry if she denies him and throwing her down and raping her to hurt her.

She has been afraid to be in this position since she woke up and started to remember. How had he caught her so off-guard and unprepared?

"Caroline? Just one kiss?"

Throat too tight to answer, she simply nods. She stares at his lips and rather than think of the hateful words those lips have delivered to her, rather than think of the way his teeth have pierced her skin and drawn blood, she thinks about the man she thought she'd fallen in love with. The man she'd kissed and made love to, before he'd become a monster.

His lips are warm and gentle. They hover so close to her own and then brush hers and pull away, and she thinks she is saved and it's over. But then they touch hers again. His lips touch the corner of her mouth and then the tip of his tongue teases the dimple just next to the corner of her mouth. He used to kiss her like this when they were younger. Before her fairytale romance became a nightmare.

She tastes the wine, the chardonnay when he strokes his tongue over her lips. She should have had some. Maybe this would be easier. When she opens her mouth to ask him to stop, he takes advantage of the moment and kisses her with passion and desire that she doesn't want to feel.

Miles had been an attentive lover when he wanted to be. He knew where to touch her, where to kiss her, when to slow down. He knew exactly what to do to make her melt down right here and lay down on the bed and beg him to make love to her.

His kiss is intoxicating. Her hands splay across his chest to push him back, but suddenly she feels her fingers twist and grasp at his shirt. His hands are inside her shirt.

"No." She pushes him back gently. "Not yet, Miles."

"Caroline, I love you. I will change for you—"

"This isn't the time." She steps away from him and smooths her shirt down over her hips. "Your parents are here, Miles. Dinner is ready downstairs."

"Tonight?"

"I'm not ready..." She can't even make herself say the words. 'Make love.' They make her feel ill.

"But a kiss. Can I kiss you goodnight?"

She presses her lips together. He's not going to let her out of this room unless she says yes.

"Of course." Her voice is gruff. She's not sure how the hell she'll get out of it later, but right now this promise is all that stands between her and a broken rib or two.

Odd, she thinks, as they make their way back down to the kitchen. Miles' parents being here had saved her from making love to him just now. Miles' mother had come between them.

Miles' mother...

Between us...

Between us, Mother....always....there....always there....like... Yes...Just like that....

"Caroline?" Miles lays his hand on her back. She blinks and realizes she is staring at the front door.

Always...involved...always there...

"I'm fine," she says slowly.

"You've gone pale again."

"No, no, I'm fine."

Always...there...

Take care of it then, Miles....take care...take care of it...

"Are you remembering something?" Miles sounds so concerned. Directly at odds with the words she keeps hearing. Dawn appears at the base of the stairs with a glass of wine in hand.

“Thought you might like some wine.” She reaches to hand Caroline the glass, but freezes when she gets a good look at her.

“Thank you.” Caroline takes the glass.

“Please come in for dinner.” Miles squeezes her shoulder and then leaves her and Dawn alone.

“What?” Caroline asks when she realizes Dawn is still staring at her. “I can’t put it all together. There’s just too much but still too little. I can’t do it—"

“Did you fuck him?” Dawn asks bluntly.

“What?”

“Just now. Did you fuck him? A quick little ride while I was down here fencing with Maleficent?”

“What the hell are you talking about? No, I didn’t. Dawn, I—"

“Save it, Caroline. Your lips are all swollen, and your face is all red with whisker burn. And now he’s all touchy feely, are you okay, please come in for dinner?” Dawn sets her own wine glass on the banister and looks around, presumably for her keys.

“I didn’t,” Caroline repeats desperately. “I swear to you, Dawn, it didn’t happen.”

“Did you fake it? Or did you come? Can he still make you come, even after he killed my husband?”

“Dawn,” Caroline whispers. Dawn finds her purse on the floor under the hall table. Caroline watches her pick it up.

“You know as well as I do how this game is played and won. Nothing happened upstairs—"

“His mouth was all over you—"

“He kissed me. That’s it.”

“If you’re lying to me,” Dawn squeezes her eyes shut, “if you’re lying to me, so help me God, I will kill myself. And then you can live with two deaths on your conscience, Caroline Wolfe.”

Caroline winces and then throws her head back. “Not two. Three.”

RAPUNZEL

FORTY-TWO

August, 2008

Springfield, IL

“Ladies?” Miles appears in the foyer again, oblivious to the tension ringing in the air. “Dinner is ready.”

Caroline stares at Dawn, uncertain where her last statement came from. What she knows for absolute certain is that she has to get out of here. She has to get away from Miles and this life she lives with him. Dawn, who is still looking at Caroline with uncertainty, is probably thinking the same thing. Get away from Miles. Get away from Caroline, the freak woman who talks in riddles and doesn’t understand them herself.

“Shall we?” Miles raises his eyebrows. Caroline clears her throat and nods. She looks back over her shoulder to make sure Dawn is following them. As angry as Dawn is with her right now and as frustrated as she is with Dawn for her suspicions, she can't do this evening without her.

Dinner is like a scene from a play Caroline is watching. She nibbles on her food, but does not taste it. Dawn appears to chew robotically, as if she has no idea what she's eating, only that she must chew before she swallows. Miles and his parents discuss the steel business, and all the while, Caroline fights an urge to tell them that the game is up and she knows they are not in the steel business. She doesn't know why she wants to say this, doesn't know what exactly she thinks they do, but she's certain their money is from something else entirely. As if the steel business, Wolfe Steel & Design, is just a dummy corporation for a money laundering scheme or something.

That's not it, though. Caroline has no doubt there is something a little off with the Wolfes, most especially Miles, but it's nothing as white collar as money laundering. Miles pushes the wine on her, but she does not drink it. She notices Dawn barely touches hers. She wonders if fear hovers in Dawn's stomach as it does her own. She wishes she could get an unobstructed view of Dawn's mind, of her *thoughts*, just once. Caroline has come to trust her, but she still wonders just exactly what Dawn thinks and feels. Is she staying to help Caroline out of a mess because she feels obligated? But why would she? Why would she believe Miles to be partly responsible for Danny's death and stay here as Caroline's friend out of obligation? Who is she obligated to? Certainly not Caroline. Miles? Is she obligated to Miles or just afraid of him?

Or does she still care? Caroline wonders what will become of their friendship once they get away from Miles. *If* they get away from Miles. That's the thing. Dawn can get away. Dawn can pack up and leave at any time. Caroline is never going to be free from him. She's certain of this. She will never get away from Miles Wolfe. Unless one of them is dead.

That thought nearly drives her to drink her wine, but she is determined not to. She needs a clear head for later, when everyone is gone, except herself and Max and Miles. Miles had asked for another kiss. It's very likely that once the house is empty and no one can come to her rescue that he will force himself on her. If she has a clear head, maybe she can talk her way out of it.

Maybe not.

Amanda quizzes Max on starting kindergarten. Caroline squirms in her chair in the dining room as Amanda recounts all of Miles' genius moments as a child. He'd learned to read before kindergarten. He was doing complicated math problems in second grade. His problem solving and reasoning skills were well beyond what typical fourth graders exhibited.

"But did you like school?" Max asks Miles. Caroline bites her lip, hoping Amanda will not shush him for asking what she would consider a worthless question.

"I did."

"What was your favorite class?" Max takes a big drink and leaves a milk moustache on his upper lip. When Max glances at her, she raises her eyebrows and glances at the napkin beside his plate. Carefully, Max wipes his mouth and then refolds his napkin. Caroline is proud of her son for his manners, but even more than that, she is remembering another family dinner when Max was no more than two. He had knocked over his sippy cup and spilled a dribble of milk on his highchair tray. After dinner while Miles' parents were outside on the patio with Max, Miles had slapped her so hard her teeth rattled. She was at home with his son to teach him good table manners, Miles had told her.

Rather than make her uneasy, the memory warms her heart. It is a memory. Of Max. For a moment, Caroline had had a clear view of Max as a baby. Sweet, soft black curls and thick, long eyelashes. Blue eyes.

"My favorite class," Miles says now as he studies Max's face and pretends to think about it. "I liked math a lot when I was younger. But I liked my college years best."

"College years?" Max repeats. "Why? Where did you go to college?"

"Illinois State University," Miles tells Max, but his eyes are on Caroline. "That's where I met your mommy."

Caroline presses her lips together. She is still emotional in the aftermath of remembering something about her son. Feeling for the first time how her son *is* connected to her. Knowing this child is hers, and she will never leave Miles without Max safely in her arms.

"And where you met Dawnie too, right, Daddy?"

"Yes, where I met Dawnie too," Miles says and turns to offer Max a smile. "Are you okay, Caroline?"

"Yes, I'm fine." Caroline looks down at her plate, but she feels Amanda's eyes on her. The woman is probably still hungry to see her miserable.

"Didn't Mommy and Dawnie have another friend, Daddy? Didn't you say Mommy had a friend that you didn't like?"

Caroline's heart punches painfully hard in her chest. She looks from Max up to Miles, curious what Miles will say. They are talking about Beth. Caroline knows she and Dawn have never talked about Beth, not in front of Max. Why would Miles talk about her?

"No, I said Mommy had a friend who didn't like me," he corrects Max. Again he looks to Caroline. "Beth didn't think I was good enough for Mommy."

"And hasn't it been decided that we're all better off without that lesbian complicating our lives," Amanda says firmly, as if she is ending all talk of Beth Summers starting now.

"Beth wasn't a lesbian, Amanda." Caroline stares at Miles, anger and hate stirring together inside her to create false bravado. "Why did you ever say that? How the hell did you ever know anything about her?"

"Really, Caroline, does it matter now? She hated me on sight, and I honestly didn't care much for her either."

"It does matter now, Miles," Caroline answers. "Beth was seeing someone when she died."

Caroline feels Dawn's eyes on her. She can't turn to look at her, but she knows Dawn is surprised to hear the memories coming out of Caroline's mouth.

"Like who? Most likely another woman—"

"Mike Garrett." Caroline throws down her napkin and stands up. Miles stops Dawn when she stands to go after

Caroline. Instead it is Miles that follows Caroline into the kitchen.

"Who's Mike Garrett?"

"I don't know."

She runs hot water in the sink. They always serve dinner on the fine china when Miles' parents are dinner guests. Miles does not want the china in the dishwasher, therefore after surviving dinner with his parents, she normally has to survive washing dishes with Amanda. Caroline washes and Amanda dries, because the woman does not want to ruin her manicure.

"She was sleeping with him?" Miles sounds very interested.

"I don't know," Caroline snaps. She turns to Miles as she squirts dishwashing liquid in the water. "I don't know. I don't remember. But I do remember her telling me one day that she was interested in him, and I know they'd gone out a few times."

"So you do remember Beth?"

"No!" Caroline slams the faucet back down to stop the water. "Yes, sometimes I do, but not really. I don't remember that much, but I know she wasn't a lesbian and I remember you saying that after we got married and she was gone and I wish you'd just stop!"

"Don't start defending Beth Summers to me or I'll—"

"You'll what, Miles? Hit me? Pick up that knife there and cut me? Guess what?" She picks up the knife and hands it to him. "Go ahead. I'm not scared of you. I've never been scared of you. You've done it all to me, and I'm still here."

"Shut up."

"What? Now I'm showing you disrespect and your parents can probably hear it? What happened to that line of shit you gave me upstairs? If I still loved you, you were gonna get help. Huh? What happened to getting help, Miles?"

"Shut. Up."

"Go to hell." She turns away from him, back to the sink. "And take your mother with you."

She doesn't see it coming. The blow to her kidney knocks her off her feet. Her knees buckle, but she catches herself and stands again.

"When they're gone—"

"What? What're you gonna do when they're gone? Wait until Max is asleep and then come to my room and beat me?" She drops her voice to a whisper. "Rape me? I got used to that too, didn't I, Miles? You got nothin' on me." She pokes her finger at his chest. "Unless you wanna kill me."

Caroline hears the chairs scraping back from the table in the dining room. Miles glares at her, looks as if he wants to snap her in two.

"Let me help you with the dishes," Amanda says as she strides into the room.

"No." Caroline shakes her head. "It's okay, Amanda. I've got them."

"Nonsense—"

"Mom." Miles takes his mother's hand and leads her out to the patio. Caroline hunches her shoulders and starts washing the one plate she's brought into the kitchen. She hears footsteps behind her and then sags against the sink in relief when Miles' dad joins them outside.

"You're crazy," Dawn mumbles. She sets a stack of plates on the counter beside Caroline.

"Maybe I am."

"What are you doing, provoking him like that? Caroline, he's gonna tear you apart tonight."

"I hate it when he talks about Beth like that."

"Look, don't get yourself killed trying to prove something to me, okay?"

Caroline swallows hard. "It's not about you, Dawn. I am so sick of living like this. I can't do it anymore."

"You'd better do it, until you figure out how to get that little boy away from him."

"I know."

Caroline washes dishes and Dawn dries them. The silence is heavy and uncomfortable, but Caroline is too tired and weary to think of something to say.

"Was Beth really seeing Mike Garrett?"

"I don't know. She kind of wanted to. I remember her telling me that. But I can't remember anything else."

"When did she tell you that?"

"You were at home that weekend."

"I miss her," Dawn says softly.

"I hate it when he talks about her like that."

"What're you gonna do? He's gonna be all over you when we all leave."

"I don't know."

"I could stay—"

"No."

"I don't wanna leave you with him—"

"No."

"He won't hurt me."

In the way...all the time...

Take care of it... Take care of it...

Caroline shakes her head, hoping to get Amanda's voice out her mind.

"Yeah, he will, Dawn. He'd go after you, before he did anything to me." She knows as she says the words that it's true. Miles would attack Dawn before he'd lift a finger to Caroline tonight.

Dawn licks her lips and pays extra attention to the wine glass she's drying.

"I'm sorry. About what I said earlier."

"It's okay." Caroline shrugs, Dawn's earlier hateful words forgotten. Her mind is in motion again. Thinking. Remembering. So much information. So close to the surface. Caroline is desperate to call it all back, but with the noise and the lights and Dawn talking, she just can't do it.

"Look. It's just that you loved him once, Car. I know what it is to love someone. I'm scared you're gonna fall in love with him again."

The wine glass Caroline holds in her soapy hands breaks.

"Shit!" Caroline takes a quick breath. A thin line of red spreads over the palm of her hand.

"Shit, Caroline, are you okay?" Dawn sets the glass she'd been holding on the counter and takes Caroline's hand in hers. The blood puddles in Caroline's cupped hand. "You're gonna need stitches. I'll take you. Let's go. I'll tell Miles—"

"Dawn," Caroline says calmly. Dawn, who has become a frenzy of movement, stops and looks at Caroline. "I will never fall in love with him again. Never."

"What did he do?" Dawn whispers.

"I don't know," Caroline answers truthfully. "But I know I will never love him again."

Dawn nods. "Okay." She squeezes Caroline's hand. "But right now, you do need stitches. And you probably need some Advil. I saw him hit you."

"I'm okay."

"Lightheaded?" Dawn wraps a dry dishtowel around Caroline's hand.

"Little."

"C'mon." Dawn leads Caroline over to the patio door. Miles and his parents sit around the table on the patio. The mood is jovial, a complete three sixty from the atmosphere inside the house. Max sits on Miles' knee.

"What's going on?" Miles calls.

"Caroline cut her hand," Dawn announces. "I think she needs stitches."

Miles does not get up and rush to her side. He simply turns his attention to Caroline. He puts his hand on Max's shoulder. Caroline sees his fingers curl in to squeeze the boy. The threat is subtle enough that Caroline doubts anyone else sees it.

She can hear it, just as if Miles is right there whispering in her ear.

Leave me, Caroline, if that's what you want. But you'll never get Max.

SLEEPING BEAUTY

FORTY-THREE

2007

Springfield, IL

Beth downs the beer in one swallow. Caroline bites her tongue. They have been at odds for so long now. Since she'd started dating Miles. Beth hates him. Caroline knows Beth wants what is best for her, and yet, she is so angry with her. What right does Beth have to judge Miles? *How* can she judge him anyway? She doesn't *know* him. Not the way Caroline does. He's a little bit old-fashioned. Waiting to make love to her until the night they became engaged. Saying that he'd prefer Caroline didn't work, especially if they had children. And yet, Caroline likes that about him. He had respected her. Waiting until they were truly in love before he made love to her. He wants a good family home for his children. How can she fault him for that?

Beth has been drinking a lot. Caroline hates that. Beth has never been much of a drinker, not since Caroline has known her. She has to be feeling really low to be drinking like this. But Caroline knows if she approaches her, if she says anything to her, Beth will lash out at her. She'll say mean things. Hateful things, even. Ask her what the hell she knows. Tell her to go with Miles. Tell her to go to hell. Maybe Caroline is taking the easy way out, but she is afraid of that confrontation with Beth. So she sits in her lawn chair at the graduation party and watches Beth drink like the well will be dry tomorrow.

Maybe if she could find Dawn. Maybe Dawn could talk to Beth. Get her to stop drinking. That's not good enough though. She's had enough. She needs to go home. Maybe Dawn would drive her home. Maybe Dawn would get Beth home and tucked in and then Beth would be okay and she wouldn't have to be angry and launch into how much she hates Caroline and Miles.

Caroline looks around. Dawn and Danny had been sitting across the bonfire from her and Miles. But they are gone now. Maybe they've gone for another beer or some snacks. But maybe they've gone home. Maybe Dawn is going home with Danny, and they won't give Beth a second thought. They shouldn't have to. Beth doesn't drink, let alone drink and drive.

Caroline glances at Miles' empty chair. He'd gotten up a few minutes ago to use the restroom. Maybe she should just go talk to Beth. Before Miles comes back. She could just go talk to her. Even if Beth got angry and caused a scene, maybe that would be better. Better than watching her drink herself sick. Better than worrying about how she was going to get home. Worrying if someone would hurt her.

“Where are you going?” Miles asks just as Caroline stands up.

“I was just...” she sighs and continues, “going to talk to Beth.”

“Why?”

“Miles, I’m worried about her. She’s had way too much to drink.”

“Beth is a big girl, Caroline. She’s here with friends. You saw her come in with those two girls and that other guy. They’ll take care of her now.”

Now. That word crawls inside her and gets stuck in her throat. Now. They’ll take care of her now, because Caroline has tossed her aside for Miles.

“Are you sure?” Caroline waffles and hates herself for doing it.

“I’m sure.” Miles answers firmly. “I think we should leave.”

“Yeah?”

“Yeah. I think we should sneak out and go to my place.”

“And then what?” Caroline lifts an eyebrow suggestively.

“We could make love all night. Or we could—"

“I’ll take door number one,” Caroline says with a smile.

...The phone rings and wakes them. It is still dark outside; the alarm clock on the table beside Miles’ bed reads 3:17. Caroline moves Miles’ hand from her waist and stretches to pick up the phone.

Beth...

Michael Ramsay...2117 Sterling Way. Michael Ramsay.

Michael Ramsay.

If she'd have just said something to her...if she'd have just walked over and said something. Even if she'd started a fight. Things would be different. Bethie might still be alive.

Michael Ramsay...

I, Caroline, take you, Miles, to be my lawfully wedded husband...

As long as we both shall live...

CAROLINE

FORTY-FOUR

August, 2008

Springfield, IL

Max loves school. Miles quizzes him every night over what he has learned through the day. Max proudly writes his name; Caroline is fascinated with each monkey tail on each letter. Her son is learning to write. He is learning letters and their sounds and learning to read. As she marvels at how the human brain learns things, Miles grumbles because his son is not learning fast enough.

Her hand itches a bit. Dawn had taken her just yesterday to have the four stitches removed. Neither of them had discussed running. Caroline still sees Miles' hand on Max's shoulder, still feels the threat reverberate in every bone of her body. She can't leave until she can get Max away too.

The bruises Miles had landed on her later that night have faded, though she is still sore. Max's excitement over learning to read letters and playing with his new friend Alex is enough to make the hurt go away. She wishes briefly that she were married to someone who loved her, not in the sick twisted way that Miles does, and that she could have another baby. She pictures Max's small hands handing her diapers and bottles for a new baby.

It will never happen. God had given her two chances. The first she'd blown and she's not doing so well with this one. Max's basic needs are met and then some, but she worries about the boy, living with a father who beats his mother and a mother who only remembers him sometimes.

Dawn is on her way over. Caroline pours two glasses of iced tea and takes them into the library. Miles would yell at her for this, but she doesn't care. Miles is at work. Dawn is coming by so the two of them can discuss new paint colors. Caroline is tired of the drab redecorating job Miles had done while she was laid up in a coma. Maybe new colors won't jog her memory, but they will go a long way toward making her happier while she lives in this prison.

The first room she will change is the lavender room. The second, perhaps, the library. She likes this room. She doesn't have a sense of being here before the accident. Nothing familiar. But it is calming to her now. Maybe the books that line the walls whisper to her and make her forget her own horror story.

Still waiting for Dawn, she tugs open the closet door. In all the time she's spent in this room since the accident, she's never thought to open the door. What could possibly be in the closet of a library that could be more interesting than the books? A vacuum cleaner. No. Not too interesting. A paper box, printer paper from Staples. Printer paper. That seems to indicate that there's a printer somewhere in the house, and she hasn't seen a computer, let alone a printer, since she's come out of the coma. Unless it's empty. Or being used to hold other things.

Like what? Caroline squats down and feels a vague ache in her leg. She's definitely improved since waking up from the coma, and yet, she still suffers enough aches and pains that she figures her body will never forget the accident and the injuries sustained.

She sees her hand reach for the box top, almost as if it is not connected to her and she hadn't realized she was going to do it. Those fingers, still strangely detached from *her*, touch the top. She studies her hand and finally her left hand joins her right and she lifts it off. From where she sits, she can't see into the box. She leans forward, kneeling now, instead of squatting and tips the box so she can see. Rolls of tape and pencils and pens. A calculator. Stapler.

Office supplies.

Caroline sits back and laughs, surprised when the laugh comes out sounding nervous. What had she expected? A loaded mouse trap? One of those toy snakes that jumps out of a can when you open it?

A smoking gun?

A smoking gun.

The hair on the back of her neck stands on end. There's something else in the closet. Something back further, behind the paper box. On her knees, Caroline crawls a foot further into the closet.

She wishes Dawn was here. Wonders what is taking her so long.

A safe.

A fireproof safe. A big, stainless steel fireproof safe. With a key lock.

Caroline feels a drop of sweat trickle down her back, but at the same time, a chill climbs her spine.

Where's Dawn?

Michael Ramsay. 2117 Sterling Way.

Suddenly, as clear as a movie screen, Caroline sees that same safe in her mind. Only it is open. As if someone had rushed out and forgotten to close it. Impossible. Miles wouldn't leave *that* door open. Miles Wolfe would never *accidentally* leave the safe open. Not the one that was in his office on the third floor before the accident. If the safe was open, it was because he meant for it to be open.

But why would he leave the safe open?

To lure someone into the office, his lair.

Michael Ramsay...

Caroline sits back on her feet again and rubs her eyes. Her head is killing her. She squeezes her eyes shut and thinks back to the conversation she and Dawn had had the day they were cleaning, when she'd recited the name and address that keeps popping up in her head.

A license. Dawn had said that somewhere along the line Caroline had seen a driver's license that belonged to

Michael Ramsay. Who the hell is Michael Ramsay and why would she have seen his license?

She hears footsteps behind her and sighs in relief. Even if she and Dawn can't make heads or tails of her half memories, they can figure something out with the horrid color scheme in this house. Caroline likes the idea of making a change. Of *owning* the change, showing ownership in the house. Claiming something as her own. She can't paint her son and claim him, though she desperately wishes she could. She has to sit and wait for those memories to come to her, because she can't change Max. But the house—that's different.

And she has to admit, she enjoys being with Dawn. She is comfortable with Dawn now, and she comes as close to *having fun* as she's going to get, when she's with Dawn.

"Hey." Caroline tilts her head and pops her neck, wishing the headache would go away. "I'm thinking some kind of almond or toast or something for my bedroom. What do you think?"

"Caroline? What are you doing?"

Even though she's trained herself not to react to Miles and retrained herself not to react after the accident, she jumps. Miles' words hang over her, while she still sits on the closet floor.

"Miles." She looks up at him over her shoulder. "What're you doing home? It's only ten in the morning." She glances at her watch, as if she's unsure and she needs to verify that it's still just ten in the morning.

"I left my briefcase in the bedroom this morning. Finished a meeting and figured I'd run home and get it. See if you wanted to grab an early lunch before I go back to work."

Caroline turns away from him. The top is still off the paper box. The safe, tucked away in the back of the closet, is screaming to her now, and it's so loud in Caroline's mind that she wonders if Miles can hear it too.

"No," she says softly. "No, I don't think I want lunch yet, but thanks for asking."

"What're you doing?"

Caroline puts the lid back on the box and then slowly pushes herself to her feet, sagging a bit against the doorframe when her legs protests taking her full weight. Her stomach clutches under the weight of the butterflies dancing there. Miles didn't forget his briefcase, and she knows it. She'd watched him carry it out to his car earlier this morning, just before coming back to kiss Max goodbye and wish him a good day at school.

Miles sits on the edge of the desk and folds his arms over his chest.

"Dawn's coming over. We're going to talk about painting the house. I'm just waiting for her."

Miles holds up a hand and shakes his head. "You're not painting the house, but tell me why you were in the closet, waiting for Dawn."

"Because in all the times I've been in this room since the accident, I've never opened that door. I guess I figured if I lived here, I could open that door."

"What were you looking for?" Miles presses.

"Nothing."

His questions are irritating her further, and her head is still pounding.

"You don't just go opening doors when you're looking for nothing."

"Actually, Miles, you do," she corrects him. "I feel absolutely no connection to this house. I don't remember living in it, ninety-five percent of the time. I like to explore and see if anything jogs my memory."

"Why don't you just talk to me? I can jog your memory. I can tell you about the night there was a snowstorm, and you and I and Max curled up in here with blankets. You read to Max. The Lion, The Witch and the Wardrobe. Very cozy."

"Sounds like it," she agrees. "And yet I still like to wander the house and just see if anything feels familiar."

"And did anything feel familiar to you in this closet?"

Their eyes meet. Caroline *knows* his question is loaded. He is asking if she remembers the safe.

"Well, I would imagine I should be familiar with the vacuum cleaner, but no, nothing is familiar." She almost holds her breath, hoping that she is as good an actress now as she used to be. But he would notice if she held her breath, and he would know why. Act normal, she tells herself.

"In the future, I'd prefer you didn't go snooping around—"

"How am I snooping around, Miles? Don't I live here? Did I live here before the accident? Or has this all just been a big lie?"

"No, this is our home. We've been here—"

"Then you tell me how it's snooping around when I open closet doors in my own home."

Miles shakes his head and stands up straight. He mutters something about how difficult she is and leaves her standing in the closet doorway. Caroline waits until she hears him on the steps before she lets out a shaky breath.

Where is Dawn? She should have been here by now. She should have been here a long time ago. Caroline closes the closet door, but she still sees the safe in her mind as she leaves the library, a glass of tea in each hand.

Why had she been so jumpy about that box? Why did the safe make her so nervous? And what the hell was in there that had Miles so interested in what she remembered?

"Caroline!" Miles yells from upstairs. His voice is muffled, but she can't tell if it's coming from the second or third floor. She hates the thought of going up there with him. The lavender room makes her sick to her stomach, even more so when Miles is in there with her. And their bedroom makes her skin crawl. The image of Miles pinning her down, hands wrapped around her neck is vivid and persistent, and it's the last thing she wants to think about.

"What?" she calls up to him, rather than go upstairs.

"Come here, would you?"

She sighs, answers that she'll be there in a minute and goes to put the glasses back in the kitchen. Miles' briefcase is on the counter. Caroline stares at it for a moment and then reaches for it. What does he carry back and forth day to day? What does he *do*?

She hears his footsteps upstairs and drops her hand away from the briefcase. She has no excuse for looking through his things, so she can't be caught even thinking about it. Instead she goes back out to the foyer and begins the long trek up the stairs.

"Where are you?" she yells as she nears the second floor.

"In the room next to yours," he answers. *Great.*

Michael Ramsay...

What had she been thinking about with that box? A thought had stirred to life inside her. Something that left her uneasy. So uneasy that she can't remember now what she'd been thinking.

Something about Michael Ramsay? No. Not when she'd reached for the box. She'd been wondering what to expect in that box. What she might find.

A smoking gun.

Her foot hits the top step. Miles is deep into the room. His old office. The one where he used to stand and watch her from the window.

A smoking gun.

Michael Ramsay.

Suddenly the image is clear—the driver's license. The file folder she'd found it in. The file folder that had been in the safe.

The picture. Blonde hair, yes. But those eyes. That cold, steel green that could cut through a person. Most people would define that sharp look as blue eyes, but Michael Ramsay had green eyes.

So did Miles.

The photo on the license was a picture of her husband.

A smoking gun…no paper trail…

The computer. There had been a computer on the desk. A slim Dell laptop. Her fingers tapping the keys…

Michael Ramsay. Killer for hire…

Michael Ramsay. 2117 Sterling Way. Bloomington, IL.

Michael. Miles.

Take care of it…

Caroline's heart pushes painfully against her chest as she steps into the room.

Miles had been supplementing his income. She remembers suspecting him of something illegal, because of the money that poured through his hands like tap water.

The safe door had been left open, as if to entice her into the room. As if he had known that she sometimes came into the room and looked out the window and wondered why he would waste hours at a time standing here watching her.

Her fingers, with their French tips, tapping away at the keyboard. Needing a password. She'd tried her birthday, Miles' birthday, Max's birthday. She'd tried every possible scramble of each of those numbers and all of those numbers mixed. She'd gotten nowhere.

But she'd found something else. In the top drawer of his desk, she'd found a dainty gold chain. With a small heart pendant. She'd recognized it. Immediately, she'd recognized that chain as the one Beth Summers had worn every day she'd known her. Her father had given it to her before he left her and her mother.

Thc chain was broken. As if it had been yanked away from Beth's neck, rather than carefully removed.

Why did Miles have Beth's chain in his desk drawer?

Killer for hire. She'd found nothing, so why were those words burned into her brain now? Killer. For. Hire.

The datebook in Miles' top desk drawer.

From 1994. Caroline had perched on the edge of the office chair and opened the slender black volume. All thoughts of Miles showing up at home early had melted away. Max was in his room. In one hand Caroline held Beth's broken gold chain. In the other, Miles' datebook from 1994.

Caroline quickly found the day of their first date. There were no marks on it. No silly hearts drawn on it. Caroline's name was not written there. But with a sinking feeling, she'd flipped through the pages until she'd come to the date of Beth's accident.

There had been a number scrawled there.

Miles had killed Beth. Plied her with liquor. Possibly drugged her. Tampered with the brakes or the steering. And then he'd used his money to cover his tracks. She didn't need a shred of proof to *know* it was true.

She'd asked him once about the money. The first time he'd laughed, sipped a tumbler of scotch and said he was a killer for hire. Caroline had assumed he was being an ass, putting her off, to avoid telling her he had an illegal money laundering scheme of some sort going on. When she'd brought it up again, he'd backhanded her.

Killer for hire.

"If you're going to paint," Miles says now, as she steps into the room, "let's start in this room."

Killer for hire.

He'd told her the truth, and the truth was so outrageous she'd assumed he was being an ass. He'd killed Beth Summers, because Beth had made it clear she was willing to come between them. Beth wanted to break them up.

"I thought you didn't want me to paint." Caroline crosses her arms over her chest.

Miles shrugs now. He watches her suspiciously. As if he knows she has just remembered everything. Or at the very least, he suspects it. God knows how many people her husband has killed on his second job. How many days he's gone off to the steel mill office and then detoured and—what? Does he shoot them? Does he carry a gun? Surely it'd be a gun. Surely hired killers don't go in for the gore—

As if it matters. As if it's any less horrible that he fires a gun, probably a gun with a silencer, instead of something barbaric like stabbing them. There's no slicing and dicing. No blood bath. He is a cold-blooded methodical killer, not a frenzied serial killer who wants to smell his victims' fear or blood.

"Maybe you're right. This color is pretty bad."

Caroline nods. "Good. I'm glad you agree with me." She smiles, praying that since this has been decided, he'll leave now. He'll take his briefcase and go away. To his office. God, but she hopes that he's only done it a few times. Just a few times.

Because what, Caroline? If he's only murdered a few people for money, that's okay? She imagines he is probably very efficient at his second job. Cold and precise. Just as when he beats her. He does not show his emotion. He can backhand her or punch her in the kidneys with absolutely no emotion on his face. And then turn around and order her calmly to fix his dinner or ask her if she'd like some ice cream.

Sociopath.

Miles Wolfe is a sociopath, and he's killed people. She wonders if he has other aliases. Others besides Michael Ramsay.

"What color are you thinking for this room?"

Caroline blinks hard and looks back at him. He is walking the perimeter of the room now. Trailing his fingertips over the walls. She swallows hard when he stops at the window, the one he used to stand by when he spied on her.

"Um. I don't know. That's what Dawn and I were going to talk about today. Just get some color ideas."

Dawn.

Danny. The fire. Miles *had* killed Danny. But why? So he could *own* Dawn too? Possess her? Run to her when he needed something different? Or because he felt like Danny and Dawn knew too much about his own marriage? Was Dawn next on his list? Or had he killed Danny, assuming he could scare Dawn into obedience?

No wonder he'd played God and had her face changed when she'd had the accident. No wonder he'd wiped every trace of their past life from this house. Miles is desperate that Caroline never remember the things he said to her and the things she pieced together on her own.

"Why do you need Dawn's opinion? We could do this together. It would be fun."

Caroline inhales sharply when Miles moves up behind her and puts his arms around her. "You're too busy," she mumbles. Her heart is hammering in her chest. Miles has to feel the erratic beat against his own chest behind her.

"I'm never too busy for you, Caroline," he answers. She closes her eyes when he presses his lips to the hollow just under her ear. "You and me. Painting the house together. You with paint drips on your bare feet. Paint on your face. We would laugh. And then we could stop and sip wine and make love while the paint dries around us."

Caroline shakes her head. "That's a fairytale thing, Miles. We've never had that kind of love."

"I miss you, Caroline," he whispers. She feels him grow hard against her back, as his hands slide up her sides to cup her breasts.

"Please don't do this, Miles."

"Caroline, it's been over a year since we've made love."

"I'm not ready."

"I won't hurt you—"

"What about the night you pinned me down and tried to strangle me? After we made love?"

"That was just a game."

Caroline doesn't answer him. She has to get out of here. She has to get away from his hands, from his hands that are now trying to slip beneath her shirt. She has to go to the school, get her son and get out. The same urgency from the day of the accident is creeping up her throat and choking her.

"You remember right? It was just a game." He kisses her again. Fear rages inside her. His hands now cup her breasts, inside her shirt. His fingers are pushing under the cups of her bra. "You liked it. It made you come harder when I did that. Don't you remember?"

"No, I don't remember that." She takes a deep breath. It's all or nothing. She'll either walk out of this alive, or Miles will kill her now. She only hopes that if Miles kills her, Dawn will take Max and run. "Maybe it was another woman? Maybe Dawn?"

"What did you just say?"

Caroline hears the way the ice coats his words. His hands are cold now, as if his fingers are not inside her bra, cupping her bare breasts.

"I said maybe it was Dawn that liked you to hold her down and strangle her." Caroline sounds lighthearted, as if she is really trying to help him remember something.

"Dawn? Are you suggesting that there's something going on between Dawn and me?"

Dawn. Where the hell is Dawn? What if—? Oh God. What if Caroline hadn't played her cards right and Miles has already done something to Dawn?

Fight. The word comes to her and before Miles can move, Caroline throws her head back and slams it against his nose.

"Son-of-a-bitch!" Miles roughly draws his hands away from her. She rushes to get away from him, from the blood gushing from his nose, but he reaches for her. Catches her upper arm in his fingers and yanks her back to him.

"Let go of me!" she screams. "Let go—"

"I'll kill you," he says calmly.

"Or die trying."

She is sorry the moment the words leave her mouth. Broken nose be damned, Miles swings and connects his left hand to her jaw. She throws her head back, but she does not cry out. She will not give him the satisfaction.

"Stupid bitch," he mutters. "Give you a second chance, and you throw it away too."

"Second chance at what, Miles?" Her jaw throbs, but she doesn't rub it. If she can get past him to the door, maybe she can run. Maybe she can jump down half the stairs and get away from him.

And maybe time will freeze and Miles will melt, like the villain in a fairytale and then she and Max and Dawn can live happily ever after.

Where is Dawn?

"Snooping around in things that are none of your business. You back talk me. Deny me—"

"Second chance at what? Being your prisoner?"

"You had it made. I gave you everything you could have wanted. Before and after—"

"Everything I could have wanted?" she laughs. "No woman wants to be a possession, Miles Wolfe. Is that even your real name? Or is it Michael?"

He backhands her across the face.

"Any young girl off the street would kill for a chance to live the life you've had. Fairytale romance, all the money you'd ever need—"

"Fairytale romance?" Caroline repeats. "What fairytale is that, Miles? Rapunzel? Even before that God-awful lavender room, I was stuck here. With you. Stuck with a man who hates humanity and thrives on killing for money. A man who'd rather rape me than make love to me—"

"Enough!" Not quite a yell, but he raises his voice and the word bounces off the walls of the empty room. "You should've left well enough alone. I could have had this taken care of after the accident. It would've been very easy to take care of. People would have believed you died from the injuries."

"Dawn wouldn't have." She's outwardly calm, but inside she's scared. Miles is going to kill her. The new face had bought her a few months, and yet what had those months given her? Heartache and headache, doing her damndest to remember who in the hell she was.

"I'll take care of that bitch when I'm done with you." Miles shoves her up against the wall and presses into her with his lower body. He closes his hands around her neck.

"This is gonna be messy," she says quietly. "It's not your style."

"Beth wasn't the first, Caroline. Don't think you know anything about me."

"I know you're the dev—"

She groans when he squeezes his fingers around her throat. She can't breathe. Miles' bloody face is less than an inch from hers. His cold eyes are hot with rage and lust. He is feeding off her panic. Maybe, she thinks as the room grows dim around them, maybe she really doesn't know him. Maybe he'd prefer hands on killing to a gun any day.

"Let her go, Miles!"

Miles stands up straight when they hear Dawn's voice. He doesn't move away from Caroline, and he doesn't release the pressure on her neck. The room is growing darker, and Caroline almost wonders if she imagined Dawn's voice.

"Shoot." He drops his hands away from Caroline, and she coughs and falls forward, clawing at her throat. "Shoot, Dawn. Ten thousand says you miss me."

Dawn pulls the trigger without hesitation. The bullet misses him by an inch. Caroline eyes where it is lodged in the wall, about a foot to the left.

“Inept,” Miles mutters. He charges Dawn, no doubt to take the gun from her. She squeezes the trigger again and hits him. In the shoulder. He doesn’t go down. Caroline watches in disbelief as he reaches for the gun. His fingers wrap around Dawn’s hands on the gun.

Dawn’s face is painted with determination. Hatred. It’s as if she doesn’t see Caroline by the wall. They fight over the gun. Caroline has seen enough TV shows to know that the gun is going to go off and one of them is going to be gut shot. Probably Dawn. Which will leave Miles wounded, but still able to turn and use the gun on her.

She could run. Right now. Slip by them and get the hell out. But she won’t. She won’t leave Dawn to fight her demon. This is her nightmare, and he always has been. It will be up to Caroline to stop him.

She scrambles around them hoping she can find something she can use as a weapon. This room is completely empty, which is probably while Miles chose it for this final scene. He’d known her well enough to know she’d fight and she’d use whatever means available to do so.

The gun goes off. Caroline screams and looks back at them. Another miss, but in the shock, Miles lands a blow to Dawn’s midsection and then knocks her off her feet. He straddles her, just as he had Caroline in that memory they’ve just been arguing about.

“I should’ve killed you with Danny,” he whispers as he

wraps his fingers around her neck. "Saved myself a hell of a lot of trouble."

"Fuck you." Dawn tugs at his hands, but she can't budge them. Caroline knows Dawn is going to blackout, if she doesn't help her soon.

Caroline spots the gun laying on the floor, about a foot away from Miles. He could easily reach over and pick it up and shoot them both. End it right here. But he wants to do this with his hands. He wants it to be personal. Wants them both to *feel* his hands take their lives.

Dawn's face is discolored, and her eyes are closed. Caroline takes a step toward then, and Miles laughs. He turns to look at the gun, still laughing at her obvious desire to get the gun. While his head is turned, Caroline lifts her leg—the one that still aches form time to time—and kicks him. Her foot connects with his jaw and there is a quiet little snick, and Miles slumps to the side. His hands loosen on Dawn, but they remain on her neck.

Dawn opens her eyes and looks up at Caroline.

"He called me."

Caroline squats down beside her, but Dawn looks anxiously toward the man still hunched over her.

"On my cell. I was half way here. He called, and all he said was he thought he just might come home and kill you. And when he was done, he was going to come after me."

"He killed Danny." Caroline licks her lips. "And he killed Beth. And I don't know how many other people."

"Didn't kill you though," Dawn whispers.

“Or you.”

Caroline pulls Miles’ hands away from Dawn, pushes him off her and helps Dawn to stand.

“Is he dead?” Dawn asks, afraid to look at him.

“I dunno.”

“We should call 911.”

“I went back for the gun.” Dawn rubs her eyes. “I’m sorry. I went back for the gun. I know you didn’t want—"

“The gun didn’t kill him, Dawn.”

“You didn’t either.” Dawn chances a glance over her shoulder. Miles has not moved. “You didn’t *kill* him. You saved us.”

Caroline nods. Calmly she leads Dawn out of the room and down the staircase. “Let’s get out of this house.”

Caroline puts her arm around Dawn’s shoulders as they cross the foyer. She pulls open the front door and walks with purpose across the front porch. “I want my son. I need to see my son.”

THE END

***

Thank you for reading Fairytale. Please take a moment to leave a review on your favorite bookish website.

Turn the page for a sneak peek at Sketching Litchfield Lake.

SKETCHING LITCHFIELD LAKE

Chapter 1

TREVOR

black water

black water lapping at his shoes

his boots

why was he wearing boots?

black water

gray black sky—

a shiver climbing his spine

the water's warm

warm and black

Trevor Gerhardt gasped awake. His heart was going to explode. Jesus Christ, he was having a heart attack. He was going to lay here and die. What if no one even found his body? Like, for days?

Bright, garish yellow light streaked the ceiling. Trevor stared at that light, wondered who in his family would be waiting for him on the other side. His heart still pounded; he could feel it in his neck and his chest and toes and fingertips. Hurt, though. His chest hurt, and he was still panting, trying to catch his breath. It was stifling in this fucking room. The air was stagnant.

Like the lake water.

The thought drove him off the bed. His foot caught in the damp sheets as he scrambled to get up. He tripped, hopped a couple of steps, and crashed into the wall by the window. The drapes shifted under his clenched fist and that streak of sunlight grew wider and brighter, and Trevor squeezed his eyes shut against the sharp pain in his head.

“Jesus, Trevor.”

Shit. He wasn’t alone. Heart still beating too fast, he bent at the waist and rested his hands on his knees. Gulped in air, but it was fetid and hot, and it stuck in his lungs, draped over his ribs like syrup.

“Shut the curtains.”

He stood up straight. Glanced at her as he rounded the double bed. On her stomach, her right arm up under her pillow, she watched him as he scratched his way down over his stomach and his dick. Dishwater blond hair matted to her head, she narrowed her eyes at him and turned to face the other way on her pillow.

Shit. He forgot her name. Who the fuck was she?

He left the door open as he lifted the toilet lid.

"Really?"

He ignored her. Felt somewhat better as he flushed. He wasn't one to look in the mirror often, but the bathroom in this apartment was so small, his nose was almost pressed up against the mirror as he washed his hands. His hair was smashed against the side of his head, too, and his skin was pasty white, and there were still drops of sweat on his forehead. He parted his blood red lips and looked at his teeth. Dropped his gaze to the sink. Saw his toothbrush. A pink toothbrush lay by his.

His heartbeat finally slowed; he was beginning to catch his breath. The room almost tilted as he turned to go back to the bedroom. She rolled over and stared at him. He hated that. He hated the way she stared at him in the mornings.

The thought startled him.

She snorted a sarcastic laugh.

"You forgot me again, huh?"

Trevor rubbed his hands over his head as he crossed the room to the bed and lifted his knee to sit down beside her. Flat on her back now, right arm still over her head, she stared at him boldly.

He watched his hand as it moved, as if it had a mind of its own, to touch her. Cover her small breast. He met her familiar gaze. Moved his hand over her, but not the way she liked it.

"Mallory."

"Jeez, Trevor, really?" She flinched when he lifted his ass from the bed and yanked his underwear off. She didn't like it like this. She'd told him that once, and he didn't mean to hurt her. But in this sleep-dream drunk stupor, he was rough, and he yanked her panties down just to her knees. She'd give it to him. She always did, but she didn't like it. She opened her legs for him, and he drove into her hard and fast.

She held on to him, fingernails scraping his shoulders as he pumped his hips over hers. He'd looked at her face once, when he did this to her, and he'd seen a mix of boredom and pain and wondered what *he* looked like when he was like this. Since then, rather than look at her, he'd buried his face against her neck, smelled the remains of the night before— whether that be perfume, sleep sweat or sex—and rode her hard until he came inside her.

The first time he'd done it that way, they'd panicked. She hadn't been on the pill then. Whatever happened between them, he sure as fuck didn't want a kid right now. He sure as hell wasn't daddy material; he wasn't sure she was mother material. She'd gotten the pill, even after she'd told him she didn't like it this way, that it hurt and he was a slob and a jerk, and so now at least when he fucked her like this, a three minute thing that left him shaking and spent and drove the goddamned nightmares out of his head, he didn't have to worry about getting her pregnant.

"Least you remembered my name before you fucked me this time."

He flopped over to lie on his back, breathless and sweaty again, and watched her roll away from him. She climbed out of bed and stalked to the shower. She could be prickly on a good day. Pissy and mean when he started her day like this. She turned the shower water on and then turned to look at him.

"What?"

He huffed out a deep breath and raised his hands. Dug the heels of his hands into his eyes.

"You want coffee?"

When she didn't answer him, he propped himself up on his elbows to look at her. She was leaning against the door-frame, the shower water running behind her. It would take a while for the water to heat up. Time enough for him to do something for her. He did that sometimes. After he mauled her, he would touch her. The way she liked. If he did that, if he made her come, she'd give in, get over it. They wouldn't have to bitch at each other the rest of the day.

He sat up. Stared at her nude body. She was a waif, all bones and hard angles. Tiny hips, small breasts. She was good in bed, and he loved the dirty things she said when she was excited, when he made her come.

Didn't have time today. He had to move. Coffee. Canvases. He needed more canvases. He had to paint. Fuck it, he should just paint now. Still had one canvas left. He could do without the coffee if he started painting now.

Maybe he could capture that weird sliver of light over the black water if he started right now. Never mind that he had nine other canvases with that same black water and that same strip of light lined up against the wall in the other room. Maybe this time he could get it right.

"You're such a dick." She rolled her eyes and ducked back into the bathroom.

***

If you'd like to read more, click here

ALSO BY TRACY BROEMMER

Women's Fiction Novels:

Luther's Cross: 10th Anniversary Edition

Just Like Them

Small Hours

Two Story Home

Say Everything

Sketching Litchfield Lake

Damsel

Picket Fences

The Valentine Suite

Truth Is, The Williams Legacy, Book 1

Other People's Ugly, The Williams Legacy, Book 2

Omissions, The Williams Legacy, Book 3

Currently Out of Print:

Every Little Thing, Lorelei Bluffs, Book 1

Two A.M., Lorelei Bluffs, Book 2

Blind, Lorelei Bluffs, Book 3

Leaving July, Lorelei Bluffs, Book 4

Hesitation Marks, Lorelei Bluffs, Book 5

Four Letter Words, Lorelei Bluffs, Book 6

See Kate, Lorelei Bluffs, Book 7

Loved You More, Lorelei Bluffs, Book 8

A Lorelei Ending, Lorelei Bluffs, Book 9

I Do, Lorelei Bluffs, Book 10

Come Home for Christmas

Ever, Again

Safe as Houses

ABOUT THE AUTHOR

Tracy Broemmer is the author of several contemporary romance novels including the 515 Whiskey Series, Shameless Santa, and the Mississippi Queen Trilogy. Tracy also writes women's fiction and is the author of the Williams Legacy series as well as several stand-alone titles.

Tracy's books have been called gripping, emotional, and timely, and readers describe her characters as real and relatable

Tracy lives in Midwestern Illinois with her husband of 32 years. For a full backlist of titles, visit her on the web at www.broemmerbooks.com

Sign up for her newsletter at the bottom of the home page.

www.ingramcontent.com/pod-product-compliance
Lightning Source LLC
LaVergne TN
LVHW041924090826
845145LV00016B/1584

* 9 7 8 1 9 6 5 3 3 1 2 4 8 *